wicked

2

Legacy & Spellbound

Nancy Holder and Debbie Viguié

SIMON PULSE

NEW YORK LONDON TORONTO SYDNEY

SIMON PULSE
An imprint of Simon & Schuster Children's Publishing Division
1230 Avenue of the Americas, New York, NY 10020

Designed by Ann Zeak
The text of this book was set in Aldine 401BT.
Manufactured in the United States of America
This Simon Pulse edition January 2009
10 9 8 7 6 5 4 3 2
Library of Congress Control Numbers:
Legacy: 2002115623
Spellbound: 2003106083
ISBN-13: 978-1-4169-7117-7
ISBN-10: 1-4169-7117-3

These titles were originally published
individually by Simon Pulse.

contents

wicked

2

Legacy

To the holder of our family legacy, Elise Jones, who is a true heroine

—Nancy Holder

To my dad, Richard Reynolds, who has always been there for me and is my truest fan

—Debbie Viguié

ACKNOWLEDGMENTS

Thanks first to Debbie, an awesome coauthor and fantastic friend. And thanks to her husband, Scott, who is the best of the best. Big, big thanks to Lisa Clancy, Lisa Gribbin, and Micol Ostow. To my agent, Howard Morhaim, and his assistant, Ryan Blitstein, my deepest gratitude. Thanks to Art and Lydia; J&M'e; Melanie and Steve; Del and Sue; AngelaBAH Rienstra and Patmom; Allie Costa; my never-husband Bill Wu; Liz Engstrom Cratty and Al Cratty; big bro Steve Perry; Kym; Karen Hackett, Lisa Bayorek, and Linda Wilcox.

—N. H.

Thanks to the two Lisas at Simon & Schuster for all your hard work and support. Thanks to Mimi Viguié for all her support and love. Thank you David and Eunice Naples for your friendship. Thanks to Ted Rallis for always listening. Thank you also to Brian Liotta for your enthusiasm and being part of my extended family. As always I could not have done any of this without the love and support of my husband, Scott.

—D. V.

Part One
Yule

☾

When the Yule Log burns bright
Witches come out to play at night
But once the year has finally turned
Witches will drown, and witches will burn

ONE

BLACK OBSIDIAN

☾

Seek and destroy, hunt and find
We will kill all their kind
They will beg and they will plead
As we drink their blood with mead

Protect us, Goddess, hear our cry
Cahors call out to the sky
Shelter us beneath thy arms
And help us to escape all harm

The Cathers Coven: London, December

The Coven was on the run.

Holly Cathers, her cousin, Amanda, and their friends were witches of the light trying to hide in the dark, in a land controlled by the Supreme Coven, warlocks who worshiped the horned god. As they trudged through the growing darkness Holly consulted her directions, frequently, desperately hoping they were nearing their destination and safety.

If there is any such thing as safety, she thought bitterly. A year and a half ago she had been a happy, normal teenager. In a horrible twist of fate her parents had been killed in an accident, the victims of a curse that all who loved a Cathers witch would die by drowning. She had gone to live with her estranged aunt and her twin cousins. It was then that all hell broke loose.

She had known for only a few short months of her true heritage as the latest in a long line of witches, a descendant of the ancient House of Cahors. Her family was involved in a centuries' old feud with another witchly house, the Deveraux. Now Michael Deveraux was hunting her and hers. Still, they had had to come here, to London, the seat of the Supreme Coven, to find Holly's missing cousin, Nicole.

After that first terrible year, in which Michael had killed Amanda and Nicole's mother, Nicole had left, too freaked out by the magic and the death to stay in Seattle any longer. She had called once, months later, to warn them of danger and to tell them she was going to try to come home. She had never made it, kidnapped instead by the Supreme Coven.

The Coven kept on going, too tired to move at much more than a crawl. Holly's nerves were frayed, worn down by months of endless fighting. The stress was taking its toll on her, and she was beginning to act in ways that would have once been abhorrent to her.

Now, as they raced to put themselves as far from danger as they could, the others moved at a distance from Holly, leaving her alone in the midst of the busy London afternoon. Just as passersby on the street instinctively avoided the cloaked witches, so the rest of the Coven instinctively avoided getting too close to her.

They're afraid of me, Holly Cathers thought as she and the members of her coven hurried down Oxford Street. *Afraid of my power, afraid I'll lose my temper again.*

They're right to be afraid.

I'm not sure I can control myself anymore. Isabeau is stirring inside, and she's driving me to disobey, and to go to Jer. Because her husband, Jean, can manifest in him, and she wants him . . .

. . . wants both to love him and to kill him, so she can rest. . . .

Bide your time, kinswoman. Let me do what I said I would.

Holly could almost hear Isabeau reply, *Then help me do what* I *said* I *would: kill my only love, my only hate.*

I must roam through time and space, earthbound, until he is truly dead. . . .

"No," she whispered, then clamped her mouth

shut and moved on. Isabeau, Holly's ancestress, had died betraying her husband, Jean Deveraux, six centuries before.

And now she lives on in me, Holly thought bitterly. *And Jean lives on through Jeraud Deveraux. The two won't let us rest.*

Isabeau and Jean had been married, pawns in a deadly game played by their families. It had been their destruction. Now Isabeau and Jean were both cursed to wander the world as spirits until they fulfilled the curse each had laid on the other . . . Isabeau, who had sworn to her mother, the fierce Queen Catherine, that she would kill Jean, was doomed to walk the world, earthbound, until she could fulfill her vow and kill her husband.

Jean had sworn vengeance on Isabeau herself, after she had betrayed his family to her mother. Thanks to her duplicity, every man, woman, and child of Deveraux blood had been put to the torch. Infants. Even their livestock had burned alive. Only Jean had escaped, and he had been horribly burned.

Now Jeraud Deveraux had been burned, just as Jean had been. By the woman he loved . . .

In each succeeding generation, Jean and Isabeau had attempted to possess members of their own families, through whom they would free themselves from love and hate, and sink into the earth for one last time . . . hopefully to find peace in the arms of angels, or in each other. . . .

Each generation had failed them.

In Holly's time, she was Isabeau's vessel, her unwilling host. Jeraud Deveraux, the son of her terrifying enemy, Michael, was the one Jean used. Passion and hatred boiled inside them both as Jean and Isabeau pursued each other through time and space, loving and hating, willing death, and forbidding it. . . .

Now Holly shook her head. Isabeau spoke to her more lately, calling to all that was cold and wild within her. It was getting harder to ignore her, harder to draw the line between them.

She glanced about, wondering how much farther she and her fellow covenates had to go. It was bitterly cold in London; granite-colored snow cascaded from skies the color of gravestones, and the bitter wind could freeze bones. Double-decker buses and old-fashioned black taxicabs slammed around overcrowded traffic circles; pedestrians slogged along, caught in a crush of steamy breath and bad tempers.

Overhead, seven falcons wheeled, minions of the Deveraux, searching for Holly and her coven. Holly had been the first to notice them, scrutinizing the birds perched on the lampposts outside Victoria Station, their beady, glaring eyes ticking as each passenger rushed by.

Back in Paris, the High Priestess of the Mother Coven had woven spells of invisibility around Holly's coven to protect them from the Deveraux—from the entire Supreme Coven, for that matter. Having no desire to test those waters, Holly and the others had darted back into the train station and quickly boarded an Underground train for Essex Square, but somehow the birds were able to sense the presence of witches, and were trailing them.

Now their wings cast deadly silhouettes against the neon signs and streetlights that were winking on, although it was barely four in the afternoon. Winter days in London were short; the night reigned supreme. Camouflaged among the dark umbrellas, the birds swooped and searched, unnoticed by the mundane Londoners because the creatures were magical and only visible to those who walked in that world. So far, the creatures still could not locate their quarry.

Now the Coven hurried along. With Holly and Amanda were the remnants of their coven: Tommy Nagai, Amanda's best friend; Silvana Beaufrere, a friend of Amanda's since childhood; and a very reluctant Kari Hardwicke. Kari had been a member of Jer's coven and Jer's lover before Holly had come along.

Holly sighed as she looked at her. Kari had never forgiven her for leaving Jer behind in the school gymnasium as it was consumed by the Black Fire conjured by his father and brother. For months they had thought Jer dead and the members of his coven had joined with Holly and her friends. Now, all Jer's coven were dead except for Kari, and she wanted out.

Kari had accompanied them to London only because the High Priestess of the Mother Coven had informed her that she would likely be killed or taken hostage by the Supreme Coven if she left the relative safety of their numbers. She wanted nothing more than to go back to Seattle and, like Nicole Anderson, forget that she had ever learned that magic and witchery were real forces in the world.

The new member of their party—if not officially of their coven—was Sasha Deveraux, Eli and Jer's mother, and the estranged wife of Michael. The lovely red-haired, green-eyed woman had asked to come with them, her mission being to save her beloved son, Jer, and to turn him completely away from the worship of the Horned God and all the darkness that entailed . . . or so Sasha hoped.

And so Holly hoped too.

But Holly had promised the Mother Coven—and Nicole's sister, Amanda—that they would save Nicole first. Once she had been rescued from the Supreme Coven—*and how are we going to manage that?*—then Holly was free to go after Jer.

I hope it's a promise I can keep.

The Mother Coven had helped ward their passage to London; they had gone by train and then by ferry, Holly remembering all the while that the curse on her family was that those who loved them would die by drowning. For that reason, she had refused to take the Chunnel, the underground tunnel that transported travelers underneath the English Channel. In the end she hadn't been sure that the ferry was any better. She spent the entire trip reliving the nightmare of the ferry attack in Seattle, when they had lost Eddie.

When I lost Eddie, she reminded herself. She was still haunted by his face and by the sure knowledge that he had died because she had chosen to save her cousin, Amanda, instead of him. It was a secret she had kept to herself. *Along with so many others lately.* She sighed, frustrated. Being a leader meant making the tough choices, the sacrifices. *Hey, whatever helps me sleep at night,* she thought bitterly. The truth was, she was beginning to scare even herself.

For the hundredth time she thought of the great battle waged on and over the Bay against Michael's legions. She remembered the promise she had made her dead ancestress, the powerful Catherine. The promise that she would be worthy.

She shivered, but it had nothing to do with the biting cold. She wasn't sure what she would have to do, how much more of her soul she would need to sacrifice to be worthy to carry Catherine's mantle. Her visions of Catherine, from her daughter, Isabeau's point of view, had been unbearably gruesome. She shook her head and glanced anxiously at the sky.

Focus; keep your mind on the task.

Holly glanced down at the slip of paper in her hand. It was the address of a Mother Covenate safe house, and the owner was putting herself at great risk by opening her doors to the Cathers coven. Again Holly noted the relative weakness of the Mother Coven as compared with the Supreme Coven—and as opposed to the violent and brilliant ghost army she herself had led into Elliott Bay to save Kialish and Silvana . . . though only Silvana had survived.

Cahors all, she thought, her heart beating fiercely. *Wild and strong and fearless. They called me their queen . . . and Catherine said I was the one who could keep the family name alive. . . .*

But I need Jer to do that. His magic combined with mine will give us the power to defeat the Supreme Coven. I feel that. I know that. . . .

Oui, ma belle, a voice whispered inside her head. *Alors, go to him. Go now. Vite.*

It was Isabeau.

Torn, Holly gestured to the others, indicating the fish and chips shop across the street. It was a landmark for them. They were supposed to turn right, then go through the second narrow alleyway. Their contact would be watching in the window for them.

Kari looked longingly at the shop—it had been hours since they had eaten—but Holly firmly shook her head. Creature comforts had to be denied until they were out of harm's way . . . or at least off the streets.

The Coven obediently turned right, hanging back from Holly. Her face burned; she was ashamed and defensive, still remembering how she had nearly hurled a fireball at them in the Moon Temple, the most sacred ground of the Mother Coven. As it was, she had insulted Hecate, one of the most revered aspects of the Goddess—and the name of Nicole's familiar, whom she had sacrificed for power.

They're shocked at me for doing it . . . and yet, it's up to me to make sure they survive the attacks from Michael Deveraux. I sacrificed a little part of my soul for them, and all they can think of is how horrible it was of me to drown the cat.

She put her hands in the pockets of her black wool

coat and ducked her head, angrily pursing her lips. *What's the saying? Heavy hangs the head that wears the crown. . . .*

Then Amanda hurried up to her and tugged at her coat sleeve. Holly glanced at her; her cousin was jabbing her finger upward, and her face was ashen.

The seven falcons had lined up on a second-story brick ledge on the opposite side of the street; they cocked their heads in the direction of the fugitive coven, their blue-black feathers shining in the street light. Catching the glow, their eyes gleamed; they clacked their beaks together softly, menacingly, and their claws jittered on the balcony as they edged along, matching the particular, quick rhythm of Holly's footsteps.

Amanda stared at her as if to ask, *What do we do?*

Holly's face prickled with fear; her heart thundered against her chest, and she clenched her gloved fists inside her pockets to keep from crying out.

Can they hear us?

Have they found us?

She didn't know if she should avoid their gaze or study them to see what they might do next. It was then that she realized that the falcon in the middle—three stood on one side of it, and three on the other—was cast in an eerie green glow; it was also larger than the others. There was something about it that differentiated it from the others; it was the leader, and it was unearthly . . . unnatural. Could it be Fantasme, the spirit-familiar of House Deveraux, that had survived through the ages partly as symbol, partly as a real, living thing? It had been Fantasme that had saved Jer's brother, Eli, from the Black Fire so many months ago.

The lead falcon screeched once, then swooped from the perch and began to fly across the street.

Holly whirled around to warn the others not to make a sound. Just in time, Tommy clamped his hand over Kari's mouth, shaking his head vigorously. Kari's eyes bulged; Tommy kept his hand over her mouth, and Holly waved both hands to tell her, *No! Stop!*

Then the whir of wings above her caught her attention. She looked up to see the falcons aiming themselves directly at them. Their claws were extended, their beaks clacking.

The falcons are attacking!

She thought of Barbara Davis-Chin, who had been attacked by a falcon after Holly's parents' funeral, and who still lay near death in a hospital in San Francisco. Little had Holly realized then that the falcons were minions of Michael Deveraux and his evil son, Eli. She had had no idea that a world of magic existed, and that she was one of the primary players in it.

Still mute, Holly signaled for everyone to run.

She didn't look back at the group as she raced down the sidewalk, hoping the others kept up—expecting them to—and wondering if she should break the edict of the Mother Coven not to use magic on the London streets unless they were in mortal danger.

"Once you spellcast, they'll know exactly where you are," the High Priestess had warned Holly. "The only chance you have against them while you rescue Nicole is to remain hidden."

And passive. And unarmed, Holly thought now. *We're in danger. Should I break the cloak of invisibility to fight?*

The lead falcon moved its head in lockstep birdlike fashion, twisting right, left, and then it swooped back up into the lowering sky. The others swooped back up in formation, forming a V behind it, and then sky-rocketed toward the moon.

Holly was so surprised that she stumbled over her own foot and fell to the ground. Her ankle throbbed as she dragged herself closer to the wall of the nearest building.

Sasha ran up to her and pointed a finger as if to cast a spell. Holly wildly shook her head, and Sasha immediately stopped, bending over and extending a hand toward Holly, a simple physical gesture to help her up. Holly gripped Sasha's wrist and let her pull her to her feet. She hissed from the pain in her ankle.

They both looked up.

The shimmering lead bird seemed almost to disappear against the moon as the others became small, moving lines . . . and then they disappeared. Whether they had truly vanished to another place or continued to fly until they were no longer visible, Holly couldn't tell.

They might come back.

Not willing to take any chances, she limped forward, gesturing with her hand that the others should do the same. She could hear their footfalls, heard one of them faltering and turned around to see Kari stop, looking panicked and confused. Tommy grabbed her hand and yanked her forward; she shook her head again and stayed rooted to the spot.

She's freaking out.

Amanda glanced at Holly with something like exasperation, then ran back to Kari and took her other hand. Silvana made encouraging gestures while Tommy kept hold of her and, together, he and Amanda pulled her forward like a horse on a lead line.

Holly glared at Kari, but Sasha gave her a little tap as if to say, *Ease up on her.* Then she slung Holly's arm over her shoulder and helped her forward.

On their side of the street, about a hundred feet away, a door opened.

A man peered around it, saw them, and raised his hand.

Sasha and Holly looked at each other. Holly mouthed, *A guy?*

They had expected a woman; the only man they had seen attached to the Mother Coven had been Tommy, in the temple for the ceremony to renew them after their battles with Michael Deveraux and the long flight in the Mother Coven's private jet to Paris from Seattle.

The man was young, maybe Holly's age, and he gestured to them to hurry. Sasha wordlessly propelled Holly along; Holly shut her eyes tightly against the pain, and glanced over her shoulder to make sure that the others were following close behind.

They were, and they had caught up with Holly and Sasha by the time the two reached the door.

The moment Holly stepped across the threshold, her ankle healed. She raised her brows in delighted surprise.

After everyone had entered the building, the man dipped a little bow and said to Holly, "Blessed be." He added, "It's safe to talk in here. The place is very heavily warded."

"Thank you," she said gratefully, skipping for the moment the traditional greeting of the Mother Coven.

That was rude. It was immature of her, perhaps, but she was angry at the Coven for not providing them better protection for the journey. "And *you,*" she said, wheeling on Kari. "Don't you ever put the rest of the coven in danger again."

"Or what?" Kari demanded, her eyes flashing. "You'll throw another fireball at me?"

"Hey." Amanda stepped between them. Then she said to the man, "Blessed be," enunciating each syllable as if to remind Holly how to say the words.

"Blessed be," Silvana and Tommy added.

Silvana extended her hand. "I'm Silvana, and this is Tommy."

"I'm Joel," he said, shaking with her. Holly detected a bit of a Scots burr in his voice. "I'm a male witch."

"As opposed to a warlock?" Holly filled in, a little perplexed.

"Aye," he told her. "I worship the Goddess."

There was a moment of silence in the Goddess's honor.

"We were told to expect a woman," Holly said. Then she realized they hadn't been actually told whom to expect. Maybe she'd just assumed it would be a woman.

He frowned. "That's odd. As you can see, I'm not one."

Holly and her coven stared edgily at him. He held out his hands; in each palm was incised a moon, symbol of the goddess. Holly remained unconvinced.

"Is there some way you're to contact the Mother Coven?" he asked. "You can check my credentials."

As with magic use, Holly had been warned that trying to communicate with the Mother Coven would alert her enemies to her presence.

She looked coolly at Joel and said, "We're staying, for the moment. But if you do anything I find the least bit suspicious, I'll kill you. Fair warning?"

"Holly," Kari protested, but Holly made no reply, only gazed levelly at Joel.

"Fair warning," he said somberly. "I assure you, we're both on the same side."

"As long as it stays that way, we'll be fine, then," Holly retorted.

He inclined his head, and a small bit of the tension escaped from the room.

Holly looked around the room and realized it was a souvenir shop. English bone china tea services sat in the front window, and the shelves bulged with dolls dressed like Beefeaters and Royal Marines, and piles of scarves in tartans and plaids.

Maybe I can find something to take home, she thought wryly. *Though I'd rather it was Michael Deveraux's head.*

She was a bit shocked to realize that she meant it.

"Please, take off your coats and make yourselves comfortable," he urged as he flipped a CLOSED sign in the front window and pulled the drapes, obscuring the view from the street. "I'll get some tea."

They began to do as he asked while he bustled off through a curtained doorway, leaving the coven alone.

"That was so scary, with the birds," Amanda said as she carried her coat to a coatrack beside the dark wood door. "I guess they couldn't quite figure out where we were."

"They were too close for comfort," Silvana observed, shaking her cornrows to dust the snow from them.

"It's not a good sign," Sasha observed. "We're supposed to be completely cloaked. The Supreme Coven must be working overtime to find us."

"Oh, joy," Tommy drawled.

"Please, come in," Joel called through the curtain.

Holly went first, feeling apprehensive. She murmured half of a spell to conjure a fireball, then pushed the curtain away.

She stood in the sitting room of what had to be his living quarters. There was an overstuffed settee upholstered in fat cabbage roses, and a dark green lounger set at a right angle beside it. On a coffee table before the settee were a ring of runestones, a burning lavender candle, and a statue of the Goddess in her incarnation as the Blessed Virgin Mary.

A space heater hummed on the other side of the settee, and Holly moved instinctively to its warmth.

Gesturing eagerly, Joel said, "Please, sit down. The High Priestess told me to make you as comfortable as possible."

He went into a small kitchen alcove. Silvana sidled over to Holly and said, "I have a good feeling about him. I'm not getting any bad vibes."

Holly cocked her head. "I didn't know you could read people."

Silvana shrugged. "Not in any mystical way. Just intuition."

Joel returned with cups of tea on an oval tray, and all the myriad things the British poured into their tea. Holly liked the richness of the heavy doses of sugar and cream.

"Can we do magic in here?" Tommy asked.

"Aye. Magic." Joel smiled at him as he set the tray down on the coffee table. Then he blushed and looked away. Tommy grinned as he apparently realized he was being flirted with.

"I've got some cots for you too," Joel said, "in my bedroom." To Holly, he added, "You can have my bed, of course."

"Royal treatment," Kari muttered.

Holly didn't react—she didn't bother anymore. Kari's resentment was very old and very boring. But Amanda, loyal to her core, snapped, "Shut up, Kari."

"Let's all stay calm," Sasha suggested, holding out her hands. She had taken off her coat. It was hard to believe she was old enough to have two children, with her soft, almost girlish face and her thin body. She had that coltish appearance many girls had in their early teenage years. Holly also had trouble believing Sasha had actually been married to Michael Deveraux. She was so nice.

"We were attacked," Holly said to Joel as she sat down on the settee. Her jeans were damp from the snow, and her boots were completely soaked through. "Did you see the falcons?"

"Aye." His shy smile returned. "I did a spell, tried to keep you cloaked."

"It worked," Tommy told him as he sat beside Holly and accepted a cup of tea from Joel. "Thank you. For the tea, too."

"Now what?" Holly asked. She was exhausted, but she was also totally wired. She lived in a constant state of tension; it was as if fleeing for her life was the only reality she had ever known, and being a girl back in San Francisco with a job at the horse stable and parents who fought a lot was some strange dream she had borrowed, for a time, from someone else.

I wonder if I'll ever be able to relax again? And even if I weren't in danger, would I remember what it's like to not monitor every situation, looking over my shoulder, sleeping lightly and not for long?

Holly sipped her tea and wondered those things. From the expressions on the faces of the others, their thoughts were similar.

Amanda glanced up at her and through the steam of her tea murmured, "Blessed be, Holly."

There's nothing blessed about this situation, Holly thought angrily. But she gave her cousin what she wanted, which was a smile—which reached nowhere near Holly's protected, frozen heart.

Nicole: London Headquarters, the Supreme Coven, December

The "honeymoon suite" at the headquarters of the Supreme Coven was decorated in nightmares.

Nicole sat with her back against a headboard carved with grotesque, misshapen human figures—imps—worshiping the Horned God, who had been carved in the center standing atop a pile of human skulls. *Lovely.* The hangings draped from the ebony canopy bed were bright crimson, sporting the leering face of Pan, forest god of lust.

At the sound of the opening door, she had bolted upright and pulled her knees to her chest, murmuring a warding spell. A gossamer rectangle of blue formed around the doorway.

James Moore, Nicole's bridegroom, chuckled as he walked through the rectangle and made a casual gesture with his left hand. The rectangle popped like a soap balloon, and the remnants winked back into the void from which Nicole had summoned them.

"It'll take more than that to keep me away from you," he laughingly told her. "Just accept it, Nicki. Your magic is no match for ours. You might as well put yourself in thrall to me willingly, because on Yule, I'm going to force you into it if you're not with me already."

He had bleached his hair white, and was wearing black jeans, a black T-shirt, and a black leather jacket. His left ear was pierced, and a black loop of metal hung there.

"I don't know why you want to bother," she said sullenly.

His smile stretched across his face. "Because you're hot."

"You make me sick."

He laughed. "No. I don't." He took off his jacket, dropped it carelessly to the floor, and walked toward the bed. "Do I, Mrs. Moore?"

I will not cry, Nicole admonished herself. *I won't do anything. I'll just sit here. . . .*

James approached her stealthily, jaguar to prey. She clenched her fists around her knees and clamped her mouth shut so that she wouldn't scream.

"I know what you did to me," he informed her as he reached down and pulled his T-shirt over his chest. "When we captured you, you put a glamour on me. I knew even then that you did it. It backfired, didn't it, Nicki? You didn't think I would actually marry you. You just thought I'd fall in love with you and free you."

"Yes," she hissed at him, breaking her promise to herself not to respond to him in any way. "I bewitched you. Or tried to. And now you've married me and you . . .you're . . ." She trailed off helplessly. "Don't you care at all that I don't love you?"

He blinked his deep blue eyes. "No. Why should I? I'm a warlock. We don't believe in love." He chuckled low in his throat and added, "We do, however, believe in lust."

Then he came to the bed, and Nicole willed herself away to another place. . . .

"Isabeau, ma vie, ma femme," Jean whispered fiercely. *"Comme je t'aime! Comme je t'adore!"*

She lay beneath him in their marriage bed, on a

mattress that was loaded to overflowing with fertility charms. Roses were strewn all over the chamber—roses in winter, forced to blossom by Deveraux magic.

As I am forced, she thought; but she was lying to herself. She was giving herself to him freely; nay, she wanted him, was taking him even as he took her—

I did not dream such passion existed, she thought, as in the candlelight, Jean's eyes lit up with fire. His face was a study in ecstasy, and triumph. *And he is the giver of it; he is the center of the fire that burns me. . . . I burn with him, I burn from him. . . .*

And in Joel's little London flat, Holly cried out and bolted upright. She was bathed in sweat, and her heart pounded.

From the doorway, Amanda flicked on the light and said, "Holly, what is it? What's wrong?"

"Dream, that's all," Holly assured her as she brushed her dark ringlets away from her damp forehead. "Sorry. Go back to sleep."

Amanda hesitated. "Are you sure? My God, you're sopping wet."

"I'm okay," Holly insisted, her voice rising. "Go. It's all right."

"But—"

"Damn it, Amanda! Leave me alone!" Holly shouted.

I want to go back to sleep.

So I can be with him again.

Stunned, Amanda stared at Holly as the other witch pointedly shut her eyes and turned on her side.

Something's happened to her, Amanda thought. *Ever since she sacrificed Hecate, she's been so mean.*

I'm scared. We all are. She's supposed to be our leader, but I'm not sure where she's taking us. Are we really going to try to rescue Nicole, or is Holly going to make us look for Jer instead?

Alas, Amanda could not see the future, and wasn't sure that she would want to even if she could. Time alone would reveal Holly's intentions. As Holly lay still, Amanda left the room and shut the door.

Headquarters of the Supreme Coven, London, 1676

Luc stood before the convened Council of Judgment as they peered down on him from a dais. It had been ten years since the Great Fire of London—as it was being called—begun by him and Giselle Cahors, as they had fought in public. Ten years that the Supreme Coven had waited for House Deveraux to provide the secret of the Black Fire in return for being restored to favor. The throne of skulls, once occupied by his family, groaned beneath the weight of Jonathan Moore, who still reigned as High Priest. The red and green of Deveraux, their coat of arms emblazoned with the fierce, proud visage of the Green Man, hung behind the throne, symbolizing their ownership of it. A hooded man stood beside the tasseled hanging with a torch, awaiting word to shame Luc by putting the flame to his family's badge of honor.

Though Luc kept his head raised high, he was terrified. Not only his life, but his soul lay in peril. And for what? An ill-conceived altercation with the Cahors witch. He had been such a fool to attack her in broad daylight, with all of London watching.

It's my hot Deveraux blood, he told himself. *The sight of a Cahors is enough to send the most stalwart of us into a frenzy of rage. They nearly destroyed us, and we have vowed to obliterate every one of them from this land and all others. We have sworn blood oaths, father to son to son to son, that there shall be no place, anywhere, that they will find safety from us. That oath has bewitched us. We cannot stop ourselves from attacking when we see one of them.*

Now he stood before the Judges. There were thirteen of them, all robed in the black gowns of their estate, heavy gold chains draping their shoulders and chest, their faces for the most part concealed by the hoods they wore. Each sat beside the other in a row of high-backed chairs with pentagrams carved into them. A long table fronted them, and at each place sat a bowl of salt, a goblet of wine, and a burning black tapir.

Behind them, a stained-glass window of the Great Horned God ate demons and humans shrieking for mercy. Flames danced behind him; and from his hollow mouth, a cascade of red splashed into a pool behind the massive ebony chairs in which sat the Judges.

Jonathan Moore smiled evilly down at him as Luc stood all alone facing his inquisitors. He knew very well that if the sentence for his misadventure had been solely Moore's to pass, he would be a writhing tower of flame right now. Satan himself would be feasting on his soul.

But Moore's was only one vote among several, and the Deveraux still had many friends. As House Deveraux rose and fell, so would their own fortunes.

"Luc Deveraux," Moore intoned. The man's smile faded, to be replaced by a scowl, and Luc's heart thudded. *It is good news,* he thought. *If it was the worst, he would deliver it to me with joy in his heart and a smile on his face.*

Luc lifted his chin and stood with his legs apart, reminding himself that so long as he lived, he would be able to come back another day to restore the

Deveraux to power. All that he need do is survive.

With a flourish, Moore unrolled a vellum scroll and began to read. "You fought in public, displaying the proof of the Black Arts to the eyes of ordinary men," he began. "You brought disaster to London Town, endangering our revered landmark, this headquarters. And to add to your list of offenses, you let the Cahors witch get away."

"That is all true," Luc said boldly.

Moore looked over the top of the scroll. What he had to say next clearly displeased him.

"Ten years ago, we informed you that all would be forgiven you, if you would but give us the secret of the conjuring of the Black Fire, a secret your family has kept from this Brotherhood for too long."

"We would willingly share such a secret, were we privy to it," Luc proclaimed. He held out his hands, which were chained together. "Alas, we know it not."

Several of the Judges looked at him askance, as if they didn't believe him. He was supremely frustrated. Deveraux had died under torture because others had believed they still retained the secret of the Black Fire. They had been persecuted, courted, and abandoned. For centuries, the belief persisted that the Deveraux kept the secret, waiting for the proper moment to conjure the Black Fire. *If only that were true,* he thought.

"Since you are so recalcitrant," Moore continued, "this is our sentence: that your family be exiled from this coven and from Europe for a period of one hundred years, at which time your House may reapply for Brotherhood. You are to have no contact with us for one hundred years. If during that time you find that you are able to conjure the Black Fire once again, you may contact us. Otherwise, we sever all relations with your House."

He stared at them in disbelief. *They are giving me my freedom?* Allowing his family to work on counterplots without being held accountable to the Supreme Coven?

Luc almost laughed in their faces. He couldn't believe their idiocy.

"Your family will be exiled to the Americas," Moore continued, "for one hundred years. You are to stay there. If a Deveraux, or a Deveraux familiar, so much as places one foot in an ocean, we will annihilate your family."

He held up a hand. "And your spirit-familiar, Fantasme, will remain here as hostage, until the one hundred years of exile have been completed. If we discover that you have attempted to leave your prison country, we will kill the bird and scatter its soul to the winds of time."

As if to underscore this pronouncement, Moore clapped his hands. Two robed warlocks rested a thick pole across their shoulders; hanging from the pole was a spiked cage. In the cage, the proud bird was capped and hobbled, huddling miserably and clearly in pain.

"What have you done to him?" Luc demanded, taking a step forward.

"Think of him as your whipping boy," Moore said, delighting in Luc's distress. "If any in your family misbehave, Fantasme will pay for it with torture."

Luc clamped his mouth shut. It would do no good to protest, or to ask for mercy on Fantasme's behalf. Besides, Fantasme was a Deveraux. The bird would sooner die a slow, miserable death than hear a fellow Deveraux plead for anything, much less his life.

"Very well," Luc said curtly, inclining his head with a regal air. "I accept the sentence of the court."

Moore broke into a smile and gave a curt nod to the robed warlock who held the torch. The man set it to the Deveraux colors. The flames caught the fabric, raging across the face of the Green Man. The smoke reached Fantasme's nostrils, and the bird tried to flap its wings and cry out. But it was tightly bound, and its mouth within the mask stayed silent.

The judges said in unison, "House Deveraux is banished. Woe unto the warlock who gives them succor, who befriends them, who aids them. House Deveraux is to us as dead."

They each took a drink of wine from the goblets before them. Then, as they swallowed, they picked up the black tapirs, turned them upside down, and smashed the flickering wicks against the surface of the table.

The only light in the hall emanated from the flames destroying House Deveraux's banner.

"Leave us," Moore said to Luc. "Turn your back and run, for you have until the next moon to be gone from these shores. If we find you among us, we will destroy Fantasme, and then will hack you and all your fellows to pieces and feed them to the Hell Hounds. We will mount your heads on the traitor's gate and we will give your souls to Satan."

Luc turned. He needed no more encouragement to be gone.

His robes flapped around him as the others watched him in silence. His boots rang on the cold stones of the Great Hall. Smoke trailed after him, accompanied by the whoosh of the fire eating up his family's colors.

By my honor, the Cahors shall pay for this, he thought. *I will hunt them down and destroy them unceasingly.*

And in time, we'll take down House Moore as well.

This I vow, by my soul.

May Satan devour it if I fail.

Attend, Cahors: We are in an everlasting vendetta. May death come to any Deveraux who spares any one of you.

TWO

MOONSTONE

☾

Casting, seeking, we hunt our prey
By the light of blessed day
We curse the moon as it does rise
With all its subtle female ties

We worship the Goddess divine
Above us, the full moon is a sign
Peace to all, friends and kin
Who hold the Goddess deep within

The Cathers Coven: London

Sasha was worried. Holly was beginning to spin out of control again, as she had in the Moon Temple back in Paris. Holly was the most powerful witch alive, but Sasha feared she was too young to carry such an awesome responsibility. Powerful as she was, though, she would still be no match for the Supreme Coven.

Joel came to sit by her side so silently, so stealthily, that she almost did not hear him. She opened her eyes and saw the concern on his face. "Well, what do you think of our little coven?"

"Most of them are . . . broken," he said, his tongue lingering on the last word.

She nodded agreement. "Holly lost her best friend and her parents, discovered she was a witch, and became head of her own coven all within a year. During that time she's been constantly battling Michael Deveraux. Now we have the whole Supreme Coven on our heels."

He raised his brows. "That's too large a burden for anybody to carry alone."

"Holly's not alone," Amanda said defensively from the doorway.

Joel inclined his head, inviting her to join them. "No, she's not, but that's how she feels."

Amanda moved toward them, arms crossed over her chest. She looked angry, but more than that, she looked frightened. Joel and Sasha moved apart so that she could sit between them. She hesitated only a moment before collapsing onto the sofa.

"She scares me," she whispered so low, Sasha had to strain to hear her. "She just really let me have it. I got freaked out. I thought, what if I piss her off *too* much?"

She began to cry softly, and Sasha pulled her close,

whispering words of healing over her. Joel joined in, his gentle brogue washing over them. Sasha could feel all Amanda's grief for the loss of her mother, her fear for her father and her sister, and her sense of responsibility for Holly and Holly's actions.

Slowly Amanda stopped crying and sat up. "What did you do to me?" she muttered. "I feel *great.*"

"Joel's a healer," Sasha said, smiling at the male witch.

"It's second nature for most Druids."

"Druids?" Amanda asked.

"Aye. I'm descended from Celts. Druids draw power from the earth and try to find harmony and balance within it and mirror it within themselves."

"And you worship the Goddess?" Amanda asked, starting to sound sleepy.

He nodded. "It's a small step from Mother Earth to Goddess. In fact, many would argue that it's not a step at all."

Amanda nodded. "Thank you. For everything you're doing for us, and me." Her words were starting to slur, and her eyes began blinking shut.

He shrugged. "I do only what I can."

Sasha locked eyes with Joel. "Feeling up to doing some more?"

He nodded.

A gentle snore emanated from Amanda. The girl had fallen asleep, her chin on her chest. Sasha and Joel stood and carefully moved her so she was lying down on the sofa.

Together they moved silently to the other room. They moved first to Silvana and moved their hands through the air above the girl's body. Sasha could feel her anxiety, her concern for her mother, who was back in the States protecting the shaman, Dan Carter, and Amanda's father, Richard. They spoke words of calming and strength over her and prayed to the Goddess to protect those left behind.

Next they moved to Tommy. Like Amanda, he was afraid of Holly. His concern, though, was primarily for Amanda, afraid that she might get hurt. His fear for her was matched only by his love for her. They murmured words of strength and peace over him that he might be a rock for her.

When they passed their hands over Kari, her terror was nearly enough to make Sasha scream. She glanced at Joel's face and saw the horror that Kari felt mirrored there. They worked for several minutes, trying to purge her mind and soul and body of the crippling fear. Sasha knew that if they couldn't, sooner or later Kari's inability to take action would get her killed.

They straightened and stared at each other for a

long moment as they each took deep, cleansing breaths. Then as one they turned toward the bed where Holly lay.

Only, Holly was sitting up staring straight at them. She smiled slowly, and the sight sent a chill down Sasha's spine.

"Please, no," Holly told them in a reasonable voice. "Thanks for helping them and thanks for helping my ankle. But I don't want you in my mind. That's private."

Sasha debated about arguing with her for only the briefest moment. She could feel the rage flowing off of Holly. The girl barely had it under control, and it would do none of them any good to push her. Sasha locked eyes with Holly for one brief moment. *In time we will continue this discussion,* the older witch thought.

Holly gave Sasha the briefest of nods to acknowledge that she understood her message.

We will never continue the discussion, Holly thought as she plumped up her pillow. She had scented it with lavender, to combat sadness, and rosemary, for remembrance. *What's in my heart is private. And I'm getting tired of Sasha trying to second-guess my every move. I said we'd rescue Nicole first, and we will.*

But if it were up to me . . . how could I choose between

my cousin and the power of a love that goes beyond me and Jer?

Stonily she closed her eyes. The daytime world would remind her that Nicole was family, blood. Jer was an outsider in more ways than one. He was from another magical House; his brother and father were bent on killing Holly and anyone she met on her path. Of all the time she had known him, she had physically been around him only a few days at most.

But if it were up to me . . .

She was drifting now, as rosy mists washed over her eyelids. Her body gently unwound from all the trials, cares, and worries. She heard the lap of calm seas against wood, a warm, soft sound like a kitten savoring cream. The sky was fresh and clear, the waters smooth and still. She was drifting, yet her little boat glided steadily for the island.

The sun glinted off the battlements of an ancient castle; wild roses enclosed it, hands to heart, nature's velvety red Claddagh rings. Each arched window was a stained-glass letter, rippling in the sun as the boat moved closer. They spelled R-E-S-C-U-E.

She was not afraid. It was going to be easy.

The island grew as she sailed to it; the shoreline was welcoming, a carpet of moss and ferns greeting the hull as her wooden boat touched land. As she stood, she looked down and saw that she was gowned in Cahors black and silver, lacy long sleeves touching the hem of her straight skirt. There was a cir-

clet around her black curly hair, and earrings that cascaded to her shoulders. A matching belt of silver hung low over her hips.

The boat was upholstered in black velvet; the oarlocks were silver. As she stepped out of the boat, a small figurehead at the bow lifted one hand and saluted her. It was a Greek warrior woman, her helmet pushed back to reveal a serene smile of confidence and pride.

Even in ancient Greece, my line had power, *Holly thought.* Our blood has ennobled women for centuries.

With that knowledge came more certainty that she was going to rescue her one true love.

Her slippered foot touched soft fern, and then . . .

. . . she was walking through the gentle forest; birdsong greeted her as she entered a glade washed with sunshine. In the center, an enormous oak rose to the heavens, its lush branches providing a canopy for the man who lounged beneath it.

It was Jer, with his dark hair curling around his ears, and his dark, Deveraux eyes. He was crowned with ivy, and he lay on a bed of oak leaves. His face was angular and slightly weathered, and he was more muscular than she remembered.

He's older. He's matured.

When he caught sight of her, his face lit up. His dark eyes gleamed hungrily, and he rose from the nest of leaves. His head was held proudly, his bearing noble, graceful.

Then he spread his wings and flew to her.

She lifted her own, and they gave flight.

"Jer," she murmured as they traveled to the moon, to the stars, to the heart of the sky. "Jeraud Deveraux, I am thine."

"Mine, *and none other," he whispered. "Et nul autre."*

In the night, in the dark, Holly sighed and dreamed. In the hall, watching her, Sasha worried.

She's going to turn against us someday, she thought, terribly troubled. Then she left her High Priestess to her dreams. That was all they were—dreams. There was no truth in them.

None at all.

The Coven of White Magic: London, December

Evil traveled best at night, and so José Luís's coven raced to cover as much ground as they could by day.

Except, it's not José Luís's coven anymore, Philippe thought. *It's mine.*

The Coven was made up of four male witches of French or Spanish heritage. The four worshiped the Goddess in their own unique way, blending it with the Catholicism practiced by their families. The most solemn of their number, Armand, had even studied for the priesthood before joining the Coven. Alonzo was older, the father figure and benefactor of the group. Pablo was a teenager, the younger brother of José Luís. José Luís's death had left Philippe in charge.

The Coven had found Nicole Anderson, descendant of the Cahors witches, and had been trying to protect her from the evil that pursued her. They had failed and the warlocks who had captured Nicole had killed José Luís during their attack. Their coven leader had been their only casualty . . . if one could use the term *only.* Losing José Luís had been like losing a brother.

He was my best friend, my copain. And they killed him.

They won't get away with it.

The others grouped behind him, as if awaiting his order to move, to breathe. Astarte, the cat Nicole had adopted a few days before her capture, purred as she settled in Armand's arms, kneading his forearm as she gazed intently at Philippe. She was clearly awaiting her orders as well.

They had driven their car to the outskirts of Paris and left it there, in case the Supreme Coven had cast finders' spells on them. They had dumped their robes into the waters of the English Channel, and warded one another with protection spells as best they could.

At each juncture of their journey, they had turned to José Luís's true little brother, Pablo, whose senses were most acute—and who could often read minds—for guidance on where to go next. It made sense that he would lead them to London, for the Supreme Coven had claimed that ancient city as their territory for centuries. After the Great Fire of London, the Mother Coven had retreated . . . and the citizens of London had paid, and paid dearly, for that act of cowardice—Jack the Ripper had been one consequence, and the many bombings perpetuated by the IRA had been another. Mad cow disease had run rampant courtesy of the Supreme Coven.

And now they have Nicole, Philippe thought angrily. *Goddess, protect her from their savagery. Deliver them into our hands and let us free her.*

"Anything?" he asked Pablo. José Luís's strong Spanish features were evident in Pablo's face as he raised his chin and closed his eyes, frowning in concentration. The others remained motionless, watching him, willing him to lead them to their enemies.

They stood at the traffic circle of Piccadilly Circus, a Virgin Megastore on their left, and a huge Grecian-style museum on their right. Directly before them, cars swirled around an obelisk topped by the statue of a war hero. Pablo had guided them here, sensing the strength of the Supreme Coven's dark influence as his compass point. It had become very strong . . . but now had disappeared.

They hide well.

Just like they kill.

When Pablo said nothing, only exhaled and gazed down at the pavement, a collective sigh went up. They were getting tired, and nerves were fraying, and Philippe knew he had to do something to bolster their spirits, keep their confidence high and their focus strong.

Then Pablo murmured, "*Momento.* There's someone . . ." He cocked his head as if listening to sounds Philippe could not detect. Then his eyes widened. "*Una bruja,*" he whispered, and pointed across the street.

At that very moment, a striking young woman half-turned, her glance brushing over the Coven as if by accident. Philippe caught his breath. *Nicole!*

Astarte's tail flicked wildly as if she, too, recognized her mistress.

The woman's hair tumbled wildly around her face, masses of ringlets and curls; she had very black eyebrows and intense eyes. She was thin, and wiry.

But she was not Nicole.

She was, however, of witchblood.

She appeared to realize that Philippe and the others were too.

Though the crowd surged around her, she remained rooted to the spot, her lips moving, making a discreet gesture with her left hand. She was casting a spell.

Then everything changed; the scene around Philippe stretched and slowed down; people walked past him in slow motion; voices dragged; even the light changed, becoming oddly diffuse and washing the scene with strange off-colors.

The witch glided toward them, although in some portion of his mind, Philippe realized that she was not moving. She was projecting her persona as a confrontation; her eyes crackled with energy. She raised her arms and asked in a strangely echoate voice, *De quien eres?*

Not, *Who are you?* but, *Whose are you?*

He responded to her, reaching into her mind: *I am Nicole's.*

That shook her; her reflected image wobbled as if it were on TV and the reception was bad. Then the scene shifted again, and she was back in her place across the street, and he was staring at her.

He said to the others, *"Bon, allons-nous,"* his gaze fastened on her as she turned her head to the right, then gazed back at him and began to walk through the crowd. She was moving toward the nearest building, which was a fish and chips shop.

She looked back at him again.

"I feel it too," Pablo murmured. *"Ella es familia de Nicole."*

She's part of Nicole's family.

Then a shadow crossed above her head like a low-moving cloud. She stumbled backward, glancing up.

Above the noise and tumult of the street, the unmistakable war cry of a falcon jittered across the winter sky. Astarte yowled angrily and swiped with her paw at the air.

Philippe jerked his gaze to the clouds. Sure enough, three enormous falcons hovered there, the largest glaring down at the lone witch. She stood stock-still; the three looped, then tipped beak-first into the air currents and began to make for her.

"Non," Philippe murmured, raising his right hand. A fireball appeared in it; he prepared to lob it, when the falcons swooped directly over the witch's head, then swooped upward again. He extinguished the fireball. Apparently, they had not been able to see her.

Or else she is their friend.

The members of José Luís's coven crossed themselves. Their Father Confessor, Alonzo, murmured, "The birds couldn't see her."

"Let's go," Philippe said, rushing toward her.

"It might be a trick. Falcons serve the House of Deveraux," Armand commented. "Perhaps they are trying to draw us out of our cloak of invisibility."

With one more glance his way, the witch darted between two buildings and was lost to Philippe's view.

"Attends!" he cried. He stepped into the street; horns blared. A man on a bicycle slammed on his brakes and began swearing at him in Farsi.

Philippe circled his wrist, creating a bubble of safety around himself as he ran against the traffic. Cars jerked to a stop; the man on the bicycle slowed, then tipped over—just in time, the man steadied himself with his foot—and all the while, Philippe knew he was being foolish. While he and his coven brothers could hide themselves from detection, the effects of his spell were laid bare for all to see—including the watchful falcons, who now grouped as a trio and began to dive toward him.

Now I've done it, he thought. They were perhaps ten meters above him. He saw their flashing eyes, could magically hear the chatter of their beaks as they opened and closed them, watched the sun glint off their talons.

Then they swooped up and flew over him as they had done with the witch who so resembled Nicole. They wheeled back around, screeching with frustration, then doubled back in the opposite direction.

When his foot reached the curb of the other street,

he saw a brief flash of blue light to his right, in a small alleyway. He ran toward it.

She was not there.

But a fresh lily lay against old stones, and as he picked it up he glanced left, right . . . and saw no witch.

As the others caught up to him, he examined the lily, and then he inhaled its scent. "She's a friend," he said aloud, holding out the flower, "and she's in danger."

Astarte stared at him with her big yellow eyes, and plaintively mewed.

Jer: Avalon, December

For the third time that day Jeraud Deveraux began counting the stones that made up the walls of his prison. He thought of his life before, at home in Seattle, where he had gone where he wanted, seen whom he desired, and done what he wished. *My, how small my life has become.*

He didn't know how long he had been on the island. He hadn't even seen more than his small portion of it, which consisted of a cell-like room with a tiny door opening onto a narrow path that led to a lone rock on a sheer cliff. Neither the six-foot path nor the cliff offered any hope of escape. He could not scale sheer rock.

Inside his cell there was only the one door, but he

was the only one who used it. The others who came and went did so right through the wall, through some kind of porthole he had been unable to find or open. He had spent days searching for another way out of the room and days more searching the cliff for a means of escape. He had finally given up.

His time was better spent trying to heal his body and mind and gathering information from the girl who brought him food. He feared he wasn't faring well with the healing part. His flesh was still mangled, and he feared he looked barely human. His mind hadn't fared much better. Every night he dreamed of Holly, wanting her and hating her. He fought himself from calling to her until he was in a fever of torment and then the real agony began. Every night in his dreams he relived the night in the school gymnasium when his father and brother had summoned the Black Fire and Holly had left him to burn in it.

On the plus side he had managed to gather a considerable amount of information. He knew that he was being held prisoner on the mythic island of Avalon. He had also managed to learn that it was the home of Sir William, the leader of the Supreme Coven, and his son, James. He had almost pinpointed the location of the island, even, through a variety of means ranging from the astrological to the magical. If his stars were right, the island was located in the Celtic Sea between Ireland and Britain. If his stars were wrong, he could be on the dark side of the moon for all he knew.

The skin on the back of his neck started to crawl. It was an intensely uncomfortable reaction that he had come to associate with the members of House Moore.

Seconds later he heard footsteps approaching. He turned and stared straight at James and Eli as they materialized inside the room. He blinked hard. He had seen people appear inside the room and it still startled him. A light blue shimmered around them and then faded within a moment. *It has to be a portal. It must be opened by magic.* If that was true, though, then how did the servant who brought him his food make it through? He had tried to follow her out once but had found himself thrown backward half the length of the room. Maybe it was keyed to certain peoples' auras. Maybe it was keyed to his.

He focused on the two people now occupying the room with him. James was the son and heir of Sir William, head of the Supreme Coven. Eli was Jer's own brother, though it was hard to believe they shared anything in common, much less parents. James strode in as if he owned the place, which, technically, he did. Still, his swagger was decidedly more pronounced. Eli slunk forward like a cur at his side.

On his left ring finger James sported a ring. It was a band of gold wrapped around a huge bloodstone. It glistened darkly against his skin. A smile spread across James's face as he saw Jer eyeing it.

"Sorry you missed my wedding yesterday," James mocked. "It was a splendid affair. The rites were observed, the wine flowed, and the bride was mute." He chuckled. "I believe you know her—she's from Seattle, after all. A pretty little Cahors witch."

Jer's stomach twisted in knots. *Holly!* What had happened to her? He was so busy fighting a sudden feeling of nausea that he almost missed James's next words.

"'Course, it's Moore now. Nicole Moore."

Jer's heart leaped. It wasn't Holly! He breathed a prayer to whatever entity would listen to keep her safe and then another one for her poor cousin now wed to James. "Why aren't you with her now?" he asked.

"Let's just say she's recovering from last night," James chuckled evilly.

Taking in a long scratch that ran from the bridge of his nose to his jaw and the way his left arm hung a little limply Jer wondered if James wasn't the one recovering. "Congratulations," Jer said sarcastically. "Now, leave me alone."

"Sorry, little brother," Eli finally spoke up. "Can't do that. We've got work to do."

Jer studied Eli quietly. His brother had dated Nicole for a long time. *What does he think of James marrying her?* Eli's face was passive, inscrutable, and it struck Jer just how much more like their father Eli looked than last he had seen him. There was something in his eyes, though. A dangerous spark. *James had better watch his back.*

"What work?" he asked, fearing the answer.

"Black Fire," James answered.

Jer forced himself not to recoil. He forced himself to sit absolutely still as though he had no knowledge, no experience, no deep terror of the fire. "Excuse me?"

James gestured as if to show the rising of flames. "Black Fire. You are going to help me conjure it."

Jer laughed in disbelief. "I'm not going to help you do anything."

"Oh, I think you will, if you want to live," James drawled.

"Kill me, you'd be doing me a favor," Jer retorted. It was a bluff. Not so long ago it wouldn't have been, but as he had been growing stronger he had begun to hope again. *Either that or it's the dreams where Holly comes to me,* he thought.

"I will, but not before I kill Holly before your eyes and Nicole's sister, Amanda, as well."

Jer licked what was left of his lips. He had sworn

once, it seemed a thousand years ago, to protect them from his father. He had pledged himself to defending the helpless. Staring into James's eyes, he did not doubt that the other could do as he threatened. Something in him gave way a little. "I don't know anything about the fire," he admitted. "Except that it burns."

The House of Moore: Van Diemen's Land (Australia), 1789

Sir Richard Moore, By the Grace of His Majesty George III, Royal Governor of Botany Bay, stared into the scrying stone that lay on the carved wooden desk before him. In ten days the British ship *Destiny* would arrive with a fresh cargo of convicts to work the lands. Among the one hundred plus men and women were convicted thieves, murderers, buggerers and, most important, six witches. Of course, they hadn't been convicted of witchcraft. Thievery was the crime they had been accused of. But he knew they worshiped the Goddess and they were on their way.

Sir Richard curled his lip. *Followers of the Mother Coven. They think to escape us and spread their filth here, among the dregs of society. But those of us who are loyal to the Supreme Coven are everywhere.*

Even though at times it feels as though we had been exiled to Hell itself . . . as I am in this vast wasteland devoid of culture and refined company . . .

No matter. My House is in ascendance. My father sits upon the throne of skulls in London Town, and I, his eldest son, come to this forsaken land in search of new magics that will add to our armory in the days to come. For while it is true that the Deveraux have been exiled these 113 years for publicly battling during the Great Fire of London, they may come back one day with the secret of the Black Fire. And then the House of Moore will have to fight to retain our crown as High Priest.

I stand much to gain if I can learn new ways of inflicting harm in this vast wasteland.

But before I do, I will take care of the minor inconvenience that these witches present. . . .

He closed his eyes and concentrated. He pictured the ship in his mind's eye. The seas were riding high, and the wind was kicking up. A storm was brewing and, with his knowledge of the Black Arts and his power, he helped it along.

Then he pushed against a seam in the ship's hull. Slowly a crack began to form. First a drop of water eased its way through, and then a steady trickle. He opened his eyes. Within moments he knew that the trickle would turn to a flood.

He turned back to the scrying stone and watched until the ship had sunk. Every man, woman, and child drowned, and he watched them all, smiling.

When at last it was over he rose, pleased with

himself. The papers on his desk relating to the running of the colony could wait. He had a meeting to attend.

The Cathers Coven: London, December

It was late afternoon, almost twenty-four hours since Holly and the others had entered Joel's safe house. Now, seated again before Joel's fire, Holly blinked and stirred from her reverie. She had had a vision: She had seen herself walking down the street near the fish and chips shop, encountering a tall man across the street, trying to communicate with him. There had been others with him. Then the Deveraux falcons had swooped down on them all, harrying them.

She didn't know what it meant, but she had a sense that the wards of the souvenir shop had been penetrated. That, combined with the unease she felt in not having known Joel was a male witch—a Druid, whatever he called himself—prompted her decision to leave.

They left Joel's home in the morning after having been given directions to another safe house in London, and a backup in another city should London become too dangerous. The city was Coventry. The irony was not overlooked by Holly, who was equally certain that it had not been overlooked by the Supreme Coven.

They twisted through endless streets until they had left Joel and his safe house far behind. A shadow brushed across Holly's mind and she turned, expecting to see something behind them. There was nothing there. She changed course, and they began moving south. With each step she took the feeling of being followed lessened. They turned another corner and took another street, which slowly began to wind its way north.

The feeling intensified, and Holly stopped in her tracks. The others exchanged looks but spoke not a word. The sensation stayed at the same level of intensity. "Does anyone else feel that?"

Sasha nodded silently, but the others just looked at her with blank faces. Holly took a step forward and the tingling along her spine increased. She took a step backward, and it lessened. Another step back and it lessened even more.

"North, I think the Supreme Coven's headquarters is north of here."

Sasha nodded agreement.

Slowly the group started forward. A half dozen more steps and Amanda spoke. "I feel it now too."

Another dozen steps and the others felt it as well.

Another dozen steps and all hell broke loose.

THREE

AMETRINE

☾

Death and destruction spread our fame
Till all others tremble at the Deveraux name
We will rule them in the end
King and serf, foe and friend

And now we claim for our own
All the power that we've sown
Goddess answer us in our need
Cause our foes to scream and bleed

"Goddess, protect us!" Holly cried as directly above the Coven, about twenty feet in the air, immense, scaly demons dressed in ancient battle armor burst from round portals shimmering with blue. Their heads were horned, their eyes red, glowing slits, and their mouths glistened with multiple rows of fangs. Their bodies were the sickly color of a bruise, purple and blue-black.

They began to drop to the ground. *It's raining fiends,* she thought, feeling an overwhelming urge to laugh hysterically. Then one of the demons landed mere feet from Holly, and the urge to laugh vanished. She leaped backward, stumbling and falling, yet she managed to release a fireball at the monster. It raised its taloned hand, grasped the fireball, and extinguished it, flinging the embers to the ground. With a roar, it advanced on Holly. Its fangs glistened with green saliva as it lumbered forward on thick, well-muscled legs. Reaching into its armor, it withdrew what looked to be the hilt of a sword. Then it raised the hilt into the air.

A black falcon shrieked as it burst from the portal. Between its clawed feet it carried a gleaming blade. With another cry, it released the blade, which whistled through the air like a bomb and then magically connected with the hilt.

As the demon swiped it at Holly, crackles of green magical energy trailed. The weapon sizzled and danced with magic, and as Holly launched another fireball, the sword sliced it into dancing shards of heat and light.

She conjured and flung more fireballs, feeling herself almost a machine, some kind of animated fighting automaton such as warring clans had possessed back in the Middle Ages. She wondered where everyone else was, aware only of chaos whirling all around her.

The demon sliced her projectiles apart with ease. Then it hacked at the air itself, and the gray, snowy sky seemed to shatter. Solid nickel-colored shards exploded outward, leaving a churning hole of fluorescent green about ten feet in diameter.

From the magical rent crawled more demons clambering over the broken pieces of sky, these much smaller and completely black, with deep, bloodred eyes and mouths that wrapped halfway around their snakelike heads. Seeing Holly, three of them leaped at her. She moved her hands and uttered an incantation, forming and sending a magical bolt of energy in their direction.

Her aim was true; she took out two of the three, and they exploded in a shower of body parts. The survivor sailed through the flying carnage and attacked her knee, clamping down hard with incisor-like teeth.

Holly screamed from the pain; it distracted her, but she managed to conjure another bolt. She flung it at the demon, and it disintegrated. She conjured more, sending them flying without aiming them, trying to wound the larger demon as it shambled toward her. The sword was no longer glowing, as if it had lost its magical charge, but the sharpness of the blade looked deadly.

"Goddess from the depths of night, banish them all from my sight," she murmured. She looked up, expecting to see the demons vanish. Instead, the demons kept coming but her vision began to blur and fade. "No!" she sobbed, frustration overwhelming her. "Goddess, now restore my sight, and kill this beast with whom I fight." Her vision was partially restored, but she was beginning to lose consciousness because of her injury. *I'm the strongest witch alive,* she thought, *but I don't know how to use my power to save myself.*

Then the monster froze, threw up its hands, and roared in agony. Slowly it began to tip forward . . . directly on top of Holly. Her fingers twitched as she whispered, *"Desino!"* Her vision blurred again as gray splotches danced before her eyes. *I'm losing it . . . Goddess, I demand protection!*

The monster froze in mid-fall. With a twitch of her finger, Holly threw it to one side, where it collapsed in a heap on the ground. Behind it stood the tall, dark-haired man in her vision. She didn't know if her magic or his had killed the demon.

"Look out," Holly rasped as another demon rose up behind him.

He wheeled around and moved his hands in clockwise motions; the demon staggered backward, then came at him again. It stuck its hand into its armor and brought out a wicked-looking short sword, glowing and crackling with magic.

Holly launched a fireball at the sword, and the

weapon burst into flame. Startled, the demon dropped it. Then it slashed at the space between it and the man, and Holly raised her hand to help him again.

But this time, more of the smaller demons pounced on her, pushing her onto her back. They began to bite. . . .

"Non, I will not die this day!" a voice shouted inside Holly's head. It was Isabeau. Latin words mixed with French poured through Holly's mind as her witchly ancestress conjured. The demons held her down, slashing at her with their teeth, gnawing on her. . . .

"Non!" Isabeau protested. *"Live, girl!"*

From somewhere deep within herself, Holly traveled to a place free of panic and pain. Everything around her was black and icy, but she herself was a light. It was as if her consciousness had been somehow crystallized, as if it were some kind of glowing entity. It flickered; then, as if ghostly lips had blown gently on it, it grew brighter.

"Speak words of magic. I will teach you. Ecoutes . . ." Isabeau urged her.

Holly listened carefully, but the words slipped away before she could make them out. They were like luminescent bubbles, each one bobbing away, then popping as she mentally reached out to grasp it. At first she was frustrated, and tried harder. Time passed; she grew languorous, realizing there was a kind of cold comfort in the black ice surrounding her. It was peaceful there, and there was no fear. . . .

"Non! You will not die!" Isabeau railed at her.

But I am *dying,* Holly thought. *And it's all right. It's better than all this running, and being afraid. . . .*

A man was running toward her, his arms outstretched. He wore a robe of green ivy and red holly. On his right arm rested a magnificent falcon, hooded and belled. In his left hand he held a warrior's sword.

Her heartbeat echoed his footfalls, which were slowed, each foot lifting up, then moving gradually downward; it was as if he were floating in the unending landscape. *"It is my Jean. Thus he has come,"* Isabeau said to her, *"through vast echoes of time, over long stretches of time apart, moons and years and centuries. . . ."*

He was coming for her now, to claim her. Surrounded by darkness, coming out of darkness, to bring her into darkness.

To rend my spirit, and send my soul to Hell . . .

Jean . . . non, ah, Jean . . . have mercy on me. . . .

Holly sensed Isabeau's confusion, her longing, and her fear. Jean de Deveraux was Isabeau de Cahors's only love, sprung from her only hate. She had sworn a vow to kill him, and had not; for that, she must walk the earth. Rather, she had died, and he had never forgiven her for either of her treacheries—the massacre of his entire family, or for dying herself. . . .

On he came, in the strange, floating gait; he was tall and dark-haired; his eyes were set deep, and his brows were fierce. There was such a look of ferocity on his face that Holly had no idea how to read it. Anger? Joy?

Through the muffled thunder of her heartbeats he came closer. By the glow of her own light his features became more visible, and her lips parted in surprise. This was no stranger; this was Jer Deveraux.

Jer! I'm here!

The man's expression changed; he looked very confused. Then he shook his head—his hair floated in slow motion, his eyes caught the light and flashed—and his voice slid toward her as if it were rolling toward her inside a crystal ball:

Holly, no! Don't make contact with me! They will find you!

Inside her head, Isabeau cried, *"Jean!"*

Still conscious of herself as a light, Holly moved toward Jer. His face shifted, took on a slightly wicked cast, and he murmured, *"Isabeau, ma femme."*

He was Jean once more.

"I did not kill you, I did not," Isabeau pleaded. *"Je vous en prie, monsieur!"*

Jean ripped the hood off the falcon's head and raised his right elbow, urging the massive bird to take flight. The creature hefted into the darkness and shot toward Holly. Its sharp beak aimed for her face; its eyes gazed evilly into hers.

Holly gave a cry of despair.

The bird soared toward her.

She tried to back away, to make herself move in any direction, but she couldn't.

Behind the bird, Jer Deveraux—not Jean—shouted, "No!"

And in that moment, Holly woke up.

Her eyes flew open. The tall man stood with his back to her, battling two of the larger demons with bolts of magic, while, beside him, another, older man held aloft a large cross. Snow was falling; soon it concealed the two men from her view; everything was a blur of snow streaked with something slimy and green, and what looked like human blood.

"Take it easy," said a voice. She recognized it as Joel's. What was he doing here? "I'm healing you."

"Jer," she whispered.

Then everything faded to black.

"Oh, God!" Kari shouted as she and Silvana fought to repel the charging demon. It was headed straight for them, and their combined magic spells had done nothing to slow it down. Above its head it whipped a morning star, a sphere of metal covered with spikes.

The demon's purple-black skin steamed in the snow; its breath reeked of death. From its glowing eyes tendrils of flame escaped, and when it opened its mouth, ash poured out.

Kari screamed and started to bolt. Beside her, Silvana tried to stand her ground, murmuring one of the protection spells Holly and Amanda had taught them over the summer, but she was so terrified, she kept forgetting the words. Silvana's *tante*—Aunt—Cecile had taught her the ways of *voudon,* not of black and white magics, and combat was still new to her.

"Kari, don't run! It'll get you!" Silvana shouted, then realized she had interrupted her own spell.

Kari did run, shrieking as she turned on her heel and raced in the opposite direction. The demon roared and flung the morning star at her. It went wide, leaving Kari unhurt as she kept going.

Silvana shouted out, *"Concresco murus!"* and to her relief—and astonishment—a barrier of glowing blue energy formed between her and the spiked ball. The morning star crashed into the barrier and was caught there.

Enraged, the demon flung itself against the barrier,

but it was deflected, bouncing backward and slamming to the icy ground on its back.

Silvana turned to the right and repeated the spell, then to the left, forming a three-sided wall of protection. The smaller demons scrabbled up against it, pounding at it with their claws and trying to rip at it with their teeth. Two of the larger ones advanced, one with a battle-ax, another with a curved scimitar. Both of them were repulsed and both of them kept trying to break through.

All any one of them has to figure out is that the fourth side is unprotected, Silvana thought, *and we're dead.*

She caught up with Kari, grabbed her arm, and said, "Move it!" As she tried to put as much distance between them and the demons, she uttered the spell again, pointing to the space directly behind them. Then she hazarded a glance over her shoulder—sure enough, she had created another barrier.

"Get me out of here, get me out of here!" Kari screamed hysterically. "What's going on?"

"I'm guessing guards," Silvana told her, wasting precious energy. "We must be near the headquarters."

"Then they probably know it!" Kari cried. "They'll be sending out reinforcements!"

As if on cue—or by magic spell—the area directly in front of Kari and Silvana burst open with a flash of blue light. Dozens of tiny bony creatures poured out, chittering and gabbling as they darted toward the two girls. They were imps, all mouth and fury, and they were coming after Kari and Silvana.

Kari started screaming again.

"Will you shut up!" Silvana yelled at her.

They both made U-turns, running back in the same direction they had come . . . until they hit the fourth barrier Silvana had created. Unable to slow down in time, Kari smacked into it, while Silvana managed to avoid a collision. Kari ricocheted backward, disoriented, while Silvana lunged forward and grabbed her, pulling the other girl against her as she held out her left hand and tried to conjure a fireball.

Her spell failed.

The imps kept coming.

Sasha stood beside a male witch whose name she didn't know—he wasn't Joel, who had silently followed them here—and together they created a thick, brilliant wall of light. The creatures of darkness that tore themselves into it were instantly consumed. It lasted perhaps ten seconds, then faded.

"Another?" Sasha queried, and the man nodded.

They extended their arms, murmured their invocations and incantations in Latin, and created a second wall. But by then, the oncoming demons and imps steered clear of it, and it faded without taking out a single adversary.

The man shouted, *"La-bas!"* and Sasha, who lived at the Mother Temple in Paris and spoke French, pointed her fingers at the ground. She willed her energy to become subject to him, to give strength to his spell, and together they incised a ravine into the snow.

The first demon to step into it plummeted downward as if into a bottomless chasm.

At the man's urging, Sasha walked backward, allowing him to use her energy once more to create a second ravine, and then a third. By then she was utterly depleted and trembling like a leaf. Her knees buckled, and he caught her up in his arms, holding her as he whirled around. She knew they had kept their backs undefended for too long, and so she wasn't too surprised to see a new kind of demon—this one snakelike, with several arms and an elongated head—whipping toward them. It extended its black, forked tongue and it snapped at the man's arm like a whip. Sasha heard a sharp hiss of burned flesh, and the man flinched but did not drop her.

The tongue retracted as the demon rushed at them.

Then the creature extended it again.

★★★

Tommy bellowed as he fought in hand-to-hand combat. He was fighting with a sword Amanda had grabbed from one of the dead demons. His opponent had just appeared, bursting through one of the portals—a skeletal warrior with green glowing eyes.

As Amanda bombarded it with waves of magical energy, it continued to attack. Miraculously, Tommy was holding his own, fighting with uncommon skill—*it can't be because of that one semester we had of fencing*—he looked as surprised as she felt. Then she realized that someone must be augmenting his skill with magic.

With an athletic lunge, he shoved the sword into the rib cage of the skeleton as if to pierce its heart, and the figure exploded in a shower of bones.

There was no time to so much as cheer. Another skeleton burst through the same portal and took up position. Before Amanda could register its arrival, a third one appeared.

Something rushed through her like an electric current, making the fillings in her teeth tingle. Her muscles jumped, her heart skipped a beat; she felt renewed and strengthened.

I've been charmed, she thought. *Someone did to me what they did to Tommy.*

With no time to take that in, she raced over to

another dead demon and picked up a sword for herself. She took a practice swing, confirming her guess that she had been magically enhanced, and raced back to Tommy's side.

He was battling the second and third skeletons, and they were beating him back. Amanda jumped in, her sword flashing, her movements so fast, she couldn't even tell what she was doing.

Bones flew everywhere as the two skeletons exploded.

We did it! she exulted.

But then a fourth sprung up inside the portal. A fifth. A sixth.

She quickly glanced at Tommy, who anxiously shook his head.

"I'm tired," he confessed.

She took a deep breath.

So am I.

The skeleton warriors leaped through.

There was screaming and fighting all around her, and Holly knew by the tremor in Joel's voice that their side was losing.

"Be well, heal," Joel pleaded with Holly. "You're our only hope."

I can't be, she wanted to tell him. *Please. Not me.*

She was in agony. She had been ripped and bitten in so many places, she had no idea how she was still in one piece. Before Joel had started performing magic on her, she had been so near death, she'd been numb; but with each renewal of his healing spell, her awareness of the pain intensified. She could hardly stand it.

She tried to fight it, to let herself die, but he gritted his teeth and said, *"Damn it, save us."*

"There's not much time," the dark-haired man shouted, flinging magic at an oncoming demon. The demon screamed and fell. The man ticked his gaze down at her, then returned to his magic battle.

Joel doggedly continued, *"Bi tarbhach, bi fallain, bi beò cath. Rach am feabhas creutar agus inntinn."*

And Holly felt herself being pulled back inside herself, to the dark, cold place. Shadows hung like frozen curtains. As before, she was the only source of light. Was it her imagination, or was that light dimmer?

A figure appeared on the landscape, and Holly shrank away. Was it Jean again? Or Jer?

It was neither.

Wearing black and silver, and holding a large spray of lilies, Isabeau floated toward her. Her hair tumbled loosely over her shoulders, and she looked wild and untamed. *"Ma fille, I have brought someone to help you."*

She extended her arm, and another figure drifted

slowly toward Holly, in the same slow-motion manner. This figure was dressed all in black, and heavily veiled. But her hands were visible; they held a gleaming dagger across her chest. Its hilt was brass-colored and encrusted with jewels.

The dagger glowed. There was something very beautiful, very hypnotic, about it. The point shimmered.

"You are going to die. But that does not trouble you. You wish it," the figure said. Her voice was deep and heavily accented, like Isabeau's.

"You are a coward."

Holly swallowed.

"Your friends are going to die. Think of that, soft young woman. In the next few moments, they will be dead."

"No," Holly whispered.

"All will be lost. And my bloodline will die out. Forever."

"You're Catherine," Holly said, realizing. "Isabeau's mother."

The figure raised its veiled head. *"The strongest witch who ever lived. Until you."*

She raised the dagger and pointed it at Holly. *"You can save everything. But you must be willing to become the witch you were born to be."*

"I . . . I . . ."

"Don't stammer, girl! It humiliates me so! The battle is being lost. They are dying."

"Then stop it!" Holly cried. "I'll do anything! I—I will!"

"Swear." Catherine held out the dagger. *"Swear by your own blood, which is mine, Holly of the Cahors Coven."*

Holly reached forward and touched the dagger; it pricked the tip of her forefinger with a sharp slice. Three droplets of her blood dripped in slow motion toward the featureless black landscape. . . .

And she was on the street.

With the others.

And she was unhurt.

She gasped; beside her, Amanda said, "What, Holly?"

There were no demons. No imps. No portals. Everyone was fine. The other members of her coven stood in the snow, watching her curiously as she turned in a circle, completely bewildered.

"Where are the others?" she asked. She was stunned. "The guys? The dark-haired man?"

Amanda glanced at Sasha and Silvana, standing nearby. Tommy came up and waved a hand in front of Holly's eyes. "Yo. Everything all right?"

"Joel?" she called.

The snow fell heavily. The wind whistled. Other pedestrians on the street passed by, oblivious to the presence of the Coven, which was warded and cloaked.

"Okay, this is very weird," Holly said slowly.

"I quite agree," said a voice as a figure stepped from the snowfall and approached her.

It was the dark-haired man. He cocked his head and studied Holly. "There was a battle," he began. He gestured to her coven. "And now . . . there is not."

She nodded, flooding with relief. Someone else knew what had happened.

From the falling snow, three other men emerged, one very young, looking confused and wary. The others were older, one of them in his forties. Holly recognized them from the battle.

"You stopped it," the man continued. "Magically." She had time to notice now that he had a very thick accent.

"Holly?" Amanda asked, her voice rising. "What's he talking about?"

"I stopped it," Holly agreed. *But there was a price . . . what was it? Another death? What have I done?*

She turned and walked north.

There was no tingling sensation, no sense of anxiety, no impending danger.

"It's gone." She looked at the dark-haired man, who was watching her carefully. "We ran into something here, and we were attacked."

Her coven members stared at her. But it was clear

the man remembered everything that had happened as well.

"We were on our way to find you," he said. He reached into his jeans pocket and pulled out the petals of a wilted lily. "You left this behind."

"I . . ." She took the lily, examining it carefully. "I had a vision. I saw you, but I never left . . . the place I was." She was careful not to mention the safe house. "Who are you?"

He gestured to himself and said, "We serve White Magic. I am Philippe. Our leader was killed by those whom you fight."

The youngest one looked stricken. "He was my brother, José Luís," he said quietly.

"Killed?" Holly gestured around them. "But the battle's . . . gone."

"There was another battle," said the oldest of the men. "There have been many of them."

"Whom do you serve?" Philippe asked, gazing steadily at Holly. "To whom do you owe allegiance?"

"Holly, don't answer that," Sasha said firmly, coming up beside her and putting her hand on her shoulder. "We don't know who these men are."

Holly pursed her lips.

"We lost José Luís during a kidnapping," Philippe

informed Holly. "The Supreme Coven took one of us." He paused, then added carefully, "Her name was Nicole."

"Nicole!" Amanda cried, rushing toward the man. "Where is she?"

Holly raised her hand. "Amanda, be careful. Don't say anything else until we know what's going on."

The man looked sharply at Amanda, who was bursting with questions. "You know Nicole?" He narrowed his eyes. "You look much like her."

Holly stepped forward. "I'm the High Priestess of this coven," she announced. "You need to deal with me."

"We are here to rescue her," the man said. The other men nodded, and the oldest one crossed himself.

"Oh, Holly!" Amanda cried.

Holly softened. She decided to trust him. After all, they had risked death to fight beside them. "So are we," she said.

After a brief discussion, Holly decided the best thing to do would be to go to the second London safe house for which Joel had given them directions.

She was worried that he had not reappeared after Catherine had eliminated the battle for them. Of everyone she had seen at the battle, he was the only missing person.

There was to be a price, she reminded herself, with a terrible feeling of dread. *If I caused his death . . .*

She could not think further about it.

She had a coven to save.

San Francisco

Tante Cecile gasped as she was wrenched from her meditations. The girls were in danger. She glanced uneasily around the Victorian house and wondered if she should go find Dan. They had been in San Francisco for several days, watching over Amanda and Nicole's father and Holly's friend, Barbara Davis-Chin.

It had been hard to be separated from her daughter, Silvana, knowing that they might never see each other again. Still, each of them did what they had to for the good of the Coven.

She closed her eyes and rubbed her temples slowly, trying to draw the images she had seen into clearer focus. *A great battle, her Silvana fighting nobly. Then, suddenly it was over, as though it had never been. Why? She saw Holly standing before a veiled woman promising her . . . what? Something.*

Her eyes flew open as her heart skipped a beat. *Oh, Holly! What have you done?*

Ametrine

London, Safe House

The second safe house was more in keeping with what Amanda had expected the first one would be like: a small London flat festively decorated for Yule with garlands of holly and ivy, and a Yule log atop a cheery mantel awaiting the birth of the sun. The flat was overseen by a female witch named Rose, who ushered in the ten fugitives and led them as far away from the doors and windows as possible.

"There's no guarantee you're safe any longer," Rose told them after Holly related the story of the battle and the undoing of it. "But I don't know what else to do."

She gave them something to eat and excused herself to figure out sleeping arrangements.

As they crowded into her sitting room, Philippe approached Holly and Sasha and said, "We must talk."

Amanda frowned, somewhat hurt by the exclusion. She was obviously not one of the inner sanctum of their group.

Then Tommy took her hand and said, "Let them deal with it for now, Amanda. Holly's our leader."

The contact of his skin, though she had felt it a hundred times during rituals, sent an unexpected shiver through her. Her mind began to go someplace that frightened her. *Tommy . . . Tommy Nagai is a man . . .*

he's a guy . . . and I . . . I'm a woman . . . we're growing up. We can . . . there are things we can do and be together, the two of us . . . if, um, he wants . . .

Suddenly she wasn't interested in what Holly and the man were talking about. She wasn't jealous that Sasha had been allowed to join in and she wasn't. She was just intensely aware of Tommy. *None of them is with him. I am.*

She looked down at his hand in hers. She felt herself flushing and said, "Nagai, you're making contact with my skin."

His smile was wicked gentle. His almond eyes were dancing. He looked as if he had swallowed a flashlight, and her breath caught. *We're so having the chemistry thing,* she thought.

"Tommy, you're . . . you're holding my hand."

"So?" He chuckled.

She gave his hand a shake. "C'mon, let me go." When he didn't, she said, "What's your deal, Tommy?"

"You are such an incredible dork," he told her fondly. "Anderson, I've been crushing on you for years. Haven't you ever noticed?"

"Oh." She was taken aback. *Tommy?*

Tommy the joker, who never took her seriously but who was always there, always listening, always commiserating over everything that ever happened to her?

Hello?

"Years," he repeated, as if trying to penetrate her astonishment. "Since we were babies, practically."

"Oh." She gave him a shy smile. "Hi." It wasn't poetry, but it was all she could think to say. Somehow, though, it was all she needed to say.

He smiled back. "Hi." Gave her hand another wag. "Not so bad?"

"Not so bad," she agreed. "But we're still babies."

"Not so much." He pecked her cheek.

"Mew."

A cat jumped up onto Amanda's lap. Startled, she jumped and then settled as the cat began to purr and curled up as though to go to sleep.

"Well, where did you come from?" she asked the bedraggled-looking feline. "Are you Rose's cat?"

"Her name is Astarte. She is Nicole's. She came to Nicole a few nights before she was kidnapped. She has joined us in the search," Pablo told her.

Amanda felt her stomach twist into a tight knot. A few nights before she was kidnapped . . . *Did this cat come to her when Holly drowned Hecate?* she wondered. A chill rippled up her spine.

Philippe looked over at Amanda and Tommy. He looked envious. "They found each other," he murmured.

"Well, they didn't have far to look," Sasha said dryly. She looked expectantly at Holly.

Holly cleared her throat. "As you know, there was a battle, and I . . . I made contact with a veiled woman. She undid it somehow."

"What was her price?" Sasha asked. As Holly flushed, she pressed; "It was worse than the cat, wasn't it?"

Holly narrowed her eyes. "That's my business."

"No, it's not, not when you're part of a coven. We all have to agree on things. It's the way of the Mother Coven."

Jer's mother was putting Holly on the defensive, and she didn't like it. Holly threw back her head and shot back, "And that's why the Mother Coven is so weak, Sasha. Look at us. They can't even protect us, while the Supreme Coven kidnaps some of us and kills others. They're lame."

Sasha blinked. "I can't believe you can say that, when—"

"Alors," Philippe said, raising his hands. He turned his attention to Holly. "I beg your pardon, but we must move to action, not discuss philosophy."

"You're right," she said tersely. "What's done is done. What I did or said . . ." She exhaled. "I'm not certain what I agreed to, in all honesty. But it saved us."

"Sometimes that's not the right thing to do," Sasha insisted.

"Well, when you get down off your high horse, let me know." Holly turned on her heel.

"Holly," Philippe called, following her as she stomped into the kitchen. She looked around, found Rose's electric kettle, and lifted it to see if there was water in it. Satisfied that it had recently been filled, she plugged it in and rummaged through the scattering of tea things on a silver tray for a tea bag.

"You're the one Nicole called," Philippe said, leaning against the white-tiled counter. "It was then that James and Eli were alerted to our location. Then that José Luís was killed."

She hunched her shoulders as she selected a Prince of Wales tea bag and smoothed the string away from the little pouch of fragrant tea. "Are you trying to guilt-trip me into saving her? Because you don't need to. I said I'd do it and I will."

"I'm only saying that I care about her. We care about her," he amended.

"No, you don't." She scowled at him. "You're just as bad as the Mother Coven. All this talking isn't going to get anyone back."

"We need to figure out who each of us is first," he replied. He gestured to the tea bag. "May I have some as well?"

"Sorry," she muttered, picking up a second bag. "There should be some cups around here somewhere. . . ."

He opened a cabinet and pulled out two mugs that said LILITH FAIR. He chuckled. "Rose is such a one who would go to a thing like that, eh? Sarah McLachlan?"

Despite herself, Holly smiled in recognition. "My mom loved her stuff. She thought that made her hip and cool."

"Moms yearn to be hip and cool." He chuckled. "My own mother is a traditional French housewife. Except that she sells magic herbs and potions to all her rich girlfriends."

"Some sell Avon, some sell love spells."

"Exactement."

She pointed to the cabinet. "You have a bit of psychic awareness. There's no way you could have known the cups were in there."

"Peut-être." His shrug was pure French.

The kettle began to burble. Holly took the cups from him and settled the tea bags inside them.

"Okay. You've broken the ice and found common

ground, thereby bonding with me. What do you propose we do now?"

"Transportation spell," he said. "Go to them."

Her grin widened. "I like that."

He grinned back and pointed to his head. "Psychic awareness," he replied. "You see? We will work well together."

"I hope so," she said as she lifted the kettle again.

He frowned. "Let it boil. Americans never let it boil."

Setting the kettle down, she folded her arms. "I'll let it boil over, if that's what it takes. To make good tea," she added pointedly.

"To make good tea," he echoed.

Jer: London

James and Eli swaggered belowdecks, pints of beer in their hands, and chuckled at the mess that was Jer, lying prone on a sleep-away cot nestled among the ship's cargo. They had taken one of the Supreme Coven's private yachts for the voyage to London—James, being who he was, commandeered it—and Jer, though in terrible pain, understood that he was being taken to headquarters to help with the conjuring of the Black Fire.

Does my father know what's going on? he wondered. *Whose side is he on these days? Will he be there?*

He knew that his days of relative isolation were over. Now he would have to earn his keep . . . and ensure his own survival.

But it was Eli and Dad who conjured the fire. I have no idea how they did it.

He wondered how Holly was. Where she was. He had dreamed of her so many times.

I hope I haven't sent my spirit out to her, but I can't be sure. I've spent so much time half-unconscious, and I know I've thought about her. They're looking for her. They want to kill her.

"Want a beer, Jer?" Eli asked, sidling over to his brother. Viciously he pressed the bottom of his beer mug against Jer's burned, swollen lips. Jer groaned in pain as his lower lip cracked and began to bleed. "Not thirsty?"

Jer was thirsty. He was practically dying of thirst.

I won't give them the satisfaction of begging, he thought. But with his next breath he moaned, "Water."

"Sorry? What's that?" Eli queried politely.

Jer clamped his mouth shut.

Eli laughed. He made a show of swigging down his beer and walked away.

"Help James and me conjure the Black Fire," he said, "and you'll have all the water you can drink."

London, Safe House

Kari sat quietly, rocking gently. She had been feeling better, safer when they were at Joel's. Now the realization that a huge battle had happened and she couldn't even remember it terrified her. *Was I going to die?* she couldn't stop herself from wondering. *And just how did Holly stop it?* Something wasn't right with that. Didn't the others see that as well?

They're too busy kissing the ground she walks on, she thought bitterly. *Well, I certainly didn't elect her as head of the Coven. I don't know why we have to do everything she says.*

Truth be told, she would much rather have Sasha as their leader. The older woman was more experienced and kinder, especially to Kari.

And Sasha was Jer's mother. Kari wasn't so naive as to believe that that didn't play a huge part in how she felt. Tears stung the back of her eyes. There was something so comforting in Sasha's presence, and she reminded Kari of Jer so much—her manners, her features.

Kari could feel the tears streaming openly down her facc now. The others didn't notice, though. They never did. Either that or they didn't care.

So many nights she had lain awake wishing she had never met Jer and been introduced to the world of magic. Then she would repent her thoughts because she couldn't imagine a life without Jer Deveraux. So many nights she cried herself to sleep praying that she would see him again.

But when she had seen him . . . he had only had eyes for Holly. Kari tried to convince herself that Holly had bewitched him. *But was I already losing my hold on him? He was so dour and withdrawn. Things were coming to a head between him and his father . . . almost as if they sensed they were going to have a showdown.*

Holly came between them and forced the issue. She's the most arrogant chick I've ever known . . . and with her power, that makes her dangerous. God, I wish I'd never gotten involved in all this crap.

I'd have a Ph.D. by now, if I'd just stayed the course.

Yeah, but I was too into Jer to turn back when I realized he really was a warlock, and there was such a thing as true magic. By then I was hooked on him, and on trying to learn how to use magic on my own. I can't blame that on Holly.

But I can blame her for taking him away from me.

Some time there'll be payback, Cathers. Count on it.

Kari balled her fists and closed her eyes.

The tears kept coming.

Part Two
Imbolc

☾

"When they hung her, I watched and laughed. She was innocent. I was the witch they sought. I sold my soul to the Devil himself, and the Devil protects his own. He protected me, and he protected the Cathers woman. She told me once she was descended from queens of powerful witchery, and I believe her."

—Confession of Tabitha Johnson, upon her deathbed

Salem, Massachusetts

FOUR

HEMATITE

☾

We lick the wounds that we have borne
As limb from limb we have been torn
But we will rise and live again
Death's the beginning, not the end

Find now the strength to change
To take our souls and rearrange
We can be as we will
We can love, or laugh, or kill

Headquarters of the Supreme Coven: London

In the clothes she'd been captured in, although freshly laundered, Nicole paced the floor of the honeymoon suite. Her dark hair was in a tangle, her thoughts as jumbled.

I have to get out of here.

The room was her prison, and she was not allowed to leave it. She had tried everything, from blasting at the door with magic bolts to hacking at the knob with a wooden coat hanger. She felt terribly inept at figuring her way out—real life certainly wasn't like the movies—and it embarrassed her that she gave up so easily.

James had been gone for two days, which was a relief, but she was unbearably tense from wondering what was going to happen next. Tension squeezed her heart as she gazed at the carved relief of the moon on the headboard of the bed. All witches knew when the full moon blazed; in two more nights, it would be Yule, one of the most sacred nights of the Coventry calendar—and the night James had promised he would force her into thrall. She would be the Lady to his Lord, and he would exploit her magical energies, use them for his own evil purposes . . . and there would be nothing she could do to stop him. It was the worst violation she could imagine.

I blew it. I should never have left the coven.

In anger, she tossed another bolt at the door.

To her shock, the section of wood adjacent to the jamb splintered from the doorknob to the top.

She gaped at it openmouthed, unable to believe it. Racing to it, she pushed on the weakened section, hearing a sharp crack as it continued to split. Her heart caught; she glanced around guiltily, listening for footsteps in case someone realized what she'd accomplished, then shot another bolt against the wood.

This time the section detached sufficiently for her to push her hand through and unlock the door on the other side. She scraped her hand on the rough wood, but she would have been willing to push her way through a broken window if it meant getting out.

Easing the door open, she peered into the hallway. There was no one there, but that didn't mean it was unguarded. For all she knew, she had already triggered an alarm and James's family's henchmen were on their way here to subdue her.

She took a step into the corridor, which was papered in black and red, and then another. She shook her head, amazed that she had gotten this far. She ticked her gaze over her shoulder, anxiously scanning for movement.

And then she ran like hell.

She had no idea where she was going, and she told herself she should slow down and figure out a plan. But how? What plan? She didn't know anything about this place except that it was home to the greatest evil force in Coventry, the Supreme Coven. That people died here.

That I might die here.

And so she ran.

★ ★ ★

Seated on the throne of skulls, Sir William cocked his head as Matthew Monroe, one of his principal lieutenants, walked into the room.

The redheaded Monroe looked bemused and said, "This is what we have so far. Someone managed to trip the alarms at the guard post in north London, but nothing happened." He shrugged. "As far as we can determine, no demons or imps were dispatched. There was no engagement, and everything seems quiet now."

Sir William shook his head. "It's not right. The only way our alarms activate is when an identifiable threat triggers them. That means a witch."

Monroe nodded. "That's true, Sir William."

"And yet, nothing happened."

"Also true." Monroe crossed his arms over his chest. "But I don't think it was a glitch. I think someone tripped the alarm, and then used magic to reset it before anything happened."

"That's the most logical explanation. But it is, of course, very troubling."

"Very, sir," Monroe agreed.

Sir William narrowed his eyes. Slowly, his human form melted away, revealing his demonic appearance. He was proud of it. His ancestors had worked long and hard to become elite members of the damned—the first had been Sir Richard, governor of Botany Bay. Sir

Richard's explorations into the Nightmare Dreamtime were legendary, and Sir William was justly proud of him.

Monroe blinked fiercely, but stood his ground, one of the few who had seen the transformation often enough not to run screaming in fear. His fearlessness was one of his more admirable traits, and one of his more dangerous. Still, Sir William trusted him as he trusted few others.

His voice rumbled in his chest as he said, "Have we located the Cathers witch?"

Monroe hesitated. "We're fairly certain she's in London. The Deveraux falcons have sensed her, but they can't seem to locate her."

With his large clawed hand, Sir William made a fist and pounded the armrest of his throne. "Damn the Mother Coven and their wards and cloaks! If they'd stop hiding, come out and fight . . ." He huffed. "I don't understand how the Cahors ever consented to become part of that group. They were far too hot-blooded." His scaly lips pulled back in the rictus of a smile. "And Holly Cathers is more of the old school, wouldn't you say?"

Monroe couldn't help but smile back. "As you say, Sir William. Particularly if she's the one who tripped our alarm and lived to tell the tale."

"She needs killing."

"She does," Monroe agreed.

Sir William chuckled. "Has my son shown up yet? Brought Jeraud Deveraux with him?"

Monroe checked his watch. "They're due within the hour," he informed his High Priest.

"Of course James thinks he'll discover the secret of the Black Fire first, use it to push me off this chair," Sir William drawled. "That boy . . . thick as a post."

"He has a lot of smart friends," Monroe reminded him. "And I still contend that Michael Deveraux is one of them."

"Michael's only loyal to Michael," Sir William insisted. "As long as I keep my grip, he'll come along."

He dug his claws into the armrest, cracking the bones, and yanked a section of it free. The splintered bone fragments resembled bits of bread sticks in his fist.

"Looks like I still have that grip."

Monroe's brows raised slightly, and his voice quavered for only an instant as he replied, "Looks like you do."

Sir William carelessly tossed the bones to the floor and said, "Use one of the more long-legged sacrifices tonight. We need a new femur for this thing."

Black and red, black and red, blackred, blackred . . .

The wallpaper was a blur. Paintings and suits of

armor were blurs as Nicole raced past them. Mirrors startled her, but she kept on.

Nicole hadn't stopped running since she had escaped from her room at the headquarters of the Supreme Coven. Her lungs ached and her throat was dry as dust; she kept telling herself to slow down and think, but what good would that do? She was as panicked as a mouse in a cage with a snake, and she knew it.

And so she ran.

Her impulse was to go down any set of stairs she found, but even in that, she didn't know if she was doing the right thing. She had never actually seen the outside of the Supreme Coven's headquarters, and for all she knew, it was built entirely underground. Warlocks preferred their ritual halls below the earth; it was witches who worshiped the Lady Moon and tried to build their sacred places as close to her as possible.

Now, in the dark, she nearly tumbled down another set of stairs, these made of stone. She took them, heaving painfully with each downward, widely spaced step. There was no banister, only a stone wall, and no light.

She was halfway down when she heard voices echoing off the hard surfaces. She froze.

". . . home sweet home now, Jer."

Nicole inhaled sharply. *That's Eli.*

"How the mighty are fallen, eh, Deveraux? Now you're down in the dungeons with the sacrifices. If you don't watch it, you'll end up like them."

And that's James.

She shuddered and plastered herself against the wall, even though there was no way they could see her from this vantage point.

But I don't know that, do I? she thought, panicking again. *I don't know anything. . . .*

She forced down the panic and tried to listen. Her heartbeat in her ears roared so loudly, she was almost sure the three men could hear it too.

"Thirsty?" James asked.

There was no answer.

"Well, I've got to check in with dear old Dad," he continued. "Then I'll go check in on my darling little wife."

Her blood ran cold. *He's going to realize I've escaped.*

"Your father's in some kind of conference," Eli said. "I saw his whipping boy Monroe go into the throne room. I've got some new arcana I need to dedicate. Would you give me a hand?"

"Sure. Nicole will wait."

They both chuckled.

Footsteps rang on the stone below. She waited

for a long time until they had faded away before she continued on down the stairs.

Can I trust Jer? she thought. *Does it matter? I need help, and he knows his way around here. He's their captive, just like me, so there's hope.*

But he's a Deveraux. How can anybody ever trust one of them?

She came to the bottom of the stairs. To her right, about fifteen feet away, stood a wall of bars divided into five or six cells; above them, a badly flickering fluorescent light. Shapes moved in the cells as she approached, and she stopped for a moment, licking her lips as she tried to get up the nerve to move forward. She was terrified that someone would give her away. *There might be a reward in it . . . what am I saying? Of course there will be a reward. As soon as they know I'm missing, everyone will be looking for me.*

She whispered, "Jer?"

There was no answer.

What did they do to him? Maybe he can't even hear me. Maybe he can't talk.

Taking another step closer, she tried again. "Jer?"

"Oh, God," a male voice cried out from the darkness. "Oh, thank God, have you come to save us? They're crazy here! They're going to kill us!"

"Ssh," she begged. "Please. Be quiet."

"We're tourists. This is insane! We're from Ohio!" The voice raised, shrill and frantic. "We thought we were buying tickets to a play, and the next thing we knew . . ." There was sobbing.

Nicole drew nearer to the cells. From the cell farthest to her right, hands poked from between the bars, stretching to touch her.

"God, get us out of here!" a woman shrieked.

Nicole made a magical gesture she had learned from José Luís and said, "Be calm."

A magical tingle prickled her skin as a soft waft of serenity trailed over her arms and shoulders. One tiny iota of tension left her. But one only. Her heart was still pounding so rapidly, she couldn't count the beats.

The woman's voice dropped to a whisper. "We're strangers here. We have no quarrel with . . . whoever you are. You have to help us." The words were slurred, almost sullen. "Or we will be murdered."

"Help us," the male voice added, pleading.

Nicole walked to the cell, bent down, and put out her hand. She stretched between the bars, worrying that in their panic, these people might grab at her and not let her go. But she felt she had to give them some kind of hope. Some comfort.

Goddess, protect them.

"I'll try," she promised, experimentally moving her hand so as to make contact.

A hand brushed her fingers. She heard the mournful weeping, but it was too dark for her to make out a face. Having no idea if the occupant could see her, either, she said again, "I promise you. I'll try."

"Nicole?"

She started. That voice had come from the other end of the row; she got up, swaying for a moment, and staggered toward it, completely winded. "Jer?"

The light was falling at a better angle near the front right quadrant of the cell, and she positioned herself to take advantage of it as she peered between the bars.

"Don't look at me," he croaked.

She wished she had listened to him.

He didn't look human. He was so badly burned that she would have never been able to recognize him if she hadn't known who he was.

"It was the Black Fire," she murmured. "Oh, Jer, I'm so sorry."

"I would've been fine," he rasped, "if you hadn't pulled Holly from me. Cathers and Deveraux together can withstand the Black Fire. But once she left me . . . there, to face it by myself . . ." He sounded hoarse and he spoke slowly. She winced at the sound of his voice; his vocal cords must have been seared; she couldn't even imagine the pain of being burned inside and out. "Deveraux have always been abandoned by Cahors."

"Oh, God, Jer." She gripped the bars and closed her eyes, unable to look at him any longer. "God, I'm sorry. I've going to get you out of here. But we have to hurry. James is going to realize I'm gone, and then we'll both be toast." She laughed anxiously. "So to speak."

"Okay. What's your plan?"

"My . . . plan." She hesitated. "Jer, I don't . . . I just escaped. I didn't even know you were here!"

"We can't just walk out, Nicole." He sounded irritated with her.

"I did," she replied. "Well, I blasted my way out. I broke down the door of our room with magic that I didn't even know I had. But no one came to see what was going on," she added hastily. "No one stopped me from coming here."

"—probably didn't bother with your room—whole place—heavily warded—figure you're harmless."

She strained to hear him, but his voice faded in and out. There was a moment of silence, and she thought he was finished. He continued, though, his voice slightly stronger. "Do you have access to James's arcana?"

"His magic stuff?" she asked, embarrassed because she didn't know the vocabulary. "Not really."

"Then you have to steal it."

"What?"

"We have to have a plan," he said. "People don't just leave this place."

"Well, I know that," she said hotly.

"Go back to your room. Let James think you can't get out."

"No way!" She took a step away from his cell and stuffed her hands in her jeans pockets. "No way on earth am I going back there. Are you insane?"

"They'll look for you. And they'll find you. And if they find you, there's no way we're getting out of here."

She raised her chin, but tears sluiced down her cheeks. *I really do not want to agree with him.*

"It's Yule in two nights," she pointed out desperately. "He's going to put me in thrall. I wouldn't be able to stand that, Jer. He'll force me to help him with his magics, and I won't be able to stop myself. You know the kind of spells they do around here. They're evil."

"Then we have one night," he told her with exaggerated patience, "to plan our escape. Now, go back."

Dejectedly, Nicole pulled her hands out of her

pockets. "I can't do it. I can't go back to him for even one minute!"

"Fine. Then let's escape right now," Jer mocked.

"James . . . he's *mean.* He . . ."

"Nicole, if you want to get out of here, you're going to have to do a lot more than freak out. *Now go back to your room."*

The harshness of his tone put her on notice. She took a deep breath and said, "I almost forgot that you're a Deveraux."

"Don't ever forget it," he growled. "I don't."

She wiped her hands; they were ringing wet with perspiration. She was shaking at the thought of returning to James.

"How am I going to know where his arcana is?" she asked him.

"Has he asked you to participate in a rite?"

"No. Not yet. But—"

"Then you're going to have to ask him to let you. Tell him you want to."

Her eyes widened. "No way. He does Black Magic!"

"Do you have a better idea?" he demanded. At her silence, he said, "You're going to have to get your hands dirty, Nicole. There's no pretty way out of this. No one's going to come to our rescue."

"The Goddess . . . ," she began. "I think she's watching over me, guiding me."

"She guided you to me, then. And I say that we have to act. We have to save ourselves."

"But . . . he *sacrifices* things. You know he does." She glanced uneasily at the row of cells, thought about the fingertips she had touched. She felt sick to her stomach.

"If he makes you sacrifice something, you'll have to do it," he insisted.

Her stomach twisted. "Jer . . . ," she pleaded.

"When you get a chance to see his arcana, look for a soul stone. You'll need an athame. He probably has an extra onc. You'll have to steal both items," he said, mentally going through his plan. "Try to get some mugwort. We always have our own back home, but in a big place like this, he might just get some from a common storage area."

"The athame . . . that's his knife, right?"

"Yes," Jer told her. "I'd tell you to take his principal one, but he'd notice that right away. A high-ranking warlock like him should have a couple of spares at least. It's got to be one he's used. Make sure."

She swallowed hard. "Does *used* mean that he's sacrificed something with it?"

Jer grunted with surprise. "You Cahors witches are

very different from us, aren't you? Of course that's what it means."

"Oh, God, Jer! I—I—"

"Damn it, Nicole! Lose the attitude. Do you want to end up like me? Get back there *now*!"

"Then what?" she cried. "What do you want me to do after I've stolen these things?"

"Bring them to me."

"But how? How will I get out again?"

"You'll have to figure that out," he said tiredly. His voice was growing weak again. "I can't exactly help you."

"Why not?" she demanded. "Aren't you a warlock?"

"I'm half-dead, Nicole."

She put her hands on her hips and glared at the misshapen thing that used to be Jer Deveraux. "And I say, *you* lose the 'tude. This is more your turf than mine, Jer. Stop laying it all on *my* shoulders."

There was a silence. Then Jer made a strange gravelly sound that might have been a chuckle.

"*Touché,* Nicole. You have a point." He let out a long, raggedy breath. "Maybe I can do something. Loosen my cell door, something like that."

"Say a protection spell over me," she suggested.

"We're not good at those, but I'll do my best."

She stood perfectly still while he chanted a few words in Latin, using a spell she didn't know—*not that I know that many*—but she felt nothing after he finished.

She said, "It didn't take."

"I told you we aren't very good at those," he reminded her from the shadows. "You should go. You have to beat him back to your room."

She grimaced. "He'll see the wrecked door."

"Can you fix it?" he asked her.

"Not magically, I don't think."

"What about your Goddess? Can she?"

"Don't make fun of my beliefs," she snapped, then realized that until that moment, she hadn't truly believed. In snippets, and in bits and pieces, her faith had grown. But it still wasn't there. She was still terrified, and she still felt very alone.

"You'll have to deal with it there," he said urgently. "Go, Nicole."

She hesitated. "I don't know how to get back."

"That I can help with. I'll do a finder's spell. Go on."

"I . . . I'll be back as soon as I can."

She turned on her heel and ran back to the stairs, taking them, rushing like a madwoman despite her exhaustion. Part of her resisted each step, each footfall forward—she was going back to James, and nothing in her wanted to do that—but suddenly she felt strangely buoyed, even energized. She knew that she was supposed to turn right; knew that at the next stairway, she needed to go left.

It's Jer's finder's spell, she realized.

Before she knew it, she was racing down the corridor to her room. The door was flush with the wall, and it wasn't until she reached it that she saw that it appeared to be untouched. It was as if she had never so much as scratched her fingernail across it.

"What?" she said aloud, then glanced around, tried the knob, and found that it opened.

She let herself in, closed it behind herself, and heard the lock click. She was effectively locked in again, with no evidence that she had gotten out.

How can this be?

Then she turned around to face the bed, and gasped.

A shimmering blue figure stared back at her. By the height, Nicole judged it to be a woman. She was standing next to the bed, a gauzy phantom veiled from head to toe in black, except for a dagger that she held across her chest. It was curved and encrusted with jewels.

An athame, Nicole realized. *Is this the Goddess?* "Who are you?" she asked aloud, sinking to her knees.

But there was something about the figure that was . . . off. She knew deep in her soul that this was not the Goddess, but a lesser being. Yet she didn't want to insult the apparition, who may have come to help her. She stayed on her knees. "Are you a friend? Did you fix the door?"

The figure remained silent.

Nicole tried again. "Are you Isabeau?" Though Isabeau had taken Holly over at a séance conducted by Tante Cecile last year, Nicole had not had a good view of her. And veiled as the figure was, it was impossible to tell her identity.

The figure still said nothing, only extended the dagger toward her. Nicole uncertainly reached out her hand. "Does it belong to James?" she asked as she got to her feet.

As if in reply, the figure inclined her head the merest fraction of an inch. Then she shifted her gaze to the headboard. Nicole followed her line of vision and walked toward the bed, nervously skirting the area where the figure stood.

"Is there something for me here?" Nicole asked.

She crossed to the headboard and touched the carving of the Horned God seated on the pile of human skulls.

It was loose to her touch.

Blinking, she grasped it between her fingers, working it gently, and pulled the figure off the rest of the frieze. A hole approximately two inches in diameter had been bored into the wood, and she peered inside.

There was a small pile of objects, including a ring, what looked to be a couple of smooth pebbles, and something else. She pulled it out and saw that it was a tiny wax figurine with hair wrapped around its head. Her hair.

She swallowed and looked back at the veiled form. "Is this me?"

The figure held out her hand.

Nicole uncertainly clasped the figure to her chest. "You want it?"

The woman moved her head. It was eerie that she didn't speak, and barely moved. Everything was happening at once; Nicole was exhausted from running and still so frightened that she could hardly stand, much less consider what was going on. She needed a moment to figure out what to do . . . but she didn't have a moment.

"But . . ." She glanced down at the figurine, at the pebbles, and at the knife. As far as she could tell, the woman was helping her; though she was not a celestial being, she appeared to be on Nicole's side, at least in some deep-boned sense that Nicole couldn't really even begin to comprehend.

Then the woman turned the knife around so that she held it hilt-first, and offered it to Nicole.

Nicole took a breath, and wrapped her hand around the hilt.

A cold, icy chill ran down her spine. And she saw in her mind's eye:

A souvenir shop, its front door hanging open, and snow pouring in. Nearby, a tea cup, smashed on the tile. A puddle of tea.

A man, his name was Joel, and he was a Druid; he had helped Holly, but now he was lying on the floor before a dying fire, his eyes wide open, his lips tinged a pale, robin's egg blue.

"Oh, my God, he's dead!" Nicole cried.

At once the shimmering figure disappeared, leaving Nicole with the knife, the wax figure, the ring, and the pebbles.

And the door to the bedroom began to open.

Quickly she replaced the pebbles, the ring, and the figure and pushed the carving back into place. The knife, she hid under one of the pillows.

She had just whirled around to face the door when James strutted in.

He said nothing, only smirked at her and shut the door. "You must have missed me," he said. "You're panting."

She forced herself to stop breathing heavily, which wasn't difficult. As he came near, her chest constricted, and it was hard to make herself breathe at all.

"There's going to be a ritual tonight," he informed her. "And you're going to participate." He smiled evilly. "An old friend of yours will be there."

Alarms went off.

Does he mean Jer?

"What kind of ritual?" she asked him.

"We're working on the Black Fire. You know, Cathers and Deveraux together is supposed to be a potent combination."

She tried to play dumb. "So Eli will be there."

"Oh. Yeah. *Eli.*"

He looked at her with a mixture of amusement and contempt. Then he crossed to the bed, sat down, and stretched out, still wearing his boots. She tried to take a steadying breath; she was growing faint from lack of oxygen, but she knew she had to keep her wits about her.

He held out his arms. "Come here, Nicole. Welcome me home."

She stared at him and gave her head a shake. *Not again. Never again.*

There was a knock on the door, and then it opened. A redheaded man stood in the doorway. He looked unaccountably nervous. He ticked his glance in Nicole's direction. His cheeks visibly flushed as if someone had slapped him. Nicole observed him carefully, intrigued.

James half sat up, frowning. "Monroe, I didn't say 'come in.'"

"Your father wants to see you," the man said. He glanced once more at Nicole, then looked quickly away. She could almost hear his heartbeat, he was so nervous.

Oblivious to the other man's distress, James swore under his breath and got up. He brushed past Nicole and headed out the door. The two left, James slammed the door behind them, and she heard the lock click.

For a moment she panicked at the thought that she was once more entrapped, and then she reminded herself that she had managed to get out once before. And now she had the things she needed.

I think I do.

"Isabeau?" she called. "Are you still here?"

There was no answer, and Nicole sensed that she was truly alone. She scrambled back onto the bed and retrieved the items from the headboard, pausing to examine the ring. The black stone was shaped like a pentagram, topped with a gold replica of the carving of the Horned God that was on the headboard.

She closed her fist around it and took a deep breath.

I'll take it to Jer.

If I can get back to him.

As the others grouped around Holly and Amanda, Nicole's cat, Astarte, settled into Amanda's lap. Holly reached out to pet her, and the cat hissed at her.

She withdrew her hand, gazing at Philippe, Sasha, and Rose, who had arranged everyone else in a pentagram surrounding the two witches. They were still in Rose's parlor; the pentagram was burned into the wooden floor, beneath her floral carpets.

"We call upon the incarnations of Deveraux and Cahors past," Sasha intoned, "that we might learn more of the blood feud between the two great houses. Let our Priestess glimpse her past and the past of her house. Let the blood of Cathers drip into the memories of Cathers hearts."

She picked up Rose's athame. Holly fearlessly held

out her hand, palm up. Sasha drew a slice down the center.

It hurt, but Holly remained still and centered.

It was Amanda's turn. When the knife ran down the center of her palm, she sucked in her breath and murmured, *"Ow."*

"Let me see," Holly demanded. "Let me live through the eycs of Cathers. And Deveraux," she added.

"No," Amanda whispered. "Stay away from them."

"And Deveraux," Holly repeated, ignoring her cousin.

There was a stir around the circle, which Holly also ignored. She pressed her palm against Amanda's—their birthmarks creating two thirds of the lily, which was the symbol of the great House of Cahors. Immediately she felt their combined strength filling her veins.

When we get Nicole back, we'll be the three Ladies of the Lily together. There'll be no stopping us from doing whatever we want to do.

"Still your mind, Priestess," Philippe urged her.

Holly took a deep breath, and did as he asked.

San Francisco

Richard Anderson sat and he thought. He didn't seem to do much else these days. He had been grieving for a long time—for years. Then one day—yesterday, actually—he just stopped. He was done. Done grieving for his wife, done grieving for his marriage, done grieving for his life. It was as though he suddenly had woken up.

He looked around, and strangers were taking care of him. He believed one of them was Amanda's friend's mother or aunt or something. He had no idea who the Native American guy was. There was much talk and concern about a Barbara, who apparently wasn't doing well.

And no one could tell him how his girls were doing.

Something had to change. He needed more information first, though. If there was one thing he had learned in Vietnam, it was that you damn well better know what was waiting for you when you leaped. The only lesson he had learned half so well was to crave safety and stability. When his wife, Marie-Claire, had met him, he had been a daredevil. He took risks. When he had come home from the war to his young wife, he had found the most stable job he could and settled down. His computer company had sprung from that, and it had never been a very risky enterprise.

She had never understood his desire for stability; he could see that now. Maybe he hadn't been exciting enough for her at that point. Instead of actually trying to talk about it or ask for a divorce, though, she had snuck around behind his back. Her fault. He had known she was doing it and had done nothing. His fault. He had been too worried about keeping her. Having two little girls hadn't helped. He had felt such a need to keep their home life secure for them, so that they wouldn't have to face risk, uncertainty.

He had sure botched that. Maybe instead he should have taught his girls to survive, to be tough. Maybe that would stand them in better stead now that they were fighting such evil. He closed his eyes. There was nothing he could do to change the past. He could, however, change the future. Maybe it was time for his daughters to discover that their old man knew a thing or two about life and war. He couldn't do magic, but he bet they'd be surprised to learn exactly what he could do.

FIVE

BLOODSTONE

☾

Harken now, there's work ahead
For every Deveraux, alive or dead
Oh, Green Man grant us this we pray
Courage and victory at end of day

Goddess help us face our fears
Drying now our angry tears
Give us the strength to prevail
As we glimpse beneath the veil

Salem, Massachusetts: October 29, 1692

Jonathan Deveraux smiled as he awoke. He could hear the rain pounding on the roof, and from afar thunder rumbled ominously. Yes, it was going to be a glorious day.

As he dressed he mentally reviewed the events of the past months. Salem had been a quiet town until January, when young Elizabeth Parris and Abigail Williams had started crying that there were witches in their midst. Hallucinations, seizures, and trances experienced by them and other local girls had been all the proof the God-fearing people needed.

What had started out as an ugly prank by a couple of bored, spiteful children had turned into an epidemic of fear and paranoia. But, more than that, it had turned into a game of chess that Jonathan and Abigail Cathers played.

When he had come to Salem he had been shocked to find a descendant of the Cahors family living there with a new name and no memory of the blood feud that had driven her ancestor from her native France. Abigail Cathers was a witch, but she never knew that he, Jonathan Deveraux, was a warlock.

So for months she had played the game, though she did not know who her opponent was. He would move a citizen of the town into a position to denounce her as a witch and she would deflect, causing another to be accused in her place. Sarah Osborne, Margaret Jacobs, and Elizabeth Proctor had all been pawns, sacrificed by Abigail to cast suspicion away from herself. The good citizens were blissfully unaware of the manipulation of their minds by the two.

But at last he had checkmated her. Today she would stand trial before the Court of Oyer and Terminer. The six remaining judges of the court, which had been set up by the governor to try the witch cases, could do no else but find her guilty.

He only wished he could be there to see the look on her face when they pronounced the sentence. Alas, the court was closed to the public. His scrying stone would have to do.

As the child Elizabeth Parris slowly and solemnly denounced Abigail Cathers, the woman turned white. Three girls sat in chairs before the judges, their faces grim but their eyes dancing with a fiendish glee. How many had died because of them?

"And she cursed my dog so she could not have pups. Every year she's had a litter and this year none. And it's all because of Abigail Cathers. Doggie barked at Abigail, and Abigail looked at her quite cruelly and said that she would never have little puppies to bark at people again."

"I have done nothing wrong," Abigail said, standing. "These children have falsely accused so many, and you have willingly believed every word. Listen to what they are saying; it is ridiculous. Why would I curse a dog for doing what it was made to do? This court has sentenced dozens of innocents to their death. My friend, Goodwife Mary Shiflett, was among them . . ." And here she faltered. Tears formed in her eyes. ". . . and you drowned her! You *drowned* her!"

"She was well accused," Samuel asserted.

She raised her chin. "True witches would not have

allowed themselves to be killed. True witches would have silenced these girls and not their miserable dogs."

She sat back down, the chains that bound her clanking loudly in the silence. The testimonies continued. The evidence was all ridiculous, highly circumstantial, and the judges were believing every word.

At last Abigail exploded. Once more, she got to her feet. Her eyes began to glow, and she shrieked, "You stupid little girls. You have no idea what a witch can do!"

Behind her the wall exploded, flinging debris into the air. Men shouted as bits of stone cascaded down upon them. Dust powdered the room. Then she was gone as her restraints fell to the ground with a loud clatter. The girls lay crushed beneath the weight of the falling stones.

Silence fell thick and terrifying upon the group of men gathered there. "Is it possible?" Samuel asked into the silence. "Could we have convicted so many innocents while we have let the one true witch escape?"

Governor Phips rose to his feet. He was pale and shaking from head to toe. "Gentlemen, I don't know the answer to Mr. Sewall's question. All I know is, I'm disbanding the court."

"But, sir, how can you even think of doing that after what we've just seen?" Jonathan Corwin demanded.

The governor held up a hand. "And how can you, sir, condone convicting more people who are probably innocent after what we've just seen? You think that a real witch would go to her death as lightly as the ones that you have murdered?"

"But the confessions—"

"There have only been a handful of those, and at this time how can we be sure that that Devil who just left here didn't bewitch them into confessing just to cast suspicion from her?" Bartholomew pointed out wearily.

That silenced them all for a moment.

John Hathorne spoke quietly into the silence. "You all know me, and you know I don't take our duties lightly. It seems to me that either this witch was far more powerful than her fellows, or we have condemned a great many innocent souls to death. If the latter is true, as I suspect, then God will judge us for what we have done."

He paused to let his words sink in. "If God is to be our judge then, let history not judge us. If this were to come to light there would be massive public unrest—upheaval, even. The authority of the law, the Church itself, could be questioned. There are many who already think we are wrong; let us not swell their ranks. We do have several confessions that shall be proof enough for most. Several have been sentenced and killed. Let us put an end then to these witch trials."

He waited for the murmurs to cease. "And let us erase all record of Abigail Cathers and what she did here today. Let us not speak of it, not even to each other."

As the dust still settled slowly along his shoulders, John commanded in a voice that shook, "Clerk, tear the pages regarding Abigail Cathers from the record. Destroy them. No one must know of the terrible things we have witnessed here."

Solemnly the young man did as he was told. After removing the pages he struck a match and set them on fire. He dropped them to the stone floor, and as they all watched them burn, the flame seemed to turn from hellfire red to black.

At last the records were but ash, and John sat back with a shudder. He felt sick.

"And what of the others we already have in custody?" Samuel asked. "If we simply release them it's as good as admitting there was no threat."

"Then they shall be tried, but not by us," John Richards said. "And somehow I think they'll be found innocent."

Lieutenant Governor William Stoughton whispered, "Amen."

Jonathan Deveraux sighed heavily as he put his scrying stone away. He had not succeeded in having Abigail killed. At the very least he had just made that task harder to accomplish since now he would have to try to find her. She certainly wouldn't be staying anywhere near the area—not after what she had done.

Ah, well. Salem would return to its same sleepy roots, and life would return to normal.

How dull.

"Thus it has always been," Sasha said to Holly as they sat back from their shared vision of the past. They were in the sitting room of the safe house with Philippe, who had participated. Rose had commandeered the others to work on fixing some food for the large gathering.

"Deveraux hunting down Cahors—or rather, Cathers, once your family changed its name—all over time and space."

Holly nodded wanly. "Six hundred years ago, Isabeau de Cahors was forced to marry Jean de Deveraux, and then she helped her family massacre the Deveraux family. There was a huge fire, and she died in it. Everyone assumed Jean died too."

"But he didn't," Philippe concluded. "She had sworn to kill him, but either she failed or she spared him. And now their spirits are intertwined, and I believe they will continue to be so until she fulfills her blood vow and kills him. And the Deveraux Coven continues to hunt the Cathers witches wherever they may be found."

"'And kills him'?" Holly repeated. "But how can Isabeau kill Jean, when they're both spirits?"

"I think you know the answer to that," Sasha said gently. She laid a hand on Holly's arm. "Isabeau has the ability to possess you, and Jean can live again through . . . my son."

"Jer," Holly murmured with a shudder. She looked down at Sasha's hand on her arm. She was grateful for the older woman's sustaining, calm presence. Though Sasha was nothing like her own mother, still, she was someone's mother . . . and Holly felt very much in need of mothering these days.

She's Jer's mother, she reminded herself. *How can she talk about this so calmly?*

"I think we can figure out a way to beat this," Sasha said firmly. "I have to believe that, Holly. I don't believe you're destined to kill my son."

"Or for your son to kill me. Isabeau may want resolution, but Jean wants revenge," Holly reminded her.

"He's still madly in love with Isabeau. They were very passionate people, Jean and Isabeau." She made a little face. "That's what attracted me to Jer's father. His passion for life." Stirring, she gave Holly's arm another squeeze. "But that's a different subject. What we need to concentrate on now is finding your cousin, and figuring out where Jer is. He keeps making contact with you, so that means he's . . . alive. . . ."

Her voice caught. Holly put her hands in Sasha's and gazed steadily into her eyes. "I've already had to do things I didn't want to do, for the sake of the Coven," Holly told her. "I'm strong, like Isabeau. I'll find him, Sasha. But I won't harm him."

Sasha closed her eyes and let out a heavy sigh.

"When Michael forced me to leave, I worried so about my boys. Not a day has gone by since then that I haven't wondered and worried about them. That's why I went to the Mother Coven—so I could learn spells to protect them and keep them safe. And then I began my online friendship with Kari, who kept me informed about her boyfriend, 'Warlock.' "

Holly flushed, feeling awkward. Jer and Kari had been hot and heavy for over a year, until Holly came along. She couldn't help her mixed feelings on the subject.

Sasha continued: "I'm sure Michael told them that I deserted them."

Holly swallowed. Michael Deveraux had indeed told his sons that their mother had abandoned them. Eli pretended not to care, but she knew it had wounded Jer deeply. As the only semi-good Deveraux in the family, Jer had suffered the most from Sasha's absence. She knew he believed that if his mother had stayed or taken him with her, he wouldn't be as tainted with evil as he was now.

I don't think he's evil at all, Holly told herself. She realized, though, that was wishful thinking, and not something she was positive of.

But I am tainted, she thought. *I have let evil come into me in order to protect my coven.*

I can't be with anyone who's completely good. I'll ruin him.

For a second, she panicked. *What have I done to myself? To my life?*

And then she raised her chin. *I did what I had to do. It's done, and there's no use going back over it.*

"Are you all right, Holly?" Philippe asked, peering at her. Then he gave her and Sasha a crooked smile. "A strange question, in these strange times."

"I'm all right," she said steadily. "I am."

"Then we must press on. We must plan a strategy," Philippe said, looking at them both. "My theory is that since you had such a vivid image of Jer when we were in the battle, it means he's nearby. If that is so, it's possible he is in the Supreme Coven's headquarters."

"But he told me he was on the island of Avalon," she argued. "He told me that himself, in a dream." She balled her fists. "He lied to me."

"Perhaps he's been moved," Sasha put in.

"Yes," Holly breathed, uncomfortable.

Philippe shrugged. "We do know that Nicole is at the headquarters. And that she is married to James. Or at least that is what the Mother Coven was told by their spies. Perhaps he is there as well."

Overhearing, Rose came over. She nodded as she said, "I can confirm that. We had a message to that effect, from someone on the inside. Someone on *our* side," she added. "I mean, that Nicole is married to James, and that she's inside the headquarters."

Philippe clenched his jaw and doubled his fists. His dark brows pinched as he gritted out, "That cannot stand. We must free her as soon as possible."

"So you know the location of the headquarters?" Holly said slowly. "And you didn't tell us?"

"I don't know the location," Rose shot back. "That hasn't been revealed to us."

"Who is the spy?" Holly asked Rose. "And if she—or he—knows so much, why don't they just give you the location?"

"We don't know who it is," Rose said bluntly. "We have a friend inside, but he—it's probably a male—has not identified himself. As for giving us the location, we're hoping that he will, in due time."

"Then how do we know this *friend* isn't just feeding

us misinformation? Messing with us?" Holly persisted.

"Pablo also confirmed Nicole's presence there," Philippe interjected. "He is a Seer. He can also read minds."

Holly glanced up sharply. "And he can't *read* the address, either?"

"Think about it," Rose said. "Such information is probably one of the most closely guarded secrets of the Supreme Coven. They've probably found a way to protect it, even from someone like Pablo. Surely they're aware that there are mind readers on our side as well as theirs."

"He'd better stay out of my head." Holly's tone was tense. Harsh. She couldn't help it. She wanted no one to know the depths she had gone to in order to protect her covenates . . . nor to grasp how far she was willing to go in the future.

I'm not even sure how far I'm willing to go.

"Understood?" she asked, even more harshly.

Philippe looked surprised, but said nothing. She could see the wheels turning, however, see his uncertainty about her.

You'd all better stay away, she thought hotly. *I'm not what I seem.* Her hands trembled at the fury—and the fear—warring inside her.

"Holly?" Amanda asked, coming up to the group. "Are you okay?"

"Yes. I'm fine," she said tersely. She turned away.

"Has Pablo been able to sense the location again?" Sasha asked Philippe, perhaps to placate Holly. Clearly frustrated, he shook his head.

"Then here's what I suggest," Sasha said tentatively. "With you and Pablo working together, we try to connect with Nicole. We work through her, try to find the headquarters again."

Amanda covered her mouth with her hands. "Nicole," she murmured. "God, I hope she's all right."

"Trying to connect like that may put her in danger," Philippe pointed out. "If they realize what we're up to . . ."

"I don't know what else we can do," Sasha said. "And she's already in danger."

Rose raised a hand. "Maybe we need to rethink. We're rushing—"

"We can't just sit around and wait for something else to happen," Holly cut in. "We have to make it happen."

"She's right," Philippe said with approval. He stood. "I'll get Pablo."

"First, we need to eat," Sasha insisted. "Holly's been working hard. She's drained, and so am I. We need to regroup."

Philippe hesitated, and then nodded. "*Eh, bien.* You're right. We need to be strong, and prepared." He looked through the doorway at Alonzo, who was handing out cups of coffee to some of the others. "We of the White Magic Coven would like to have a Catholic Mass. Do you object?" he asked Holly, Sasha, and Rose.

"Not at all," Rose replied. "The more blessings on us, the better."

"I'll speak to Alonzo," he said, rising.

Sasha watched him go. She said, "We're lucky that they found us." Then she turned to Holly and said, "Tell me more about how the battle *vanished.* We need to know everything we can about their magics."

A cold knot wound in Holly's stomach. She said, "Isabeau came to me while I was hurt. I was dying." She swallowed. "She told me she could help us. Then . . ." She took a breath. *Should I tell her everything?*

"Go on," Sasha prodded.

"Her mother was there."

Sasha looked surprised. "Catherine?"

"Yes. She appeared to me once before." Holly thought a moment. "But she was a corpse the first time. This time she was veiled."

And then she knew: *Isabeau lied to me. That wasn't her mother. It was the Goddess as Hecate, Queen of Witches.*

Hecate still hasn't forgiven me for sacrificing Nicole's familiar, Hecate. Her statue on the grounds of the Mother Temple wept at the sight of me.

If I'm right, I sacrificed Joel to her. That was my second sacrifice to her. Maybe even my third, if Kialish's death counts. And any witch knows that the more sacrifices you give to one manifestation of the Goddess, the more that manifestation owns you, controls you.

She set her jaw.

I am controlled by no one. Not Hecate, not anyone. I am my own mistress.

"Never mind," she said aloud. "Forget all this. It's time to look for Nicole. Now."

"But . . ." Sasha looked confused. "You need to eat, and the men want to have the Mass . . ."

"Who's in charge here?" Holly asked shrilly. She got to her feet and called, "Philippe! Change of plans!"

After Nicole was certain that James was gone for good, she tried the door again and found that it was locked. Before she hurtled magical energy at it, she tried using the athame on it. The ultra-sharp and sturdy weapon stripped the doorjamb as clean as a bone, and she pushed out of the room and into the corridor as before. She stuffed the stones, the figurine, and the ring in her pockets.

Instead of running, she tiptoed stealthily, wondering if Jer's spell would help her find her way back. The headquarters of the Supreme Coven was enormous; the architecture spanned centuries.

Allowing her intuition to guide her, she wove her way down innumerable passageways, some so narrow, she had to turn sideways to get through. Cobwebs stretched across walls of stone; she panicked as she realized she was in unexplored territory, not retracing her steps from the first time, and then she reminded herself that she didn't need to go the same way. She only had to find Jer.

Time was ticking by, and she was still wandering; then, just as she began to lose hope, she heard voices.

Intrigued, frightened, she drew close to a wood-paneled wall and put her ear against it. Then she realized that farther up on her right was a sort of balcony, and she dropped to her hands and knees and crawled to the low wall.

". . . traitor," a voice said from a distance below her location. She cringed. That was Sir William. *My father-in-law.*

"No, I swear it. I'm loyal to the Supreme Coven. Why would I want to see the Mother Coven in ascendance? I'm a warlock. That would be madness!"

The speaker was the man who had come to their

room. *Monroe.* The one who hadn't been able to stop looking at her in her room. He sounded terrified. His voice was shaking.

"Monroe, do you take me for an idiot?" Sir William demanded. "I watched you with my scrying stone. You thought your mind was warded, hidden from my gaze. How dare you underestimate me! You've been feeding information to those bitches for nearly a year! All your family has betrayed us, for centuries! And you thought the time was right. You let down your guard and contacted them. I've been watching all this time."

"No, Sir William! There's been a terrible mistake—"

"Indeed there has. And you made it!" Sir William boomed.

There was a horrible scream. Nicole covered her ears, but the sound penetrated. It went on and on and on until she thought she would scream as well.

And then there was silence. After that there was a thud, as if a body had fallen down.

"Clean it up," Sir William commanded.

For a moment, Nicole was so frightened that she couldn't see, couldn't breathe. Then she scuttled as fast as she could on her hands and knees until she could stand up again. She doubled over and retched; then she started running, praying to the Goddess to get her to Jer before whatever had happened to the man named Monroe happened to Jer, or to her.

She found stairs and raced down them; she was gasping for breath as she rounded a stairwell and flew down another set of stairs. She groped in the darkness, hearing that heartrending scream in her mind.

Straight ahead, a light hovered about two feet off the ground.

She froze, backing away, shaking so hard she could barely stand.

A voice emanated from the center of the light.

"Nicole?"

"Holly," Nicole whispered. "Holly!" She ran toward the light, praying it wasn't a trap, and whispered, "I'm here! It's me!"

"Stand in the light," Holly said. "It's a teleportation spell. We'll get you out of there."

Nicole began to obey. And then she hesitated and said, "Jer's here, too. In the headquarters. But he's not with me."

There was a pause. Then Holly said again, her voice steady, "Stand in the light, Nicole. We'll get him later."

"But—"

And then she heard footsteps coming down the stairs.

She ran forward to the light. But just before she stepped into it, it vanished, utterly. Now she stood in pitch darkness, blinking at the afterimage of the bright light, completely disoriented and beginning to panic again.

The footsteps were nearing the bottom of the stairs. They were heavy, a man's footsteps; was it her imagination, or did they sound like James's?

Her heart pounded. She looked back over her shoulder and saw a small light, like a candle or a flash-light, bobbing as whoever was approaching took the last step. By the unhurried pace, Nicole assumed the intruder hadn't seen her yet.

She moved to the left, finding nothing in her way, and began to walk as quickly and as quietly as she could. Her shoulder bumped into a wall; as far as she could tell, she had moved into a corridor. She kept going, biting her lip to keep from crying out when something scurried over her shoe.

Then she sloshed into foul-smelling water; she slogged through it until it splashed around her knees. Nearly choking from the odor, she pressed on, fear-fully glancing backward. She was making too much noise, but she couldn't make herself walk any more slowly. She was too frightened.

At last the water grew shallower; then she was out of it. The corridor let out onto another stairway and she took it, tired and sore and beginning to lose hope that she would ever find Jer. She kept hearing the horrible scream; it was all she could do to force herself not to imagine what Sir William had done to the man named Monroe who had been branded a traitor.

Then all of a sudden she realized she was standing on the landing of the last stairway before the dungeons, and as she stepped down she saw again the watery light and the row of cells.

Her heart leaped and she broke into a run, giddy with relief and wobbly with exhaustion.

"Jer!" she whispered sotto voce. "Jer, it's Nicole! I have the stuff!"

She reached his cage just as the familiar sphere of light appeared inside and Jer, apparently not having heard her, stepped into it.

Then it disappeared again, and Jer with it.

Leaving her behind.

She stepped toward the cage and reached out a hand. The cell was completely empty. "Hey," she whispered. "Jer? Holly?"

"Hey, yourself, baby, what's going on?" drawled a voice.

Nicole whirled around.

Eli and James stood less than three feet away, grinning at her.

SIX

JADE

☾

Quietly now, grind their bones
Our eyes set on the throne of thrones
We crush them now as we rise
Use them as stepping-stones to the skies

Weave and work and cast a spell
To send the Deveraux straight to Hell
See the fear in their eyes
As they watch House Cahors rise

Holly: London

As Holly stood in the bright light, she could barely make out the shape of another figure inside the blazing whiteness with her. She reached out a hand and whispered a name that had rested on her lips for more nights than she could remember.

"Jer."

Speaking his name aloud was like casting a spell. He was there with her at Rose's house; he really was, alive and safe. She felt his warmth, smelled his scent. She could hardly stand up, she was so amazed and happy. He put his arms around her and crushed his mouth against hers; his lips were chapped, but she didn't care; she held him tightly as he kissed her, reveling in his nearness, so overcome that she burst into tears. *He's here, he's all right. I have him at last. Thank you, thank you for surviving. And for loving me. By the Goddess, Jer, I love you. . . .*

The light abruptly vanished.

They tumbled from the magic portal Philippe's coven had helped her coven create in Rose's sitting room, both landing hard on the carpet. Then Jer roughly pushed her away, rolling into a ball and hiding his face in his hands as she lay there, stunned.

"Jeraud!" Sasha cried, running to him. She threw her arms around him and held him, but he kept his frozen position, refusing to move.

"Don't look at me!" he shouted.

"Jer? Sweetheart?" Sasha said, astounded. She tried to pull his hands from his head, but he held firm.

And then Holly saw his hand, and caught her breath. It didn't look human. It was nothing but scars upon scars, wrapped around bone. Her stomach turned at the sight. "The Black Fire," she murmured, looking at his mother, who was stricken. "You were so badly burned."

"Yes." He cleared his throat. "Could someone get me something—a blanket, a towel?"

Holly understood his humiliation, and she looked searchingly at the others, who were standing around dumbfounded. Philippe glanced from Holly to Jer to Sasha, his brows knitting as he frowned in bewilderment. "Who is this?" he demanded.

Then Amanda took a step toward her and shouted, "Holly, you liar! *Where's my sister?*"

"I have to go back for her," Holly said, her emotions twisting her voice. She couldn't stop staring as Rose hurried to Jer's side with a large bath towel and draped it over his head.

Finished, Rose took a step backward, whispering to Kari, "Who is he, Kari?"

Kari was crying hard, her sobs coming in large, hot gasps. She turned on her heel and ran out of the room; seconds later, they heard a door slam.

"Oh, my God, what if she's gone outside?" Silvana asked. "What if the birds see her?" She hesitated, then rushed after her. "Kari? Come back!"

Alonzo regarded Jer as the younger man fumbled his way to the settee and sat heavily down. "This is a warlock," he announced.

"Holly, damn it! Where's Nicole?" Amanda's voice shook. "You go get my sister! Now!"

“I will,” Holly said, taking a deep breath. “Philippe, we have to re-create the spell.” She looked at Amanda. “I saw her, Amanda. I’ll get her.”

“Why didn’t you this time?” Amanda shrieked at her. *“Why did you bring him instead?”* Her hand trembled as she pointed at Jer. “It’s always the Deveraux! Always Jer who comes first!”

“She wouldn’t come without him,” Holly answered weakly, but she knew that that answer wasn’t worthy of her. *I found Jer, and I didn’t give him a chance to say no. I pulled him in. He didn’t even know what the light was.*

“And this is how you repay her for being so kind?”

Amanda’s accusations were cutting her to the quick—or maybe they were just hitting too close to home.

“Philippe, make the portal!” Holly shouted. *“Now!”*

Rose joined Philippe, Alonzo, Armand, and Pablo as they made a circle and began to chant in ancient Celtic. Sasha pulled Amanda to the circle, and each of them joined hands with Rose. A pinprick of light formed in the center of the circle, about three feet off the ground. It began to shine more brightly, and to grow. A low, almost subaudible hum emanated from the light.

The light expanded into an ellipse, then split into

rings, then split again. The individual rings began to shimmer and rotate as the hum increased in volume.

There was the sound of a crash, and then the sphere became an elongated oval, pulsing with light from inside it.

The portal had been successfully created.

Now it was up to Holly. She closed her eyes and concentrated on Nicole, on merging with her vibrations, on becoming one with her. She was the only one in the group powerful enough to achieve such a union, and she knew why Amanda was so upset: Her entire concentration should have been filled with nothing but thoughts of Nicole, and yet she had obviously been thinking of Jer as well . . . for here he was.

Then Holly saw Nicole in her mind's eye . . . and what she saw, she did not like.

Her cousin was dressed in ceremonial robes of black and red and bound onto an altar, her eyes staring unseeing as Eli Deveraux, and a man Holly didn't recognize, both stood over her, chanting. "No," she murmured.

"What? What's wrong? What do you see?" Amanda cried, stepping forward toward Holly, but Sasha firmly touched her shoulder, keeping her from breaking the circle.

"Don't break her concentration," she warned. "Help us, Amanda."

Amanda shut her eyes and took up the chant, which Rose and Philippe had pieced together from two spells, one from the Mother Coven's tradition and one from that of the Coven of White Magic.

Holly rode the strength of Amanda's sure image of her sister, using that to make herself connect more fully with her. Then she concentrated on Jer, who had draped the towel over his head, since he had just been with Nicole in person.

Then, when she felt the most in communion with her cousin—*who's been drugged!*—she stepped into the portal—

—and Jer jumped in after her.

"Jer," she gasped as the intense white light surrounded them. She couldn't see his scars in the light, just his vague outline. She could feel him, though, both his physical presence as well as his spiritual one.

"Where is she?" he demanded.

"Bound to an altar. Your brother's there, and some other man—"

"I'll fight them. You free her."

Jer leaped from the light. Pulling her wits about herself, Holly followed after.

The darkness of the room disoriented her; it was as

if dozens of flashbulbs had gone off in her face and she stumbled, trying to clear her vision with a hasty spell.

It worked a little; she squinted hard and rushed toward the altar, seeing Jer and the other two men in a filmy blur. Jer was hurtling fireballs at his brother; then he picked up an athame from the altar and was slashing it at the man Holly did not know. Eli deflected each projectile from his brother's fists, laughing as he did so.

"So, little brother, playing the white knight?" he taunted. "Or have you tricked Holly into racing right into our clutches?"

With that, Eli flung a magical line of energy in Holly's direction. It circled above her head, then plummeted downward over her arms. Instantly, it began to divide into more lines until she was captured in a glowing web.

"Holly!" Jer cried, running toward her. But James forced him back with a barrage of pulses of magic that threw him across the room. She watched helplessly as Jer smacked the wall with a sickening thud and landed in a heap on the floor.

"Goddess, give us the help we need, infuse him now with strength and speed," she prayed, imploring the Goddess to strengthen Jer.

Then Eli yanked on the end of the line, dragging her to her knees. She forced her head back so she could see what he was doing as she slid along the stone floor. With a crackle of energy he created a grappling hook and launched it at her. "Die, witch!" he shouted.

The other man just watched with an amused expression. But while he was concentrating on her, Jer leaped to his feet and rushed the man, grabbing him around the shoulders, and hurled him at Eli. The momentum knocked Eli's hand and the grappling hook sailed wide, clattering with a metallic sound against the wall.

Jer shouted something in Latin that she didn't understand, and the web disappeared. Then he flicked his fingers at Holly and she was hoisted as if by invisible hands to her feet. She raced to Nicole and snapped her fingers at the black velvet ropes around Nicole's wrists and ankles, and they fell away.

"Guards!" the other man shouted. "We have intruders!"

Now it was Holly's turn to defend them; she caused a blaze of fire to explode along the floor, creating a fiery barrier between the two men and her and Jer. Jer leaped to the altar and scooped Nicole up in his arms, then laid her over his back fireman style. As he raced toward the sphere of light, he cast another, stronger barrier behind Holly's firewall. "Come on!" he shouted.

Holly turned and joined him and Nicole in the portal. With a flash of energy, they disappeared.

Once more she and Jer fell back into the sitting room; once more he fumbled for cover while Philippe ran to the inert Nicole. Her eyes were still open but frighteningly vacant.

"Ah, ma belle," he whispered, enfolding her hands in his. He brushed her masses of black curls from her forehead. "Has he put you in thrall?"

"It's what she was most afraid of," Jer said.

Jer's mother knelt beside Nicole and studied her eyes. "No," Sasha said finally. "She's not in thrall. She's been drugged." She looked at Rose. "Do you have oak to burn? We need chamomile and rosemary. A quartz crystal," she said briskly.

"Of course." Rose nodded and hurried to her pantry.

Amanda plopped down next to Philippe. "Nicki," she called, "wake up!"

"I'm going to burn some sage as well," Rose called from the back of the house.

"That's a good idea," Sasha replied. She rubbed her hands briskly together; a heady mixture of cinnamon and ginger filled the room. After she opened her hands, Holly saw the spices smeared on her palms. She leaned forward over Nicole and cupped Nicole's eyes, murmuring words of healing.

"What was going on back there?" Amanda asked Holly tearfully.

"She was on an altar," Holly told her. "Eli and some other guy were there."

"James Moore," Jer filled in. "Heir to the throne of skulls."

"What were they going to do to her?" Amanda persisted.

Jer shrugged beneath the towel he had found to conceal his disfigured features. "Sacrifice her, probably. They were going to try to conjure the Black Fire."

"Oh, my God," Amanda said, covering her mouth. *"Nicole."*

"They were going to force Jer to help," Holly guessed. She hesitated. "Or do you know how to do it? Conjure the Black Fire?"

His head swiveled toward her. For a moment he said nothing, and then he shook his head. "I don't know anything about it." After a moment he added, "But I will tell you one thing. You're not safe in London anymore. They'll be coming after you."

And you, Holly filled in. *Are we going to be hunted for the rest of our lives? Is this ever going to end?*

Kari had run two long London blocks before Silvana had managed to catch up with her. Kari had been crying bitter tears, hunched and sobbing as she ran, and Silvana felt sorry for her. Nobody seemed to get that she really loved Jer Deveraux, and she hated all the witchcraft and Holly, who had come between them. Holly and Amanda were cruel to her, and Sasha and Tommy politely tolerated her. Of all the Coven, Silvana herself seemed to be the only one who had any empathy for her tough situation.

Silvana had tapped her on the shoulder, saying, "Kari, it's me."

Kari turned abruptly, sliding in the snow. Her face was blotched from crying. "Did you see him?"

"Yes, yes, I saw him," Silvana soothed, holding out her arms.

Kari stayed where she was, cupping her face and wildly shaking her head. "He looks like a monster!"

"I know, Kari."

"It never would have happened if Holly hadn't moved to Seattle," she said. "We were happy. Studying at school, making love . . ."

Silvana hadn't known them then, but she had gotten the distinct impression that Jer had already started to get tired of their relationship before Holly had shown up. But she said nothing about that now. She tried another tack. "Kari, we can't be out here. It's dangerous. The falcons are looking for us everywhere.

Now that . . . this has happened, our enemies will be searching for us even harder."

"I don't care!" Kari yelled. "I'm so sick of all of this!"

"Kari, *please,*" Silvana tried again. "We have to be careful."

"Why? We're going to die, anyway! Eddie's gone, and Kialish, and Amanda and Nicole's mother. . . . They're just picking us off one by one." Her voice rose to a thin, high-pitched shriek. "I can't stand this anymore!"

Then she broke down, bursting into heavy sobs, this time allowing Silvana to bundle her up into her arms and hold her. No one on the street noticed them—*we must still be cloaked,* Silvana thought gratefully—with passersby unconsciously skirting around the area where they stood.

Nevertheless, Silvana was anxious as they stood out in the open. Her heart pounded, and her gaze swept the area while she waited for Kari to calm a bit. The street was busy with last-minute Christmas shoppers hurrying through the snow. Silvana felt a brief, sharp pang for Christmases past—simpler days—then sternly reminded herself that self-pity was a luxury she could not afford. Nor could she let Kari indulge herself for too long.

"Kari . . . ," she began, and then she froze, listening.

She thought she heard a strange scuttling noise against the brick face of the building behind them.

She turned, to see the shadow of something rapidly climbing an old drainpipe. It was too dark to make it out, but as she raised her head to follow the shadow, she heard the flapping of wings above the roof.

"Let's go," she said urgently, and her tone must have alerted Kari that she meant it.

The other girl lifted her head, looked up at the roof, and peered hard. Her lips parted, and she gestured with her head toward the roof. She must have seen something, for her swollen eyes grew wide and she looked back at Silvana with real fear.

Watching us, Silvana mouthed.

Kari swallowed hard and nodded.

Yes, Silvana mouthed.

They hurried together back to the flat, awkward in the mushy gray city snow. Silvana looked over her shoulder, but saw nothing more.

Kari pulled open the door, and Silvana brought up the rear, shutting the door and leaning against it as if to keep out the shadows and the danger with the force of her weight.

"Did you see anything?" Silvana asked her.

Kari shook her head. "No. But I thought I heard a . . . bird?"

"Me too," she said grimly.

"Deveraux falcons," Kari murmured. "Or something else from the Supreme Coven. You tried to warn me. Once again, my freak-out endangers the whole coven," she said bitterly.

"They've never picked up on us yet," Silvana reminded her. "But we have to let Holly know."

"Oh, God," Kari moaned as she took off her jacket and put it on a hook beside the door. "She'll probably turn me into a toad." It was meant as a joke, but Silvana could see that she was genuinely afraid. With good reason: Holly was not the same kind and gentle girl Silvana had met last year.

They trudged into the sitting room to find Nicole propped up with pillows on the settee. A crocheted afghan was wrapped around her shoulders. Philippe sat on an ottoman pulled up beside her and he was holding a cup of something hot and steaming.

Holly glanced over at the two as they entered, her lip curling at the sight of Kari, and Silvana was disappointed all over again at the way she treated Kari.

"Nicole," Silvana said warmly. "How are you?"

Nicole winced. "Headache. But I'm alive, so I can't complain."

Philippe touched her cheek. *"Grace a Dieu,"* he murmured. She smiled gently at him and took the cup from his hand, sipped.

Kari looked around the room and said, "Where's Jer?"

"Lying down," Holly replied frostily. "In my room."

God, Holly, lighten up, Silvana told her silently. Then aloud, she said, "Something may have noticed us." At the flash of anger on Holly's face, she caught her breath. Then she raised her chin and added, "And we heard bird's wings."

"Great," Holly bit off. "Thanks, Kari."

Silvana took a step forward.

Holly glared at her.

"Kari's been through a lot. We all have."

Holly opened her mouth to say something more, but Sasha came up and placed a restraining hand on her shoulder. "Holly, why don't you get some of that tea Nicole is having?" she asked pointedly. "It's very soothing. There are more cups in the kitchen."

Frosty with silence, Holly jerked away and swept out of the room.

Sasha grimaced apologetically at the two girls. "She's . . . tense."

"No kidding," Silvana grumbled. "That still

doesn't give her the right to be so mean to everybody."

Sasha exhaled slowly. "No. The fact that she's High Priestess of our coven does, though." She added under her breath, "Unfortunately."

"I don't believe that," Silvana insisted. "Hey, I didn't elect her leader, and I say—"

Sasha put up a hand. "That's right. We didn't elect her. She's High Priestess by right. She can't step down even if she wants to. As you have seen. So . . ." She moved her shoulders. "She gets a few privileges. Which include bad manners."

Kari rolled her eyes. Sasha wagged her finger at her and said in a low whisper, "I'd be a little more cautious around her, Kari. The pressure's getting to be too much for her. Now," she continued in a louder voice, "tell me about the bird."

"We think we heard the Deveraux falcons," Silvana began. "We think we're all in trouble."

Kari nodded in agreement. "Big trouble," she said.

Michael Deveraux: Seattle

As Michael stood on the widow's walk of his home in Lower Queen Anne, the December fogs wrapped around him and held him like a lovesick woman. Night moisture glistened on spiderwebs and encircled the streetlights like faery rings. He stood, listening to the night, wondering what was going on in London.

I should be there, he thought, frustrated. *I'm out of the loop.*

He had thrown the runes and read the entrails of a great many number of animals, and all the signs pointed to his staying in Seattle. *But nothing is going on here. Everyone is in London, including Holly Cathers. And I swore to Sir William that I would kill her.*

He sighed and resumed his pacing. He was uneasy in his skin. Two more nights until Yule, both his sons were gone, and he was at a distinct disadvantage in the game they all were playing.

Clouds cloaked the moon, casting him in darkness. It was cold, and there was snow all around him on the widow's walk. The air smelled crisp, and he closed his eyes, remembering for a moment a child's delight at the layers of white all around his house, and the hope of a day off from school. His father, a powerful warlock in his own right, used to take credit for those days of freedom, assuring his little son that he himself had caused the snow to fall, just for him.

There was no reason not to believe that. The Deveraux had done far more powerful things, and recently.

Last Beltane, we conjured the Black Fire, he reminded himself. *I assumed the reason my spell finally worked was because we three were together, my sons and I. But we haven't been able to do it since. I know. I tried, and failed. . . .*

"Laurent," he called to his ancestor, "will you walk with me?"

The stench of the grave heralded the materialization of the great duke who had ruled the Deveraux family when the Cahors had massacred them. Laurent had conjured the Black Fire that night, and it had been by the black flames that Isabeau had died. Finally, last year on the six hundredth anniversary of the massacre, he had revealed the chant to Michael that would call it forth. And it had worked.

Now, nothing.

Michael didn't know if Laurent had anything to do with the failure, if the phantom warlock was blocking it or had withdrawn his influence in some way. He did know that Laurent was as interested as he was in having a Deveraux ascend the throne of skulls in London.

He also knew Laurent did not particularly care if the victor was Michael himself, one of Michael's sons, or another Deveraux who had not yet been born. Time was on the side of the phantom, and he was a patient and cunning creature—so unlike Jean, his son, who had been so rash and impetuous.

As Michael watched, the mists swirled around a figure that slowly gained mass and solidity. Laurent's skeleton appeared first, and then bits of muscle; when Michael had first begun working with his ancestor, Laurent could only appear to him as a desiccated corpse. But now he had amassed enough life energy to walk the earth again in the guise of a vigorous and very formidable man.

He did so now, wearing black jeans, a black T-shirt, and a black leather jacket. Broad-shouldered and heavily muscled, he towered over Michael, very much a Deveraux with dark hair and eyes and beard, and looked with humor on his living kinsman as he said, "You're alone here in Seattle. They've all run off to London to see the Queen."

"Yes. This is ridiculous," Michael pouted. "I'm wasting my time . . ."

And then his words trailed off as Laurent raised his hands and clapped them together twice.

In the distance, the answering screech of a falcon heralded magic in the air.

As the silvery clouds drifted away from the moon, the silhouette of an enormous bird cut across the glowing sphere; the flapping of the wings made the snow flutter and the wind blow. A huge, proud creature, its wings swept silently up, down, as it drew near the widow's walk.

On its back rode Michael's imp, the one who had

revealed to him the Curse of the Cahors—that those they loved would die by water. As it spied Michael it threw up its hands and laughed maniacally, as it was wont to do. Its chattering teeth gleamed in the moonlight; its pointed ears stood up like two feathers on either side of its head.

The bird was Fantasme, spirit-familiar of the Deveraux, and as it swooped toward the walk, the imp slid off its back and landed on the wooden railing.

"Where have you been?" Michael demanded. He had thought the creature was down in his chamber of spells, where he kept it.

"Holly Cathersss has taken your ssson from Headquartersss," the imp said. "No Jer Deveraux tonight, no Black Fire tonight." It rubbed its taloned fingers together, its repulsive, leathery face drawn back with glee. "Now we bring her back! Now we kill her!"

"What?" Michael was stunned.

Laurent raised a brow. "They were going to create the Black Fire?" he asked the imp.

"Yessss. Going to try," the imp reported, grinning evilly. It bobbed up and down on the railing, skipping along the thin piece of white-painted wood with no care for the thirty-foot drop to the ground.

"Do you know how they hoped to accomplish it?" Laurent pressed. He had assured Michael that he had no idea why the spell to conjure the fire was not working now. Michael only half believed him; only a fool would trust a Deveraux. In their family, blood was not thick at all. And it was the cheapest of commodities.

"No," the imp replied, completely unconcerned. Michael wondered if it was lying to Laurent—if, later, it would tell Michael everything. Michael had no idea why this imp had come to him, had chosen him to serve, and it had occurred to him more than once that it might actually be a spy—sent from James Moore, perhaps, or even Sir William.

"She rescued him," Michael mused. "Rescued my son."

He couldn't help his admiration, but he prayed he did not reveal it in his tone. Little in this world infuriated Laurent as Holly Cathers's continuing ability to thwart them at every turn. But though his ancestor insisted that she must die, Michael had not given up the idea of making her his consort. A strong witch like her in thrall, and Cahors and Deveraux together again . . . it could prove to be exactly what he needed to take over the Supreme Coven and conjure the Black Fire alone.

The imp nodded eagerly. "Now we lure her back!"

It jabbed a talon downward, and Michael understood.

Lying in rows in his basement and in boxes in his chamber of spells, and resting impatiently in graveyards and mausoleums, his army of the dead awaited their marching orders. He had begun animating them months ago, biding his time, waiting, too, for the moment to strike.

Duke Laurent smiled broadly. "Excellent," he said. "I will enjoy that."

"And Sssan Francisssco," the imp reminded Michael, "where the three are hiding."

Michael knew he was referring to the shaman, Dan Carter; the voodoo woman, Tante Cecile; and Holly's uncle, Richard Anderson, the husband of Michael's dead lover. He sneered. Killing Marie Claire's husband would be ironic. As he had torn the two apart in life, he could cause them to be joined together in death. "San Francisco as well," Michael assented.

"It's a fine time to be a Deveraux," the Duke said approvingly. "A fine time for revenge, and death."

The imp chittered gleefully, and Fantasme flapped his wings as he soared in mockery at the Goddess Moon.

Michael glided along the widow's walk with a lighter step.

★ ★ ★

From her perch among the mists of time and magic, Pandion, the lady hawke of the Cahors, woke from her seemingly eternal slumbers and cocked her head. She sensed a battle was at hand, and her heart soared.

It had been too long since she had dined on ashes and blood.

Centuries too long.

SEVEN

AMBER

☾

Passion now begins to wake
And whom we desire, we will take
Then we'll cut them down to the quick
Love itself, the cruelest trick

Moved we are by love's sweet song
Though it plays not for long
We can blow on embers bright
Till passion overtakes the light

Cathers Coven: London

They were alone. Seated on her bed, Jer was hidden in his blanket. He remained silent.

Holly kept her eyes fixed on her hands, which were shaking badly. Her knees wobbled, and she sat on the other side of the bed; it was narrow enough that she could feel his body heat as he moved uncomfortably away.

She blurted, "Jer, I didn't mean . . ."

"I know." His voice was a cruel parody of his old voice, the one that had not been burned with Black Fire.

"I didn't mean to leave you alone in the fire," she cut in, speaking more loudly than she had meant to. "My cousins didn't know what would happen to you."

"Doesn't matter, does it?" He kept his back to her. The blanket stretched across his broad back. She remembered what it felt like to put her arms around him. His lips on hers had been soft and warm, and then, as desire mounted, more insistent. She remembered all this, and her hands shook even harder.

I've dreamed of this moment for so long. But it's not at all how I thought it would be. I'm glad he's safe. So glad. But . . . he doesn't love me anymore. If he ever did.

I can make him love me, she thought fiercely. *I'm a witch.*

She balled her fists, resisting the temptation. That would be a hollow victory. "I . . . we can work on your . . . on your scars," she ventured.

"Just stay away from me," he croaked. Then he said, "Eddie and Kialish are both dead?"

"Yes." She closed her eyes, remembering Eddie's last moments. He had screamed for her to help him as the sea monster had advanced on him. But she had chosen to save Amanda instead, even though she had been afraid that Amanda was already dead.

His silence condemned her. Then he said, "This is all because of us. My family. The Deveraux."

He said his own name as if it was a curse; to Holly's way of thinking, he was right.

"My father will rule the Supreme Coven, Holly. He'll do whatever it takes. He won't stop until he's sitting on the throne of skulls, either he himself or Eli. And he needs Black Fire to get there."

"I know," she said softly.

"He doesn't care about people. About . . . me." Jer drooped forward; the blanket shifted, and she realized he was burying his head in his hands. "My God, I've become such a whiner. I'm a friggin' wimp."

"No." She put her hand on his shoulder.

A shudder ran through him and he jerked away. She clasped her hand against her chest, afraid she had harmed him. "I'm sorry," she whispered.

"Me too." He took a deep breath. "Please, Holly, I need some time. Alone."

The moment widened to a minute. Then Holly rose unsteadily and walked from the room, shutting the door behind herself.

"How are you doing, *ma belle*?" Philippe asked quietly as they sat beside each other on the settee. The others were milling around, talking about what Kari and Silvana had or hadn't seen, beginning to look for things to eat for dinner. Holly had slammed into her bedroom, where Jer was, and had not returned.

Nicole nodded slowly. "Good, but only because you're here." She looked at him wonderingly. "You actually came after me."

He smiled. "Did I not promise that I would? We of the White Magic Coven always keep our promises."

He leaned down and kissed her, and she couldn't help but smile. There was a promise in his kiss, and she knew that he would keep it.

"I love you," she told him when he pulled back. "You're what kept me alive the last few weeks."

"And do you know that I love you and will do everything in my power to keep you safe?"

She nodded happily. "Yes. I can feel that."

Then Astarte sidled up to her, meowed, and leaped into her lap. To her surprise, she began crying.

"Oh, cat," she said fondly. "My sweet cat."

And she realized she was weeping for Hecate, who was dead. As if Astarte understood, she put a paw on Nicole's cheek, catching a tear, and cocked her head. There was tenderness in the gesture, and sympathy, and Nicole stroked the cat's head as she leaned against Philippe, resting against his chest as the cat began to purr.

"You are well loved," Philippe said.

Nicole closed her eyes. "Yes." Then she swallowed. "I have to talk to Holly. It's about Joel."

He raised a brow. "What?"

She took a deep breath and started to rise. Her knees were a little wobbly. Philippe assisted her.

"Thanks." She hesitated. "You can come with me, if you want."

"Of course."

He slid his fingers through hers; holding hands, they walked out of the sitting room and toward Holly's closed door. Nicole began to tremble; she was more afraid than ever of Holly, even though Holly had just risked her own life to save Nicole's.

She raised her hand and rapped softly on the door. "Holly?"

The door opened. Holly had been crying. She made no mention of her tears, only narrowed her eyes as if she were irritated by the intrusion. "What?"

Nicole glanced around her; she couldn't help her revolted fascination with Jer. He looked so horrible, it was hard not to fall into something like a hypnotic spell and gaze at him, as if something were hardwired in her brain that said, *Pay attention. Don't let this happen to you.*

He was lying with his face to the wall, the covers

pulled up to his chin. She couldn't make out his features.

As if she sensed that Nicole was gawking, Holly scowled at her and came into the hallway, shutting the door behind herself. She crossed her arms across her chest and squared her shoulders.

Nicole wanted to say, *Holly, it's just me.* But she didn't. What she did say was, "I had a vision. There was a man named Joel, I think . . . I think he's dead, Holly."

The other girl visibly paled. Nicole reached out a hand and steadied Holly by the shoulder. Holly looked past her, as if to a distant place only she could see, and bit her lower lip. Beneath her hand, Nicole could feel Holly trembling.

"What did you see?" she asked finally.

"He was in his house. On the floor. The snow was coming in."

Holly ticked a glance at Philippe. "Go and check," she ordered him.

He nodded. "I'll need the address."

"I'll go with you," Nicole said.

"No." Holly shook her head. "You'll stay here."

Nicole frowned. "But—"

"She's right, Nicole," Philippe cut in. "You stay here. I'll go alone."

★★★

Philippe was gone nearly an hour. When he returned, Holly was waiting for him in the entryway. Her face was ashen, and there were circles under her eyes. He hadn't realized how tired she looked, and his heart went out to her. She looked thin in a baggy sweater, and he guessed that the Capri pants she was wearing shouldn't be as loose as they were on her frame. *I wonder if she's eating?* he thought. She was in a nearly impossible position; he didn't know how she was managing as well as she was, and he admired her for her strength of will and her courage.

She looked at him, then dropped her gaze as his expression told her the bad news. Joel was indeed dead, and had been lying just as Nicole had seen him in her vision.

Holly was silent for a time. Then she murmured, "He healed me. During the battle that went away, he saved my life. And I . . ."

"Sometimes there is a bargain," Philippe said gently. "If that was the case, it was the right one to make. You are the High Priestess of a coven, and a powerful and important witch."

She stared up at him, her eyes glittering like hard, brittle glass. "If I'm so damn powerful, why did I have to make such a bargain?" she demanded. Then she softened a bit. "What did you do with him?" she asked.

He hesitated. Then he said, "Witches are generally cremated. But I couldn't do that for him. I simply called the police. His death appears as a heart attack, no foul play."

"But you didn't wait for the police."

"*Non.* They won't find me," he assured her. "They won't find *us,*" he corrected.

"Good." She swallowed. "Thanks."

He inclined his head. "You are welcome, Holly."

She blinked as if she was almost shocked by the kindness in his voice. His compassion for her increased.

Then she shrugged as if to deny the dent he had made in her armor, turned on her heel, and left him alone in the entryway, where Nicole found him.

She put her arms around him and pressed her face against his chest.

"You found him," Nicole said brokenly, "as I saw him."

"Oui."

"Oh, God, I hate this. All of this," she whispered. "I want it to be over."

Philippe stroked her hair, and let her cry.

Tante Cecile, Dan, and Richard: San Francisco

Cecile Beaufrere had found several boxes of Christmas decorations in the attic of the small San Francisco house she, Dan Carter, and Richard Anderson had been living in for the last few weeks. They had discussed living in Holly's home, or the home of Barbara Davis-Chin, but in the end, had decided that they had to stay as low under Michael Deveraux's radar as possible. She and Richard had enough money to sustain them for a few more months—she had never liked using magic for personal economic gain—but she wondered when this ordeal would be over.

If it's ever over. The battle between good and evil is eternal. Are we destined to be part of that battle from now on?

Despite her *voudon* roots, she had always kept Christmas back home in New Orleans. She did the same now, though it seemed forced: Richard was still numb from the shock of discovering the realities of the magical realm, and sick with worry over his daughters. He seemed to be rallying somewhat, however, and talking about making plans "to help out." She had cautioned him to be very careful; they were in hiding, and he shouldn't do anything that might allow Michael Deveraux to locate them.

Dan was still mourning the death of his son, Kialish—and Kialish's partner, Eddie, too—and Cecile was well-aware that this was the first Christmas without them.

The year of firsts is the hardest, she told herself as she quietly decorated the Christmas tree. *The first birthday, the first anniversary . . . the first time you walk into a room and realize that he will never be in his favorite chair . . .*

. . . oh, Marcus . . .

Cecile had lost her own true love many years before. Marcus, Silvana's uncle, had been a fabulous man—creative, artistic, and very kind. A professor at Tulane, he had died of a brain embolism when Silvana was an infant. Cecile had had no warning, and despite all the magical work she had done to keep her family safe and well, she and her niece had lost him in a matter of heartbeats.

Now she was charged with protecting someone else's loved one—Richard—and she was not certain she was up to the task.

"That's pretty," he said now, walking into the living room. Nicole and Amanda, his daughters, were going to be terribly shocked when they saw him again. His hair had gone completely white.

And they will see him, she vowed firmly. *We will all be reunited. My* loa *will help guard them and guide them home.*

"Thank you." She smiled at him and held out a small box of colored glass ornaments shaped like Christmas stockings. "Would you like to help?"

"Maybe in a little while." He eased himself slowly into a recliner facing the tree, folding his hands over his lap, and smiled vacantly at her.

"Wish I had some eggnog," he added. She said nothing. What he wished he had was the whiskey that went in the eggnog. By mutual agreement, neither she nor Dan purchased alcohol when they went to the grocery store—and Richard never went. They saw to that.

Tomorrow night the moon would be full, and witches and magic users everywhere would be celebrating Yule. The winter solstice. Ironically, Yule had roots as an Egyptian solar festival, a twelve-day holiday to celebrate the rebirth of Horus, son of Isis and Osiris. The magical properties of the season were still recognized in their various forms, with many traditions being celebrated in many ways. The American secularized forms, together bundled as Christmas, had always held their appeal for Cecile, and she had no problem participating in the many rituals and traditions, drawing the strength of community from them.

But now she was isolated from her community. Now she was a stranger in a strange land, drawing strength only from Dan Carter. The two kept the flame alive as they waited for those in Europe to find and save the lost ones, put an end to the Cathers-Deveraux vendetta, and hopefully, return home.

What I fear, however, is that the Deveraux have convinced the Supreme Coven to make the private vendetta their public war . . . pulling in the Mother Coven as well. And then it will never end, because the two larger forces will paint the confrontation as the war of good versus evil. When in truth it's not that at all. The Cathers were never entirely good.

And if the love Jean held for Isabeau is to be accepted as real, the Deveraux were never entirely evil. . . .

She sighed and placed another metallic Christmas stocking on the tree. Her spirits drooped, and she wished—as she often wished—that she and Silvana were back home in the French Quarter, blissfully unaware of all the trouble that had been brewing in Seattle.

But that was a coward's thinking, and she knew that those blessed with communion with the *loa* had grave responsibilities in this world.

I should give thanks that Amanda called me, she thought. *I have been called to my highest and best purpose.* But in truth, she really couldn't. *My niece-daughter is with the Coven, and I'm as worried about her as Richard is about his girls.*

Sighing, she plucked another ball out of the box.

That was when she saw the shadows flitting across Richard Anderson's face.

Wings.

Several of them, flapped in silhouette across his pale features, and then against the tan leather of the recliner. They glided silently over the flocked wallpaper, sliding menacingly along.

As was Cecile's habit, the drapes were pulled across the windows. The silhouettes were magical, emanating from no natural source.

Drawing in breath, Cecile set the box down and whispered to her *loa,* "Guardians, come. Guardians, take the magic from this room and use it for protection."

Still, the silhouettes slid without sound over the walls, then dipped downward toward the floorboards, stretching over the hardwood floor. The shadows moved toward her; she got up on the ladder she had been using to decorate the tree, standing still and praying for protection, for strength, for annihilation of all evil.

At that moment, she heard Dan Carter shout from upstairs, where his bedroom was. It was a cry of surprise. His footsteps sounded across the floor; then his door opened. She held her breath as he raced down the stairs.

She called out, "Stop!" when he began to race into the room.

Seeing the menacing shadows of wings, he halted, frozen to the spot. Then he made a series of hand motions and plucked something from the leather bag he had had the presence of mind to bring with him—his medicine bag—and sprinkled it in front of himself on the floor.

The shadows broke up as they hit that portion of the hardwood. He sprinkled more on the floor, and then into the air in front of him, and in that way, created a safety zone for himself as he walked toward Cecile. As he progressed, he gestured for her to stay silent.

Finally he stood at the bottom of the ladder. He flung magical dust at her, then reached out his hands and gestured for her to come to him. She let him pull her from the ladder and drape her body over his shoulder. Saying not a word, he backed slowly out of the room.

That was when the shaking began.

The entire house quaked, once to the left, and once to the right. The windows rattled. From inside the chimney, birds shrieked.

Then ghostly hounds began baying, their howls terrible and fierce, their invisible toenails skittering over the wooden floor as they raced after Dan and Cecile. Cecile smelled their wet fur and their dragon-hot breath, but saw nothing. They were invisible. But as they rushed past Richard's recliner, they tipped it over, throwing Richard to the floor. Invisible maybe, but not insubstantial.

Richard got to his feet, then was hit dead-on by something. With a shout he fell to his knees and began wrestling with something he couldn't see. He yelled, "Run! Get out of here!"

Dan ran-walked backward. Cecile scrabbled out of his arms and raised her hands to Heaven, summoning the forces of Baron Samedi, King of *voudon,* to aid her. Rushing winds gathered between her palms and she sent them to Richard to aid him.

Then the door slammed shut, separating her and Dan from Richard.

"Richard!" she shouted, pounding on the door with her fists. Dan began to chant as he worked the doorknob, straining to get the door open. The invisible hounds scratched and bayed on the other side, and the door bowed toward her and Dan.

There was a crash, and then the door burst open and Richard shot across the transom. Dan slammed the door behind him.

Richard shouted, "Keep going!"

His face was cut and bleeding, and a hank of his hair had been yanked from his skull; he looked partially scalped.

The three raced down the hallway toward the stairs, Cecile in the lead, Dan next, and Richard bringing up the rear.

Dan yelled to her, "Upstairs!"

Halfway there, mist began to gather around their ankles; it was dark brown, hot, and poisonous. It attacked them, swirling around their legs. Blisters broke out on her shins and thighs, and Cecile cried out, shocked by the pain.

Dan grabbed her hand and yanked her toward the stairs, pushing her in front of him and propelling her upstairs. She stumbled several times, but he gave her no chance to right herself. He kept pushing and pushing until she reached the landing. Richard charged up close behind.

"My room!" Dan shouted. "Go, Cecile!"

Speaking her name was like breaking a spell; as she raced down the hall she began to babble, saying, "What's happening? What's going on?" even though she knew: They were finally being attacked. By the Supreme Coven or Michael Deveraux, she could not say. She had anticipated this for a long time, waited for it, braced herself for it.

I finally let down my guard, and now, it's here.

But how? How did they find us?

She threw open the door to Dan's bedroom and ran inside. The other two came in right behind her and slammed the door.

Dreamcatchers hung from the ceiling, and feathers

and bones; they whipped about as the three of them ran for the wall opposite the door and flattened themselves against it. She prayed to her *loa* and Dan called upon Raven, his totem, while Richard pushed Dan's dresser in front of the door. The house was booming as if someone were bowling with cannonballs, and the door was rattling practically off the hinges.

That was when the window shattered, and an enormous black falcon soared into the room.

"Look out!" Dan cried, throwing himself over Cecile in a shielding embrace. They flattened against the floor, he with his weight on top of her, as the shards flew in all directions and the bird screamed with pain.

She hazarded a glance at it, peering through the jumble of his arms. It had been aiming at Richard, but it had narrowly missed him. He had ducked, and the bird had pinioned itself in the wall. Blood was gushing from the bird's beak and it was struggling frantically to get loose. It flapped its wings and batted its head, but still it stayed stuck, and it was rapidly losing blood.

Dan was murmuring words at it; she joined in, in French, willing it to die and for its essence of hate to return to its master. Still, the bird thrashed, flapping its wings.

Richard picked up the brass lamp on top of the

dresser and began slamming it against the bird's body. It screamed like a human being; he kept hitting it, with a strength Cecile hadn't realized Richard possessed, until the creature hung limp from its beak. Then it detached from the wall and slid to the floor, dead.

That was when the imps started pouring in through the broken window. Hundreds of them, tiny, scaly creatures that jittered and cackled as they crawled over the shards, mindless of the injuries they inflicted on themselves. Some lost limbs, some taloned claws, and still they jabbered and clattered, dropping onto the floor like cockroaches or rats, and scrambling toward Dan and Cecile.

That was when Cecile sent out a mental message: *Holly, help us! We're under attack!*

She had no idea if the girl would hear them.

But Dan shifted his attention toward her and said, "Yes. Good, Cecile."

She felt his own vibration as he joined her.

Help, Holly!

Save us!

We have been found!

The Tri-Covenate: London, Yule

It was finally Yule. Sasha smiled at the two pairings who had volunteered to put themselves into thrall—

the Lady to the Lord—in order to multiply their magical powers. As an official of the Mother Coven, she had the ability to perform the rite, and she knew that now, more than ever, those she traveled with had need of more power. The forces of the Supreme Coven were gathering all around them, and she knew, in her heart, that their days of safety were numbered.

So she stood on the night of the full moon before the door to Westminster Abbey with two couples bound together with herbed ropes, ready to slice their palms so that their blood might mingle.

One of the pairs was Nicole and Philippe, which did not surprise her. But the second had made her smile wistfully for lost days of innocent love: Tommy Nagai had declared his love for Amanda, and she, apparently, returned it.

Life is full of surprises, she told herself. *Many of them sweet and winsome.*

But as with life, so with the ritual: She had assumed that Jeraud would agree to accept Holly in thrall, and he had refused.

"My blood is tainted," he had told his mother. "I am a Deveraux."

That was exactly the point, Sasha had tried to explain to him. He was a Deveraux.

Ashen, Holly had absorbed the blow of his refusal

as best she could, but it was clear she had not been prepared for what was, ultimately, a rejection of the most intimate connection witch and warlock could undergo. She loved Jer, plain and simple. And she had assumed that he would consent to place her in thrall. After all, she had braved much to rescue him—the enmity of the Mother Coven, her own life, and that of her other loved ones.

But all Jer said when he refused was, "I am a Deveraux."

So Holly stood beside Sasha, acting as her assistant while she bound the ropes around the wrists of the others. Nicole and Philippe were filled with passion—Sasha could feel it—while Amanda and Tommy were newer, shyer, more childlike with each other.

"By the Goddess, I charge thee, turn to each other in times of peril," Sasha intoned. "By her mercy, draw strength from each other, the Lady to the Lord, the Lord to the Lady."

"Blessed be," the onlookers intoned. Alonzo made the sign of the cross over them while Sasha dipped oak leaves in water and sprinkled them.

"May the Lord draw magical blessings from the Lady, and may the Lady do the same."

"Blessed be."

Holly choked back tears as Jer stood in the

shadow beyond the reach of the Lady Moon. His scarred face was hidden from her view, and yet, she had memorized each rivulet of flesh, the way his eyes pulled downward as if his face were melting. Her heart understood why he had refused to place himself in thrall with her, and yet that same heart was breaking.

It's our turn, she mentally told him.

But she understood the danger as well—what if Isabeau took possession of her, and demanded Jean's death? What if Jean finally exacted his revenge?

And yet, her yearning for him was unbearable.

Jer, I would die for you. I would forsake all these others for you. And she meant it too. *Goddess help me, I mean it.*

He kept his face turned away from hers, as if by looking at her he might weaken. So she kept staring at him, hoping to make eye contact.

But through the long ritual, he kept his face averted.

His heart averted.

I love you, she called out to him.

And she knew he answered, *I know.*

She endured her pain during the ritual, as Amanda and Tommy and Nicole and Philippe entered into a union more profound and intimate than Christian marriage: Their magical essences were united, and they were, in a sense, one combined source of magical power. She saw the light in their eyes, saw the soft glow of magic surrounding them, and she could hardly bear to be in their presence.

Then Sasha announced, "It is done. They are in thrall."

And Nicole and Amanda both gasped and said in unison, "Seattle is under attack!"

It was true. Back in the safe house, Rose turned on the news. Seattle, in the state of Washington, was under siege. No one knew what precisely was going on, but floods rushed through the town; squares of city blocks were on fire; and people were being devoured by "packs of dogs" the likes of which the city had never seen. Bodies by the score were being discovered, both on land and washing up on the beaches. And numerous eyewitnesses had claimed that the dead were walking. . . .

"It's Michael," Holly angrily announced. She didn't need scrying stones and runes to tell her that, although she did consult them. "He wants us back there." *Though I have no idea why.*

"What about San Francisco?" Amanda demanded, frantic about her father. Silvana was equally worried about Cecile. But the news was only about Seattle.

While they watched, Jer came up to Holly. As if to underscore his reasons for not joining her in thrall, he let her see his hideous face. *If only Joel were alive, he could probably do something to heal him,* she thought bitterly. The Black Fire that had burned him was magic, and it would take incredibly strong healing magic to even begin to heal the damage done to him. Alas, healing was not one of her gifts. *Cahors seem better equipped to inflict pain and suffering than to heal.* She did her best not to react, but her stomach churned at the sight of him. As if he read her expression, he gave her a sour smile.

Then he said loudly, "I'd like to propose that we three covens unite. We'll be a Tri-Covenate, and there's very little stronger than that."

Sasha came over, listening carefully. She nodded at his words and said to Holly, "He's right. We have your coven, the Coven of White Magic, and the remnants of Jer's Rebel Coven—he and Kari."

At this, Kari took a breath. She said, "I wouldn't be here if I could help it," she said a bit sullenly.

"I know." Jer put a hand on her shoulder. When she visibly shuddered, he removed it with a sigh. "But you're still part of my coven. I haven't released you."

Philippe and the other members of his coven shared a silent look before he answered, "The Coven of White Magic agrees to this union."

"Even though I'm in thrall to you, Philippe, I'm still part of Holly's coven," Nicole said.

"Yes," Sasha agreed. "One of the three Ladies of the Lily."

She pointed to the scar in Nicole's palm. As Nicole held out her hand, Amanda walked to her and put her hand beside her sister's. Holly joined them, and together, the imprint of a lily was formed in their upright palms.

"When we place it together, we make very strong magic," Amanda said, smiling at them both.

Nicole lowered her gaze and sighed—whether out of guilt that she had abandoned the other two, or with resignation that she couldn't outrun her obligation, Holly didn't know. A rush of pity shot through her for Nicole, and Kari—for them all, in fact.

It would have been so nice to grow up innocent of the Coventry world, she thought. *To not know there was power like this. To not need it.*

"Let us go outside, then, so the Lady Moon will shine down on us," Sasha urged.

They did as she bade, finding a place behind Rose's flat where they could perform the ritual unnoticed. Holly stood, a little anxious at the thought of binding her coven to the others so formally. *Not the kind of binding ritual I was hoping to do tonight,* she thought, looking at Jer.

Sasha opened her arms. "Let the leaders come forward."

Holly, Philippe, and Jer stood in a triangle, each with his or her hands on the shoulders of the others. Sasha walked slowly to each of them, picking up each hand, slicing the palm and replacing it on a shoulder. In the end the blood of each was upon a shoulder of the other two. Rose took a silk cord and wove it in and out of their legs, binding the three of them together.

Then Sasha bade each person stand behind the leader of his or her coven. Rose pricked their fingers with a pin, and they each squeezed a drop of blood onto the head of their leader.

Sasha spoke, her voice reverberating with authority and power: "Now these three lives and these three fates are bound together as are these three covens. Each High Priest or Priestess bears the responsibility for their own coven. The blood of each of their covenates is on their heads. Each High Priest or High Priestess also bears the burdens of the other two. You place hands on shoulders to support and to guide one another. Your burdens are theirs as your blood is now theirs. Your legs are bound so that you may not turn from one another in adversity, never flee from your brothers and sisters, but will stand beside them to protect them. You are three."

Sasha placed her hand on Jer's head. "You are fire."

Holly winced in unison with him as he heard the word. Fire had nearly been his destruction. Fire had cost him so much. How then, could he be fire?

Sasha moved to place her hand on Philippe's head. "You are earth."

Then it was Holly's turn. Sasha placed her hand upon her head. "You are water."

Dread filled Holly. *No! How can I be water, the thing that destroys those I love?* As she thought back upon all that she had done, though, the "sacrifices" she had made, she could see the truth of it. The pain wrenched her heart.

Sasha removed her hand and continued. "You three stand in need of a fourth. Let the Goddess dwell with you and fulfill the circle. Let the Goddess be the very air that you breathe."

A chill wind whipped suddenly through Holly and the others, cold enough to take her breath away. Then, as quickly as it had come, it was gone. *The Goddess has spoken.*

Sasha held out her arms and sent beams of magical energy into the center of the triangle; they filled the space between Holly, Jer, and Philippe, until Holly sensed Jer's magical essence, and Philippe's, too, and allowed hers to mingle with theirs. The result was an increased magical presence, much greater than the sum of its parts, and she wondered, *Is this what thrall is like? Is it even better? Because this is pretty wonderful.*

As if in answer to her question, Philippe glanced lovingly at Nicole, and she at him, and the moment was so private that Holly began to cry.

Sasha whispered in her ear, "Someday, Holly, I promise."

But Jer overheard her and looked at his mother steadily, offering no such words of encouragement. Holly had not felt so alone since her parents had died on the river . . . at the hands of a Deveraux.

Maybe he is his father's son, she told herself, which was a foolish thing to think, but she knew what she meant: Maybe he was more Michael's son than Sasha's, more evil than good.

"It is done," Sasha declared, and the energies that crackled in the middle of the triangle dissipated. Holly let her hands fall off of Jer's and Philippe's shoulders and she stepped back, shaken.

"We need to get back to the States," Nicole proclaimed. "We have so many people to protect."

Holly nodded. Then she reached out a hand to Jer.

But it started to snow, and he took advantage of the curtain of white to pretend that he didn't see her outstretched hand.

★ ★ ★

As before, the Mother Coven offered their private jet, but no other support. No soldiers, no weapons, nothing in the battle against evil that was raging in Seattle.

As soon as they alighted from the plane, the Tri-Covenate was under siege. The weather was horrible—thunder and lightning, incredibly heavy rains that turned the streets to frothing seas, chaotic with an undertow of cars, newspaper kiosks, street signs, and even streetlights. As the waters poured down the hills of Seattle, they began to drag wide-eyed bodies with them, and the corpses of innocent animals caught in the magical onslaught.

Worse were the fires raging all over the city, which the rain couldn't dampen. The flames soared into the sky like demonic aurora borealis; the tongues of fire scorched vast skyscrapers and entire city blocks; there was so much devastation that the news stations had stopped taking count, apparently deciding that they might as well wait until it was all done, and the death and devastation would no longer be a moving target but a quantifiable tragedy.

As Holly and the others tried to grab a cab or even a bus to the Anderson home, they couldn't believe the throngs of panicked crowds trying to catch flights out of the city. The airport was jammed, and people were so terrified that they put their humanity on hold: They lost their sense of accountability, and forgot that once this was over, they would have to live with their own actions. No one could think that far. No one could think at all.

"We're all going to Hell!" a collared priest informed Holly as he pushed past her and the others as they went down an escalator.

Another man said, "We're *in* Hell, brother!"

Staring at the others, Holly walked through the automatic sliding-glass door and stepped into the storm.

Wind and rain pulled at her, the air howling like a banshee. She caught at her coat, huddling against the clements as Alonzo struggled to hold his umbrella over her. She thought of her parents' funeral—how lightning had struck a tree—and she felt a thick, cold loathing for Michael Deveraux that she knew would only be lost upon his death.

By the Goddess, I will kill him before the next moon, she vowed, her hands clenched.

And then the loathing grew, and Holly thought she would lose another shred of her humanity, another piece of her soul. She knew it, and she was glad.

Witches in my position can't afford the luxury of softness. I have to be hard, so others don't have to be. Jer's worried that he's too dark, too evil to ally himself with me. He doesn't even know evil, the things I've done to protect my people.

And in that moment, Holly allied herself with the darkness. She felt herself yield to it, go over to it, and there was one last instant of regret.

I will never know the pleasures of ordinary people again, she realized.

Jer must have sensed her capitulation. He glanced at her and murmured, "Holly, no."

"You could have saved me," she flung at him.

Then she turned her back on him and began looking for a taxi.

They grabbed two minivan cabs, and the drive into Seattle was like a nightmare. People ran in mindless terror. Buildings burned. And the torrents of water washed down the streets and gutters, floodwaters such as God had called down when Noah had built the ark.

"Look, Holly," Amanda said, pointing upward through the cab's front window.

Huge flocks of birds flew across the fiery, rain-soaked skies. They were falcons.

"All this can't be because of Michael," Holly murmured. "He's not that powerful."

"He's one of the most powerful warlocks who ever lived," Jer countered, seated in the cab beside Holly.

She turned and glared at him. "You sound proud of him."

"I don't mean to," he told her honestly, "but maybe I can't help it."

The cab driver was courageous, winding through the city at a snail's pace because there was so much chaos and danger that he couldn't have gone any faster if he had wanted to. He muttered from time to time, stroking an icon on the dashboard of the vehicle as though its presencc could protect him. "You must be the only people coming into the city," the driver noted.

"We have business to take care of," Holly answered.

They were lucky to have gotten the cab, let alone two. Indeed, these were the only two taxis that had been willing to drive as far as the Anderson home. The price for the courage of the two drivers was not coming cheap, though. Holly had paid each driver five hundred dollars before they would leave the airport terminal.

Behind them, the other cab, transporting Nicole, Philippe, Alonzo, Armand, Pablo, and Kari, blared its horn as a whitish-blue figure lurched in front of its headlights.

The walking dead, Holly noted. *Michael has created himself an army.*

Thus it was that she wasn't surprised that when the taxis dropped them off at the Anderson home, it was under attack by zombies. The two minivans roared away, careening wildly down the street.

Huge sections of the covered porch had been pried away, and the large chunks of wood boards and posts were in the hands of the dead, who were destroying the ground-floor windows and doors in an effort to get in. She saw in the moonlight and firelight their slack faces, their unseeing eyes, and she thanked whatever manifestation of the Goddess that had inspired her and the others to send Richard, Tante Cecile, and Dan Carter out of town. As it was, it was almost more than Amanda and Nicole could bear, watching their home being taken apart piece by piece.

Like crazy whirligigs, falcons careened overhead, squawking and chorusing a cacophony of triumph. Their blank, beady eyes bored into Holly's as she began to lob fireballs at them, making her mark more often than not. Jer and Armand joined her; still, the birds flew, increasing in numbers, until the night sky was filled with them. They buzzed the house, swooping down on the Tri-Covenates, their talons gleaming and their beaks sharp as they attempted to rip and tear at the humans on the ground.

Then, directly in front of Holly, the earth began to quiver, and as she watched, hands and heads emerged from the mud, and the dead began to walk. Movement caught the corner of her eye, and she turned to look down the street. "Oh, my God, Nicole, don't look!" she begged her cousin, but it was too late.

The emaciated corpse of Nicole and Amanda's mother dragged itself into view. There was so little flesh left that the skeleton lurched awkwardly like a puppet on strings, a creature whose arms and legs were far too large for its body. Her face was half-eaten away by worms, and one eye was missing. The other was milky white.

Nicole began screaming. Philippe grabbed her to his chest and held her. Tommy did the same to Amanda.

Then Philippe lobbed a fireball at the hideous thing and, despite the buckets of rain, it ignited like a piece of paper and burned down within seconds. The bones were charred; there was nothing else left, and the remains fluttered to the mud and rested there.

There is no reason to be here, Holly realized. *Nothing to be gained.*

Then a man she didn't know ran up the street. He waved his hands wildly over his head; he was bellowing with terror. He zoomed over to Alonzo and flung his arms around the man, shouting, "You've got to help me! It's my daughter! She's in trouble!"

And Holly understood that Michael Deveraux was

going to make it very, very difficult for them here . . . and perhaps even more important, it was going to be nearly impossible for them to leave.

The waters of Elliott Bay churned and frothed as monsters came forth. Giant squid, schools of large, biting fish, and more of the enormous sea creatures that had ripped Eddie to shreds emerged from the restless waters. News helicopters and Coast Guard boats combed the area with searchlights; no one could believe what they were seeing.

Holly stood beside Jer on the cliffs, watching the unfolding nightmare, and she wanted more than anything to lean against him and feel his strength. But he held himself aloof from her, and she had to handle it all on her own. She remembered how the last time she had stood on these cliffs, she had commanded a phantom army. But now, she was drained; there was nothing in her that could command anything. And Isabeau was not with her.

She looked up at Jer, who was wearing a ski mask, and said, "Is Jean with you?"

Wordlessly he shook his head. His eyes were dull, and she thought she detected an air of shame about him. After all, his father was responsible for everything that was going on around them.

"I don't know why he isn't," he said finally. "The Deveraux love this kind of insanity."

"So do the Cahors," she said miserably.

He began to reach out to her—she saw the gesture plainly—and then he pulled back his hand. They stood side by side, yet they couldn't have been further apart.

He said, "I'm sorry, Holly. That my father is this kind of man. That I'm . . ."

"You're not," she said, laying a hand on his forearm. Though he wore a thick black sweater, he shifted under her touch, as if she could see how hideous he looked. "Jer, you're good."

"I'm not." She saw the pain in his eyes. It was the only part of his face that she could see. She realized it was a miracle that his eyes hadn't been burned out of his skull. "And," he said slowly, "neither are you. Are you, Holly? You've paid a price to keep these people alive."

She sagged. "Yes," she admitted. "I have. Can you tell, Jer? Can you see it?"

"I can feel it. There's a coldness around you that didn't used to be there."

It was her turn to apologize. "I'm sorry."

"I'm not." He paused and added, "You're not so untouchable, so innocent. Before, you seemed out of my reach."

"But not now?" she asked, her voice husky.

He shook his head silently.

That gave her pause. *I wonder if Isabeau influenced me to lose part of my soul,* she wondered, *because she had already lost part of hers. Murdering her husband took away a large chunk. But she had committed many other sins. Murder for her and her mother was a way of life.*

"You know why he's doing this, don't you?" he asked her.

"Because he's an evil bastard?" she replied.

"To distract you. To keep you here."

She caught her breath. "To keep me from going to San Francisco?"

"Yes," he said. "Cecile, Dan, and your uncle." He shook his head at the carnage unfolding before them, then looked back at her. "Divide and conquer. That's an old Deveraux game."

"I should go there," she realized.

"Some of us should. And some of us should stay here," he told her. "He'll keep the stakes high, try to take advantage by destroying all of Seattle if he has to."

Holly caught her breath. "Is he capable of that?"

Hidden in the ski mask, Jer pursed his lips together. "Oh, yes," he said solemnly. "He certainly is." Then his mouth curved into a sharp, bitter smile. "But I'll give him a run for his money. What's the saying? 'The apple never falls far from the tree.'"

"Please, be careful," she breathed.

He shook his head, and his eyes burned into hers. "No way."

Then he was reaching for her, pulling her close. His lips were crushing hers. She groaned in her soul and clung to him, needing him more than she had ever needed anyone or anything.

Then, just as she began to lose herself, he let her go and stepped back. "Leave me," he said roughly.

She opened her mouth to protest and realized it was useless. She choked down a sob and turned away.

This might be the last time I ever see him alive, she realized.

She looked over her shoulder.

He was staring at her.

She caught her breath and half raised her hand. Then he deliberately turned his back and walked in the opposite direction, toward the bay. Kari saw him coming and held out a hand to him, defiantly glancing in Holly's direction.

Jer took her offered hand; his own hand was gloved. They fell to talking earnestly, gesturing toward the bay. Planning strategy, perhaps.

Stuffing her hands in her pockets, the most powerful witch alive slunk away, feeling as ridiculous as a lovesick twelve-year-old.

EIGHT

WHITE OPAL

☾

We dance beneath the sun-drenched sky
And worship the day as it passes by
The sun renews and gives us life
And guides us through our daily strife

Cursed sun, go away
Arise, oh, Goddess, and kill the day
Take the light's wretched lies
And hide them within midnight skies

Holly and Silvana: San Francisco

Silvana insisted on coming with Holly, and she consented. Frankly, she wished they could have brought more of their coven members with them, but they had more than enough to do in Seattle, and Holly wanted to try for a surprise attack if and when they needed to.

Getting a flight out of Seattle had been an act of the Goddess. Magic alone had gotten them through the crowds, who were turning on one another like caged animals. And when the rest of the flights were grounded because the weather became just too severe, magic convinced the air traffic controllers and the pilot that their flights could take off safely. And, thanks to magic, it had.

On their flight to Oakland, which was a more convenient airport, Holly performed a finder's spell in order to locate the house where Dan, Tante Cecile, and Uncle Richard had been living. By tacit agreement, she had not tried to find them before now. Ignorance would serve as their protection.

But now, on the plane, she saw their house and she was alarmed at what else she saw: imps and falcons descending on them, tearing out their hearts and setting the house on fire.

Goddess, prevent this, she begged. *Prevent this, Hecate, and I will do and be whatever you want.*

They landed, and she magically arranged for the woman at the car rental to "see" that Holly was twenty-one on her driver's license, thus making her old enough to rent a car. She also "provided" herself with enough funds to cover the fees, even though she had used up all her money securing the plane tickets. She saw Silvana's small reaction of displeasure and silently challenged her to protest. Many witches would condemn her for creating wealth—it wasn't done—but she didn't care.

This is about survival, not manners.

While Silvana stared at the map and tried to guide them, Holly prayed to the Goddess to give her a sense of direction. The fog was thick as soaking wet wool, and she realized that in the year she had been away, she had forgotten how to drive in San Francisco weather.

A year, she thought dully as they crept along. *I feel like I've never lived here. I feel like a stranger.*

Seattle has become my home.

Silvana sat beside her, murmuring spells, and to Holly's relief, the fog thinned. She looked over at Silvana and said, "Thanks." She flushed and said, "I'm not thinking clearly. I could have done that, lifted the fog."

Silvana tried to smile, but she couldn't manage it. "Just get us there, okay?" She looked out the window. "Oh, God, Holly, what if something's happened?"

Holly pursed her lips together. There was no good answer to that, and she didn't feel like mouthing some meaningless words of comfort.

Dismayed, Silvana glanced at her, then back at the window. "Hang on, Tante," she whispered.

Holly thought, *I've grown so cold. Am I cold enough to cool the blood of a Deveraux?*

As she drove on, the pale moon trailed after them in a sky of clouds and mists.

Then she turned to Silvana and said, "I forgot. We have to cross the Bay Bridge."

Silvana regarded her steadily. "You're thinking about the curse. That those close to you die by drowning."

Holly nodded. She looked to the side of the road, narrowed her eyes, and pulled over. They sat in front of a Burger King. "Get out," she said. "I'm not taking you."

"What?" Silvana frowned at her.

"I'm not taking you across the bridge." Holly pulled on the emergency brake and crossed her arms, the engine idling.

Frowning, Silvana reached for the brake. Holly flicked her fingers in her direction, zapping her with a tiny bolt of magical energy.

"Ow!" Silvana cried. "Holly, stop it!"

"Get out." Holly raised her chin. "I mean it, Silvana."

Something in her look persuaded the other girl that she was all business. Silvana pulled back slightly and said, "Holly, we're talking about my *aunt;* she's like my mother."

"I won't ever get to her if I have to save you from

drowning. For all we know, the bridge will collapse or I'll drive over the side. You're staying here." She gestured to Silvana's purse. "You have some money. And a cell phone. If you get tired, go to a motel. I'll call you when it's safe."

Silvana stared at her. "You're serious."

"Get out of the car or I'll make you get out."

Her beaded cornrows clacked together as Silvana yanked open the door and got out. Angrily she slammed the door.

Without so much as a good-bye, Holly took off the brake and peeled out.

Grimly she drove on, watching for road signs, looking up for falcons, to the sides of the road for other evidence that Michael Deveraux was waiting for her. *Maybe he thought I'd come in on a broom,* she thought hotly. *Everyone keeps telling me how powerful I am, but I don't know how to use that power. I don't know that many spells.*

I need help.

She kept going, the fog nearly impenetrable as she remembered to use only her low beams. She went through the tunnel, and then she moved with the traffic onto the bridge.

A deep groaning sound seemed to emanate from one of the steel girders as she passed it, and the hair on the back of her neck stood on end. "There is no one around me that I care about, all right?" she said aloud, as if she had to address the curse like a person. "So don't even think about it."

With the rest of the traffic, she traveled over the bridge, her face prickling with anxiety as she made it across; her nervousness did not lessen even after she got to the other side. If anything, it increased. Her intuition was guiding her to fork to the right, and she knew the finder's spell was working. The longer she drove, the closer she was getting to the epicenter of whatever bad magic Michael Deveraux was wreaking on people she cared about very much.

Those I love are back in Seattle, battling dark magic indeed. . . .

Then she felt the house rather than saw it, and realized that it was cloaked from the gaze of the rest of the neighborhood. She murmured a Spell of Seeing and it rippled into view: a small house on a rise, set apart, separated from a group of houses lower down the street by what appeared to be storage sheds and rows of oleander bushes. The rooftop was glowing with green energy and as she pulled the car to a stop and opened her door, she heard the shattering of glass.

She climbed out of the car. Then a wild wind whipped up, smashing into her and flattening her against the car as the door slammed shut. She moved her hands and murmured a spell, and the wind separated on the other side of her body as she moved away from the car and began to run to the structure.

Glass was flying everywhere, which her spell deflected. There was loud pounding and the rushing of wind.

She took the steps to the porch by twos, hordes of tiny imps streaming around her feet like tiny horses on stampede. Perhaps recognizing her as the enemy, they began to clump around her ankles, scratching and biting her, and she cried out and hurtled a fireball toward her foot, careful not to harm herself as she took the majority of her attackers out.

She flicked a wrist at the front door and it opened with the burst of a howling wind from the other side. She was pelted with dozen of bodies of dead imps, which she deflected with a protection spell; they hit an invisible barrier in front of her, dropping to the stoop and piling up. With a flick of her wrist the pile shifted to the right, and she shouted, "Dan! Tante Cecile? Uncle Richard?"

She could barely hear herself over the noise and confusion, much less anyone else. She raced across the threshold and stood in the foyer. The ghostly baying of Hell Hounds warned her of their presence; she flung herself against the wall as their toenails clattered on the wooden floor. She warded herself, placing another barrier between herself and the hounds, and felt a spray of hot breath before the spell took hold.

There was a loud crash, followed by a shout on the second story of the house. Holly turned and raced up the stairs, to find her uncle in the hallway, swinging an ax at a large, scaly demon sprouting a crown of horns from its head. Vaguely human-shaped, it stood on two clawed feet and swung at Richard with long, taloned hands. It was slathering and drooling.

Richard lunged and swung his ax, then ducked to a squatting position as the demon swung. Then he swung again from the awkward position and, this time, sliced the demon across its bony kneecaps. The creature roared and staggered backward; Richard pressed his advantage and sprang at the monster, pushing it to the ground, where he swung the ax again and brought it across the demon's neck. Its head rolled off, and green blood sprayed the hallway.

Sickened, Holly ran to her uncle's side and threw her arms around him.

"Holly!" he cried, embracing her. "Thank God! Where are the girls?"

"Seattle," she said. She pulled away. "What's going on?"

"We think it's Michael." He pointed to the opened doorway a little farther down the hall. "Cecile and Dan are in there."

She nodded and barreled into the room with Richard following behind.

It was total chaos. More demons of many varieties and monsters she had never encountered before were overwhelming the two magic users, who had crouched behind a dresser that had been pushed into the middle of the room. They had shielded it with energy, but Holly could see that the field was weakening.

Cecile turned her head, saw Holly, and shouted. "Thank goodness! Holly, stop them!"

Holly lifted her arms and opened her mouth.

And that was when she froze.

Cecile frowned. "Holly?"

Her mind was a blank. She couldn't think of a single spell, couldn't feel magic anywhere in her being.

What's wrong with me?

"Holly!" Cecile shouted. She waved her hands in her direction. "Have you been bewitched?"

I don't know, she thought, bewildered.

Then she had a sense of something crowding inside her mind, of a presence like a shadow looming over her; although there was nothing there when she glanced left and right. She was cold; she began shivering as goose bumps broke along her arms.

Then the coldness slipped inside her, as if she had swallowed a glassful of ice.

Before her stood Isabeau, perhaps more solidly than ever before, as if she was not quite a part of the material world, but more than she had been.

Not actually before me, Holly realized, *but in my mind's eye.*

A veiled woman stood beside Holly's ancestress.

Hecate, Holly thought.

Imperiously, the Goddess bowed her head, acknowledging her name in her incarnation as the supreme deity of witches.

We can help you, Isabeau said. *Michael Deveraux has sent these creatures to harass and kill you. Without your witch sisters, you are not enough of a match for him.*

"Holly, help us!" Dan yelled at her. "Damn it!"

As Holly blinked, it was as if she could see the room through Isabeau and Hecate; she was aware that the battle was escalating, and that her side was losing.

You want more of me, Holly accused Isabeau. *Want me to make another sacrifice, ensnare myself more deeply in Hecate's service . . . have you made some sort of bargain with her yourself?*

Isabeau made no answer, but a smile played at the corners of her mouth, and her eyes glinted.

There was a huge blast, followed by another. Holly looked through the two women to see three enormous black shadows burst through the walls of the room. They were at least eight feet tall, and covered with scales; their eyes glowed red, and their hands ended in talons like scythes.

They stood for a moment in a row, and then they hurtled themselves toward Holly, Dan, and Cecile.

Without thinking, Holly raised her hands and thundered, *"Begone!"*

The room exploded. Flame, whirlwind, a rushing torrent of water and stone . . . all cycloned around Holly as energy shot through her body, making her convulse. Her eyes rolled back, and she shouted in a strange language she did not know; she was tumbling end over end in the chaos, every part of her sizzling. Her hair was on fire; her eyelashes danced with sparks. Her teeth smoked. Blue flames crawled and danced along her skin.

Someone screamed her name, over and over and over.

The shadows grabbed at her, roaring in fury . . .

. . . talons sliced at her, and missed . . .

. . . and Holly woke up on her hands and knees in wet sand.

She raised her head and opened her eyes.

It was night, and she was on a beach. Tante Cecile lay beside her on her back. Dan lay on his side facing her, surf washing over his body. Holly looked around and spotted Uncle Richard draped over the hood of a car in a parking lot approximately twenty feet behind her. He lifted his head and regarded her.

Slowly the others moved, Cecile sitting gingerly upright, and Dan rolled over again onto his stomach, giving a short shout as a wave crashed over his back. Then he pushed himself back onto his haunches and awkwardly lurched to his feet.

"What did you do?" Cecile asked Holly, her voice cracking as she stared at her. Her eyes were wide.

"I don't know," Holly replied honestly. *But whatever it was, I did it by myself,* she thought with wondering satisfaction. *I didn't sacrifice anything to the Goddess.*

She rose to her feet. "Let's go," she ordered the others.

"Where?" Cecile asked her. "Back to Seattle?"

"The hospital first," Holly said. "To Barbara."

"Of course." Cecile stood. She gazed at Holly and said, "You've claimed your power. I can see it. It's crackling around you."

Holly glanced down at her hands. A blue fluorescence gleamed along her flesh, then gradually dissipated.

Were Isabeau and Hecate blocking me somehow, so that I would have to ask the Goddess for help? she wondered. *And so I'd keep making sacrifices to her?*

She lowered her hands. "You're right," she told Cecile.

After using a pay phone to call a cab, Richard rented a car. Holly connected with Silvana, who ordered take-out that was ready by the time they picked her up. Silvana and Tante Cecile embraced tearfully. Holly was pleased by the look of gratitude on Silvana's face when she looked at Holly, but even more pleased by the forgiveness in her eyes. *Not that I need anyone's forgiveness,* Holly thought, feeling suddenly defensive.

They devoured hamburgers and fries en route to Marin County General. Although it was well past midnight, it was easy for Holly to "convince" the night nurse to lead her to Barbara Davis-Chin's room.

"I need to warn you, she's comatose," the woman—whose name badge read ADDY—said cautiously. "She won't know you're here."

Holly nodded absently, her gaze fixed on the half-opened door. It was painted a soft green. In the center of it hung a clear plastic rectangle containing a manila chart affixed to a clipboard. The chart read, DAVIS-CHIN, B. Holly had a flash of a mental image of her mother hurrying down the corridors of the emergency room with an armload of similar charts, consulting the names of her patients as she approached their beds. It had always been so amazing; her mom took care of people for such a short time, and yet she made certain she knew their names, bonded with them, focused on them.

I miss her so much, Holly thought with a sharp pang.

Then Holly pushed open the door, and nearly fainted.

Barbara Davis-Chin lay in her bed as Holly remembered her from her last visit: pale and thin and hooked up to machines. But this time, a nightmare sat on her chest.

It was a hunched, evilly smiling creature with pointed ears and a face as sharp and angular as a skeleton key; it was the color of dirty coins, and covered with filthy gray hair.

Its fist was sunk deep into Barbara's chest, and Holly could see that its filthy fingers were socketed around Barbara's beating heart, squeezing poison into it from its own veins and arteries, which pulsed and rivuleted on the exterior of its body.

All the while it cackled maniacally, and Holly realized that no one could hear it except her.

She thought of running back to the waiting room

where Silvana and the others were waiting, then steeled herself to turn to the nurse, who was still bewitched and obviously did not see or hear what Holly saw and heard, and say, "You can go back to the nurses' station now."

"Yes," the woman said.

As the nurse drifted away, Holly steadily walked toward the creature. It jutted its bottom lip toward her—it was a brilliant red, as if it were bleeding—and began to growl.

Holly began to intone a protection spell, then realized that each time she prayed to the Goddess, she had to sacrifice a tiny part of her soul; she wondered if this was the price other witches paid, or if this was a cost she bore alone. But knowing it, she kept her mouth shut and decided to deal with the imp—if that was what it was—on her own terms.

She moved toward it; it smiled at her, completely unruffled by her presence.

Holly stared at it, her focus centering on it; then, in a strange juxtaposition of her senses, she was aware of the thrumming of Barbara's pulse, the loud drumming of her heartbeat—*kathum, kathum,* then she was a sight, not a person, careening down the arm and then the fist of the creature, slamming inside Barbara's heart—

The heart of darkness; this is the center of the evil, of the dreams, of the sickness that is killing her . . .

. . . all around Holly floated nightmare shapes and tortured landscapes; she whirled around in a circle with her mouth open screaming in silence—

STOP IT!

And then she was back at the doorway, staring at the imp, which grinned back at her and then chittered happily, drawing Barbara's heart clean out of her body and displaying it to Holly. She thought of Hecate, the dead familiar, and how Bast had presented the dead falcon to her and her cousins as a trophy; only now, it was Barbara's diseased heart being presented to her; her heart that was bleeding and in such misery—

STOP IT!

The creature disappeared . . . but Holly sensed its malevolent presence. Even if she could no longer see it, it was still torturing Barbara.

She rushed to the waiting room, all eyes upon her. "We need to get Barbara out of here."

Uncle Richard ceased his pacing and fixed his eyes on her. "Sit, rest, I'll take care of the paperwork." He took off.

She sank into a chair and accepted the coffee that was offered her by Tante Cecile. She was tired, and very worried. The lines were being drawn . . . across living bodies and through living hearts.

This is a deadly game Michael Deveraux is playing, she thought. *And I can't afford to lose it.*

Wearily she closed her eyes.

How many generations of Cathers and Deveraux have kept this up? It's got to end. We've got to win.

Johnstown, Pennsylvania: May 31, 1889, 2 P.M.

The lake had risen two feet overnight. The dam at South Fork groaned against the weight of the extra water. The dam was old and in need of repair. No one seemed to care, though. Everyone expected the dam to go on doing what it had always done. Every year after the rains, people would scratch their heads and marvel that it still stood, but they did nothing to help it in its battle to contain the lake.

Fourteen miles below the dam the town of Johnstown sat in a flood plain. The good citizens occasionally made rumblings against the owners of the dam, but the rumblings meant nothing. They were just a way to pass the time, something to speak of besides the weather.

And so, year after year, the town rumbled and the dam groaned and nothing was done. The water pressed harder, the lake rose higher, and in the dam a tiny fracture became a crack.

The crack had been noticed, and several men now struggled to relieve the pressure on the dam. They tried, among other things, to open a new channel to allow the water someplace else to go. Their efforts were too little, too late, though. The dam groaned as it tried to hold back a wall of water sixty feet deep.

Claire Cathers was happy. The thought took her by surprise as she was sweeping her front porch. She stopped and leaned for a moment on the handle of her broom as she stared idly out into the wet street. It was nearly sunset, and the rain had let up for a few minutes. A couple more hours and her husband and daughter would be home.

She smiled at the thought of Ginny. The little girl was beautiful, headstrong, and passionate—a Cathers through and through. Of course, that was to be expected. Cathers blood always seemed to prevail, and Virginia had a double dose of it.

Five years earlier if someone had told Claire that she would marry her third cousin, Peter, the one who had tormented her as a child, she would have called them crazy.

Old Simon Jones stopped before her and tipped his hat. "Afternoon, Mrs. Claire."

"Afternoon, Simon. How's the day shapin' up?"

"Tolerable so long as the dam holds."

She chuckled good-naturedly at the joke. The dam had been the subject of much concern, talk, and humor for as long as she could remember. Still, the old structure held.

The sky darkened perceptibly, and a few fat drops of water splatted on the ground.

"Have a good evening, Simon," she called after his retreating back.

"Good Lord willing and the creek don't rise. Well, at least not more than it has."

She smiled. Life was good. In fact, it had turned out altogether differently from what she had expected. Her mother had died when she was very young. Her father had always been a sternly disapproving man. In most matters he always acquiesced to his two older sisters, and he had taken that frustration out on Claire. He had taught her to act like a lady, and that meant being humble and submissive; matter of fact, they had been married an entire year before she could bring herself to look Peter in the eye.

Peter was a salesman. Most Cathers were, and had been as long as anyone could remember. They were all smooth talkers and quite persuasive, but none was quite as silver-tongued as her Peter.

For all that, though, he was a gentle and loving

man. He had vowed to her on the day she gave birth to Ginny that he would raise his daughter differently than her father had raised her. He had kept his promise. He always said to little Ginny that a woman was the equal of a man. Even though she was tiny he took her everywhere with him. He even took her on sales trips like the one they would be home from soon.

Claire pressed a hand tight against her stomach. Tonight when Peter arrived home she would have another surprise for him. She smiled as she prayed that God would give her a son. The local midwife had given her some herbs to put under her bed, that she might have a boy. Claire protested that she didn't believe in such superstitions. She had put the herbs under her bed, anyway, though, she wanted a son so badly. *God willing, maybe I will have one.*

The skies opened up and the rain began again. Claire, having swept the debris and excess water from her porch, hurried back inside. She added more wood to the fire in an effort to battle the chill damp in the air. The streets were flooding, an annual occurrence in Johnstown.

Everywhere businessmen were transporting their wares to the second stories of their buildings. Husbands and wives were carting furniture and food upstairs in their homes. Claire had already moved upstairs everything they would need earlier that day.

She glanced back outside at the sheets of rain pelting the street and for a moment felt uneasy. Something didn't feel quite right, as though there was a strange energy in the air. She shrugged it off with a whispered prayer for the safety of Peter and her little girl. She began to wonder if she would see them both within the hour or if they had stopped along the road, seeking shelter.

Then two young men ran down the street, shouting, "Dam's breaking! The dam's breaking!"

The taller of the two ran into the blacksmith, who threw up his hands and said, "Heard that before, young feller!"

"It's true, it's happening!" the shorter lad said. Then they raced on, bellowing at the top of their lungs, "Dam's breaking!"

"Must be foreigners," the blacksmith said to Claire. "Crazy boys."

She nodded vaguely, not really listening. Her ears were attuned to another sound: a strange, distant roar, like that of . . .

. . . of what? An ocean?

Then she saw the wall of water raging down the hillside. Its immensity shocked her into incomprehension; she had never imagined such a flood in her life; never seen such a thing as the vast, churning waters as they mowed down trees as if they were dandelions. For a moment the sight made no sense to her; she stood in her everyday gingham dress and her second-best white apron, staring. "My God!" she screamed, and she began to run.

She raced past houses where families were scrambling to their second stories; a tree shot through the gully to her left, bounding through a gush of water. She heard the flood behind her, and directly before her stood a house with an open door. She headed toward it, not sure why she did; in her panic she could no longer think clearly.

From behind her she heard screams, heard thunder, and then . . .

"My God, no!" Peter Cathers cried.

He stood at the rim of the canyon, looking down on the destruction of Johnstown. Swaying with disbelief, he held his child in his arms and screamed for his wife as the waters engulfed everything in their path, then spread out in all directions with grasping, merciless tentacles. Rooftops poked above the raging waters, then disappeared. Whole tracts of trees shot down the hills and slammed straight through buildings.

Bodies of people and animals floated like corks.

"Claire! Claire!"

★★★

He was unaware that as his little daughter closed her eyes to the horrors, her world within telescoped into a strange world of gray mist, rolling across an image: a sailing ship, sails bursting with wind, and a little girl—

—She looks like me!

—tumbling over the side into the ocean.

And a woman on deck shrieking, held back by sailors, as she struggled to free herself and leap into the sea after the girl.

The mists roiled and thickened, then rolled away, and Ginny heard the thoughts of that woman, as if she were standing next to her, speaking directly to her:

Now we are three, we "Cathers." I have no daughter to carry on the family line, but the boys have at least some magic. Mayhap 'tis just as well. Perhaps it is a sign from the Goddess that House Cahors is truly dead . . . and that the magick should die with me.

Then two little boys rushed up to her, shouting and throwing their arms around her knees and her waist. The smaller of the two stared straight at Ginny; in her mind, he opened his mouth and, in an eerie, otherworldly voice, said directly to her, "Virginia, I am your ancestor."

Then Ginny's eyes snapped open and her small

child's hands grabbed up lanks of her father's hair as she buried her face against his shoulder and sobbed, "Papa, Papa, the lady is scaring me!"

And then little Ginny saw another thing: a letter, and it read:

> Know this then, Hannah, my darling wife, we did not hang them all in Salem. Some—and I am so ashamed to say this—we ducked some, as they did in the Olde World. That is to say, we tied these poor women to stools, and put them in the river. And if they sank, we declared them innocent. Aye, if they drowned, I mean to say, we consigned their souls to God. . . .
>
> Then Abigail Cathers showed us true witchr'y, and I knew we had murdered innocent women who had no more knowledge of witchcraft than you or I.
>
> God have mercy on me, I cannot bear this guilt any longer.
>
> Adieu.
>
> Jonathan Corwin

Then in her mind she saw her own mother bobbing in a room with many chairs, and a table, all underwater. Her mother's eyes were open, and her hair blossomed around her head like a halo.

Ginny burst into tears and moaned to her father, "Mama has drowned, Daddy. She has drowned!"

At Johnstown, ten thousand were said to have lost their lives. Though Claire Cathers's corpse was never found, she was declared dead, and Peter Cathers decided to go West, to take his daughter from that place of watery death and find the driest country that he could.

The things that Ginny had seen, she never spoke of again, and in due time, she forgot.

California proved not to be the place for fortune; Cathers father and daughter determined to go north, to Seattle, a place said to be rich in everything but men.

They loaded a wagon with their belongings, mostly mining equipment they no longer needed, for there had been no gold for them in California, and began a long journey toward the Pacific Northwest. Ginny was almost nine then, and considered by all who knew her to be of keen intellect, and a beauty to boot.

Stopping one evening in an encampment, where there was beef stew with real beef and potatoes and onions and carrots, the rough men there spoke of Dr.

Deveroo, a seller of patent medicines that could cure what ailed a man.

"He's comin' tonight with his travelin' show," one of the miners told Peter while Ginny scooped up the last of her beef stew with a hardtack biscuit. They sat side by side on long trestle tables beneath a canvas canopy strung above their heads. The place was lit with lamps, and Ginny thought it looked like a fairy land. "First there's fine entertainment, and then he sells his patent medicines." He gestured to Ginny. "She looks a bit peaked. She might could use a few spoonfuls."

Peter shrugged. "We'll see."

"Oh, Papa, can we see the fine entertainment?" Ginny begged.

Peter smiled indulgently. "I suppose, Ginny." He picked up his tin cup of coffee and sipped it appreciatively. "There's no charge for the entertainment, I take it?" he asked the miner.

"None, sir," the man replied. "Deveroo sells his elixir; that's how he affords the rest."

About an hour later, as two brightly painted wagons pulled into the encampment, a cheer rose up around the camp. Peter put Ginny on his shoulders so she could see.

"He's got black hair and black eyes," she reported.

"Black hair and brown eyes, I reckon," her father corrected her.

"No, Papa. They are black as coal. And he's staring right at me."

Peter felt a little chill; he didn't know why. He said, "I'm here, Ginny."

"I know. Oh, and now he's smiling at everyone."

"Please, friends!" boomed a voice. "Esteemed and illustrious gentlemen! Please have a seat so that all may see our most amazing presentation! My companions and I have traveled the length and breadth of this great land, and we have seen many remarkable sights, some of which we will present to you this very night!"

Everyone settled back onto their seats at the trestle table, affording Peter a look at Deveroo as the man stood up on the buckboard of his wagon. He was a tall man, broad-shouldered, dressed in a black suit of clothes with a black waistcoat and a white shirt. He wore a top hat, which he doffed, and his curly hair brushed his shoulders. He wore a drooping mustache . . . and indeed, his eyes were very black. Peter had never seen the like in his entire life.

The wagon itself was decorated with faces of a strange man made of leaves. The grotesque faces were strangely contorted, appearing rather evil, and Peter wasn't certain that this "fine entertainment" would prove to be something his daughter should see.

The other wagon was painted with wild swirls of green and red, in no discernible pattern. A very muscular bald man dressed in a leopard skin held the reins, which he put down with a flourish, rose, and picked up a concertina, which he began to play. The squeeze box looked like a toy in contrast with his massive stature.

Two ladies in elaborate golden dresses appeared from the back of the same wagon, lightly tripping down a set of wooden stairs until they alighted on the earth. They began to dance, and Ginny caught her breath, enchanted.

After their dance was concluded, the man in the leopard skin performed many amazing feats of strength, including hoisting two miners seated in chairs over his head. He bent a man's shovel and twisted a bar of steel into a knot.

"Sandor the Strong Man drinks three tablespoons of my patented life elixir every morning, noon, and night!" Dr. Deveroo proclaimed. "Such a bottle can be yours for only one paltry dollar!"

"Papa, you should buy some," Ginny told her father.

"Perhaps another time. A dollar is a lot of money," Peter told her.

Many of the miners did purchase bottles, and

some proceeded to begin their three-tablespoon regimen immediately upon receipt.

"And now, watch, my friends, as I amaze and astonish you with feats of magic!" Dr. Deveroo exclaimed.

He clapped his hands and snapped his fingers, then flicked them three times. Flames formed along his fingertips, outlining his hands with fire.

The crowd gasped.

Then he raised his hands above his head and waved them, and the flames extended upward, shooting into the sky.

Peter blinked, astonished. Ginny sucked in her breath again and said, "Papa, how did he do that?"

The flames extinguished, and the man bowed at the audience as the miners broke into wild applause. Then he extended his hands toward the two beautiful ladies, who twirled and curtsied, both smiling so prettily at him.

Slowly, the two rose into the air, still twirling, until they hung high above the wagons, bobbing like golden butterflies.

The crowd fell silent, each man thunderstruck.

"It's wires," Peter murmured.

Ginny leaned down to hear him. "Not magic, Papa?"

"Of course not." But his voice was shaky, as if he didn't believe what he was saying.

Slowly the ladies floated toward the ground. The men began to applaud, then to hoot and holler. They stamped their feet. They whistled.

"Gentlemen, I thank you!" Dr. Deveroo said, sweeping off his top hat and laying it over his chest. "Now, please lend me your ears as I tell you of the wonders of my patented elixir, which will cure all your ailments like magic. But science is at work here, my friends, not pixies and elves! Science, which paves the new frontier with wonders like my Patented Elixir of Life!"

One of the two women glided toward him carrying a green glass bottle topped with a cork. She handed it to Dr. Deveroo as if it were a precious gem.

He pulled the cork off the top and put the bottle to his lips. "This will make you stronger than ten men! It'll put hair on your head and a shine in your eye!"

He took a gulp of the liquid. Then he reached forward and put his hand around the woman's waist. As the crowd watched, he easily lifted her up and held her above his head while he took another swallow of the elixir.

"Yes, gentlemen!" he cried. "Dr. Deveroo's Patented Elixir of Life will fill you with life!"

He put the lady down and jumped off his wagon. Then he made a show of walking to the back of it. He put both his hands beneath the end of it, squatted, and lifted it up off the ground.

"Papa," Ginny breathed. "Papa, how can it be?"

Peter guffawed. "It's all tricks," he said uncertainly.

"Take me off your shoulders," she begged. "I don't want him to see me."

"There's nothing to be afraid of, Ginny," he assured her.

She hesitated, and then she said, "Papa, he's so strong, he could make the dam break."

"Oh, Ginny," Peter said softly. "Oh, my girl."

Then Dr. Deveroo's gazed swiveled toward her. He gazed directly at her; she felt his dark stare as if it were a slap across her cheek. His eyes narrowed, and his heavy brows met above his nose. He looked like a devil just waiting to grab her and eat her up.

She clung to her father and wailed, "Papa, get me out of here!"

Heads turned in their direction; a few men smirked, amused by the little girl's terror as if they, rational men all, had not gaped in silence at the astonishing feats of prestidigitation of Dr. Deveroo mere seconds before.

"Relax, girlie, it's just for show," a well-meaning man ventured. He was gray and leathery and had no teeth. He reached out a hand and patted Ginny's leg, and she writhed as if she had been burned.

"Papa, please, Papa." She scrambled to the ground, landing hard, and raced into the crowd of men.

"Ginny!" Peter shouted after her. He broke into a run, muttering, "Excuse me, 'scuse me, please, pardon," as he eased men out of his path. "Ginny!"

How could he have lost her so quickly? But no one could tell him where she had gone. He looked everywhere, all over the camp; and as the show went on and most of the miners lined up to purchase a bottle or two of Dr. Deveroo's elixir, Peter became more and more frantic.

"Might I help?" Deveroo asked finally, once the last bottle had been sold and the ladies had disappeared back inside their wagon. The man in the leopard skin sat on the buckboard, wolfing down some beef stew.

"I've looked everywhere," Peter confessed, wiping his face.

Then he looked into the eyes of the man. Peter's lips parted; he felt dizzy all over. Not just dizzy, but rather ill. The man's eyes . . . they were completely black. There was no color to them. And if one gazed into them long enough . . . one would . . . would . . .

Peter shook himself. He tipped his hat and said brusquely, "Thank you, sir, but this is a family matter. I'll find my girl myself."

Dr. Deveroo inclined his head like a king. He said, "As you wish, Mr. . . . ?"

And to his dying day, Peter had no idea why he said, "Cavendish. Martin Cavendish."

"Cavendish," Deveroo said slowly. "Nice to make your acquaintance, sir." Deveroo doffed his hat once more. "Well, if I may be of service, please don't hesitate to call on me. My troupe and I will be camping not far from here."

"Thank you kindly, sir." Peter inclined his head and moved away. He was uneasy in his skin; he could barely stand to look at the man, though he had no idea why. He turned his back and quickly strode away.

Ginny. She's hiding in our wagon.

Suddenly he knew it as certainly as he knew that she was right to be afraid of Deveroo.

Something is amiss here. We are in danger.

Without another look back, he hurried to the wagon, got in, and picked up the reins. Luckily he had not unharnassed the horses. He called over his shoulder, "Ginny? You in there?"

"Papa, ssh," she hissed back. "He'll hear you!"

"It's all right, girl. We're getting out of here."

He flicked the reins, and the horses began to move. As they galloped away from the encampment, he saw Deveroo in the process of climbing into his own wagon. The man took off his hat and stared after Peter's wagon; in the darkness, Peter could not see his face, but he imagined him fiercely glaring at him. A shiver ran up Peter's spine; he didn't know why. But he flicked his reins and called, "Hee-yah!" to the horses, and they escaped into the night.

And I'm not stopping until we get to Seattle.

Dr. Deveroo, whose name was actually Paul Deveraux, narrowed his eyes as the Cavendish wagon raced down the trail. Silhouetted by the black night, its plain wooden sides illuminated by stars, it carried interesting cargo: a man and his little girl tetched with witchblood. He could feel it on them, practically smell it on the girl.

Cavendish, he thought. *That's a name I'll have to remember.*

In the ensuing months he traveled the land, performing his magic and selling his elixir. In San Francisco, he received a letter from friends within the Supreme Coven, loyal to the House of Deveraux and eager to dethrone the Moores. The Moores were still running things, still boasting how they could use the

Nightmare Dreamtime that old Sir Richard Moore had learned about down in Van Diemen's Land to get rid of their enemies.

What the Moores did not realize was that through their friends, the Deveraux now possessed the secret of the Nightmare Dreamtime as well.

All we need is the Black Fire, and we'll be on the throne again, Paul Deveraux reminded himself as he read the letter by the light of a campfire.

His confederate, one Edward Monroe, wrote: *We have heard stories of a medicine man in the timberland, who claims to know how to conjure something his people call the Dark Cloud Fire. Perhaps this might prove of interest. The place is called Seattle."*

"Seattle," Paul Deveraux mused. "Sounds interesting."

NINE

PERIDOT

☾

From earth we are, to earth we go
And so the cycle will always flow
Shine upon us, Great Horned God
Let us dominate this land we trod

Goddess, hear us as we pray
Wash the past clean away
Renew us now and give new birth
To family coven, hope and mirth

Holly was tired, and her nerves were stretched thin. Leaving San Francisco had been hard, in some ways harder than it had been when she had first left a year ago. Back home on the Bay she had felt an intense sense of safety. She knew that it was illusory, but when she closed her eyes it was impossible not to believe that the last year had been a bad dream.

That was gone, though, left behind with her house, the hum of the city, and the fog that blanketed it all like a thick curtain that separated it from the rest of the world. Now, together with Tante Cecile and Dan, she was trying to smuggle Barbara Davis-Chin and Uncle Richard back into Seattle.

Didn't we just get him out of this place? she thought about her uncle.

But Uncle Richard had changed; he was in a far better place than she had ever seen him before. He was strong, and though afraid, not afraid to face whatever came his way.

The same could not be said for Barbara. The doctors had only protested weakly when Holly had decided to move Barbara. The truth was that she had been in a coma for over a year and they had no idea what to do to help her.

It was dangerous to return to Seattle, but it was time for the Tri-Covenate to prove its worth. They were stronger together than separate. At least, Holly hoped so. With James and Eli teamed up with Michael, they were going to have to be.

It wasn't far now, maybe ten minutes. Holly willed Dan to drive faster but knew that if he did he would only draw more attention both from the mundane and the magically inclined.

Nothing seemed changed in Seattle since she had managed to leave. *Escape was more like it,* she thought, reliving the violence she had seen in the airport. The city was still under siege. Michael Deveraux had thrown down the glove, and it was up to her to meet the challenge.

First things first, though. She had to make sure her coven was safe and she had to find a way to heal Barbara.

She glanced out the window fearfully, looking for falcons. The clouds hung heavy in the sky, dark and lowering, gathering strength for another deluge. There was no sign of birds of any kind. Beside her, Tante Cecile was murmuring low incantations to stabilize Barbara. Richard was watching the landscape intently.

Holly began murmuring her own spells, wards to strengthen those already surrounding them, wards to make them invisible to all. Suddenly something like a cold wind rushed through her mind. *Michael!* She knew it with all her being. He was alerted, knew that she was coming! She gasped as fear crushed her heart. A lone bird appeared in the sky, wheeling slowly lower, ever closer to the car.

Suddenly, a ward shimmered blue in the air, just outside the glass of the car. She held her breath as the bird cast about for a few moments before flying slowly from sight. She sank back in her seat, relief flooding her. Moments later they pulled up outside of Dan's cabin.

Philippe and Armand emerged to escort them inside. "You?" she asked Philippe, referencing the ward that had saved them.

He shook his head. "Pablo sensed you were in danger. Armand and Sasha cast the spell."

That made sense. Mother Coven members were nothing if not good at wards. She would have to thank them and Pablo. She still bristled, though, at the thought of Pablo sensing them, her. His gifts made her uneasy, and she had done everything that she could to shield her mind from his. She wasn't sure she had been successful, though. Still, whatever secrets the boy knew he seemed to keep hidden beneath his austere surface.

Amanda and Nicole both flew to hug their father, and Tante Cecile and Silvana embraced as well. Kari hugged Dan and murmured words of welcome. Holly noted the tears streaming on all the faces and couldn't help but feel a bittersweet pang. There was no one to welcome her. Jer just stood in a corner, immovable and brooding.

"We were getting worried about you," Amanda told Holly as she released her father.

"Not as worried as I am about all of you now that I'm here," Holly answered. "I think Michael knows we're here."

Nicole turned white, and Holly couldn't help but feel her pain. *She's still so very afraid of James . . . and with good reason.*

"He might think, but he does not know, yet," Pablo answered quietly.

A chill danced up Holly's spine as her eyes met Pablo's. The thing she had to do was focus on the good the boy did for the group and not the danger he represented to her.

Richard had forced himself to not react as he saw his city under attack. He had lived through enough battles to know a siege when he saw one. There were forces at work here that he did not understand. "Know thy enemy and know thyself; in a hundred battles you will never be in peril." Sun Tzu was right.

He'd continued to stare out the window. He had found himself again and knew well his own strengths and weaknesses. His enemy was another story, but he was learning.

His throat had constricted painfully at the thought of seeing Nicole and Amanda. He hadn't been there for them when their mother died. He would spend the rest of his life trying to make that up to them. Holly had told him that they were alive and well. He wouldn't quite believe it until he could see it with his own eyes, hold them in his arms. He took a deep breath and willed himself to be patient.

At last they'd pulled up outside a house he did not know and two strangers rushed outside to help them in. He eyed the newcomers and liked what he saw. Especially the one who spoke briefly with Holly. He had a strength to him and a strong jaw and firm gaze.

They moved quickly inside and then he saw Amanda and Nicole. They flew to him, and he felt the tears rolling hotly down his cheeks. They were alive and they both had a glow to them that he did not remember. He crushed them to him and murmured, "I love you," over and over to them both.

Never again would he let them down. Never again.

As the others talked and rebonded, Dan approached Holly and said, "I think you need some time in the sweat lodge. Some time to pull yourself together. To reflect."

She nodded gratefully. "That's exactly what I need. Thank you."

Quietly she slipped from the room.

She undressed and made her way into the room. Dan had already lit some wood, providing the sacred smoke and heat. Holly squatted by the fire and shut her eyes; she inhaled slowly, clearing her mind.

Her hands were clenched, her spine stiff. She tried to convince her body to relax, but the concept had become foreign to her. She had two states of being these days: high alert, or exhaustion.

All I do is react, she thought. *We have to make a plan of attack, figure out how to take the bad guys down.*

Sweat rolled down her forehead and her chest. She moved away from the smoke and concentrated on her breathing.

And then she realized she was not alone.

She started; then a hand moved over hers, and she knew it was Jer. "Oh," she whispered.

He put his finger to her lips. She fell silent, every cell in her body focused on the contact. She opened her eyes and, in the pitch darkness, imagined Jer as he had been, handsome and sensual, and reached out her free hand to touch him.

As if he could see, he caught her hand and flattened it against his chest. His heart was beating fast and hard; she thought of the wings of the Deveraux falcons and began to lean toward him, silently begging him to kiss her. "Jer . . . ," she murmured.

And then she was alone.

"Oh!" she cried, startled. She moved her hands through the darkness, searching for him.

He was not there.

Did I dream it? she wondered.

Unsteadily she rose, finding the light switch and flicking it on. There was the fire in the brazier; there, the towel she had brought with her. Self-consciously, she covered herself with it and minced toward the door.

She opened it and peered into the hallway. No one was there.

Then Dan appeared at the other end and said, "Finished?"

"Where is . . . ?" she began, and then she nodded. "The fire's still going."

"I'll take care of it," he told her. "Go get your shower."

He withdrew to give her privacy as she lurched a few more steps and then walked into the bathroom. She shut the door. Her hands were shaking.

Then she began to shower.

Nicole woke by Philippe's side. His body was warm against hers—solid and comforting. He had fallen asleep with his arm around her after having given her the most passionate of kisses. Something had woken her but had left Philippe undisturbed.

She reached out with her senses, stretching her

mind carefully so as not to awaken Philippe. Holly and Amanda were performing a ritual, Nicole could feel it. Magical energy crackled in the air setting off sympathetic vibrations along each of her nerve endings. She closed her eyes and she could feel the power surging through her and around her—so familiar, and yet, somehow, new.

She had to go to them. She rose from her bed and was moving before the thought had completely formed. Their blood called to her, the same witch-blood that sang in her veins. Trying to deny it had only brought more fear and pain then she could have imagined.

Passing the spare bedroom, Nicole saw Pablo's eyes blinking at her, shining in the dark like a cat's. His head was up. He looked at her for a moment, nodded slowly, and dropped his head back down to his pillow. His eyes closed, and Nicole glided on.

No, it was time to embrace her gift, her heritage, her destiny—no matter what it might be. Her sister and cousin looked up as she entered the room. Candlelight flickered eerily over both their faces.

Amanda's eyes were warm, forgiving, and in a moment Nicole realized she had always underestimated her twin sister. *Amanda's the strong one. She's been there for Holly. And she'll be there for me.*

Holly's eyes were bright, knowing, as though she could read Nicole's innermost thoughts. *And Holly is the flame who has drawn us all together—lit our path and shown us the way.* Nicole remembered once hearing an old adage, something to the effect that the brightest flames only shine for a brief while before burning themselves out. Holly was on the edge, Nicole could sense it. This was the first time she had actually met her eyes.

Three candles stood forming a triangle—a strong symbol. A candle sat before each of the other girls. One candle stood before an empty place. *My place,* Nicole realized.

She sat down before the candle and stared solemnly at the leaping flame. This was her place. Without her, the other two had been weaker. No more.

The candle flames leaped in unison, straining toward the sky and burning white hot.

"We three come before thee, Goddess," Amanda intoned. "I offer my soul."

"I offer my heart," Holly intoned.

And what did Nicole offer? The one thing she had always held back. "I offer my mind."

"We bind ourselves to you and to one another. We are soul sisters and witches of the blood."

"I am the mouth that I might speak the truth," Amanda offered.

"I am the eyes that I might see our foes from afar," Nicole answered.

"I am the hand that smites those who raise a sword against us," Holly declared.

Next to each girl a cat appeared, silently on whisper paws. Bast and Freya had accepted Astarte, welcoming the newcomer. Nicole silently intoned a prayer for Hecate, her departed familiar. She was overwhelmed with an image so powerful, so clear. Hecate sat at the feet of a beautiful woman—the Goddess in one of her incarnations.

Tears stung her eyes as a weight lifted from her shoulders. She had felt guilt for so long over leaving her familiar behind when she ran away. Hecate had not deserved that. There had been no real way to take the cat with her. Worse, because of Hecate's connection to the magic Nicole had done, she had not wanted Hecate around as a constant reminder of the life she had been hoping to forget.

"Peace," Amanda murmured, waving her hand over her candle. Nicole hastened to follow suit, intoning the word with Holly.

Amanda had known that her sister would join them in the circle, but she couldn't stop herself from smiling when Nicole appeared in the doorway. It was good to have her back. When Nicole had left it was as though she took all of Amanda's bad memories and anger with her.

Now Nicole was back and, without all the years of built-up resentment getting in the way, Amanda was able to discover a real love for her twin sister. She thanked the Goddess for the second chance, knowing that things could have worked out much differently.

After all, Mom and Uncle Daniel didn't talk for years. Holly hadn't even known her dad had a sister.

Maybe it was true that time heals all wounds, but Amanda knew the real change was the one that had been wrought in her. Over the past year she had grown, let go of her childish jealousy of her sister, and learned the value of family.

Nicole seemed changed too. Her time in Europe sounded like it had been a living nightmare. *I can't believe she had to marry James Moore.*

Amanda shook her head slowly. She would not have wished such pain on her wayward sister even when she imagined she hated her. As she gazed at Nicole across the circle, Amanda felt complete.

Each girl took her candle and lifted it slowly into the air. A hot wind rushed through the room and fanned the flames until they leaped high above their heads. Suddenly the flame from Nicole's candle jumped, arcing between hers and Amanda's. Amanda's flame jumped, connecting it with Holly's. Holly's flame arced toward Nicole's until a solid ring of fire hovered above their heads connecting and enveloping them.

"No matter what each of us can do, we are made stronger by the others," Amanda whispered in awe.

As Nicole nodded agreement, Holly smiled faintly. It was good that the circle was complete again and that her cousins found strength in it. She loved them both, but the chasm between her and them was slowly widening. The others were frightened of her. That was why she would never tell them that she had caused the ring of fire to appear. Best to let them believe in the power of teamwork, the magic of three.

Kari's eyes ached from hours of staring at the computer screen in Dan's small cubby of an office. Books on shamanism lined one wall. Dreamcatchers and medicine bags were piled inside a small cube.

She heard the floorboards creaking and knew that some people were up. Casting spells, probably. Her throat began to burn, and she swallowed down the urge to vomit.

One last thing and then I'm out of here, she promised

herself. She didn't know where she would go, but it would be far away, school and everyone be damned. *Hell, half the school has burned down and no one here cares about me.* She felt a hot tear begin to roll down her cheek.

Earlier Pablo had been able to connect with Barbara's mind for the briefest moment. What he had described had sounded very familiar to Kari, who had spent years studying myths, religions, and the occult. Given what he had seen and what she remembered of Australian lore, she had had a starting place.

From there she had gone to the net. She had steered clear of all the high-traffic sites and chat groups, ferreting out those few sites that contained more esoteric, arcane knowledge, knowledge one had to specifically look for before one could find it.

At last with a triumphant sigh she sat back in her chair and rubbed her eyes. She knew what was wrong with Barbara and what they had to do to save her. Discovering that had been the easy part. What was coming next wasn't pretty.

Part Three

Ostara

☾

If one dies while in these other states of consciousness, one dies indeed.
This begs the question: Are dreams truly only ever dreams?

—Cesar Phillips, 1874

TEN

SODALITE

☾

Fire without and fire within
We'll burn them now and watch them spin
They dance for us, plead and moan
As they burn both flesh and bone

From earth we spin and strain toward sky
Trying to touch Goddess on high
Leave behind this mortal coil
As witchblood now begins to boil

Van Diemen's Land, 1790

"Sir Richard," the fawning convict murmured as he scraped and bowed at the doorway. The Cockney's clothing was in tatters, and he had lost all his teeth. He was a most disgusting man. But as he had been crippled when he had been arrested back in London—for stealing a loaf of bread—he was no good for farming or cutting timber, and so Sir Richard Moore had taken him on as one of his house servants.

Richard looked up from his letter and raised his brows.

The convict ducked as if a lash had been laid across his back . . . which it had been, many times, until the creature had learned how to show proper respect to his betters.

"The Abo woman as you wished to see is 'ere."

"Excellent," Richard Moore said. "I shall see her in two minutes."

"Yes, sir."

The convict backed out and then respectfully shut the door.

Richard returned to his letter, which was filled with good news. It was from his young brother, Edward.

> *We Moores remain in ascendance within the Coven, and it is due in no small measure to the wond'rous magic you have found in that forsaken land to which you have been dispatched. Father awaits your next discovery, as do I.*
>
> *The Deveraux press on in the Americas, their quest for the Black Fire fruitless thus far. They are the laughingstock of the Coven, and I believe we have naught to fear from that quarter. The Horned God*

continues to favor our House and to scorn the sacrifices of the Deveraux. For which I do tender all thanks.

E.

"Excellent," Sir Richard murmured. He refolded the expensive paper and unlocked the top drawer of his desk, where he kept all his private correspondence. Retrieving a bundle of letters fastened with a bright red ribbon, he untied it, added his brother's missive to the top of the stack, and retied it.

He was in the process of replacing the bundle in the drawer when there was a knock on the door.

"Enter," he said pleasantly.

"'Ere she is, Sir Richard," the Cockney man announced as he opened the door.

Richard was startled. The Abo woman was the most beautiful woman he had ever laid eyes upon, and never in his life had he considered that such a gentleman as he would think such a thing. She wore European clothing of fine material—a navy blue dress with a fichu of lace, and a mobcap such as any genteel lady might wear. As she swept a graceful curtsy, his blood was stirred, and he deigned to favor her with an incline of his head.

The Cockney backed out again, and Richard said, "Shut the door."

The woman regarded him. He saw that her eyes were a very startling green.

"Your name."

"You may call me Aliki," she said, and grinned at him coquettishly. "It is the way we say 'Alice' in my language."

"There is a joke in that," he ventured, not following her meaning.

"There will be a famous story of Alice one day, a girl who enjoys adventures in magical places," she said. "But not yet."

He regarded her, still uncertain of his place in this conversation. "I see. And will the story be about you?"

She shrugged. "Perhaps. It will be of no import to me, however."

Feeling a bit put off, he decided to get straight to the point. "I have heard of your powers of witchcraft."

Saucily she put her hands on her hips. "And I have heard of your interest in such powers."

He cocked his head. "Have you altered your appearance in order to be more appealing to me?"

She laughed but made no reply. Then she looked around the room and said to him pointedly, "I am tired and thirsty, Sir Richard."

He summoned the Cockney, who brought a chair and a bottle of Portuguese and two goblets. Sir

Richard poured, and he toasted Mistress Aliki.

She sipped in a most refined way, her gaze over the rim of her goblet quite warm and inviting. Then she settled the goblet against her fichu and said, "I can show you the mysteries of the Dreamtime."

"Indeed?" He leaned forward, fascinated.

"Indeed," she promised. "Tonight."

Tri-Covenate, Seattle

Jer could hear his heart pounding. Whether it was caused by the presence of Holly or his participation in the Aboriginal blood rite, he wasn't sure.

Standing together in the center of Dan's main room, they were wearing simple leather loincloths and, in Holly's case, a T-shirt. Both were barefooted. Kari had insisted that they dress as closely as they could to the Aboriginal custom.

Dan solemnly stepped forward and began to paint on Holly's face. The patterns and lines and symbols were unfamiliar to Jer, but he knew they were Aboriginal in origin. Dan and Kari had spent a long time, each researching in their own way, discovering the secrets of Alcheringa, the Dreamtime. When he was finished with Holly, Dan began to paint the patterns on Jer's face. Jer was acutely aware of how ugly he was, and that the paint only added to the macabre effect.

If he understood everything that Kari was so solemnly telling them, the Dreamtime was the time before history before the creation of the world and man. It was somehow, though, inexplicably tied to the land, and in specific places it resonated more strongly, as though the fabric between past and present was very thin. The Aborigines also claimed that the land told the stories of the early days of creation and that certain landmarks, such as Ayres Rock, were testimony to them.

"The native peoples believe that each place is connected to its history, and it has a physical being and a spiritual being," Kari finished.

"So it's like an astral plane?" Holly asked.

"Yes, but it is more than that. It's like an astral plane for another dimension."

"What do you mean?" Nicole asked.

Kari sighed in exaggerated frustration. "If you were simply astral traveling in this dimension, everything you see would be what is familiar to you. You would go outside this house and you would see your neighbor's house, the cars parked on the street. Your spirit is just walking about without your body.

"In the Dreamtime you might see a few familiar landmarks, like the Bay, or a mountain, but it will exist in an entirely different environment. There won't be houses, or if there are, certainly not like the ones we can see out the window. There might not even be people. It might be populated by creatures we are completely unfamiliar with."

Holly shook her head impatiently. "Whatever. We'll cope with whatever we come across. We'll just find a way to free Barbara and we'll get out."

Kari nodded, though Jer recognized an angry spark in her eyes. "Fine. Do it fast—you don't want to spend any more time there than you have to. There's a reason places like this are only dreamed about. Remember, you have to exit where you enter."

"And that will be somewhere in Australia?" Jer questioned.

Kari nodded. "We really should be in Australia to be trying this, but Barbara is here with us and somehow she's been trapped there, so I figure with the help of a little magic we should be able to send you there too."

"Anything else?"

"There is one other very important thing: Remember, the mind has power over the body in this arena. Whatever happens to you there, happens to you here. If you cut yourself there, your body will bleed here. If you die in the Dreamtime, you die for real."

There was silence for a moment. Dan stepped back slowly, his work done.

"All right, let's get this over with," Holly muttered.

Armand stepped forward and solemnly made the sign of the cross over both of them. Jer felt intensely uncomfortable. He hadn't yet adjusted to the beliefs of the Spanish Coven. Still, he dipped his head in a silent gesture of thanks. After all, they were going to need all the help they could get.

The others stepped away and formed a circle around them, hands joined. Jer and Holly both lay down in the center, their backs on the ground and their heads supported by small pillows. With a word, Nicole cut the lights and Philippe set the candles around them glowing. The smell of incense filled the air, sweet and light.

Jer closed his eyes and began to take long, deep breaths. The others began to chant softly, rhythmically. He willed his spirit to leave his body. His fingertips tingled where they brushed against Holly's. Slowly his mind emptied.

He felt as though he were floating, hovering an inch, just an inch, above his body. He stretched out with his mind and his spirit. A great light rushed toward him, engulfing him, and he gave himself up to it wonderingly. The light started pure and soft and then expanded until it burned his eyes through his closed eyelids. Pain seared through his body, and he heard Holly cry out even as he did.

His eyes flew open. He was standing in the middle of a great desert. The sun burned down so hot that he flinched back, throwing his arm in front of his face. The Black Fire! He forced his heart to stop racing. *It's only the sun.*

He turned to look at Holly. She was squinting into the light, her hand up to shield her eyes.

He turned slowly, wondering where exactly they were. He froze halfway around. "Look," he pointed.

Before them rose a large, square mesa. It towered above the surrounding desert like some mighty giant.

"Uluru," he said. "Ayres Rock."

A movement caught the corner of his eye, and they turned together to see something loping toward them. "And, that, I believe, is Yowee."

The creature was obsidian, shiny and evil-looking. Its eyes glowed like the fires of Hell. It scrabbled toward them on wickedly clawed feet that made no sound. A hot wind flew before it, blowing sand into Jer's eyes. He blinked desperately.

Yowee was the spirit of death.

Holly conjured a fireball and threw it at the creature. It passed right through him as though he were a ghost. Jer threw up a powerful ward and it passed right through.

They turned and ran. Ayres Rock loomed before

them. The desert air made it appear as though they were right at its base, but Jer quickly realized that was not the case. Behind him he could hear nothing, but he didn't dare risk a look back.

Before him he could see the wind that preceded the creature whipping up the sand. The blast became stronger, and the hairs on the back of his neck stood on end. He ducked just as a tentacle—*Where the hell did that come from?*—cracked through the air above his head.

He began to zigzag back and forth while still trying to head for the rock. He could hear Holly panting beside him. He couldn't turn to look at her, though, because he was too busy driving his own body forward.

I shouldn't be able to run like this, not with these burned, scarred legs, he thought. *Maybe I'll stay in this Dreamtime. It's not such a nightmare for me.*

At last they made it to the rock and began scrambling upward, the Yowee following behind.

They reached a plateau and found themselves face-to-face with a beautiful dark-skinned woman dressed in colonial garb.

The woman's eyes were ancient. Her hair was wild, flying about her like a lion's mane. She reached out and touched them both.

Remember, here the mind holds sway over the body. Her

lips had not moved, but her words sounded clear in Jer's mind.

He twisted, looking down at the Yowee. He closed his eyes, and in his mind he pictured the creature losing its handholds and falling backward to the desert floor. Then he opened his eyes and saw it happen. Holly must have caught on as well, because the creature suddenly exploded in a shower of gore and body parts.

He felt his body slump. *Mind over body. That must be how I was able to run.* Slowly he and Holly turned back to the woman who had helped them.

"Thank you."

She nodded gravely.

Jer realized that she was connecting with their minds so that they might understand her.

I'm Aliki. I taught Sir Richard Moore the secret of this place. And for my help, he exiled me here. Her smile was bitter. *It is a just punishment, I suppose.*

Holly swallowed. "Then if *you're* trapped. . . ." She took a breath and glanced at Jer. "A creature sits on the chest of a friend of ours, squeezing her heart. She's been trapped, and—"

The woman raised a hand. *There are very few who know of this place, fewer still who know how to use it. I can help you.*

"We would be very grateful," Holly told her.

Describe her, please. If her spirit is held captive here, it will appear to us as her physical form.

Holly nodded and described Barbara in detail, both her physical appearance and her personality. Aliki closed her eyes and seemed to retreat inside herself. Time passed, and she did not move.

When her eyelids fluttered open, her eyes were blazing with green light. *You are in luck. She is imprisoned inside one of the caves at the base of the rock.*

"Then let's go," Holly said, turning.

Be careful. There are things much older and far more terrible than the Gate Guardian you just killed. I'll go with you to help you find your path.

Holly nodded understanding and started back down. The woman followed her, and Jer brought up the rcar. When they reached the bottom, Aliki led them around the side. They walked for nearly half an hour before reaching a small aperture in the rock. It looked too small to be the opening of a cave, but their guide ducked her head and squeezed inside. Holly followed, and Jer anxiously ducked down and entered as well. Once inside, his skin began to crawl in a way that he recognized well. His family had cast its spell here; their magic crackled in the walls and turned his stomach.

Every fiber of his being shouted out for him to

turn and flee, but he doggedly followed the two women. The passageway was narrow, and his shoulders scraped painfully against the walls as they passed through. At last they rounded a corner and a cavern was revealed. Jer exited into it with a feeling of relief.

Blue flames leaped into life all around the perimeter of the cave. Pictographs graced the walls, standing out in stark relief and seeming to blaze with a life all their own. Several passageways led off the cavern into darkness, and once more Jer shuddered. The feeling of evil was overwhelming.

In a dark corner of the cavern a green light shimmered. Holly moved toward it slowly, as though something was pulling her. Jer hung back instinctively. When Holly drew close to it, she gasped. "Barbara!" Holly raced forward and fell to her knees before the light.

Cautiously, Jer crept forward. An old woman with tortured eyes looked up at him from the green mists of energy. She seemed half-spirit, half-flesh. Her mouth formed silent words, and her eyes pleaded with them.

Holly reached out a shaking hand as though to touch her.

The mists swirled and coalesced on top of her chest, becoming a hideous, dark shadow. The shadow was blurred, but Holly could trace the silhouette of the creature that tormented her.

Take care, Aliki warned as she glided up beside her. *She has been here for some time. You must be very gentle and very precise or she will die.*

Holly nodded slowly. "Tell me what to do."

In the old days, leaders of my people came here to seek enlightenment and to commune with our gods. She frowned. *I showed these secrets to Sir Richard in return for favor. We had a ritual for coming and a ritual for going. You have used the ritual for coming or you would not be here. You will have to do it for yourselves as well when you want to go. This is where she entered this land and so this is where she must leave. You must leave where you entered.*

"Why haven't you performed this ritual for yourself?" Jer asked.

She looked at him sadly. *I have the House of Moore to thank for that. Someday, I'll free myself. But for now, I'm trapped here.*

She bent swiftly and drew a circle around Barbara. *Watch carefully,* she instructed.

She began murmuring a spell in a beautiful language. Jer struggled to hear the words, to remember them.

The image of Barbara shimmered once and then returned. Aliki nodded as if to herself.

Kulpunya still holds her here. He is a spirit-dingo. He was originally sent to Ayres Rock to kill the people who lived there by their enemies. He can be forced to obey with a chant. She narrowed her eyes and set her jaw, as if coming to some kind of decision. *I will teach it to you.*

Holly glanced at Jer apprehensively. "Two chants?"

Jer said to Holly, "You remember one, and I'll remember the other." He paused. "I'll learn the one to tame Kulpunya."

The woman held up a hand. *If you mispronounce even a single word, you will free Kulpunya from his bondage, and he will try to rip you to pieces.*

"Then I'm *definitely* the one learning the chant," Jer said.

Holly looked alarmed. "Why can't you say it for us?" she asked the woman.

I am of this place now, she replied. *My magic won't work on him.*

Then she hesitated. After a moment, she drew Jer a distance away from Holly and stationed him so that her back was to Holly. She said to him in a quiet voice, not using her mind, "I need to warn you. Your spirit and hers, they are at war on another plane." She touched his face, tracing his ruined flesh. "She did this to you."

He licked his lips, felt the scarring on them with the tip of his tongue, and sighed heavily. "I know."

And yet . . . you love each other. This passion . . . it can rip you apart as surely as Kulpunya. It can rip her apart too.

He cocked his head, aware that Holly was staring at them. He steadily returned her gaze.

"I know that, too."

"Jer?" Holly called.

He said to the woman, "Teach me the chant." He held a hand up to keep Holly at bay. Holly's mouth dropped open and she stared at him, fuming.

"All right," the woman said. "Let us begin."

She began to chant. Jer listened carefully as her voice took on a strange, hypnotic drone, and soon the rhythmic syllables began to make sense to him, as if she were speaking English. Mental images of the nightmare creature stood out in sharp relief as she took his arm and led him back toward Barbara, still encased in green energy. It was hunched on top of her chest; and as Jer watched, it plunged its hand into Barbara's chest and squeezed her heart.

He was not aware he was speaking until Kulpunya jerked up his head and drew back fangs in a rictus snarl. Jer continued the chant, aided by Aliki, his voice drawing strength from hers, until their voices took on a bizarre, humming quality like a didgeridoo.

The monster growled deep in its throat and squeezed harder. The form of the aged, weakened Barbara threw back its head and whimpered in pain.

"Jer," Holly murmured. "Jer, are you doing it right?"

He ignored her, continuing the chant with Aliki. She steadied his arm, raising her voice with his.

Then she turned to Holly and said, "Get ready. When I tell you, say your chant."

Jer's voice continued to thrum, louder, louder still, as the monster's eyes narrowed. Blood and saliva dripped from its jaw. Its shoulders rounded, and the muscles in its legs bunched as it shifted its weight on Barbara's chest, preparing to spring.

Reflexive fear shot through Jer, but he kept his place in the chant.

Then it leaped at Jer.

Aliki shouted, "Now!"

Holly began her chant as Aliki bellowed at Jer, "Use your mind!"

As Kulpunya slammed into Jer and flung him to the floor of the cave, demons exploded from the dark passageways.

Seattle

Deep within his chamber of spells, Michael Deveraux looked up from his altar and smiled. "Well, well," he said. "Someone's released Kulpunya." He picked up a scrying crystal and gazed into it.

He turned to the other two participants in the night's ritual. "Care to make a journey with me?"

His son, Eli, and James Moore both nodded.

Amanda sat beside Tommy on the couch opposite Barbara Davis-Chin. Holly and Jer had been gone a while, and everyone had scattered around the room, resting and waiting and watching. Fear nibbled at the corners of her mind as she prayed protection spells for their absent comrades.

Tommy slid an arm around her shoulders and she stiffened, acutely aware of his touch. Deep inside her a new warmth began to spread, a feeling of well-being that belied their circumstances. Her skin tingled where it met Tommy's. He gave her a gentle tug and she leaned back gratefully into the circle of his arms.

She sighed and leaned her head on his shoulder. She felt so good that a twinge of guilt touched her. Who was she to feel so happy when her cousin and friend were in such terrible danger? Still, she could not stop the slow smile that spread across her face.

They sat that way for what seemed a long time. Slowly Amanda could feel the tension oozing from her body. She met Tommy's eyes and saw something beautiful shining in them. Slowly he bent his head toward her to kiss her. And then Barbara Davis-Chin began to scream.

Australian Dreamtime

Michael Deveraux smiled as he opened his eyes and found himself in Australia. *Well, not exactly Australia, but close enough.* He turned and saw James and Eli beside him. Eli looked disoriented and a little unnerved. James, on the other hand, appeared completely unruffled.

Michael narrowed his eyes. He was beginning to think that maybe, just maybe, he had underestimated Moore's kid. He would bear watching. There would be time enough for that later, though. For now, they had a witch to kill.

Michael turned slowly. Ayres Rock, desert floor.

And I know just where to start looking.

He had known Holly had returned to Seattle, but his falcons and scrying stones had been unable to locate her. When she had entered the Dreamtime, though, he had known it. She must have come trying to rescue her friend, Barbara, whose spirit he had exiled here. House Moore didn't claim an exclusive understanding of Australian magic.

As they began walking toward Ayres Rock he glanced again at his companions. Eli had been a lot quieter the past few weeks. He wondered if it had anything to do with the Cathers witch that James had married out from under him. Michael was unsure where Eli's loyalties lay anymore, but he was sure there was a resentment of James that would work to his advantage.

When they reached the base of the rock, James commented, "They are inside it."

Michael nodded. "That's where I had their friend trapped."

"It's a big rock," Eli said flatly.

Michael could feel himself growing irritated. "It's more than just a rock. It's a living thing."

"Legend says that the rock was formed because two serpents were battling each other and became frozen together, locked in combat for all eternity," James explained.

Michael nodded. "Let's wake them up."

The demons flew from everywhere, and Holly threw three fireballs before she remembered that in the Dreamtime the mind was what mattered.

The hideous monster Kulpunya had pinned Jer to the ground; he had one hand around the creature's jaw, and blood was gushing down his arm.

"Jer, use your mind!" she shouted to him.

Kulpunya jerked his jaw free and dove at Jer.

"Your mind!" Holly shrieked.

At the last possible instant, the creature exploded. Gore splattered across Jer's face and arms, and Holly fought the urge to vomit as she dispatched another demon in a similar manner.

Aliki was also fighting, taking out demon after demon. While Holly hazarded a glance her way, a demon seized the opportunity and charged her. Before she could stop the creature it hit her *and passed right through!*

Holly doubled over in pain, feeling as though every one of her internal organs were ripped to shreds. It was then that she saw the demon carrying a scythe in each hand. Too late, she shouted out a warning. Aliki turned just in time to see the creature as it sliced her in half.

As Holly groaned, the two halves of Aliki's body hit the dirt and vanished. *She was more spirit than flesh,* Holly realized. She had little time for reflection, though, as she straightened up to face another assault.

Suddenly the earth shook violently and it threw her face-first into the dirt. She heard a heavy thud and guessed that it had knocked Jer off his feet too.

Earthquake?

As she pushed herself to a sitting position, the ground shook again. She glanced up and saw Jer rising unsteadily to his feet. All the demons had vanished. *Not good.*

Ulu had lain in the sand a long time, so long that he had forgotten how many millennia had come and gone. Even now as he shuddered and the dust of ages fell from him, his mind quickened, flitting back through time, searching for a purpose, a meaning to it all. He groaned and stretched out sinuously. His long tongue slid out between his fangs and tasted the air, savoring the sensation. He felt bruised and scarred but above all he felt alive. He took a deep breath that rumbled in his lungs and exhaled slowly. Then he remembered Ru.

His eyes flashed open, seeking those of his brother. Ru stared back with cold, unfeeling eyes. Slowly the other snake began to uncoil and Ulu felt the almost forgotten sensation of hatred coursing through his veins. *Kill Ru,* his mind urged his body.

He pulled his head back and opened his mouth. Long fangs dripping venom extended downward, but Ru was ready for his attack and when Ulu struck, Ru was not where he had been. Instead, he feinted to the side and then came in, sinking his own fangs into Ulu. Ulu wrapped his body around Ru and began to squeeze as hard as he could.

★★★

Jer fell outside, and rolled as quickly as he could away from the heaving rock. Several feet away he managed to stagger to his feet and look up. His jaw dropped at what he saw.

There, above him, two enormous serpents were battling each other. Each was the red of the rock that moments before Jer and Holly had been inside. Holly, who had come tumbling out after him, joined him in looking upward, her face bearing a mixture of fear and awe.

"It will only last about another minute. Enjoy the show while you can," a familiar, mocking voice advised.

Jer whirled around to find himself facing his father, brother, and James. He clenched his hands into fists at his side as rage tore through his body.

James smirked at him, and the hairs on the back of Jer's neck lifted.

We're screwed.

His father gestured to the serpents behind him.

"The effects of the restoration spell are only temporary. The two beasties will be as frozen as stone again in a few more seconds." An amused smile crossed his face. "I wonder, though, if they will freeze in the same shape, or if Ayres Rock is about to get a makeover. That would shake up things back home, I imagine."

"What are you doing here?" Jer hissed.

"Come on, Jer, your brain didn't fry. I'm here to take her out." Michael glanced at his comrades. "We all are."

Jer took a step toward his father. A sudden, startled cry from Holly caused him to turn around just in time to see one of the giant serpents lunging for him. He tried to run, but it was too late; the giant mouth closed about him. First there was a fiery blast; then a sharp, stabbing pain, and then all was darkness.

Holly watched in horror as the snake swallowed Jer. She rushed forward, too hysterical to even think of magic. The creature was attacked by its comrade, though, and it turned away from her and back to the battle.

She rushed forward. The snakes began to slow, and suddenly they dropped down to earth, the head of one along the back of the other. Before her eyes they began to morph into something else. . . .

She ran into one of the monsters, fists flying. Pain exploded up her arms. What had seemed flesh only moments before had turned to stone. Before her was only Ayres Rock—and Jer was trapped somewhere inside it.

ELEVEN

CITRINE

☾

Our magic lasts beyond the grave
With the power to destroy or save
This will be our finest hour
When we crush the Cahors' power

Witchblood flows through our veins
We dance wherever the Goddess reigns
Though our power seems to fade
Deveraux throats will taste our blade

"No!" Holly screamed as she pounded her fist against the rock.

Behind her she heard a low chuckle. She turned quickly.

Michael, Eli, and James grinned back at her.

"Now, that's fitting, isn't it?" Michael drawled. "You free one loved one from the Rock only to lose another to it. I believe that's what they call *dramatic irony.* We have to be going soon. One shouldn't stay too long in this place—it does things to the mind. We wanted to leave you a little present, though, before we go."

James and Eli started quietly chanting. Michael lent his voice to theirs, and the words seeped into her mind. *Where have I heard them before?*

She remembered—a split second before the Black Fire burst into life.

Tri-Covenate, Seattle

Amanda leaped up from the couch with Tommy beside her. The others came running as well and they all crowded around Barbara. The poor woman was babbling incoherently between sobs. She looked up at all of them and began screaming again.

"Barbara?" Amanda asked, fighting the hysteria she heard in her voice. "Can you understand me? Did you see Holly?"

Barbara just kept babbling and sobbing. Alonzo waved his hand in the air above her head.

"Peace, rest, and be restored."

Her body instantly slumped and her eyes turned glassy. She stared at each one of them for a long moment before closing her eyes and drifting off to sleep.

"At least they found her," Nicole said into the silence. "Hopefully it means that they're on their way back too."

Amanda nodded agreement, but the sinking sensation in the pit of her stomach told her otherwise.

Australian Dreamtime

The heat of the flame scorched Holly. She watched helplessly as Michael, Eli, and James turned and ran. She tried to reach out with her mind, to will the flames to be extinguished, but she quickly realized it was no use. If the Black Fire was terrible in its destructive power in her world, it was tenfold as devastating in this one. Flames rose as tall as skyscrapers within seconds.

She began to run around the base of the rock, praying the flames would not follow. All the while her eyes scanned the impassive face of the rock for caves, crevices—anything that might lead her to Jer.

"Goddess," she murmured, then clamped her mouth shut. When had the Goddess ever freely helped her?

Her lungs burned from the smoke-laden air and the exertion. Her eyes began to tear up until she could barely see. She lost her bearings until she couldn't have told from which direction she had come.

At last, something in the stone caught her eye. She blinked fiercely trying to clear her vision. Slowly she reached out to touch the rock face. A tiny portion of the rock face was raised, as though something had pushed it outward from the rest of the stone. The raised section of stone was in the shape of a handprint.

She placed her palm against the stone hand, and electricity shot through her. "Jer!" she cried.

It was him, she could feel it. He must have pushed his hand nearly through the beast before it had frozen. She held her breath and reached out with her mind, trying to connect with him as Doña Rosalind had done with them.

Something faint came back to her—an echo, really. Still, it was proof that he was there and alive. She pushed harder, trying to reach him, trying to reach . . .

"Jean!" Isabeau sobbed his name over and over as she lay beneath him and the Black Fire rolled over them. She could feel the rage pouring out of him, heard the mixture of hate and love in his voice as he told her that he would pursue her for all time.

She loved him, Goddess forgive her. She loved her greatest enemy, her husband and Lord. Yet she would rather doom herself to wander the earth for all eternity than harm him.

Yet was there hope for them both yet? The fire burned around them. Isabeau could feel its heat, but they remained untouched. What sort of magic was this? It was Cahors and Deveraux magic, working together, fueled by passion and love.

Jean looked deeply into her eyes and she could see that he realized what was happening too. His lips moved. What was he saying?

Oh, Jean, I love you. We shall stay in the fire together, you and I, and let the whole world burn around us.

Then, suddenly, he was yanked from her arms. She looked up in time to see one of his servants wrestling with him. She screamed and held out her hands to him. It was too late, though; the Black Fire descended upon her and began to consume her. She felt her flesh ignite and her bones begin to melt. She died sobbing, reaching out for her beloved. . . .

You must go now or all is lost! The words pierced Holly's mind. She could hear the roar and crackle of the Black Fire scarce feet away, and the heat was singeing her hair. *Hurry, run!* She sobbed, trying to press her hand even closer to Jer's, willing the contact to be enough to keep them safe.

It wasn't enough, though, and she knew it. The thin sheet of rock that separated them might as well have been a foot deep. Without his flesh touching hers she could not survive the fire. Crying, she turned and began to run, praying the Goddess to light her way back to the place where she had entered the Dreamtime.

The desert landscape was on fire, but in her mind all she could see was the school gymnasium and Jer standing in the middle of the Black Fire, his flesh melting from his body as Nicole pulled her away.

"Not again!" she shrieked. "Goddess—Hecate—not again!"

But the Goddess wasn't answering. Either that or Holly wasn't listening, because the world kept burning and she kept running farther and farther away from Jer. Farther from her beloved. Just as Jean had run.

His heart wrenched with horror even as he ran. Isabeau was dead; he had stayed long enough to see her body ignite and turn to ash. And there was nothing that I could do. It is not just, *he thought savagely.* I should have been the one to kill her, for betraying me and my family. The witch deserved to die, but her life was mine to give or take. Just as her body was mine . . . and her soul . . . and her heart.

Even through his rage he could feel another emotion, just as powerful. She was gone and the despair crushed his lungs, making it nearly impossible to breathe. What was she trying to tell me? *he wondered.* Not that it would have made any difference. Would it?

He could feel his own flesh searing and melting as the fire burned so close. The servant who had pulled him from Isabeau had already been killed by it. It was a kinder death than I would have offered him.

At last he made it to the river and he threw his body head-

long into the water as the Black Fire rolled over the top of it. The river began to boil, but Jean stayed where he was, knowing that there was only death on the surface of the water.

As he began to run out of air he thought, Damn you, Isabeau. I will kill you, if not in this life then in the next.

And he was killing her. Isabeau—no, Holly—ran, trying to outrace the fire that swept along behind her, harrying her. Tears streaked her face as her eyes stung from the acrid smoke. It seemed the whole world was on fire. It filled her vision, her senses, until there was nothing left. No past, no future, there was only the fire. It seemed it was all she had ever known.

As she ran, the world around her seemed to be melting. Was the fire that powerful? Or was this what Michael had meant about people spending too long in the Dreamtime? Deep chasms seemed to open at her feet, yawning gulfs that stretched forever. If she fell down one of them would she come out on the other side of the earth? Or, maybe, like Alice, would she find herself in a world even more fantastical than this one?

Rabbit holes and stopwatches. I'm going to be late. I'm going to be very late. The others will be wondering where I am and why I didn't bring Jer back. I'll just have to tell them, he was lunch for the White Rabbit, I mean the Great Snake. It doesn't do to have tea with a snake, they spill the cups. Just like

Joel spilled the cup when I killed him. No, when Catherine the Goddess killed him. That didn't seem quite right.

Holly shook her head to rid it of the colliding thoughts. The fire was close; she could feel all the moisture evaporating from her skin. *If I had sunscreen I wouldn't get burned. That's what the bottle says. SPF 60 stops everything. I'll have to start carrying some with me. Since the fire is always there, it only makes sense.*

And suddenly she was back where she had started, which wasn't such a bad spot after all. The fire hadn't burned there yet. "Maybe it shan't, maybe it can't," she chanted to herself, swaying slightly. Then someone was screaming and she wasn't altogether sure it wasn't her, but since her mouth was closed she suspected that it might not be, so she turned around.

"Lots of people screaming," Holly noted.

There before her were a thousand creatures, driven as deer before a forest fire. There were people, or at least husks that must once have been human, small creatures with many eyes and long arms, and demons. There were dozens and dozens of demons. Holly felt sure she recognized a couple from the battle in the cave.

"That was before the cave came to life and you all died."

She frowned. That wasn't right. If they had all died

then they couldn't be here. She swayed. Maybe they were all dead, even her, and that's why they were here.

Focus, a voice hissed in her ear. A circle, the lady had said something about a circle. Holly picked up one of the smaller demons that had long, pointy claws. She grabbed him around his fat torso and squeezed. He made a rather pleasing gurgly noise. She let his claws dangle in the sand and slowly spun around until the ground had been scarred in a circle.

She set the fat demon down and he bit her leg, but she didn't notice. *Too many things to do. Where will I find the time to get married?* She felt tired. A nap sounded good; she lay down in the middle of the circle. A lullaby, she needed a lullaby. What had the nice lady taught her?

One of the demons she knew she recognized from the cave jumped on her chest and seemed to dissolve right into her body. Holly giggled because it tickled. Another joined in and another.

"I am the lifeboat!" she screamed out, though she wasn't sure what the *Titanic* had to do with anything.

Suddenly there was a sharp, stabbing pain in her brain and it jolted her. What is going on? It felt as though she were being pushed out of her own mind, quite a feat given that she was already out of her body. Wasn't she?

She struggled to push back, to fight. For a moment she felt as though she had been shoved into a tiny corner and was watching several little creatures fight over making her mouth move, her arms and legs.

No! she screamed. They didn't seem to hear her. Or maybe they were ignoring her. *I have to get out of here!* She struggled to gain back control of something, one thing. Her mouth, if only she could say the words.

They came pouring out. She couldn't remember if they were the right words, or even what words were really, but it sounded good. She could feel herself being sucked backward as though into a vacuum. As everything faded to black, she shouted, "Jer, forgive me!"

Holly sat straight up screaming. Freaked, Amanda started screaming as well. Then, as suddenly as she had started, Holly stopped, and collapsed backward on the ground. She began making low moaning noises and rocking herself. Saliva poured out of her mouth and rolled down her cheeks to mix with tears.

Amanda turned to glance at Jer's body, waiting for some sign of life from it. Blood trickled slowly down his arm, they had not seen it earlier for staring at Barbara. A minute passed and there was nothing. Stunned silence filled the room.

Kari finally broke it. "Where is he?" she shrieked.

Amanda turned to look at her. Silvana had her arm around Kari, but she shook it off and lunged forward. She knelt by Jer's body, her hand shaking as she reached to touch his scarred face, then pulled it back uncertainly. *"Where is he?"* she demanded, looking at Holly.

Holly just continued to rock and moan. Kari leaped over Jer's body and seized Holly by the shoulders, shaking her hard. "You tell me where he is!" she screamed. Holly didn't answer, but her head banged against the ground like a rag doll as Kari shook her.

Before Amanda could overcome her shock and move to stop her, Silvana stepped forward and grabbed Kari firmly by the shoulders.

"Kari, let her go! She can't hear you!"

"Where, where, where!" Kari shouted, tears streaming down her face.

Alonzo darted forward and pulled Kari's hands from Holly. Holly slumped back down on the floor, her eyes glassy. Alonzo yanked Kari to her feet; she balled her hands into fists and started punching him in the chest and shoulders.

He signaled for Silvana to let go of her. Reluctantly she did and stepped backward. Alonzo let Kari hit him a couple more times before finally catching her flying fists in his hands. "Why? Why did she leave him there?" Kari sobbed.

"We don't know what happened yet," Alonzo said quietly. "He might be fine."

"He's not. I know it!" Kari cried.

Alonzo pulled her into his chest and wrapped his arms around her. Great heaving sobs wracked her body and as she glanced at Tommy, Amanda felt a twinge of sympathy for the other girl. *It must be terrible to lose the one you love to somebody else, and then believe he's dead, only to have him come back and then disappear again.*

It didn't make her like Kari any better, but at least she felt a little sorry for her. Tommy grabbed her hand and squeezed it as though to reassure her that she had nothing to worry about.

TWELVE

AMETHYST

☾

The stronger we grow, we can't be stopped
Deveraux strength cannot be topped
Flowing, twisting from within
A reflection of all our sins

Blessings, cursings all must flow
As we await our greatest foe
The sleeper walks, but we must wait
For she alone can determine her fate

Michael was the first to open his eyes. He leaped to his feet, immensely pleased. Eli and James were conscious a moment later. Michael couldn't help but smile at the wary look in James's eyes.

That's right, boy, just remember that I could have killed you at any time I chose. You'd do well to stay on my good side.

James rose quickly, his features taut. Eli did not fare so well. He lay unmoving for several minutes. His eyes didn't even blink. Just when Michael started thinking he might have to do a healing spell just to get his son off his carpet, Eli sat up with a yelp.

James sneered, and Michael felt a twinge of embarrassment for his eldest. *Or is it embarrassment of my eldest?* No matter. There would be time to take care of the two young men later. But for now—

"Time to celebrate," he announced with a laugh.

"I can't believe we did it," Eli said, shaking his head as he slowly got up. "We conjured the Black Fire and killed Holly."

"A day to be remembered in history." James smiled.

"As will be the day when we put you on the throne of skulls," Michael commented.

James flushed but met Michael's eyes. The kid knew that Michael would probably kill him. He also knew that Michael needed him, for now.

As long as we have an understanding.

Michael rubbed his hands as he walked toward the window. Outside he could see the smoke from the dozens of fires plaguing Seattle. The effects of the torrential floods were also in evidence. Yet his own house and his block had remained untouched by the destruction. *Good neighbors are hard to find,* he thought sardonically.

He rubbed his hands together. "I'm feeling generous, boys." With that, he waved his hands and everything stopped. The ocean monsters disappeared back into the sea, the fires were snuffed out, and the rain ceased. The clouds parted, and thin watery sunlight started pouring through. Michael stretched his hands toward its life-giving rays.

"It's good to see you, old friend; by God how I've missed you."

And the sun shone down on Michael Deveraux, casting its life and approval on all his plans, all his work. And he smiled as the people of Seattle dropped to their knees and offered prayers of thanksgiving to whomever had stopped the carnage.

Tri-Covenate, Seattle

"I don't like it," Sasha announced as she turned off the television.

"Thousands dead? What's to like?" Amanda muttered.

"No, not that," Sasha said, waving her hands in the air. "It's the fact that he just *stopped*. Why?"

"He feels he has accomplished his purpose," Pablo answered quietly.

"But how can that be?" Nicole asked. "Holly's alive."

"We know that, but maybe he doesn't," Tommy

suggested. "I mean, it would make sense. From some of the things she's said, we figure that he showed up there in the Dreamtime. He must have thought that she was killed."

"By the Black Fire," Armand supplied. "She's been muttering about that constantly."

Amanda shuddered. "It's a terrible thing to see," she said, her voice holding both awe and fear. Tommy wrapped an arm around her.

"He must think he killed her, and in the state that she came back, she's probably not registering on his radar," Silvana said carefully.

A hush descended on the group. In the silence they could hear Holly muttering to herself. Each fought the urge to look, but looking at her was like watching a car accident. It was such a horrific sight that it was hard to look away.

Simply put, Holly wasn't herself.

Specifically, she seemed to be possessed by so many demons that no one was sure if Holly was truly even in there. She sat in a corner, bound in a strait-jacket that Alonzo had found at a local hospital. At the same hospital he had managed to liberate some tranquilizers and had given one to Kari.

With a collective shudder they turned back to one another. "We have to do something. We can't just leave her like that," Amanda protested.

She held out her hand to her sister. Nicole looked down at the birthmark in Amanda's palm, then at her own. Holly bore the final third of the lily. Together, they made a powerful triumvirate.

Firmly, she put her hand against Amanda's, and then the two of them reached out toward Holly.

They were rappelled against the wall, and slid crashing down to the floor.

"Okay, okay," Amanda said unhappily. "I don't think we're going to be able to get near her."

"Then we need to try something else," Nicole said.

"Yeah, but what?" Silvana asked.

"An exorcism." Sasha said the word they had all been trying so hard to avoid. "We're going to have to try to drive the demons out of her."

"Can it be done—I mean, truly?" Nicole asked, turning to Philippe.

Philippe raised an eyebrow. "I have heard of such things, but I have never actually seen it done." The others of his coven nodded agreement.

"I saw one once when I was very small," Tante Cecile offered. "My grandmother cast a demon out of a man. I remember how terrified I was."

There were a few murmurs, and then the group turned to Sasha. With Holly incapacitated and Jer missing—well, his spirit, anyway—they had all seemed to look to her for leadership. By right, Philippe should have taken up the reins, but he had subtly deferred to her.

It's not because he's afraid of leading, she thought. *He just knows that he and his group are the relative newcomers and that the others would feel more comfortable with me leading, partly because I've been here longer and am older, and partly because I'm a woman.* She shook her head. Truly he was wise beyond his years.

"Amanda is right. We must try." She glanced at Holly. "And soon. It's too dangerous to leave her like this for long; she has too much power to have it uncontrolled, or, controlled by the wrong forces." She took a deep breath. "Tonight, we'll try tonight."

Michael, Seattle

"Tonight," Michael declared, smiling at Duc Laurent. "We'll deal with the rest of the coven tonight."

His ancestor nodded. "I understand your wife is among them."

Michael knotted his jaw. "Ex-wife. I figure she and I are long past due for a talk."

Duc Laurent chuckled. "You know, in my day, there was no such thing as ex-wives. Either your wife was your wife, or she was a sacrifice."

Michael smiled. "You know, I think you had something there. Yeah, I think it's time we get back to good old-fashioned family values."

"Speaking of family," Laurent added, "you should keep an eye on your older son."

"Eli?" Michael made a dismissive gesture. "He's harmless. Besides, he wouldn't dare lift a finger against me."

"Don't be too certain. Your leaving Jeraud to burn in the Dreamtime doesn't sit well with him."

Michael laughed. "I have a hard time believing that. The boys hate each other. I have it under good authority that Eli even tried to kill Jer several times the last couple of months. I believe poison food was the last attempt. . . ."

"This may be true, but I would watch very carefully." Laurent raised one brow as he gazed at his living relative.

Michael pursed his lips. The Duc wasn't often wrong. Still, it seemed implausible. He would have to think about it later. Now, he had to prepare for the night's sacrifices.

Eli turned his athame over and over again, watching how the sharp edges caught the light. He remembered the day he and Jer had blessed it, feeding it their own blood, together. *Deveraux blood.*

Angry, he slammed the dagger down on the table by his bed. For months he had been trying to kill Jeraud. Now, his brother was most likely dead and yet he was not rejoicing.

Dad shouldn't have left him. Jer's always been his favorite.

If Michael Deveraux could leave his Jer, a son he had begged Sir William to save, where did that leave *him*? Eli had always known his father was ruthless, that he had best watch his step. He just hadn't believed his father would kill Jeraud. Now Eli was faced with the realization that neither was he safe from his father's sword.

Michael was powerful, but Eli was certain that he still couldn't take down Sir William by himself. *He needs James and me to create the Black Fire. So long as he can't do it himself, I'm fairly safe. I just have to watch my step. Of course, I could always stand with Sir William against Dad.*

Eli shuddered. If there was one person who frightened him more than his father, it was Sir William. He shook his head, unwilling to ally himself with the leader of the Supreme Coven outside of the usual hollow protestations of loyalty expected of the coven members. *Better the devil you know . . .*

He picked the athame up again and watched the

jewels refract the light. *I'm going to miss that bastard,* he thought, surprised. At least with Jer he had always known where he had stood. Also, hating Jer had given him focus, a focus he sorely needed now.

He glanced at his watch. He was due to meet James in a half hour. It would take that long to meditate enough so that he wouldn't try to rip his throat out upon seeing him. *At least Jer never took my women,* he thought bitterly.

Tri-Covenate, Seattle

Sasha's hands were sweating and she dried them yet again against her robe. Half an hour before, Pablo had informed the group that he thought Michael was stirring, preparing for something.

Could he be about to attack? All the more reason we need Holly to be herself. Sasha took several deep, cleansing breaths. The furniture had been cleared from the center of the room, and candles had been laid out on the points of a pentagram formed from herbs spread on the floor. She clutched her silver dagger tighter. She was sorry now that Kari was upstairs in a drug-induced sleep. They really could have used some of her research skills for this.

Armand and Tommy carried Holly into the room and placed her on the floor in the center of the pentagram. Her eyes were glazed and she was still muttering quietly to herself. She rocked back and forth slowly.

The others filtered into the room slowly, each holding a candle and each standing as far back along the perimeter as they could. No one was sure what exactly was going to happen, so Sasha had decided that they should stay as far back as they could. She noticed that along with the candle, each of the men, with the exception of Dan, carried a cross. Tommy lifted his in a salute with a smile that seemed to say, "What can it hurt?"

When at last they had all taken their places, Sasha began. "Goddess, hear us, your servants, as we form a sacred circle tonight. Bless us, and bless your chosen one."

"Blessed be," the others murmured.

"We place her in the center of the pentagram and we recognize the five points of balance. Fire, we call upon thee to drive out those creatures that have taken up residence inside this body. Mighty wind, we pray thee sweep them back from whence they came. Earth, heal this body whose life springs from you and ground her spirit that it might stay. Water, nourish her spirit, for she has been wandering for far too long in a dry and desolate plane. And last, we call upon the spirit, the fifth and final element. Return to your rightful place. Holly, be with us once more!"

The herbs caught on fire, and the pentagram burned and shone with an unnatural light. Holly had stopped muttering and was looking down at the fire. Suddenly the head snapped back, and the eyes, which had looked so glossy and vacant, filled with a malicious hate.

"No!" The voice that came out was not Holly's. Amanda screamed and clapped her hands over her ears. Wind whipped through the room, extinguishing all the candles.

Holly's face contorted and changed into a snarling mask with two-inch fangs and glowing red eyes. "We will kill it first," hissed a serpentine voice.

"Yes, yes, we will," confirmed another.

Holly began to seize uncontrollably. Her bowels released, and a putrid stench filled the air. Red fire blazed from her eyes as she dug at her face with her fingernails. The saliva that rolled down her chin was green and fetid. As though she were a doll, she was flung around the room.

"Holly, hear me, I know you're in there! Fight it!" Sasha shouted above a keening sound she had heard only in her nightmares.

★★★

Holly was asleep. Or, at least she thought she was. Someone was trying to wake her. They pushed and she pushed back. She opened one eye and saw the woman with red hair. Who was she again? She was somebody's mother, Jer, Jean . . . she couldn't remember. Couldn't be that important if she couldn't remember. She closed her eyes again.

Holly's mouth gaped open, and Sasha watched in shock as two spirits pulled themselves out of her chest. They were scabby, hideous creatures with snakelike skin and jaguar claws. Once outside of Holly, they flew, circling the room at an impossible rate. She tried to track them with her eyes but failed. She didn't even see them when they slammed into her, one on each side.

She fell hard and she heard the sickening sound of bones snapping. She began to scream as she could feel their claws digging into her throat and chest. One was trying to punch its way through her stomach. The other began to climb inside her mouth.

Frantic she stabbed at them with her dagger, slashing herself in the process. She heard the others screaming, and someone caught her wrist in midair as she was about to bring the knife down into her chest to kill the demon riding her there.

"Get it off!" she sobbed. "Kill it, kill it! And if you

can't, kill me!" Then there were hands everywhere, helping her, holding her, and the demons left. Slowly, she sat up, pain knifing through her cracked ribs. She glanced over at Holly and froze. Holly's face was frozen in the look of a death mask, but from the open mouth emanated loud, hysterical laughter.

As she watched Sasha stabbing her own body with the knife in an effort to kill the demons, Tante Cecile felt like she was five again. Images from the exorcism that had been long suppressed came flooding to her mind and she fell to her knees retching. As the others scrambled to help Sasha, she tried to push her mind into the memories, to remember what her grandmother had done, how she had defeated the demon.

She muttered a calming spell over herself, but it did no good. She glanced over to see Sasha sitting up, clutching at her ribs. She was bleeding from half a dozen wounds in her chest and stomach region. *Let them all be shallow,* she prayed. Alonzo helped her out and ushered her quickly from the room. Pablo was huddled in a corner, his eyes wide with terror, rocking himself. For one terrible moment she thought that he, too, was possessed. Then she remembered that the boy could read minds. The horrors he must be seeing in Sasha's and Holly's!

The others looked just as shaken and confused as she felt. "Time to finish this," she muttered, turning to face Holly and her demons.

"We'll kill you and then her and then all the rest," the demons chortled. "There are too many of us for you to stop."

"I can stop you and I will," she countered. "Holly, Holly, sweetheart. You must come back. Fight them, fight, fight!"

The face slowly began to contort back from a demonic one, to Holly's. The head lulled to the side, and Tante Cecile held her breath, hoping that Holly had heard her and was coming back to them.

Irritated, Holly realized that someone else was calling to her. She tried to put her hand over her eyes, but her hand wouldn't move. Panicked, she opened her eyes and looked down. She was wearing some quite white thing, and her arms were pinned inside it. The words *fight, fight,* echoed inside her head.

She panicked. *Are we under attack?* How could she fight if her arms were tied?

She muttered a couple of words, and the jacket fell off her. That was better; now that she could move her arms, she swung the left one slowly forward. Good. Now, what about a fight?

She closed her eyes. It would have to wait.

She needed a nap.

The straitjacket fell from Holly moments before her face changed back to its demonic appearance. A hideous snarling demon came to the front. Holly's arm jerked upward awkwardly, as though she were a marionette. Slowly her finger extended toward Tante Cecile.

"Muerte," the voice hissed.

Nicole watched in horror as Tante Cecile fell to the ground, clutching her chest. Her skin was ashen, and her lips stood out like a bruise. Her eyes bulged in terror and suddenly fixed, rolling back into her head.

Silvana began to scream.

Nicole took a step toward what used to be Holly. "I command you to release my cousin!" she cried, her voice shaking with wrath.

For a moment the world seemed to slow, and she could feel power, real power, rushing through her like a hot wind. The witchblood sang in her veins, and for one moment she understood all too well what it was like to be Holly.

"You will release her," she thundered, her voice exploding the windows.

"My, my, how the rose has blossomed," James chuckled.

Nicole gasped and spun around, her concentration shattered.

THIRTEEN

LAPIS LAZULI

☾

Air and water, earth and fire
All tools of our ire
Death and destruction are what we bring
The only chorus that we sing

Goddess, Priestess, now we plead
Both our souls and bodies feed
High Priestess, watch over all us keep
Wake now from your hateful sleep

James and Eli stood leering just outside the front window of Dan's cabin. Shards of glass were still falling.

"What do you want, James?" Nicole demanded, although where moments before her voice had been trembling with power, now it was trembling with fear.

"I should think that would be rather obvious," he answered, allowing his eyes to travel the length of her body.

She flushed, but stood her ground. "Get out."

He gave her a mocking bow. "But, of course, honey. I just came to deliver a friendly warning."

He and Eli turned to go. Against her better instincts she asked, "What?"

He turned back to her. "Oh, it's just that Eli's dad has amassed quite an army of the Deveraux dead. He'll be attacking you in, oh"—he checked his watch—"about fifteen minutes." With that, he turned and he and Eli disappeared into the darkness.

Nicole's legs started to buckle, and Philippe caught her. She glanced around the room at the stricken faces. All of them were staring at her except for Silvana, who was weeping over the body of her aunt and Holly, who was laughing at the sight. The noise was too much for her. She waved a hand in the air and it was as though she had hit the "mute" button on the TV. Silvana still cried and Holly still laughed, but she couldn't hear them.

Philippe lowered her slowly to the ground and she clung to his arm. In fifteen minutes they were all going to be as dead as Tante Cecile.

Holly heard explosions. She opened her eyes groggily, aware that she was having to fight to do so. *Where am I?* In a flash it came back, the Dreamtime, the demons. Had she made it home? She glanced slowly around. She could feel taloned fingers wrestling with her, ripping at the borders of her consciousness.

Her eyes fell on Silvana. The girl was hunched over Tante Cecile, sobbing. *Is Tante Cecile sleeping?* Holly wondered. From the way the body lay, she would guess the older woman was actually dead. She heard them scrabbling at her mind, gnawing at the edges like rats. She heard their little claws clicking around. Everyone was looking at Nicole. Everyone but Silvana. Silvana's hair was getting wet from her tears.

Holly began to laugh.

"What are we going to do?" Amanda asked, bewildered and shaken.

"I don't know," Nicole admitted as she held her head in her hands.

Alonzo came in from the other room. Then, suddenly in their midst, stood a woman Nicole had never seen before. Given how the rest of the evening had gone, she wasn't surprised.

Anne-Louise Montrachet stood unsmiling. "You need our help."

Nicole stared at Amanda. "Who is this?"

Amanda's jaw was set in a tight line, but there was

no disguising the look of relief in her eyes. "Anne-Louise. She's from the Mother Coven."

Nicole nodded and turned back to Anne-Louise. The other woman nodded cursorily at her. *She doesn't like us much,* Nicole thought.

"You're safe for now. The wards will hold."

Nicole raised an eyebrow questioningly. Before she could ask, though, Amanda told her, "She's good at that sort of thing."

"The best," Anne-Louise answered. "But that doesn't matter. Michael Deveraux's army is coming. There's going to be a battle."

Amanda took a deep breath. Tommy appeared from the other room, came to her side, and held her. He said to the woman, "Did you bring help?"

Anne-Louise nodded. "We will do what we can."

"I only pray to the Goddess that it is enough," Tommy said quietly.

In the distance, footfalls rumbled and birds shrieked. The ground began to shake.

The others looked at one another, then at Anne-Louise.

But Anne-Louise was staring at Holly, whose face had resumed its demonic cast.

"We may have to . . . to kill her," she murmured.

Amanda and Nicole stared at her.

"They're coming," Pablo announced.

The dead marched for Michael Deveraux. From the graveyards they rose, their burial garments caked with mud and decomposition. From the bay they fought their way through shipwrecks and kelp beds to break the surface, needing no air, and crawled up the embankments. As they marched through the darkness—and then through the rain—parts of them detached and were abandoned: arms, ribs, in a few cases, heads.

In the terrible rain and the thickly forested gullies, monsters broke loose from other dimensions and tumbled toward the cliff where Michael Deveraux waited. Flurries of falcons blackened the moon; imps rode winged nightmares whose talons dripped poison and blood.

They converged on the hillside where Michael waited, his arms spread, chanting in ancient languages. Demons in full armor raised their spears and shields to him. Enormous creatures—scaled, fanged, horned—lumbered through the mud, the white-blue lightning strobing on their teeth and red, glowing eyes.

Hovering above the bacchanal, Fantasme screeched

and capered with eagerness for the battle to begin.

Laurent stood beside Michael, his arms crossed, nodding his approval as the army massed. They were a short distance from the shaman's cabin, where the witches were no doubt quaking with fear.

"This is going to be over fast," Michael said smugly.

Laurent raised one brow. "Where are your son and James Moore? They should be at your side." He cleared his throat and added, "I warned you to watch him."

Michael concealed his embarrassment; he didn't know where they were, and Laurent was correct: They should be here. It was galling to endure Eli's obvious lack of respect for his own father and his High Priest as well. It could also prove disastrous—if Laurent decided Michael was too weak to act as the head of the Supreme Coven, he could simply wait for another generation of Deveraux to grow up, and select one of them.

Damn you, Jeraud, he thought. *Why did you have to be the rebellious one?*

You would have made a fine leader.

Laurent raised a hand, and the sky above them burst with light, creating a vortex of energy that swirled and throbbed. From it fell more warriors, including knights on horseback and men in modern combat gear: the Deveraux dead of generations past. Scores of them descended from the vortex, joining the army at the base of the cliff. None spoke, but their armor clanked and their weapons knocked against their sides as they looked silently up at Michael.

Michael had not forgotten that Holly had been able to raise an army of her own dead. Nor that she had managed to defeat him with it. Taking the battle to the water had not deterred her.

But this time, she's not here, he thought.

In the cabin, Anne-Louise invoked the Goddess, and from a wavering mist just outside the cabin, the warriors of the Mother Coven took their form.

They were knights in armor, and soldiers, and amazons and Valkyries. But they were not fully solid.

Nicole glanced at Anne-Louise, who looked both embarrassed and frustrated until she realized Nicole was looking at her. Then she raised her chin and continued her chant.

More fighters appeared—there were hundreds—each as insubstantial as the others.

She stopped, then turned her attention to Holly,

encasing her in a bubble of green energy. Holly cocked her head as if she didn't understand what was happening, then erupted into screams and began to throw herself against the barrier. "Let me out of here, witch!" she shrieked. "I'll kill you!"

Amanda pressed her face against Tommy's chest. Then she squared her shoulders resolutely and said to Nicole, "We're in charge now, Nicki. It's up to us."

She held out her hand. Nicole placed her palm over Amanda's, and two thirds of their lily brand were joined. Energy sizzled up and down their arms.

Together they faced the doorway. Dan and Uncle Richard joined them.

Then the cabin began to shake with the force of the rain and the wind outside, and Tommy whispered to Amanda, "I love you."

"Attack!" Michael shouted, and the dead swarmed toward the little cabin of the shaman.

From his vantage point atop a spectral tank, he watched his forces swarming toward their ghostly opponents. *Mother Coven forces,* he thought, sneering. *Of very little use.*

Sure enough, the enemy was engaged, and the massacre began. The warriors of the Mother Coven simply weren't as strong as his own troops. Some of the Mother Coven fighters put up a struggle, but many simply faded from existence, or disappeared in a shower of sparks. Before long, his monsters, zombies, and demons had cut a swath through them and were converging on the cabin.

He chuckled, and Duc Laurent, standing on the tank beside him, wagged a finger. "Don't get too cocky," he warned. "The witches have not yet shown themselves."

Holly, whispered the woman inside her head. *Holly, we can save you.*

"Go away," Holly hissed. "Go away, go away!"

She burst into fresh laughter. As the people who had imprisoned her looked at her, she flung out her arms and shouted, "I foreswear you, all of you! Go to the Devil! Go to hell!"

"Oh, my God," Richard murmured as the magical barrier his daughters had erected began to wobble. Flashes of magic burst at the shield over the broken window, and at the covers over all the other windows. The door was about to give way.

All the magic users in the room were at work,

strengthening the wards while outside, the soldiers of the Mother Coven were being eliminated. The battle was perhaps thirty seconds old, yet it was nearly lost.

Richard flexed his arms, ready for whatever came next, hoping there was something he could do to hurt the enemy before they took him down.

"I can't deal with this anymore," Kari cried as she crumpled into a ball. The others glanced at her, wondering when she had woken up.

"I should have given her a stronger tranquilizer," Armand muttered.

Then a light flashed to the right of her, became a portal, and James and Eli tumbled into the room.

"Grab them!" Philippe shouted.

Richard rushed at the two men but was flung across the room by James before he could get anywhere near them. Tommy tried next as Dan, Amanda, and Nicole aimed magical energy at them.

James and Eli deflected it all easily. Laughing, they both strode to Nicole, grabbed her arms and, before anyone else realized what was happening, they tossed her into the portal and barreled in after her.

It disappeared.

"No!" Philippe shouted. "No!"

Then the cabin exploded.

The tank rocked with the explosion. Michael was laughing so hard, he nearly fell off, and Laurent had to steady him.

"Mop it up!" he shouted to his warriors. "Take 'em out!" He grabbed his ghostly ancestor's arm to keep his balance and said, "To quote the kids, 'This rocks!' "

"Indeed," Laurent agreed.

Despite the rain, the forest had caught fire. The trees showered sizzling branches on the ruins of the structure. Smoke clouded his vision, and Michael strained to see if there were any survivors.

The tank rolled through the mud. *"Alors,"* Laurent said loudly. He pointed. "Look!"

Michael's mouth dropped open.

Hovering above the destroyed cabin floor, a green sphere held a single inhabitant who was pounding against it.

Holly.

Her face was a contorted mass of terror. She was shrieking wildly.

Laurent snapped his fingers at her, and she collapsed to the bottom of the sphere.

He and Michael climbed down from the tank and slogged over the bodies of dead demons and deanimated corpses as they made their way to the sphere.

Holly looked up at them. Her terror grew.

As well it should, Michael thought, preparing to annihilate her. He raised his hands.

"Make it stop," she whimpered. "Make it stop."

"Oh, I will," he assured her. He began to conjure a fireball.

Then Laurent held up a hand.

"Attends." He leaned toward Holly. "Do you know who we are?"

She shook her head. "Make it stop. Make it *stop-makeitstopmakeitstop!*" She threw back her head and screamed, "Help me!"

The two Deveraux stared at each other in wonder.

"Well." Michael raised his brows. Then he turned back to Holly Cathers, the strongest Cahors witch since Isabeau. "All right," he said brightly. "I think we can work out some arrangement, *Holly.*"

They ran through the forest as the evil army pursued them. Lightning and fire crackled over the heads of Tommy and Amanda as they raced for their lives.

"Who else?" Amanda gasped. "Who else made it?"

She caught her breath as another scream of agony pierced the chaos around them. "Did you hear that? They're still torturing Holly!"

He raised a hand. "Look! It's Philippe!"

"Philippe!" she cried. She allowed Tommy to drag her along as they caught up with Philippe, who embraced them both.

"Is Pablo with you?" he demanded, looking wildly around.

"No. And what about my dad?" Amanda murmured. "And what about Sasha?"

In the distance, Holly screamed again. Amanda cried out and turned in her direction. Tommy held her fast.

"We can't go back for her," Tommy said. "We can't go back."

"He's right, *petite,*" Philippe said, his face bloodless, his eyes filled with sorrow. "For now, we must stay alive, so we can save the others."

Tears streamed down Amanda's face as she turned back around.

Someday I will, she promised Holly. *I will come back for you. And for Nicole, too. I swear I will.*

Or I'll die trying.

★ ★ ★

From her perch in the mists of time, Pandion, the lady hawk of the Cahors, stirred from her perch and rose above time and perdition; above those damned and doomed to struggle and strive. She was the mystical symbol of the strongest witchblood line in all of human history, and as she soared and danced in the sky, she heard the screech of her immortal enemy, the hawk of the Deveraux, whose name was Fantasme.

Just as certainly as if they were enshrined in marble effigies, the players of life's pageant held their poses, frozen against rainbow-hued chronicles of what had already happened in the tangled tale of Cahors and Deveraux, and what would come to pass.

Worries were like mice to Pandion; fears were greater prey. She was of witchblood the greatest of all familiars, and so her motives could never be said to be purely good. The hunt stirred the blood; the pursuit was what propelled her essence from one century to the next. So it was with witchery and warlockhood—indeed, with all coventry—passions and hatreds, ambitions and thwarted dreams, kept the great Houses alive, whether they knew it or not.

And so, because Pandion so loved the Cahors, she was determined to rout their complacencies. They must not content themselves with small victories only, or they would fade with time. All would be dust.

This could not happen to those whom she was sworn to serve.

And so Pandion swooped and danced against the moon, celestial home of the Goddess, and prayed for obstacles, for thorns, for snares. Else, the most beloved of all witches—Holly Cathers, the heiress apparent of the throne of Cahors—would succumb to the tortures of Michael Deveraux, and all would be lost.

Despair would be Holly's lot, but not defeat.

With a cry of triumph, Pandion demanded that of the Goddess.

And winking in the cool ice light of a winter's Yule moon, the Goddess assented.

Holly Cathers was not yet done.

Nor were her covenates.

Nor was her love.

wicked

2

Spellbound

For those who hold me spellbound: Elise and Hank, Skylah and Belle, Teresa and Richard, Sandra and Belle . . . and our David, always. We all miss you, sweetie.

—Nancy Holder

To my mother, Barbara Reynolds, who has always loved me, encouraged me, and believed in me, thank you for everything.

—Debbie Viguié

ACKNOWLEDGMENTS

First of all, thank you, Debbie Viguié, for your friendship, your talent, and your dedication. And thank you to her husband, Scott, for your shoulder, your ear, and your wisdom. Lisa Clancy and Lisa Gribbin at Simon and Schuster, thank you both for all your care, editorial and otherwise. I have so much respect and affection for my agent, Howard Morhaim, and his assistant, Ryan Blitstein. For my many friends, I am so grateful—Dal, Steve, Lydia, Art, Jeff, Maryelizabeth, Melissa Mia, Von and Wes, Angela and Pat, and Liz Cratty Engstrom. Kym, you're the It girl. Thank you.

—N. H.

Thanks to my friend and coauthor, Nancy Holder, you are one in a million! Thanks, as always, to the fabulous team of Lisa Clancy and Lisa Gribbin at Simon and Schuster—what would we do without you? Thank you to Lindsay Keilers for your friendship. Thanks to Morris Skupinsky and Julie Gentile for all your love and support and my lucky contract/book-signing pen! Thank you to Super Librarian Rebecca Collacott (sorry for giving away your secret identity!). Thank you also to Michael, Sabrina, and most especially, Whisper.

—D. V.

Part One
Earth

☾

From the earth below we come
And upon its breast we live
We feed it with our death
Our bodies all we can give

Ashes to ashes and dust to dust
In Mother Earth we place our trust
And as we cycle through our years
We water it with blood and tears

ONE

ISIS

☾

We've scattered now all their bones
Ruined all their lives and homes
None can now escape Deveraux irc
As we burn them with midnight fire

Goddess hear us in the night
Save all Cahors within your sight
Help us not to count the cost
As we survey all we've lost

Seattle: Amanda and Tommy

The whole world was on firc. Trees exploded in showers of sparks, and bits of burning leaves fluttered toward the ground. They landed on Amanda Anderson's shoulders as she ran, and she did not have time to snuff them out. She could smell her hair burning, but she could not stop. She was being run to ground just like a wild animal, and she felt as small and insignificant as the squirrel that raced past her and shot up a tree, fleeing the smoke and the flames.

Behind her, unearthly screams pierced the night, howls of pain that could have come from either beast or man. She didn't turn around. People were dying, and she could not save them.

Beside her, her soul mate, Tommy Nagai, ran for his life, his breathing labored. His lungs were being seared by the same acrid smoke that was burning hers. Through the smoke she had lost sight of Philippe, her sister Nicole's true love; she hoped he was still beside Tommy, or at least behind him.

Goddess, keep us together. She sobbed, bereft and terrified, wondering if there was anywhere on the planet that such a prayer could come true. From Seattle to Paris to London and back again, Amanda and the other members of the Cahors Coven had run from Deveraux warlocks. Michael Deveraux had probably engineered the deaths of Holly's parents and attacked their family friend, Barbara Davis-Chin, so that the teenage Holly had no one to turn to except Amanda and Nicole's family in Seattle. Then he had had an affair with their mom, and Amanda was certain he was responsible for her death as well. He was closing in on Holly from all sides.

Michael's son Eli had been Nicole's "bad boy" boyfriend for a couple of years, but he had helped

James Moore, son of the Supreme Coven, kidnap Nicole and force her into marriage with James.

And now they've kidnapped her again.

And Jeraud Deveraux . . . who could say how much of all this was his fault? His own brother and father had burned him with Black Fire; he was hideous now, horribly scarred. He claimed to love Holly, but he was still a Deveraux warlock . . . and the vessel through which Jean Deveraux could attempt to finish the vendetta between the ancient, noble Deveraux and Cahors witch families, by murdering Amanda's cousin, Holly Cathers.

Michael Deveraux had won the battle, won the war. He and the forces of evil had been too powerful. Even with the Mother Coven helping them, Holly's coven had never stood a chance. Now almost everyone Amanda loved in the entire world was either dead or missing.

When Michael attacked them with his army and set their safe house on fire, Amanda had prayed all the spells and charms she could think of as her covenates scattered, racing from the burning cabin into the night. She didn't know if, with their own magic, the others had saved her and Tommy, or if it was just sheer luck that she and he had escaped into the trees relatively unscathed.

Whatever the reason, I am so grateful. So very, very grateful.

As she staggered along, defeated and terrified, she wasn't sure what she believed anymore. She used to think that the Goddess would protect them no matter what, that their powers could match that of Michael Deveraux.

That was before tonight, when James Moore and Eli had kidnapped her sister, Nicole, right out of the stronghold of the coven.

She used to believe that she could count on Holly to know what to do, even if it wasn't always what Amanda herself would have chosen. That was before Holly had been possessed by demons from the Dreamtime and had lost Jeraud Deveraux in the process. *We could have used him to fight his father,* she thought bitterly. Now she didn't even know if he was alive. *Just like everyone else.*

She used to believe there was safety in numbers, but even all the reinforcements sent by the Mother Coven had been helpless before the powers of darkness wielded against them. Now, for all she knew, she and Tommy were alone, the only two survivors of a very bad night.

We tried so hard. We tried for so long. How can it be that we failed? Doesn't right eventually prevail?

She wished she could ask Tommy some of these questions, but she couldn't spare any precious energy to speak. The flames were on their heels, racing all the faster because of the magic that was fanning them. They had to keep running. She could feel the heat fanning her back, burning her with its intensity. She glanced at Tommy. Sweat poured down his face, which was flushed. Her fear isolated her from him; though she loved him, she realized now that his love had limits, just like all love. He couldn't save her life simply by loving her. He couldn't make everything better.

But he can help me give it meaning, she thought, watching his strong back, barely visible through the smoke. *There are people worth living for. And dying for. And that's the blessing the Goddess has given us . . . and the curse. It makes us keep going . . . and makes us want to give up.*

She was exhausted. She hadn't slept in longer than she could remember, and it seemed like all she had been doing her entire life was fighting and running. *Especially running.* Maybe she should just stop and let the fire catch her, or Michael Deveraux, if he was back there. It would be so much easier. She was tired and sick of it all.

But the strange thing was that no matter how much she wanted to give up, she couldn't. A tiny spark flickered deep inside her chest—she could sense it rather than feel it—and she had no idea if that was her soul or her conscience or some other magical part of her.

I am a Lady of the Lily, she thought. *One of the Three Sisters. Holly carries most of our magic bloodline, but not all of it. I am one of the Cahors witches, even though my last name is Anderson, but Nicole and I are Cahors descendants, same as Holly.*

If something happens to Holly . . . if Nicole isn't . . . if she is dead, then I'm the only one . . .

She choked back a sob and violently shook her head. She was overwhelmed. She had already lost her mother. She refused to even consider that she might have lost other loved ones.

Nicole and I were finally getting close. She can't be dead. She has to be alive, because I can't stand any more dying.

Skeletal branches grabbed at her hair and ripped her clothes to shreds. Blood dripped down her forehead into her eyes, turning the world into a sea of heaving red. Still, she ran, and Tommy with her; and she was beginning to lose hope for Philippe.

Then, behind her, another explosion split the night air. She risked a glance back. It was massive, fissuring the earth like a nightmare earthquake. The tall copse of trees closest to her immediately burst into flames, and fireballs of branches and pinecones plummeted from the sky.

The resultant magical shock wave from the explosion threw her to the ground with such force that her ribs snapped, one by one by one, as if someone were ripping them from her backbone.

Somewhere nearby, Tommy screamed in agony.

The world was exploding; everything was blazing, even the ground. She looked up; a wedge of birds burst into flame and, screaming as one being, dropped into the firestorm that the forest had become.

Desperately she grabbed fistfuls of dirt and screamed, "Goddess help me!"

Though the fire raged around her, a centering quiet seized her thundering heart. As fear drained from her, the lack of tension was for a moment more unnerving than the terror had been. As lassitude crept over her, she felt vulnerable to further attacks.

"Be still," came a voice, a woman's voice. *"Be still; I will not leave you."*

"Goddess," she whispered. "Goddess."

"I will not leave you."

Amanda wearily closed her eyes.

Maybe you won't leave me, she thought, *but will you actually help me? Can you save me?*

Then she let the darkness take her, her last thought for Tommy.

If you can't save me, can you save him? Goddess, he is my life. Can you save him? I will do anything . . .

Anything . . .

"Ssh," the Goddess urged her.

And Amanda obeyed.

London, the Supreme Coven: Sir William

Sir William Moore, descendant of Sir Richard Moore, the famed Australian governor who had brought the Nightmare Dreamtime to the arsenal of his house, sat on the skull throne and chuckled. As head of the Supreme Coven, master and servant of evil, he was exhilarated by the death and despair that coursed through his very veins as, halfway across the world in Seattle, witches died. Michael Deveraux had done well.

But not well enough. For while it was true that many of the forces of light had been extinguished, there were three yet alive whom Sir William willed dead: Holly Cathers, and the twin sisters, Amanda and Nicole Anderson.

I can change that.

And I will.

Filled with confidence and grim purpose, he rose, his ceremonial midnight robes swirling around him. He was not surprised that Michael had failed to kill the three Cahors witches. It was clear that the warlock wasn't putting his heart into it. *He still believes that an alliance between the House of Deveraux and the House of*

Cahors would give his family enough power to overthrow me. Sir William chuckled again. Michael Deveraux was about to outlive his usefulness.

He is living on borrowed time, anyway, to borrow a cliché. I'm not sure he is aware that the threads of his existence have never left my fingers . . . and that my athame can cut a man's life to ribbons with unbelievable speed.

Sir William entered a tiny stone room that was empty save for a stone washtub and a chair upon which was folded a simple white garment. He disrobed and stepped into the warm water. Magics that required ritual purification were not to be taken lightly, not even by the leader of the Supreme Coven. The water for the bath had been brought by an innocent, a young serving girl unaware of the dark purposes of her master. Likewise the pure white robe had been brought by a delivery boy who had been instructed to place it in the room so that no other hands would touch it.

As soon as each of them had left the room, their throats had been cut by Sir William's favorite, one Alastair, and their bodies hefted into the dungeon. Nothing would go to waste; the Supreme Coven's *Book of Shadows* contained spells requiring all sorts of interesting portions of the human body . . . and the skull throne could always use another head or two. . . .

The stone room and everything in it was clean and

undefiled, and unknown to the outside world. Now it was Sir William's turn to be cleansed.

Clearing his mind of all emotion, all volition, all cognition, he scooped up the water and turned to the east. He sluiced it over his head, a mockery of Christian baptism, and allowed his muscles to slacken. In the spiritual form of freefall, he humbly submitted to the Dark God, who loved him and provided for him.

While in this limbo state, he allowed the dark forces to penetrate him, and to lift from his essence another small portion of his soul. He could sense their presence, feel the removal. There was a sharp pain for a moment, like a pinprick, and then it was over.

He had very little of his soul left, but so far, he had not missed it much. In truth, from what he had seen of those who were not children of the Horned God, souls weighed heavily and drained the joy and pleasure from their hosts.

Restoring himself to his own senses, the warlock performed the same obeisance to the west, the north, and the south, to the many aspects of the God: the Green Man; Pan; the Horned One; the Outcast Son of Light.

The purification and obeisance complete, Sir William donned the white garment—*interesting that both sides use white to much the same effect,* he noted idly, *the absence of prior limitation*—and imperiously waved his hand.

A section of the wall disappeared to reveal another room. It was brilliantly clean and devoid of any contents, save for a dozen life-size clay statues of men lying in four rows of three on the stone floor.

My Golems, he thought eagerly. *So useful, so professional. I love using them as minions.*

He rewalled the room and walked to the statuary. Though they currently reclined passively on their backs, they reminded him of the massive army of Qin dynasty terra cotta figures discovered in China three decades before. Though modern archaeologists had not realized it, Sir William knew the figures served a similar purpose as the dozen now lying before him: the bidding of those who knew how to control them.

Each statue was approximately six feet tall, each one clearly distinguishable from his fellows. Their faces were fierce and battle-ready; their expressions leered and spoke of violence and evil and a love of the hunt. On each of their foreheads was inscribed the word *emet,* which in the tongue of the ancients meant "truth."

He put his hand inside his white garment. Sewn into the skirt was a pouch, and in that pouch lay twelve pieces of vellum stolen from the Cathedral of Notre-Dame in Paris during one of the Supreme Coven's many aborted raids on the Mother Coven's Moon Temple.

Inside the mouths of the Golems he placed the strips of vellum. The creatures had no teeth; they expelled no breath. Once he brought them into life, the paper would still stay in place, as Golems had no voices with which to speak. It was the only flaw in otherwise perfect creatures.

While the houses of Deveraux and Cahors had spent centuries trying to destroy each other, House Moore had spent the time studying every form of magic known to man. It had been a wise and mature path . . . and one that was personally very rewarding for Sir William, for all their knowledge had all been passed down to him. He knew the secrets of the Australian aboriginals; the holy words of the Middle East; the rituals of shamans from countless different tribes . . . and he knew the secrets of the Kabalistic schools.

Golems sprang from that tradition: the veneration of the word. From thought to word sprang all creation—the earth, the heavens, and life within shapes of clay.

Sir William slowly walked around his unholy dozen, chanting in Hebrew. He called out the seventy-two names of God recorded in the Talmud. He did so carefully, precisely, for to make a slip would mean certain death to him. Each name corresponded to a limb or organ of the creatures on the ground. Each name called a part of the clay beings into life. To mispronounce a name would result in that organ or limb being misplaced on his own body.

Into the clay creatures he poured his spirit, his will, even as he breathed words of life over them. Ancient rabbis had created Golems for holy purposes. Ancient warlocks had learned how to twist that act of creation to their own dark purposes. The Golem became an extension of its creator, and any sins it might commit were placed on the head of the "father." Sir William could not hold back a smile. *It is a good thing I don't care about sins.*

At last the final name was pronounced. With a flourish, Sir William stepped back. *"Abracadabra,"* he intoned—a sacred word used so often, it had become a shorthand parody of magical forms. Few who spoke it mockingly understood that each syllable carried within it enormous potential for destruction . . . or grace.

The twelve forms on the ground shuddered into hideous life. Slowly, one by one, they rose, terrible in form, with blank, uncomprehending stares. Truly they were empty vessels waiting to be filled, to be commanded, to be given a purpose.

Sir William waved his hand at the four of them on

his left. "You, you will seek out the witch known as Nicole Anderson, of the ancient house Cahors. Destroy her."

The four beings nodded, their eyes filling with a flicker of intelligence as they grasped their duty. Faithful servants, they would obey him.

He turned to the four on his right. "You four shall seek out the witch known as Amanda Anderson, of the ancient House of Cahors. Destroy her."

Those four nodded as well. Their faces reflected an eagerness to please, like that of dogs willing to die or kill for their masters.

He faced the four directly in front of him. "And you four shall seek out the witch known as Holly Cathers, of the ancient House of Cahors. Destroy her. Grind her bones until they are dust and then scatter that to the winds."

They nodded eagerly, flexing the muscles along their shoulders. Sir William was pleased as he looked upon his creation. They would do their job well, never stopping, never resting. They would be completely relentless, fixed on one goal only. And when they had achieved it, the three witches would be dead.

He slowly lifted his arms into the air. "Now go, my children, and do my bidding."

He tapped each one on the chest, infusing them

with magic power. Each now had the ability to teleport through space. Slowly, the creatures vanished from his sight. When the last had gone, he smiled to himself. *Let's see the Rabbis top that.*

Four of the Golems didn't have far to go. The island of Avalon was heavily warded, though. Centuries of magic protected the place from all prying eyes and intruders. It wasn't by chance that no ship had accidentally run aground on its shores. The magics used to protect the island were powerful and indiscriminate.

Therefore, when the Golems tried to teleport there, they were repulsed—violently. The four creatures stood up on a distant shore, only slightly dazed, and shook themselves off. Then, with the single-minded unity of a common purpose, they headed off in search of a boat to try to reach the island.

Seattle: Richard

I'm back in the jungle again, knee-deep in the hooplah, and it's raining hell.

That was all Richard Anderson could think as the smoke stung his eyes and the sound of explosions pierced the air. He crouched down, the years seeming to fall off him as he zigzagged his way through the underbrush, the unconscious Barbara Davis-Chin draped over his shoulder. His eyes roved back and forth, probing the darkness.

By the time Dan Carter's cabin exploded, dozens of witches Richard had never seen fought valiantly to protect Amanda, Nicole, and everyone else trapped inside. The warrior witches had failed; and many had died while he was making his break for the tree line. One of the foreign men in the cabin had died horribly, cut in half by a pincered monster. Richard was sure more of his people would have been slaughtered if the witches hadn't come to their aid.

Thank God you showed, he thought. *Thank God you fought. I'm going to make damn sure your sacrifice was not in vain.*

Without a moment's hesitation, he'd hoisted Barbara over his shoulder. One of the European men gathered Kari Hardwicke into his arms and took off without a single look back.

Richard had seen Amanda and Tommy escape toward the north. He himself was moving east to force the enemy to divide its forces. His strategy was simple: to increase the number of targets for whoever was attacking them. If everybody moved in one large group, it would be easier for the enemy to pick them off.

Where's Nicole? he wondered now. *Where's my other little girl?*

A tree exploded in a shower of sparks to his left, and he jerked his face away, shielding his eyes. A distance behind him, a woman screamed, high and shrill. Her voice was cut off suddenly, in a gurgling rasp.

Oh God, don't let that be one of mine.

Forcing himself to move on, he stepped on a branch that cracked like a rifle. Wild animals shrieked with panic as the fire burned them out.

Richard stumbled over a smoking tree root; then, as he caught himself, the ground erupted with fire. A white-hot rock smacked him on his cheek. He flinched but stolidly kept going. A second explosion shot a tree into the air like a missile; then, from the gaping hole it left behind, a scaly demon with long ebony claws yanked itself from the earth.

Richard shifted Barbara's weight and kicked the creature in the jaw so hard, its head snapped back. Another kick snapped the bones in its neck; with a shriek, the thing collapsed on the ground, a jumbled heap of bones and horns. Richard leaped over it and raced on.

Another demon jumped in front of Richard, howling like a banshee. With his free hand, Richard unsheathed a knife with a wicked four-inch blade from his belt. He lunged forward and, in a merciless arc, slashed once at the creature's throat. It staggered to the side. He didn't know if he had actually injured it or just startled it. He didn't stop to look; he kept running.

A roaring sound punctuated by sharp snaps propelled the air behind him. The sap in the burning trees exploded like gunpowder, and Richard ducked as a branch went sailing over his head. It flew smack into the face of another demon, who hurtled itself toward Richard.

He changed directions and kept running.

He didn't know where the others were or if they were even alive. There would be time enough to worry about that later. Behind him he heard another unearthly shriek and felt something swipe at his back. Something like a claw scratched his skin. He did the only thing he could do: He kept running.

Seattle: Michael Deveraux

Holly Cathers was nuts.

As Michael's surprise began to ebb, a malicious wave of joy took its place.

The strongest witch on earth had lost her mind. And she was begging her mortal enemy for help.

It was too delicious. But it was true.

Standing beside him in the ashes of the cabin where the witches had made their stand, his ancestor, Duc Laurent, of the House of Deveraux, gave Holly an appraising once-over, then chuckled and shook his head. He locked gazes with Michael, obviously savoring the moment with the living, titular head of his family dynasty. For six hundred years, Laurent had waited for a moment such as this.

The Duc looked good for a man dead six hundred years. Then again, it helped that he had managed to give himself a new flesh-and-blood body so that he was no longer appearing as a moldering corpse.

"Possession," he intoned in his medieval French accent. "How did you manage it, my boy?"

In wonder, Michael shook his head. "I didn't. The God has smiled on us, Laurent."

Holly burst into pitiful, houndlike howls and clawed wildly at her face. She smacked her bleeding cheeks, yanked at her hair. Then she sank forward and buried her face into the smoking earth that bore the ashes of her coven. Abruptly she jerked up again, sobbing and waving her hands.

"Stay free of contact," Laurent warned him. "It's like a contagion. She could infect you."

Michael took that in; he knelt cautiously beside her, careful not to touch her or get in reach of her flailing hands.

"Make it stop," she whimpered, looking at him out of wild eyes. It was obvious she had no idea who he was. Wisps of hair were plastered to her face by streaks of blood. Saliva dripped from the corners of her mouth. "Make it stop, please." She threw back her head and screamed, "I can't bear this!"

"We can," Michael assured her. "We can make it stop."

She sobbed and began blithering, swaying like a cobra, lacing and unlacing her hands as she whispered to herself, "Make it stop, make it stop, make it stop . . ."

Tears sluiced down her cheeks. She was filthy, and she stank.

"I'm supposed to kill her," Michael said, bemused. "Sir William will be much happier with me once I do." He cocked his head, watching her. "If I *cure* her . . . aren't I aiding and abetting the enemy?" He smiled. "Holly Cathers, begging me for help. Begging me for anything."

"*Oui*. It is a moment," Laurent concurred. "But if you kill her, *mon fils,* the best you will be is Sir William's loyal follower. You will lose this compelling opportunity to raise our House to its rightful place."

Laurent was telling Michael nothing new. And he already knew what he would do. Still, it was so pleasant to have this special time, and to share it across the spans of time and space.

"Make it stop," she hissed, "stop, stop, stop."

Michael nodded at her. "I will," he said slowly and

deliberately, hoping his words could find a way to sink into her boiling brain, "but you have to do everything I tell you. You must obey me without question. Do you understand?"

She nodded fiercely. "Yes, I'll do anything you say, anything. Just make it *stop*!"

"Perhaps something in the Nightmare Dreamtime crawled its way into her mind. Several somethings, by the looks of her," he said to Laurent. "Could that be so?"

"*Vraiment.* I would assume so."

Michael wondered idly if his son, Jeraud Deveraux, was still alive. Jer and Holly had been in the Nightmare Dreamtime, trying to rescue one of Holly's loved ones, when Michael had finally managed to create the Black Fire again. It had been a triumphant moment . . . much like this one.

Michael nudged Holly with the toe of his expensive Italian boot. She didn't even notice, just moaned and kept rocking back and forth faster and faster. He had never seen anything quite like it.

He stood slowly and stared around at the hell that surrounded them. Fire blazed everywhere, escaping into the forest. It was too bad about the trees, really; they had been quite lovely. *More casualties of the Deveraux-Cahors war.* He bowed his head for a moment in the appearance of reverence and muttered a prayer to the God to allow quick rebirth to the trees.

He smirked to himself. *What was it that Treebeard said in* The Lord of the Rings*? Ah yes: A wizard should know better than to destroy the forest.* Unlike Saruman, Michael refused to incur the wrath of the forest gods and guardians.

New trees would spring up, though, from the ashes. That was the beauty of nature, the cycle always continued. He glanced down at Holly, and a smile twisted his lips. For Holly and her friends, though, there would be no renewal, no rebirth—only death.

That's fine by me.

Seattle: Amanda

The new day dawned at last, and the sunrise dripped with ravishing colors—prismatic, jewel-toned hues of tangerine and vermilion refracting on the smoke.

Amanda was surprised. She had thought it would never come, or if it did, that she wouldn't be alive to see it. Yet, the sun was there, shedding watery sunlight on the charred bones of what had once been an exquisite forest. By its light, Amanda could see a little motel, perched just beyond the edge of the trees. Exhausted, bruised, and broken, she began to limp toward it.

Beside her, Tommy shuffled along, dragging himself painfully along. He had stayed with her throughout the night, and she knew she owed him her life for that. Had he not been there she would have lain down and died any number of times. His strength had buoyed her, saved her. Now, as she detected his gasps of pain in every step he took, she knew she must do the same for him.

She clasped his hand and willed her energy to mingle with his, willed her battered body to aid his so that they might share each other's pain and help heal each other. A strangled sob from him was proof that it was working, and tears stung her eyes as his pain washed through her. He, too, was bruised and broken, and her cracked ribs groaned in sympathy with his.

He has borne so much for me, because he loves me. Tommy didn't have to be here, but he was. With a rush of conviction she knew that he would always be there, and that with the last breath he drew he would be calling her name.

Somehow that made things a little bit better. Nicole was gone, kidnapped by Eli and James. Holly was insane and perhaps dead by now. Tante Cecile, a woman who had been almost an aunt to Amanda herself, had died trying to save Holly. The Goddess alone knew where the others were, including her father, and if they were even alive. Still, Tommy was here.

And so was the Goddess. Lying in the dirt for hours, Amanda had heard the still, small voice that so many others had claimed to hear. The soft female voice whispered words of encouragement to Amanda, commanding her not to give up, to keep going.

She had always believed that the Goddess existed. *It's kinda hard to question when you can suddenly levitate stuff and dead ancestors start speaking through your cousin.* Still, despite all the supernatural stuff, the Goddess had never appeared or spoken to her. She had only appeared to Holly. At first, Amanda had been jealous, and then, as things got really crazy, relieved. Sometimes it was just easier not to have so much . . . reality to deal with.

Amanda had never been a leader, but she knew that was going to have to change; the Goddess had told her heart that, had spoken to her and lifted her to her feet back in the forest when all she'd wanted to do was lie in the dirt. She felt like either laughing or crying, and she wasn't sure which. She was an unlikely leader, as the only one who had ever followed her anywhere was Tommy.

Now she turned to look at him. They were in thrall, the Lady to the Lord, and she was so very, very happy about it. Whatever magic and strength each of them had at their command would be shared with the other. He looked like he was going to drop from exhaustion. That was pretty much how she felt. They both needed rest, and soon.

She squeezed his hand. The motel didn't seem so far off; she figured if they could just hold on for five more minutes, they would make it.

He turned to her and said, "Agreed."

Her lips parted. "Did you read my mind?"

Tommy smiled faintly. "I've always been able to read your mind, Amanda. In my own way."

"I was pretty clueless about you," she confessed.

"I know. But now—"

"Now." She leaned toward him for a kiss. It was a very sweet moment.

They trudged on, though she was buoyed as they stumbled the last of the distance in silence. Amanda gradually became preoccupied with willing one foot to step in front of the other, and her thoughts about the Goddess and Tommy faded into the background until they were nothing more than a gentle hum in the back of her mind. A few more steps and they would be there.

She looked up and spied a lone figure staring at them. It was hard to tell through the torn clothing and the burned hair and face, but he looked familiar. They staggered to him, and her heart jumped. It was Pablo, the youngest member of the White Magic Coven. The boy looked wild, and his left eye gazed fiercely at her. His right eye was swollen shut.

Relief flooded through her to find someone else alive. She nearly ran the last couple of feet, dragging Tommy behind her.

At last they stood face-to-face. For a moment, no one spoke.

Then tears welled in Pablo's eyes. "I could feel you," he said, his voice sharp, almost accusing. "Back in the forest I could feel you. I couldn't reach you, but I knew that you would end up here, so I came."

"How long have you been waiting?"

"A few hours."

She stared at him. Pablo had a gift that none of the rest of them did: He could read minds, feel people's thoughts, even track people using them. She felt her throat constrict as she asked, "And the others?"

He shook his head slowly. "I do not know. Once, I thought I felt Philippe, but *duende,* his life force, was flickering." He took a deep breath. "I have felt no one else since the cabin."

She nodded her head slowly.

"We should get cleaned up and try to get some rest," Tommy ventured. His voice was hoarse, barely a whisper, and the sound startled her.

"You're right," she said, looking uneasily toward the lobby. "I don't have anything with me, though—no identification, no credit cards."

"Good." Tommy was grimly satisfied. "We don't want to use anything that can be traced."

"But, I don't have any cash, either. Do you?" she asked.

He shrugged. "Nope."

"Then how will we pay?" she protested, wrapping her arms around herself in an effort to keep her ribs from shifting.

Tommy turned and looked at her fondly. "Ms. Anderson, I've always been a standup guy, right?"

"Yes," she said, somewhat confused.

"You've never known me to steal or cheat or lie?"

"No, never."

"Then take that into account when I tell you this. We don't have any money? Not a problem. You're a witch. Do a damn spell."

She nearly laughed in shocked embarrassment. Of course Tommy was right. They had just survived a war, and the three of them needed shelter. She set her jaw and turned on her heel, leaving the two guys behind.

She marched up to the front desk and looked the startled clerk straight in the eye. "I need a quiet room with two beds."

"I'll need a credit card and some identification," the clerk stuttered.

"I already showed them to you," she told him, her voice dropping lower. She willed her words to wash over him and through him, imbued them with the power to cloud his perceptions of reality.

His eyes glazed over slightly. "I'm sorry, you're right. How long will you be staying?"

"I'll let you know," she assured him.

He nodded absently and handed her a room key. She took it, gave him one last mental push for good measure, and walked out the door. Outside, her knees shook a little, but she kept walking.

She collected Tommy and Pablo, and they all made it to the room. It was clean and much larger than she had expected.

She turned and took her first good look at Tommy since the entire thing had begun. He stared back at her with eyes open wide, and she felt a strange urge to laugh.

Tommy's eyebrows were completely gone, sacrificed to the fire that had tried to consume all of them. Without them, his face looked almost comical. Reflexively she put her hand to her own brows. They felt like they were still there.

With a puzzled look, Tommy mimicked her

motion. His eyes widened when he realized what she had been staring at. He turned and gazed at himself in the bathroom mirror. "Talk about playing with fire," he quipped.

Amanda felt an intense surge of love for him. Tommy had always known how to lighten her mood. She slowly turned her head until she, too, faced the mirror.

She didn't recognize herself. Staring back from the mirror was a young woman with tattered clothes. Dried blood soaked what was left of the material in several places, most noticeably over her ribs on her right side. What wasn't covered with blood was caked with dirt. Her eyes were wild, flashing underneath a mop of burnt hair. The left side of her face was completely covered in blood.

No wonder I freaked out the guy at the front desk.

Silently, Pablo came to join them, and the three stared at their battered reflections. Amanda's throat tightened. *Is this it? Are we all that's left of the coven?* She willed herself not to cry. Her face already had enough gunk on it; the last thing she needed was to wet it all down and have it everywhere.

Reflected in the glass, tears began to slide down Pablo's face. She put an arm around him as she began to lose it too. Tommy put his arm around her. For a moment the trio continued to stare into the mirror. It was like a warped family portrait. A collective shudder went through the group, and then they collapsed on the floor, hugging and crying and screaming.

TWO

HECATE

☾

Thorns twist and pierce the flesh
Keep the wounds nice and fresh
Count the bodies one through ten
Then bleed them all once again

Tears we cry for the dead
With our hearts full of dread
Goddess fill us with your power
Even in our darkest hour

Avalon: Nicole Anderson

The more things change, the more they stay the same, Nicole thought bitterly as she glanced around the bedroom. So much had happened in the last few days and yet here she was, right back in James's bedroom as though nothing had happened. At least this time it was a different bedroom. She didn't know for sure where she was, but she knew it wasn't the headquarters of the Supreme Coven.

Tears of frustration stung her eyes. She had been reunited with her sister and her father, her cousin had been possessed, and she had been put in thrall to Philippe. *Philippe.* Now she didn't even know if he was alive, much less whether she would ever see him again.

Meow!

She glanced down at Astarte. The cat was gazing up at her intently, and her tail was curling and uncurling around Nicole's left ankle. The cat had jumped into the portal after her when James and Eli had kidnapped her from the house in Seattle. She picked the cat up and pressed her to her cheek.

"Last time I left Seattle, I left my cat, Hecate, behind. She died. You are my own sweet cat, now, and you won't let me leave you, will you?"

The cat batted her nose with a paw and purred contentedly. Nicole kissed the top of her head. Astarte had come to her in the Spanish countryside when she had been running from the Deveraux. Philippe had taken care of the cat after Nicole had been kidnapped by Eli and James the first time.

Eli and James. They had pulled her through the portal and they had landed back on the island. Without a word, Eli had left and James had escorted her back to his bedroom before locking her in. This time he had placed magical as well as physical barriers on the door.

It's a new doorjamb, she noticed idly. She had destroyed it when she'd escaped the first time. *Either that or he used magic to fix it. . . .*

Astarte twisted in her arms, and Nicole put her down, before she straightened wearily and sat down on the bed.

There had to be something she could do. *I'm a witch, for goodness sake. I should be able to help myself.* She closed her eyes and forced herself to breathe deeply.

"Goddess, now hear me cry, protect me now, don't let me die, I lift my face to the moon and beg you grant deliverance soon."

The words filled her with power, or, at the very least, a new courage. She turned and opened the hidden compartment in the headboard. It was empty. James was too smart to put his ring and other things back there, given that she had tried to take them before. She turned and spied a small table standing in the corner. She crossed to it and pulled out the single drawer. There was some paper, a pen, and a handful of candles. *At least it's something.*

She picked up the pen and carefully, methodically drew a pentagram upon the ground. "Earth, wind, fire, water, spirit," she blessed each point of the star as she drew it.

She stepped back to observe her handiwork. The

circle around the star looked more like an oval, but given what she had to work with, she figured the Goddess wouldn't mind.

Next she selected five white candles and set each one of them at each point of the star. Once finished, she sat down in the center. She closed her eyes and reached backward in her mind, back past all the pain and terror. When she practiced magic with Amanda and Holly it was so forced, as though she were making everything happen by sheer strength of will.

She fought to remember a different time, one of innocence, before the darkness had come. Back when she hadn't known of her witchly heritage, back when her mother was still alive.

Magic had been so simple then, when she hadn't known what she was doing. She sat quietly, trying not to force the magic, but just to let if flow through her and around her. She felt the warmth of Astarte's body as the cat came to her and curled up in her lap.

She slowly opened her eyes. She placed her finger on the candle before her. Fire jumped into being. Quietly, she moved her finger from candle to candle until all five were ablaze.

"My will is strong, my purpose right, protect me now from evil's sight. I call upon thee, Goddess fair, hearken now to my prayer. Keep me safe from beast and man, I entrust my fate to the Maiden's hand."

A rushing wind filled the room, making the candles' fire dance, though they did not extinguish. She gasped as the wind rushed through her, filling her in a moment with a peace she had never known.

Deep within the castle, on a table in the wizard's workshop, the sorcerer's hat began to glow.

Seattle: Michael Deveraux

Michael placed his scrying stone down with a loud *thump*. He had been trying to use it to find his son, Eli, and James Moore. It had not worked. *They must be blocking me,* he thought angrily. With Holly subservient to him, it was the perfect time to try to claim the Throne of Skulls, leadership of the Supreme Coven. Unfortunately, he needed Eli's and James's help to do so.

"If only I could summon the Black Fire by myself." He sighed, more to himself than to the imp chattering away on the back of the sofa in his living room.

He turned and gazed at Holly for a long moment before shaking his head. The girl was huddled in a corner with her knees tucked under her chin, muttering to herself. Even if he could explain to her how to help him summon the Black Fire, it would be too dangerous with her in this condition. No, he would just have to find his son.

He observed Holly quietly for a moment. Her magic and her potential were nearly boundless. If only he could find a way to merge it with his own. Fortunately the insanity that made her unpredictable and dangerous also kept her unfocused enough to diffuse her power and some of the spells she sent out at random intervals. It was almost safer for him to have her in this state. *Tell that to my lamps,* he thought with a grim laugh. The one thing she seemed hell-bent on avoiding was the light. *Is that the witch in her or the demons?* He didn't know. She had managed to destroy several valuable antique lamps before he had subdued her. He was lucky, though. If the insanity hadn't kept her energy unfocused, she would have destroyed the entire building they were standing in. *And us along with it.*

If I could harness her power, I would be unstoppable. It would be easy enough to place her in thrall; there is no will there to circumvent. He knew that Jer had passed up an opportunity to be put in thrall with Holly. *Fool. He didn't understand the kind of power he was turning away. Together they could have destroyed me.*

He crouched down and approached her slowly, palm extended, as if she were a wild animal. She shrank away from his hand when she saw it, retreating even farther into her corner. He sat quietly, waiting.

He could be very patient when he wanted to be. He had wooed many a wild woodland animal in just such a manner, building trust with them until they would come to him.

The bloodstains on his altar could attest to that.

Mother Coven: Santa Cruz, California

People went to the Santa Cruz Mountains in search of peace and quiet, a deeper communion with nature, or a place to hide. A person could lose themselves on any of the dozens of tiny nameless streets or winding access roads. The mountains were home to executives from Silicon Valley seeking a higher standard of living; old hippies in denial of the fact that the sixties were over or hiding from a government they thought still cared about finding them; and witches.

Up at the very top of Summit Road was a tiny dirt path that led even higher up the mountain. It wound through the trees, hundreds of feet above the last of the Christmas tree lots that covered the mountains. At the end of the dirt path was a driveway, guarded by two giant stone cats. The cats looked Egyptian, with their long necks and alert sitting posture. At the end of the driveway, guarded by cats and wards and the Goddess herself, was a house.

A visitor—if any ever happened to come to the

wild and isolated place—would have an overwhelming sense of peace and life. The spirits of the woods and streams were alive here. Even the very trees seemed to breathe upon one, their breath the silvery mist that draped the land.

The tranquillity without the house was unearthly. The suffering inside it was unreal.

The closest thing to what it was, was a field hospital in a war zone. This hospital was owned and run by the Mother Coven, and the suffering women inside it had fought Michael Deveraux and his family to save Holly Cathers and her coven.

Lying in a bed in an upstairs room of the house, Anne-Louise was lucky she wasn't dead. The same couldn't be said for dozens of her sisters. Yet, as she lay in bed nursing thirty broken bones, she didn't feel lucky. Actually, she felt pissed. The healers of the coven were working overtime, not just on her but on others as well. Still, it would be a couple of weeks before she or the others would regain any semblance of normalcy.

She glared at the High Priestess of the Mother Coven, who was standing at the foot of her bed. The other woman actually looked nervous. She had not been present at the slaughter. In fact, of all the witches of the Mother Coven, only a small percentage had been present, and most of those were the weaker covenates.

Still, the High Priestess was standing before her, murmuring platitudes. "We did the best we could—"

"Really?" Anne-Louise managed to ask, her voice a throaty whisper. Her vocal cords had been badly burned, and there was a chance they might not recover—even with witches for her healers.

"The forces allied against us were too strong. We must conserve our strength now, prepare for battle—"

"While our enemies only grow stronger?"

The High Priestess remained silent, her eyes skittering away toward the door and then back again.

"You want to know what I think?" Anne-Louise asked. She continued, not waiting for an answer. "I think the Mother Coven has no intention of trying to save those three girls or their coven. I think you're just hoping that Michael Deveraux kills them all. Then the Mother Coven can return to 'business as usual.' If the Mother Coven were truly opposed to the Supreme Coven, we would have acted against them years ago."

The High Priestess seemed to bristle at that. "The Mother Coven has always stood against the Supreme Coven," she hissed.

"Really? Then how come the Supreme Coven is still standing? How come both Covens are still around if they are so bent on destroying each other? No, I think that having a visible enemy to point to has been good business for both sides. It keeps us from fighting amongst ourselves, and questioning the leadership of our superiors."

The High Priestess blanched, and if Anne-Louise wasn't mistaken she saw fear creeping into the other woman's eyes. She pressed on.

"If not, then why did you only send the weakest of our coven to fight, or those who held any sympathy for the girls at all, *or those who ever questioned anything you do?*"

Silence, pregnant as the full moon, descended on the room. Anne-Louise stared at her leader. She had probably shocked the other woman. Anne-Louise had been orphaned at a young age and had been raised in the coven. She had always been the good little witch, doing as she was told, going where she was ordered, even studying only that which she was instructed to.

Now she didn't care. Maybe it was the pain, maybe it was the aftereffect of witnessing the slaughter of her friends and sisters, maybe it was a lifetime of unasked questions that finally demanded answers. Whatever it was, she knew that she had hit a nerve with the High Priestess. The woman was in danger of losing her place in the coven. Anne-Louise wasn't the only one questioning her judgment since the battle.

She continued to stare at her, when six days ago she wouldn't even have met her eyes. The world had changed, though. *I have.* She had always viewed the High Priestess as the anointed of the Goddess, almost a deity in her own right. Now she just saw a tired woman, one who looked more frightened than any of the young women who had faced death two nights before.

All Anne-Louise knew was that she would not blink first. The High Priestess lifted her chin slightly, seeming to rally her mystique back around her. Her eyes began to flash with heat and power, *real* power.

The door opened, and three witches glided in, shattering the moment. They closed the door, and the High Priestess turned to formally greet them. They all dipped their heads in acknowledgment.

"You are to come to work some more on Anne-Louise." It was a statement, not a question. The three nodded their heads and moved to the bed.

"I will leave you then to their ministering," the High Priestess informed Anne-Louise. She smiled coolly and left the room, gliding through the closed door. It was a simple show of power, but one that Anne-Louise had to admit was quite effective.

She closed her eyes as the healers laid their hands on her broken body. She could feel heat flashing through her, agonizing in its intensity. Dislocated shards of bone began to right themselves in her body, tearing even more flesh and muscle as they did so. Soon, they would begin to knit back together, but not today. They first had to find all the bone fragments.

Anne-Louise lay quietly. The healers had gone again, for a while at least having done their best to numb her pain. Still, it hurt to move, to even breathe.

Mew!

She opened her eyes just as a gray cat leaped up onto the bed beside her. The cat stared at her with large, unblinking eyes. "Where did you come from?" she asked in a tortured whisper.

The cat began to purr as it continued to stare at her.

"Do you have a name?"

Whisper.

"Whisper, yes, that does suit you," she said, feeling herself grow groggy.

The cat curled up against her side, lending her body heat to her. A feeling of well-being began to spread through Anne-Louise, and she fell asleep with a smile touching her lips.

Tri-Coven: Seattle

Amanda awoke to the sun streaming into her eyes. She rolled onto her side with a groan but quickly sat up as her cracked ribs screamed in protest. She choked back a sob. Next to her, Tommy stirred. She glanced at the clock. It was nine A.M. They had been asleep nearly twenty-four hours.

She glanced over and saw Pablo sitting on the other bed. His face was scrunched up like he was in pain.

"Are you okay?" she asked, her heart starting to pound in fear.

He looked at her and his eyes were glazed over. He nodded slowly. "Someone is close, one of ours. I'm not—" He stopped. "I'm not quite sure who. They don't feel . . . right."

"Then how do you know they're one of ours?" she asked, heart pounding faster.

He shook his head. "That's the only thing I can read clearly."

She nodded. She would just have to accept that. It didn't make her happy, but Pablo's gifts were not hers to understand. At least he was sure that it was a friend. She felt a ray of hope. Maybe it was her father, or maybe Nicole had escaped. *Or it could be Holly.* She shuddered and instantly felt ashamed of herself. She didn't wish any harm to Holly, but in her cousin's possessed state, Amanda also wasn't sure she could face her. *Not just yet.*

"Are they close?" she asked Pablo, praying to the

Goddess that they were. She would rather know soon than spend hours wondering.

"*Sí,* about a mile away." He stood up. "I will go and see."

She stood, too, doing her best to ignore the fire in her side. "I'll go with you." She glanced at Tommy. "We'll let him sleep. He's earned it."

Pablo nodded sympathetically. "We all have, *señora,* we all have."

She was about to correct him, to tell him that since she was not a married woman, she was a *señorita*. Then she glanced at Tommy. They had been placed in thrall, the most sacred ceremony between a man and a woman in Coventry. A lump formed in her throat. Pablo then was correct in a way. In his eyes, those of a young man born and raised in Coventry, she was a *señora*.

She scribbled a note to Tommy on the hotel stationery in case he awoke and she was not there. Then they exited the room, locking the door behind them. She warded the door, something she should have done the night before. *But all the wards in the world didn't save us,* she thought, remembering the cabin and the demons breaking into it.

She shuddered and almost couldn't leave. She began to panic. What if she didn't come back? Or worse, what if she returned to find Tommy dead or gone? She didn't know if she could handle that. In an agony of indecision, with tears sliding down her cheeks, she reached for the doorknob.

Pablo gently grabbed her wrist, stopping her. "If anything is going to happen, it will happen whether you are here or not," he told her. "Perhaps he is even safer without you."

She stared into Pablo's eyes. He was a couple of years younger than she was, but the wisdom of a far older man shone forth from his eyes. She knew that he was right.

Together they turned and headed back to the forest from which they had dragged themselves the day before. When they reached the timber line, they stopped.

"Can you tell where they are?" she asked.

Pablo closed his eyes for a moment, then opened them and nodded. "They're closer. Maybe half a kilometer away."

She tried to ignore the chill that danced up her spine, but she couldn't quite do it. Pablo stepped into the trees and began walking. She squinted for a moment along the direction he was traveling, but couldn't see anything. Heart in her throat, she followed.

Pablo was like a bloodhound, stopping every minute or so as if to pick up the scent. Every line of his body was taut, alert, and she couldn't help but admire him. He was more in touch with his instincts than anyone she had ever seen. Suddenly he stopped, head up, and held his hand up for her to listen.

She couldn't hear anything. She closed her eyes, trying to *feel* something. There was nothing. She opened her eyes. "Where?" she finally whispered.

Pablo shook his head. "Here."

The hairs on the back of her neck stood on end. "Where?"

"Right here," a voice said, nearly in her ear.

She screamed and jumped toward Pablo, twisting in midair.

A massive creature with dull black skin and flashing eyes stood before her. It was over six feet tall, with a hump on its back, and bulging muscles. A loincloth was wrapped around its midsection.

It opened its mouth and spoke again. "Hello, sweetheart."

Amanda blinked. "Daddy?"

The creature nodded, and she took a closer look. It was indeed her father. He had something slung over his back and he was coated in soot and mud from head to toe. Relief flooded through her.

"Daddy!" she cried, flinging herself against his chest. He wrapped an arm around her and hugged her tight. For a moment she was five again. Her daddy was there and he would make everything all right, he would protect her from the world.

"Princess," he said at last, bringing her back to the present. "We need to keep moving."

She pulled away slowly and only then realized that what he had slung over his back was Barbara Davis-Chin. Startled, she looked back to her dad. "Is she—"

"She's alive."

"Come with us—we have a place," Pablo said. He headed off back toward the motel.

They fell into step behind him. Amanda walked beside her father, touching his arm from time to time to assure herself that he was real. Within ten minutes they made it back to the motel.

Inside, Tommy was awake and he broke into a huge grin when he saw them.

Richard slowly lowered his human burden onto a bed and then straightened. He stared Tommy in the eyes, and then reached out to embrace him. "It's good to see you, son."

As they embraced, Amanda began to cry. She moved forward, and they welcomed her into their circle until the three of them were hugging and crying.

Tears flowed along with warmth; the three of them were bonding, becoming a new sort of family.

This is a gift from you, Goddess, Amanda acknowledged. *Thank you.*

Richard finally pulled away, and Amanda and Tommy sank down onto the bed beside Barbara's inert form.

Pablo was already inspecting Barbara. The three looked on while he completed his exam. "She's good. In her soul."

Richard nodded. "A couple of times she came to, and then passed out again about three hours ago. She seems more at ease."

"She needs rest. You, too," Pablo said pointedly.

"I need a shower first, if no one minds," Richard said, already heading for the bathroom.

Amanda sat quietly for the next twenty minutes. Twice she heard the water in the shower turn off only to be turned back on again. At last it turned off and stayed off. After another minute, her father reappeared with a towel wrapped around his waist.

Scars shone on his chest. Some were small, barely visible. Others were larger, some the size of a quarter. One in particular caught her eye. It was a long, jagged scar that stretched from the area above his heart to the middle of his stomach. With a start she realized that she had never seen him with his shirt off. Even when they used to go on vacation when she was little, he had always had a tank top on when he'd gone swimming.

He smiled grimly as though sensing her thoughts. He sat down on the other bed and threw another towel over his shoulder, partly covering his chest. "They're from the war, honey. They're a part of me that I tried for too long to leave behind." He glanced down for a moment and then looked back at her, a faraway look in his eyes. "Maybe if I hadn't, your mom would have—"

He stopped abruptly with a quick shake of his head and plastered a smile on his face. Amanda grimaced. She knew he was talking about her mom's affair with Michael Deveraux, who had later been instrumental in killing her. Back then, her dad had been what could only be described as "boring." Marie-Claire, ever the exciting and flamboyant parent, had sought excitement elsewhere. Amanda herself had often wondered if her mom would still be alive if her dad had only been more exciting—or, at least more vigilant in guarding his wife from other men.

She, too, shook her head. It was too late to change the past. Maybe her mom's death had been inevitable, anyway. She might have died any number of times or a number of ways since, like others had a few days before.

She glanced at Pablo. The others of his coven,

Philippe, Armand, and Alonzo, were still missing. She wondered if he could feel anything from them. If they were dead, he would be alone in the world. *Except for us.* She grimaced. *We might all be dead soon enough.*

Her thoughts drifted to the others who were missing: Sasha, Silvana, Kari, Holly, Dan, and Tante Cecile. *No,* she corrected herself, *Tante Cecile is dead, killed by the demons possessing Holly.* The reality of that hit her hard, but she had to let herself care. *Otherwise I'm no better than Michael Deveraux.*

Then there were the two who were certifiably missing. Jer Deveraux was still trapped in the Dreamtime, where he and Holly had gone to rescue Barbara. The Goddess only knew if he was alive, but Amanda prayed he was. The other, Amanda's twin, Nicole, had been kidnapped by Eli Deveraux and James Moore right before the battle had broken out. Amanda clenched her fists at her side. *I swear I'll find you and get you away from those monsters.*

Richard spoke, interrupting her thoughts. "All right, first thing's first."

He retrieved his wallet from Barbara's pocket. He pulled out several bills. "Tommy, you look more presentable than the rest of us. Go buy some clothes for everyone, including the others. We also need medical supplies and food."

Tommy took the money and saluted. "I'm on it," he said, already heading out the door.

Amanda felt herself starting to panic as he left, but her father's voice snapped her attention back to him. "Amanda, I need you to look after Barbara. See if there's anything you can do to help her, a spell or something. We need her intact, both body and mind. Also, can you set up an alarm, sort of a magic-motion sensor, to let us know if anyone is coming?"

She nodded. "I think I can do something like that." Her stomach started doing flip-flops. She was not at all sure she could do as he asked. Holly was the strongest of them. Still, she would try.

"Good, get started," Richard instructed his daughter. He saw the fear flashing in her eyes, but he saw resolve there as well. That was good. It was best to give her a challenge, something for her to worry about besides Tommy's safety.

He turned to Pablo and sized up the young man. "I understand you can sense others?"

The boy nodded. "That's how I found you."

"That's what I figured. From what I heard Nicole saying, you can also keep others from finding us?"

He nodded. "I can keep them from finding us using magic means, but not ordinary ones."

Richard nodded. "That was our mistake with the cabin. It was an obvious place to look for us. This, at least, is a little less likely. There are dozens of places we could have come out of the forest that were a lot closer to the cabin, in case they're looking for us. We should be safe for a little while, at least."

"I don't think he's looking for us yet."

"Good. Now, have you felt any of the others?"

Pablo shook his head glumly.

Richard reached out and squeezed his shoulder. "Try, Pablo, please."

He didn't tell the boy that he had seen one of his coven die. Until Richard knew who it was, he wasn't going to upset him.

No sooner had the thought entered his mind than Pablo glanced at him sharply, eyes narrowing. He felt pressure, as though, someone were pushing against his brain, trying to get in. He pushed back. *Don't go there, boy.*

Looking startled and guilty, Pablo dropped his eyes. Richard gave his shoulder one last squeeze before standing up. He moved as far away from the others as he could in the cramped quarters.

Tommy returned sooner than Richard had expected. Amanda called out an alert, and a moment later there was a knock on the door. Even as Richard opened it for Tommy he knew they had to have a lot more warning than that in case the next arrival was not so friendly.

The young man dumped his findings out on the bed not occupied by Barbara. He had several sets of sweat-shirts and sweatpants all sporting the logo WASHINGTON. He also had socks, a newspaper, a small first-aid kit, and a bag full of groceries. "There's a general store right next to the lobby," he explained.

Richard nodded, grabbing a pair of sweats and some socks and heading to the bathroom to change. Clean and now warm, he emerged feeling like a new man. Amanda headed for the rest room next and while she was in there, Tommy and Pablo also took the opportunity to change clothes.

When Amanda reappeared she gave Tommy a fierce hug, which Richard dutifully appeared not to notice. Amanda had always been his baby. Nicole had been flamboyant, wild, more like her mother. Amanda, though, had always been strong and steady. For years it had been the two of them against the rest of the world. As happy for her as he was, it was still hard to see his little girl as a woman.

Pablo broke into his thoughts. "I feel people!" he said, his voice cracking with excitement.

"How many?" Amanda asked.

"Two. I feel Armand and Kari."

★★★

Kari stumbled along, Armand's strong arm supporting her. The last thirty-six hours were a blur of pain and confusion. She didn't even remember leaving the cabin. Armand had spoken only a few words to her. All she really knew was that the cabin had caught fire, he had carried her out, and the others might be dead. Several times she fell and thought about staying down, but every time, he picked her back up and spoke a few encouraging words.

So, she marched on, unsure what the future held, or if there would even be a future for her. How had she gotten herself into this mess? She was just a grad student; she studied the occult, she didn't participate in it. That had all changed, though, when Jer Deveraux had introduced his dangerous world into her life. Not like she'd given him much choice.

She didn't dare ask Armand if he knew what had happened to Jer's body when the cabin caught on fire. Jer's spirit was on an astral plane, trapped in the Dreamtime. At least, she hoped he was just trapped and not dead. If his body had been destroyed, though, it was moot. If he had no body to return to, his spirit would wander forever. *Or maybe it would just vanish instantly,* she thought.

She tried banishing such thoughts from her mind, but it wasn't easy. Love was hell and she was the queen of the damned.

Seattle, 1904: Peter and Ginny

Ginny stood on the train platform as the tears coursed down her cheeks. Her husband, George Morris, was already on board, waiting for her. In moments they would be steaming their way toward Los Angeles, leaving behind everyone else she loved.

Her father, Peter, wrapped his arms around her. Together they had been through so much: the death of her mother in the Johnstown flood, the journey west to settle in Seattle, and the tears and pain and unexpected joy when he had found dear Jane, who had become his second wife.

She stepped back, wiping the back of her gloved hand against her nose. It was an unladylike gesture, but she didn't care. Peter touched his hand to her cheek, and she closed her eyes, imagining that she was once again small and that he would always be beside her.

"Los Angeles is not that far away," he tried to reassure her, his voice cracking.

It was a lie, and not a very convincing one. Los Angeles was a world away, and the thought of leaving him and her half-sister was overwhelming. As though sensing her thoughts, Veronica spoke up.

"I will come visit you when you are settled, I promise."

Ginny looked to her sister and saw her pain mirrored in the girl's face. She had the eyes of a child and the body of a grown woman. How easy it was to forget that they were a few years apart in age.

Then Veronica flew into her arms, and they embraced tightly, each fearing to let go. At last Ginny whispered in Veronica's ear, "I know you are young, but Father will accept Charles and permit you to wed if you just give him a chance to see how good he is to you."

Veronica's slender form began to shake, racked by sobs that she muffled against Ginny's shoulder. They stood for a moment more until the conductor shouted the last call.

Ginny reluctantly pulled away and quickly kissed her father's cheek before stepping up onto the train. She clasped the rail with one hand and waved fiercely with the other as the train groaned and began to slowly move.

Her father and Veronica waved back, and Ginny kept waving until they were lost from her sight. Tears streaming down her face, she turned and entered the car. Her husband, George, was waiting for her and held out his arms to her. She sank down into the seat beside him and spent her tears upon his breast. He stroked her hair gently, murmuring words of love and comfort that she scarcely heard.

"I am eager to start our new life together in Los Angeles, but I'm afraid that I shall never see Father again," she whispered.

"Nonsense. He can come visit us anytime he likes, and we shall be back soon to see him," George tried to reassure her.

His words brought no comfort, though, for she had seen something when she'd kissed her father's cheek: a gravestone with his name on it. He was going to die soon, she could feel it.

Be at peace, my sister. The gentle words whispered in her brain in Veronica's voice. *All will be well and we'll be together again soon.*

She fervently hoped so, and she felt herself relax slightly. Since she had been born, Ginny had been able to hear Veronica's thoughts. It didn't happen all the time, just when Veronica was concentrating and Ginny's mind was open. It didn't go the other way, though. Veronica had never been able to hear Ginny's thoughts.

She sighed and looked up at her husband. She and George had been married for only four months, but it seemed like they had known each other forever. *I wish*

I could read his thoughts, she fretted. She pressed her hand against her stomach. *I wish I knew what he is going to say when I tell him about the baby.*

"Is everything all right?" he asked suddenly enough to startle her.

She stared into his eyes, searching. Was it possible he had heard her? His eyes were clear and innocent, though, with no mysteries or knowledge hidden within them. No, it was a coincidence. She forced herself to smile. "As long as we are together, it is."

He gave her shoulders a squeeze, and she felt warmth spreading through her. It was good to be in love.

Mother Coven: Santa Cruz

Luna, the High Priestess of the Mother Coven, was in trouble and she knew it. One by one, every woman who had survived the massacre had questioned her *or had thought about it.* Anne-Louise was the most vocal, but everyone was wondering what had gone wrong and beginning to doubt their High Priestess's intentions.

Truth is, they're right to doubt, she thought. *Holly Cathers and her coven are an inconvenience, to say the least. Then, House Cahors has never played by anyone's rules but their own. Still, maybe I've judged them too harshly. Amanda seems like a departure from the rest of her families. She's gentle and eager to please the Goddess and others.* Luna sighed. For Amanda's sake, if nothing else, she should act. Besides, the covenates were restless, and that was never a good thing.

That was why she was sitting alone in her chamber surrounded by purple candles and burning mugwort and wormwood. She had to find Holly Cathers and she was going to need magic to do it.

She sat quietly, a bowl of water before her ringed with even more of the purple candles. She hummed softly to herself as she pricked the tip of her forefinger with a needle and squeezed three drops of blood into the bowl.

"One for Holly, one for me, and one for the Goddess," she murmured as she did so.

She stared at the crimson spot in the water for a moment and then closed her eyes. She breathed deeply.

"Goddess, I come to you seeking that which was lost, that it might be found, a Cahors witch is somewhere around, grant me sight that I may see, where on earth this witch could be."

In her mind's eye, a face appeared and she gasped in surprise. *It was not Holly's.*

THREE

DECHTERE

☾

Within the fire we dance and laugh
We sacrifice on the God's behalf
Light the pyres and ring the bell
Summon all the fiends from hell

Surround us now in cloak of night
Rejecting the Horned God's light
Death we are and death we bring
Striking from the sacred ring

Veronica Cathers Covey: Los Angeles, September 21, 1905, 11:00 P.M.

"Must you really leave in the morning?" Ginny now asked, as she hugged her sister in the lobby of the Coronado Hotel. It was a large, spacious place, and there was an actual cobbled walkway in front of the entrance. Ginny and Veronica had spent their childhoods in much lower-rent neighborhoods in rainy Seattle, where even boardwalks were a rarity . . . making mud a commonplace.

Veronica tried to laugh lightly, but it came out

more as a sob. "If I could stay, you know I would, but I must get home to Charles and the baby."

"But Seattle is so far away!"

Veronica's tears fell on her sister's dark curls. It seemed ages since they had last seen each other, and who knew how long it would be before they were again reunited? "I will see you again soon, I promise."

Ginny nodded and finally pulled away from her. Tearfully, she turned and walked inside. She threw a last look over her shoulder and waved before stepping into the carriage.

Veronica continued to wave until the carriage was out of sight. Then she turned wearily toward the front desk. *At least I will be soon home with Charles and our son, Joshua.* She smiled, buoyed by the thought. She headed for the staircase.

"Ma'am?"

She turned and saw the night manager walking toward her, a telegram in his hand. Puzzled, she took it from him. He nodded briefly and then returned to his duties. Clutching the telegram, she hurried upstairs.

Inside her room, she sat down on the settee across from the lavatory. Her eyes dropped down to the name of the sender: Amy. Her sister-in-law.

With shaking hands and a sinking feeling, she tore open the telegram and began to read it in a whisper.

"DEAR VERONICA. STOP. COME HOME AT ONCE. STOP. CHARLES DROWNED THIS MORNING. STOP. JOSHUA IS SAFE WITH ME. STOP. ALL MY PRAYERS. STOP. AMY."

A cry ripped from the very center of her heart. She got to her feet and flung the telegram across the room. It fluttered like a hapless paper boat and sank to the wooden floor. "No," she whispered.

There was a soft knock on the door, followed by a man's voice. "Madame, are you okay in there?"

Numbly, she opened the door. She stared at him, her mouth working. For a few seconds, no sound would come out. "No," she said. Then she sank to the floor.

Something burned Veronica's eyes and nose; she bolted upright to discover herself reclining on the settee with a small crowd around her. A mustached man with a shock of white hair was tapping her wrist. A stout woman beside him moved a vial of smelling salts from beneath Veronica's nose, once she realized Veronica had been revived.

"My husband," she managed.

The woman nodded kindly. "I read your telegram. Hope you don't mind none."

How can he be dead? There was so much left to do, to experience. We were going to have another child. . . .

"Drink this. It's laudanum. It'll help you sleep," the man with the mustache ordered as he held out a glass of milky liquid. More gently, he added, "I'm a doctor. And permit me to introduce my wife, Mrs. Kelly."

Mrs. Kelly's eyes shone with tears. "You dear girl," she said. "You dear, sweet girl." She gestured to the glass. "Drink up. Get some rest. I'll stay with you until you sleep."

More in shock than anything else, Veronica gulped down the draft. Then she lay numbly against the pillow and closed her eyes.

She woke much later, to discover that the Kellys had left. Groggily, she sat up, then swung her legs over the bed. She found her slippers, slid her feet into them, and rose.

The room tilted and spun, and she grabbed hold of the bedpost. She put on her peignoir, then silently glided to the door.

Something whispered to her to open the door. She frowned, knowing that to walk the halls of a hotel in the dead of night wearing nothing but her sleeping clothes was not something she should do; and yet the little whispers persisted, urging her to act.

Before she realized it, her hand turned the knob. In a daze, she began to walk down the empty hall. It was as if someone walked beside her, guiding her, whispering directions to her in her ear.

After a time, she realized she had found her way somehow to the fourth floor. A chill swept through her, and she turned around, shivering. The door at the end of the hall seemed to shimmer briefly in her sight. She wanted to turn, to run down the hall, but she didn't. Instead, she found herself drifting toward the door, pulled as though against her will. At last she stood before it and she could feel someone, *something,* on the other side.

Of its own accord, her hand lifted. She tried to stop it, but she had lost control. Fear washed over her, leaving her stomach churning and her knees trembling.

Touch the door, a voice inside her mind commanded.

"No," she whispered. But the choice was not hers.

Her fingers brushed against the wood, and the contact sent electricity shooting through her arm. She pressed her palm against the door and felt, for a moment, the thing that was on the other side. There was rage, and hatred and . . . curiosity.

Suddenly it was as if her will was hers again, and she snatched her hand away with a cry. She turned and, picking up her skirts, fled down the hall. As she reached the top of the stairs she heard the door open; the sound lent speed to her feet.

She raced blindly down the stairs until she reached the first floor of the Coronado. She glanced toward the double entrance doors. *No.* It was the middle of the night, and she would be exposed outside.

She needed somewhere to hide. She was terrified, quite overcome; she wondered briefly if it was the laudanum, but she doubted that. Her Cathers intuition had come on full throttle, and every fiber of her being shouted that she was in real danger.

A door caught her eye and she raced to it, yanked it open, and found another set of stairs. Skirts held high, she bounded down the stairs, her heart pounding and lungs burning.

She shot into the basement. The light from a single lantern tried to push back the darkness and failed woefully. She stopped, took a few deep breaths, and looked around. *There must be somewhere to hide.*

But why do you want to do that? It was the soft, insistent voice again, the one that had spoken to her outside the door upstairs . . . only this time so loud, she could hear its timbre. It was a woman's voice.

"Who are you?" she whispered. "Are you angel or demon?"

I am Isabeau.

"Isabeau?" She tasted the name on her tongue. It seemed very familiar to her, although she could never remember hearing it before. "But . . . who are you?"

Before the voice could answer, the door at the top of the stairs opened. Footsteps followed, echoing loud as thunder.

There was a pile of rags on the ground; maybe she could hide in them. Before she had taken a step toward them, though, a voice boomed, "Stop!"

She turned, the hairs on the back of her neck lifting. She was pinned to the spot by a pair of smoldering eyes. The firelight danced across his hair, and his features twisted demonically.

And yet, there was something strangely compelling about this dark, hard-featured man. . . .

"Well, well, looks like I found myself a Cahors witch," he said. "One of two remaining, if I'm not mistaken. And their father, of course."

"Y-you are mistaken, sir," she stammered. "My name is Veronica Cathers, and I am certainly no witch. And . . . and neither is my . . . fath . . . anyone I know."

For a moment a shadow of doubt crossed his face. Then he shook his head. "Your name doesn't mean a thing to me. I am concerned with who you are, not what you call yourself. And, my dear lady, you are a witch."

"I am no witch," she cried again, moving away from him. *I'm a widow,* her mind wailed. *A widow. Oh my God, my family is dead! My true love . . .*

My true love . . .

Jean . . .

The darkly imposing man smiled and lifted his right hand. A ball of fire danced in it, and he lobbed it at her slowly. She opened her mouth to scream, but instead, words strange to her ear came out, and the fireball fizzled, dissolving in midair.

She was so astonished that her legs gave way; she grabbed on to a chair for purchase, panting wildly. A cold sweat burst across her forehead, and she was terribly hot, though she wore only her nightdress and peignoir.

The man chuckled cruelly. "You see? A witch."

Her mind raced. She backed away further. "Go away. Please."

He smiled. "Not for all the tea, sweet lady. Allow me to introduce myself. I am Marc Deveraux, of the House Deveraux, a warlock, and your sworn enemy."

"My . . . enemy?" she said slowly.

Did he have something to do with the drowning? Did he kill . . . did he . . . murder . . .

Non, *he is Jean, my love, my enemy, my husband,* the voice whispered. *Jean comes to me through him. You will stay. You will allow him to touch you, to kiss you, to make love to you.*

And then . . . you will kill him.

For me.

Marc Deveraux cocked his head to the side, and his eyes took on a faraway look as though, he, too, were hearing something. "Isabeau," he whispered.

"Jean," she answered.

His face softened. He reached out a hand. "My love. *Mon amour, ma femme, tu est ici, avec moi . . .*"

"*Oui,* I am here . . . *je suis ici, mon homme, mon seigneur . . .*"

She moved toward him as if in a dream. Her hands raised toward him.

"No," she whispered. And then again, more fiercely, "No!"

The shout punctuated the air, and Marc's face snapped back into sharp focus. "Then die!" he shouted.

He raised his hand and sent a fireball her way, full-speed this time. She cried out and ducked to the side. The fire landed in the pile of rags that she had thought to hide in. Within moments they were blazing out of control.

From somewhere deep inside of her, Veronica recalled a half-memory, shadowed in the fog of her early childhood. It was of a beautiful woman with flowing hair muttering in a foreign tongue. Veronica opened her mouth, and the same words came pouring out of her, the memory growing stronger. A fireball appeared in the air before her, and she willed it forward.

Marc leaped to the side, but the fireball caught the sleeve of his jacket and the fire began to burn. Raging, he shouted in French as he peeled the jacket off his body.

They faced each other for a long moment, circling warily. Veronica could feel the heat of the fire as it spread to other parts of the basement. It was licking at the roof of the room in the corner. She tried to edge nearer to the stairs and safety. There was a popping sound, and it was followed by a far-off scream.

Maybe someone will find us, she hoped. Suddenly Marc shouted, and the room began to disintegrate around her, turning into a whirling dervish of tools, cans, and wood. She ducked as the lantern whizzed through the air where her head had been.

She took a step backward, and the backs of her ankles hit the stairs. He started toward her. There were more shouts from upstairs.

Part of the ceiling in the corner collapsed in a

shower of sparks. The door to the basement opened, and she heard a man shouting, "The fire's down here!"

She turned and ran up the stairs as fast as she could, with Marc on her heels. He reached out and grabbed the hem of her robe, and she heard the rending of cloth. Part of her skirt ripped free, and she burst past the man at the top of the stairs who had shouted.

He swore under his breath and then yelled, "Lady, what's happening?"

She ignored him and kept running. She hit the front door and burst outside into the fresh air. Her lungs were burning, and she felt like her heart would explode from her chest. More shouts began to come from the hotel behind her, but she didn't look back.

She kept running until the night had swallowed her.

Marc Deveraux tried to fight off the arms of those who were holding him back, asking him questions about the fire. He seethed, ignoring them. The witch had gotten away. He held the piece of skirt that had ripped free in his hand and rubbed it slowly between his thumb and forefinger.

Heat, which had nothing to do with the flames that were beginning to engulf the hotel, filled his being. *Veronica Cathers, we will find you, Isabeau,* the voice in his head sobbed. *Come back, my love. Come back.*

Dechtere

Tri-Coven: Seattle

The band—Kari, Tommy, Amanda, and Nicole—left Barbara behind in the motel to inspect the ruins of the cabin. Though they hoped to discover more survivors, death hung in the charred landscape like a pall. The twilight sucked whatever color might have been left, and they walked in an alien landscape that mirrored Amanda's notion of limbo.

Amanda found Silvana lying at the edge of the trees. Her eyes were fixed wide, her face frozen in terror. She fell to her knees beside her. For years, Silvana had been her best friend. She and her aunt had come to help when all the craziness had started. Now, she was gone—they both were. *They are dead because of me.*

She balled her hands into fists. No, not because of her—because of Michael Deveraux. His evil had brought pain and death upon them all.

She could not tell what had killed Silvana. She reached down and lifted Silvana's head into her lap. Something sticky coated her hands. She began to wretch when she realized the cause. The back of Silvana's head was gone.

Rage ripped through her. Silvana had not deserved to die. A shout from Tommy pierced through her fog of pain and brought her to her feet.

He was standing amid the smoking ruins of the

cabin. He was frozen, staring down at something she could not see. Picking her way carefully across the field of debris, she joined him. He was standing in front of a bookshelf that had been snapped in half and fallen in a tepee shape.

There, wedged between and underneath the two halves, was a person. Amanda reached out to touch the bookshelf, but was painfully repulsed. The space was heavily warded. "Is—it—alive?" she asked, not even sure if it was human, let alone whether "it" was male or female.

"I don't know," Tommy answered quietly. "I couldn't touch it either. We need help."

"Have you found anyone else?"

He shook his head. "You?"

"I found Silvana's body—what was left of it."

He grabbed her hand and gave it a fierce squeeze.

"Has anyone else had any luck?"

"I don't know, let's—"

He was interrupted by a loud, keening wail—as if it were an animal's. Tommy shot her a grim look, and they hurried toward the sound.

They found Pablo a little ways off. He was kneeling by a fresh mound of dirt. Two sticks had been tied together with a strip of cloth to form the shape of a cross. The cross had been driven into the ground at one end of the mound. In the dirt on the mound a pentagram had been drawn along with other symbols unknown to Amanda. She grasped Pablo's shoulder. "Who is it?" she whispered.

"Alonzo."

The oldest member of the Spanish Coven. Tears stung her eyes. Another dead. Pablo bowed his head and sobbed.

A thought struck her: *If Alonzo is buried, who did it?* A ray of hope shone through. *It must have been Philippe.* He alone of the missing covenates would have thought to adorn the grave with both Christian and Wiccan symbols.

"Pablo!"

The boy looked up, startled.

"Can you sense Philippe? He must have buried Alonzo."

The boy closed his eyes. After a moment, a look of frustration crossed his face. He put out his hand, touching the symbols marked into the dirt. His eyes flew open, and he nodded eagerly. "Yes, and he is not far away."

As if on cue, a branch snapped behind them. They whirled around to see Philippe emerging cautiously from the trees. Pablo leaped to his feet and flew to him. Philippe clasped him tight. Amanda approached more slowly. When she had reached them, Pablo released Philippe, who in turn hugged Amanda.

"It is good to see you."

"And you," she told him.

"Armand?" he questioned.

"Safe. He saved Kari as well."

Philippe sighed deeply, as though a burden had been lifted from him. "And the others?"

"Dan, Holly, and Sasha are still missing. Silvana and Alonzo are dead. Everyone else is alive."

"Have you heard anything of Nicole?"

She shook her head. "No, not since James and Eli took her."

Tommy broke in. "We did find someone, or something, in the debris. It's warded, though, and we can't reach it."

"Show me."

Minutes later they were all gathered before the broken bookshelf. Armand, Kari, and Richard had joined them, and they all took turns peering into the recess. Finally Philippe observed, "The wards are strong. It will take all of us to break them."

Amanda agreed. The others, except for Richard, formed a chain with Philippe at one end and Tommy at the other. They began to chant quietly, each in his own way but with a common purpose.

Philippe and Tommy each laid a free hand on one of Amanda's shoulders. She could feel the group's power washing over her and through her.

She took a deep breath and reached through the ward, which had already been weakened by the chanting. She grasped the creature's arms and tugged. The body moved only a little. She tensed all her muscles and yanked. The body flew out and into her arms.

She stumbled backward, and the group caught her. Tommy relieved her of her burden and lowered the body to the ground. It was Sasha.

Everyone pressed forward to look at her. Her eyelids flew open, and everyone jumped back. Sasha gazed up at Amanda and asked, in an eerily normal voice, "What happened?"

Amanda couldn't help herself, she started to laugh. And then, as a portal opened up in front of her and four lumbering gray creatures exited it, she began to scream.

Philippe hurled a fireball in the blink of an eye, but it had no effect on the creature it struck. He threw another and another with no effect. As the group stumbled backward, Amanda threw up a barrier. The first of the creatures hit it, and simply opened a portal on the other side of it.

"What are those things?" Amanda shrieked.

"I don't know, but we have to get away from them!" Philippe answered.

"To the woods, everyone, quickly!" Richard yelled, voice booming.

They turned and fled, the creatures pursuing. Another portal opened in front of Amanda, though, and the creatures just cut them off.

"They're after Amanda!" Tommy shouted, yanking her away from a reaching arm.

"Armand, do something!" Philippe shouted.

The other witch nodded and raised his arms. Suddenly, the creatures stopped. The one closest to Amanda cast its head back and forth as though looking for a scent it had just lost.

"What, what's happening?" she asked in a whisper.

"He's cloaking your energies from the creatures, making it so they can't sense you."

"But they know there are people here—they see us!" she hissed.

"Yes," Tommy whispered. "But I think they're only after you."

"That is correct," Armand said through gritted teeth. "Now, everyone, just move quietly away. Try not to attract undue attention, and don't distract me!"

They did as he said, moving steadily away from the creatures. Amanda could feel her heart pounding in her chest. *They're after me! Why not everyone else?* She turned once to look back and saw the creatures standing around, looking for all the world like lost puppies.

"We had the hotel warded, blocking our presence. When we came out in the open, I think they were able to pick up on you and come to where you were," Philippe said after a brief exchange with Pablo.

Amanda shivered. "Remind me not to go anywhere without Armand again."

She glanced at Tommy, and his eyes were bulging out. "Anywhere?" he asked, sounding forlorn.

She picked up his hand and squeezed it, appreciating him again. "Well, I'm sure he can block my vibes just fine from the next room."

Tommy smiled. "That, I can live with."

"Did anyone see any sign of the cats?" Amanda asked.

"I have not seen them," Philippe answered. "I saw their tracks, though, I believe they escaped."

Goddess, go with them, Amanda prayed. *Lead them to young women who need their strength and guidance.* In her heart she knew she would not see them again, but she also knew, somehow, that they were safe, and that made it a little easier.

The hair on the back of her neck suddenly stood on end, and Amanda swiveled her head to the side. She gasped and stopped in her tracks.

There, his back to a tree, was Dan. He was covered in dried blood, and flies were buzzing around him.

Her father moved quickly to him. "Dead," he announced, without even touching the body.

Tears sprang to her eyes. "Too much death," she murmured.

"He must have put up one heck of a fight," Richard noted.

"It didn't save him, though," she whispered.

"Come on, Amanda, we have to keep moving," Tommy reminded her gently as he wrapped an arm around her shoulders.

When will it all end? she thought in despair. *And how many more of us will die?*

Seattle: Michael Deveraux

Michael Deveraux slammed his fist down on his altar. Bits of broken glass embedded themselves in his flesh. He raised his hand slowly, savoring the pain and the sensation of the blood dripping down his hand to land on the altar. He slowly picked the glass, left over from last night's sacrifice, from his hand.

He knew that members of the Cathers Coven had survived the fire, but his scrying stones, his imp, and all his magic had been unable to locate them yet. That was going to change. What he had planned would not only enhance his power, it would also give him a unique insight into the workings of the Cathers and their pitiful little coven.

Chittering to itself, his imp appeared in the room. Michael watched it silently for a moment. He had still never discovered the creature's motivation for attaching itself to him. Then again, with imps, one rarely knew why they did much of anything.

"Well?" he asked.

"Everything is ready," the imp chortled, clearly pleased with itself.

Michael smiled. Seattle was an interesting town, a hotbed of supernatural activity. It was only natural that the Deveraux and the Cathers had both chosen it as home. There were haunted places that made even his hair stand on end.

One of those places was his destination tonight. A delicious shiver ran up his spine, and he took a moment to savor the sensation.

"Is Holly ready?"

The imp jumped up and down, wagging its head in glee.

Michael nodded. "Let's go."

Holly was in the backseat of the car, heavily tranquilized and drooling slightly. The imp jumped up and down on her, even hopping up to perch on her head, and she took no notice. Michael glanced in the rearview mirror and smiled grimly. The night sky was clear, and the stars shone brightly. The cursed moon was nowhere to be found. Michael had planned to conduct the rite on a moonless night, better not to have that symbol of the Goddess present. He would have preferred to hold the ceremony when the God reigned supreme in the midday sky, but discretion had dictated that the cloak of night hide him. Thus, when he pulled into the parking lot of the Baptist church, there was none around to see.

He got out of the car slowly, almost reverently. His actions had nothing to do with the current function of the church, but with its older uses. It had once been a Masonic church, and rumor had it that sacrifices, both animal and human, had been made there. He had never been able to verify the identity of those making the sacrifices, but he had seen enough in the walls of the church and in hidden rooms beneath to know that far worse things than human sacrifice had occurred there.

He opened the back door and dragged Holly out. She wobbled when he tried to stand her up, so after a moment he just slung her over his shoulder and, with the imp prancing at his side, headed for the side door of the building.

The door was unlocked—*Christians can be so trusting*—and he slipped inside. Once inside the door, he headed for the usher's closet, trying to avoid touching the pews as he passed them. The closet door was unlocked, and the imp held it open while Michael walked inside, Holly still slung over his shoulder.

He set her down, propping her in a corner in the hope that she wouldn't fall. He then knelt carefully by the back wall and ran his fingers under the edge of the carpet. It lifted up, and with a mighty tug he pulled, folding it back onto itself and revealing a bare floor with a trapdoor.

After securing the carpet so that it wouldn't fall back down over the trapdoor, Michael opened it and picked up Holly once more. The imp grabbed a flashlight and staggered down the steps before them, the flashlight beam waving drunkenly from side to side.

Down they descended into a darkness so thick, it made Michael wonder bemusedly if they had reached hell. Violent odors assaulted his nostrils, dank air carried the scent of blood and death. Then the stairs finally ended, and they were standing in a basement the little Baptist church above knew nothing about. Evil coated the walls and seeped up through the floor. Michael shivered as it washed over him, and the hair on the back of his neck stood on end. This was a dark place, an evil place, that had seen worse things than any he had ever done. It frightened him and, since so little did, he reveled in it. He had been here once before when he was a child. His father had brought him, and the entire experience still lived crystal-clear in his memory. How his father had first found the place he had been too afraid to ask.

He stood Holly up once more on her feet and put his arm around her to keep her standing upright. She turned and looked at him with great wild eyes and began to coo softly. It almost sounded as though she were singing a children's nursery rhyme. She laughed, loud and hollowly, and the sound echoed off the walls, coming back wilder and deeper.

He shivered again as he searched her eyes. She looked . . . happy . . . as though whatever had possessed her had found this place to its liking. He was glad it approved. The imp flitted here and there, setting everything up just so. At last he was finished and came to stand beside Michael. The strange little creature pulled itself up to its full height and bowed very slowly and with more dignity than he would have thought it capable. Truly it was a momentous occasion.

An upside-down pentagram had been drawn on the wall opposite of where they stood. The symbol had been inscribed with fresh blood—whose, he did not know. The figure of an old man suddenly appeared, coming from the wall and passing through the pentagram so that blood from the five points rested on his clothes.

Michael had seen him before when he had come with his father. The old man was some sort of dark priest—or, at least, the ghost of one. He performed rituals for those who needed them and haunted the Christians above when he was off duty.

"What do you seek?" he asked, his voice creaking.

"I seek to have this woman placed in thrall to me."

The old man drifted closer, his eyes burning. "To such a one as this?" he questioned, lifting Holly's chin with a long, bony finger.

"Yes."

"Carefully should you do this. She is not of your kind."

Michael smiled thinly. *A ghost and a Yoda wanna-be on top of it.* "Neither is she of her own mind."

"True, true. But you should be wary of the day that that changes. Whatever I bind to you, you are also bound to."

"I accept the risk," Michael told him.

The old man nodded slowly, and Michael could hear the creak of brittle bones. The priest's pale fingers reached inside his ancient robes and pulled out an athame. It glowed wickedly with a light of its own, and Michael could hear the sounds of faraway screams coming from it. *A reminder of sacrifices past,* he thought.

The old man reached out and slashed first Holly's palm, then Michael's. Michael couldn't help but hiss slightly at the pain. He was used to being cut ceremonially, but this pain was somehow different, as though it were amplified by the place, the time, and his intention.

The old man peered at him from beneath bushy brows. "To be in thrall is to share each other's power . . . and pain."

Michael hesitated, wondering fleetingly what that would mean when the time came to kill Holly. He shrugged, though, dismissing the thought. Thousands of witches and warlocks had gone through this ceremony, and it was rarely more lasting for them than marriage was for mortals. He was sure he could find some way to break the contract.

The priest took their bleeding palms and pressed them together until Holly's blood flowed in his veins and his in hers. Next the priest took a black silken cord from the imp and lashed their hands together.

"Blood to blood, magic to magic, in this very hour you double your power. As Eve bound herself to the serpent, so this woman is now bound to you." The priest then walked slowly around each of them, slashing at their clothing with his athame. At last, hands still bound, they both stood naked and bleeding from several shallow cuts from the blade.

Michael stared at Holly and could feel lust spreading throughout his body. He hadn't given much thought to this part of the ceremony, obviously an oversight on his part.

"Take her, for she is yours," the priest commanded.

Michael stepped forward to do just that, but Holly tottered and slumped to the ground, unconscious. The force of her fall undid the black cord binding their hands together, and Michael stood staring down at her.

She was his, and he would have her . . . but he would find no pleasure with her unconscious. He'd learned that the hard way, with Holly's aunt Marie-Claire—the mother of the two other Cahors witches, Nicole and Amanda Anderson.

He sighed. "Bring the change of clothes," he commanded his imp as he turned his back on Holly's inert form.

Seattle: Tri-Coven

Richard paced the floor like a caged animal. He felt as though the walls were closing in on him. He could feel his daughter's eyes on him. The woman, Sasha, was staring at him as well. They three alone were awake, keeping watch in the night while the others slept.

Now that they had accounted for all but Holly and Nicole; the others had started talking about rescue missions. Sasha was particularly insistent that someone should try to go into the Nightmare Dreamtime to find her son, Jer. If he was still alive. His body was, at least. They had found it a few yards away from the ruined cabin. Someone had carried him that far.

Considering that Holly had come back from the Dreamtime insane and possessed, almost everyone was disagreeing with Sasha. He could see her point, though. If he was alive, they needed to at least try to rescue him. If he was dead, then they could all move on and put their energies elsewhere.

Sasha interrupted his thoughts. "You saw a lot of pain during the war."

It was a statement, not a question, and he glanced at her in surprise. "Is it that obvious?"

She smiled slightly. "It is to me. But then, I know something about pain."

He stared at her. Amanda had told him that Sasha had been married to Michael and had had to give up both of her children when she'd fled from him and his evil. He guessed that she did know something about pain . . . and loss.

He pulled up a chair and lowered himself into it deliberately, though he only perched on the edge of it. "Yes, I believe you do."

Amanda glanced from one to the other of them with a bewildered look on her face.

Richard leaned forward. "I spent a year in the jungle. Very little food, less sleep, friends dying every day. Just when we thought we'd gained a couple of hours' peace, a chance to rest, the VC would be there, all around us, and the sounds of gunfire would all but drown out the screams of the dying. And in the night when I didn't know if I'd live to see another sunrise, all I had to hold on to was the hope of making it home and spending the rest of my years in peace and quiet with my wife."

He glanced at Amanda and saw the tears streaking down her face. "I guess we know how well that plan worked out," he said sardonically.

"Mom didn't understand," Amanda whispered brokenly.

"No, she didn't. But I think you do," he said, touching his daughter's cheek. "I'm so sorry, baby. I'd give anything to have spared you this kind of pain and fear."

"I know, Daddy," she choked. And then she flew into his arms, and he was holding his daughter as they cried together, for themselves and each other. Sasha placed a hand on his arm, and he could feel her pain, too, and the grief that she suffered for them as well. In that moment, he knew he was going to find her son.

Santa Cruz: Mother Coven

Luna, High Priestess of the Mother Coven, was stunned. She had asked the Goddess to help her find Holly. Instead, the Goddess had shown her another Cathers witch.

"Goddess, how can this be? Who is this witch I see?"

A gray cat with great yellow eyes scampered into the room and proceeded to sit down before her. Then the cat opened its mouth and a resounding female voice poured forth:

"What you seek has been lost for a century. Two sisters, removed from one another, one to dwell in the City of Devils, and the other to stay with her father. Death came to both, and the menchildren they bore lost their way, so that their descendants forgot who they were. House Cahors was all but lost."

Luna sat, stunned, barely able to breathe, let alone speak. The Goddess had only come to her in this manner twice, long years before. She bowed her head, feelings of unworthiness washing over her.

"My Goddess, I was seeking Holly."

"And to find her you must first find her counterpart. Seek the other witch in that city where darkness dwells. Look for the name changed once again from the ancient. You seek a Carruthers who alone may help to restore Holly's mind."

The cat stood, blinked once, and left the room, leaving Luna shaken and humbled. "To the City of Devils I will go," she vowed.

She could swear she heard the Goddess sigh in answer.

FOUR

ARTEMIS

☾

Triumphant now, Deveraux reign
Nothing will ever be the same
Cahors moan and Cahors cry
In death throes beneath the velvet sky

Everything pure is but a ruse
And love is naught but the excuse
We make for all the things we do
There is little good and nothing true

Seattle: Michael and Holly

Michael thought Holly might actually be looking better. Then again, it was so hard to tell. Her eyes were bright . . . *she could have a fever, or one of the hell-beasts in her could be ascendant*. She wasn't drooling on herself . . . *maybe she's dehydrated.* She had actually managed to eat some food on her own . . . *she got more on her face than in her mouth.* He sighed. There was only one way to know for sure.

She was sitting on the couch, contemplating her

knees. He warily sat beside her. "Holly, do you hear me?" he asked.

She nodded briefly.

"Do you understand me?"

She looked at him and again nodded.

Ah-ha, progress! "Holly, I want you to listen very carefully to me."

Her eyes were still on him. It was a good sign. "Holly, I want you to kill Amanda and Nicole Anderson."

He waited for a moment while she seemed to think about that. "Kill Amanda and Nicole," she said slowly.

He felt like holding his breath. The connection was tenuous, but it seemed to be there. He reached out to her with his mind, gently pushing. *My will to yours.* It was the way of thrall.

Aloud, he asked, "Holly, can you do that?"

She raised her hand. "Kill," she whispered. Every lightbulb in the room exploded at once.

In the sudden darkness, Michael could think of nothing else to say but, "Very, very good."

Luna: Los Angeles

Luna, High Priestess of the Mother Coven, stared out the window as the plane circled over Los Angeles

International Airport. Heavy, poisonous smog hung over the city like a shroud over a decaying corpse. The earth, the sea, the air itself were poison here, and all the people were walking corpses, shells of human beings, hollow and empty. That didn't account for the darkness, though, the darkness that she could see but most could not. There was a pall that lay over the entire area, black and twisting like so many shadows. The evil seething from the buildings, the people, the very earth was overwhelming.

She moved her lips in supplication to the Goddess, for protection and for guidance. Her skin crawled as the plane began its final descent. The teenager sitting next to her shifted uncomfortably in her seat and moved away from Luna. *She thinks I'm crazy,* Luna thought sadly. She looked at the girl's revealing clothes, her soulless stare, and the features perfected by plastic surgery. *In reality she is the crazy one, sacrificing her youth and her soul to this city of evil, which has devoured so many before her and will devour so many after her.*

Luna turned back to the window. The plane hadn't even touched ground, and yet she already felt tired, drained, old. She continued her prayers, fortifying her mind and trying to calm even the cells in her body, which were shrinking from the horrors below.

When the plane landed, she felt sick inside and

out. It took fifteen minutes to reach the gate, and when the FASTEN SEAT BELT sign was finally turned off, the girl beside her leaped from her seat and headed toward the front of the plane. The door opened, and the air from the terminal rushed inward, mixing with the air from the plane, and Luna felt her stomach twisting with nausea. She glanced around her; everyone else seemed unaware of the change as they struggled with their bags. She sighed deeply and closed her eyes. *Sometimes it's hell to be a witch.*

She made her way through the airport as quickly as she could. Even here the seedy underbelly of the city flourished. Beggars walked around selling stickers and other trinkets, pushing their presence into the faces of all. Luna shook her head slowly at one of them. The young woman made more in a year from her begging than most of the families trying to escape on vacation who threw guilty dollars her way.

When the woman pressed up to her, Luna stared into her eyes. "I think you should go home. Stop being a burden on society, work to better it."

Dazed, the young woman nodded slowly and turned to go. The mesmerism would wear off within a few hours, but at least she had purchased a few moments of peace for the young couple from Ohio who would have been the woman's next mark.

Luna continued on to ground transportation, her overnight bag held tightly in her hand. Los Angeles was a dangerous place, even for a witch. And somewhere, amid all the chaos and insanity, was a young man she needed to find. She only prayed that his heart had not been twisted by the evil around him. She prayed that he served the Goddess. She prayed that at least he did not serve the Horned God . . . *or something worse.*

Outside, the tangled cars vied with one another for positions at the curb. The honking horns and shouting voices mingled with the shrill whistles of the parking police to form a cacophony of sound that was deafening.

She hailed a taxi and stepped inside. It took all her powers just to communicate with the driver the name of the hotel she wished to visit. The Wilshire Grand Hotel was one of the most prestigious hotels in Los Angeles. She didn't know why, then, she had such a problem explaining her destination. She sighed and sank back into her seat. It was not going to be an easy trip.

Half an hour later, the taxi pulled up to the hotel and Luna pulled her nails from the seat of the car. *I must have lost ten years of life,* she thought bitterly. The drive had been enough to turn the most hardened warrior green with motion sickness and pale with fright.

She checked in and was shown to her room. She did not have much to unpack. Still, she took the time to ward the room and place various magic arcana around.

She ordered a light dinner from room service and ate it leisurely. Once finished, she dressed for the evening. She donned a simple white gown that she decorated with silver moon-shaped jewelry. She took one look in the mirror before heading for the door. It was time to go the theater.

Within minutes she was at the Ahmanson Theatre. She accepted her program and found her seat about ten minutes before the show was to start. She took the time to read her program.

The historic Ahmanson Theatre had been the site of the West Coast premier of *The Phantom of the Opera.* Now the musical was back, with a fast-rising young star playing the role of the Phantom. She read his bio with an amused grin. Alex Carruthers had been mesmerizing audiences across the country with his portrayal of the tortured Phantom. Alex had been acting since the age of seven, when he played Winthrop Wallace in a local theater's performance of *The Music Man.* He had attended a prestigious acting school in Los Angeles after high school. At twenty-three, he was the youngest actor to star in *The Phantom of the Opera*.

The lights in the theater dimmed briefly, signaling theater patrons to take their seats. Five minutes later, the curtain lifted. By the time the first act ended, Christine, the beautiful heroine of the story, was not the only one under the Phantom's spell.

Alex Carruthers had mesmerized the entire audience.

Alex Carruthers played the crowd and they ate it up. Luna watched him as the Phantom. By the time he was singing "The Point of No Return," trying to seduce the young actress playing Christine, the sexual energy flowing off every woman in the room was overpowering. And at the end of the final act, even the grown men were weeping.

Five curtain calls later, the house lights came up and the rush to leave the theater began. Luna sat for a moment, waiting for her row to empty out.

The young man was powerful. If he had any other skills that could match his ability of mesmerism, he would be a formidable force indeed. *Now it's time to find out whom he serves.*

She rose and made her way toward the stage. "Cloak my passing from all eyes, make invisibility my guise," she murmured. She smiled at herself. When she had become High Priestess, she had ceased needing to speak her spells aloud. All of the upheaval in the coven must be upsetting her more than she'd realized.

She took the stage and slid behind the curtain, walking past stagehands already putting things away for the next evening's performance. As she drifted by one of the dressing rooms, the actress playing Carlotta glanced up suspiciously. *She's a witch and she can feel me. She does well to be worried; she has a lot to hide*. In a twist of irony, the actress playing the diva that the Phantom despised couldn't actually sing well. She glamoured her voice so that it would appear passable. Luna paused for a moment as a new thought occurred to her: *Or perhaps someone glamoured her voice for her.*

She moved on; the woman was not the one she sought. When she stopped outside the men's dressing room, Alex was waiting for her. He rose from his seat and glided toward her. He alone saw her; the rest were still blinded to her presence. *Walk with me.*

She fell into step beside him. Within moments they had reached his private dressing room and entered. Once in the room, she allowed her invisibility to drop from her, so that he could see her clearly.

He was tall, just over six feet. He had white-blond hair, and blue eyes that crackled with energy. *He looks nothing like a Cahors, and yet I can feel their blood coursing through his veins*. There might not be a physical resemblance, but the psychic one was undeniable.

He sat down and motioned her to a seat as well. She took it and began probing his mind even as he was probing hers. She freely opened areas of her mind where she wanted him to go, and reinforced her mental blocks around the things she was not ready to share with him. He did the same, and they danced back and forth, thrusting into each other's minds and parrying the other's attacks.

At last, a truce was called, and just in time; he had nearly torn down her defenses. *By the Goddess, he is strong!*

"Why have you come?" he asked simply.

"To see you."

"Whom do you serve?" he asked.

"I belong to the Goddess. I am Luna, High Priestess of the Mother Coven." She lifted her chin. "And you?"

"I am Alex Carruthers, of the Coven of the Air. I serve the Goddess as well."

She narrowed her eyes as she studied him. Somehow, she didn't think that that was entirely true; it didn't feel like the first response that had come to his mind. She glanced around the room. On the back of a door hung a dark blue silk robe with a large moon on the back. A small statue of Aphrodite rested on the dressing table. Other than that, the room was bare of magic symbols.

She forced herself to relax slightly. *These are both Goddess symbols. If he has not benefited from formal instruction, there might be some slight variations in the way he worships, and that might be what disturbs me.*

She smiled grimly. Just as the Goddess had many forms, there were many ways to worship her, different ones adopted by different cultures. In the end they were more alike than different, and they worshiped the same being. *It's like Protestants arguing over whether they're Lutheran or Methodist.*

Alex smiled disarmingly at her. "I believe we worship the same Lady?"

She nodded. "The others in the troupe—they are your coven?"

"Some of them," he admitted. "We of the Craft must stick together."

"And the actress playing Carlotta—you were the one to glamour her voice?"

He sighed in a frustrated manner. "Yes. She's a marvelous actress, and she's always been like an aunt to me. She just can't sing."

"No one in the audience would know that."

"Except for you," he pointed out.

"Except for me," she admitted.

He gazed at her for a long moment. "You said you

came to see me, Luna of the Mother Coven. What is it that you wanted?"

She smiled and leaned forward. "I want to reacquaint you with your roots."

He frowned, and she could tell that she had truly surprised him. After a moment, he spoke: "I discovered at the age of five that I was different, that I could make things happen. When I was ten I realized I was a witch and that my mother had been one. I joined my first coven a year later, and by the time I was fifteen I was the head of my own. I am a witch and have had to hide this fact from a society that really has not moved much past where it was during the Salem witch trials. What more could you possibly have to tell me?"

She chuckled softly. "Everything."

Tri-Coven: Seattle

Holly, or what was left of her, stood outside the hotel room where the others were hiding. She cocked her head to the side, listening to the multitude of voices within. Something was being said about death.

There were barriers around the hotel, but they were weak—at least they *felt* weak. She raised her hands, whispering, "Kill them, kill them all."

Fireballs appeared in the air before her, hundreds of them, shining and pulsing with deadly energy. They quivered, eager to be unleashed upon their target. *"Aggredior!"* she cried, and the fireballs whizzed through the air like flights of arrows.

The first wave exploded against the wards, weakening them. The second wave punched holes through the wards, and they shimmered briefly before vanishing. The third wave assaulted the building, setting it instantly ablaze.

There were shouts from within and doors flew open, the covenates burst from the building, lobbing fireballs of their own as they scrambled for some kind of cover. Holly laughed and raised her arms to send another volley their way.

Before she could, something tackled her from behind and knocked the breath from her. She lay on the ground for a moment, stunned. *Get up, get up,* a voice hissed in her mind. Was it hers? She didn't know. *Run quickly. No! Stand and fight, destroy!*

She clamped her hands over her ears and screamed. The voices were arguing, urging her to do one thing, then another.

"What do you want from me?" she shrieked. "Leave me alone!"

"Holly!" she heard a voice cry, far away and muffled, as though it were underwater. "Holly, look out!"

What do they want from me? she thought, angrily

raising her head and turning to look. What she saw made no sense. A giant man-beast of gray hovered over her.

She rolled to the side as a massive fist crushed the earth where she had lain. She breathed, and fire exploded from her fingertips, engulfing the creature.

The fire didn't phase it, and it just reached for her again. It picked her up and began to squeeze, crushing her ribs. She let her head fall to the side as her vision dimmed.

The end at last . . . thank the Goddess.

No! Kill it. Destroy it.

I don't know what it is.

Golem. Erase the first symbol on its forehead.

Holly reached up with her hand and jabbed her thumb into the *e* of the word *emet* on the thing's forehead. She ground at it. It howled in anguish and dropped her, hands flying to its head.

She scrambled to her feet, ready to finish what she had started. Another voice inside, more insistent, screamed, *Run!*

She did.

Amanda stood panting, watching helplessly as Holly ran off, pursued by four great lumbering creatures.

"What, what are those things?" she gasped.

"Golems," Sasha answered solemnly. "Creatures made of clay and imbued with the will of their creator."

"Who made them? Michael?" Philippe questioned.

Sasha shook her head slowly. "To make one of those takes years of serious study in the Kabalistic teachings. It is one of the most difficult and dangerous pieces of magic one could ever do. Michael doesn't possess the knowledge of such teachings to have done it."

"You're sure of that?" Richard questioned sharply.

Sasha nodded. "His magic isn't based on that, and from all that I know, he has never reached into other religions with enough zealousness to learn such things."

"If not Michael, then who?" Philippe asked.

"I don't know, and that's what frightens me."

"The leader of the Supreme Coven," Pablo whispered, so softly that they barely heard him.

Armand nodded. "You said these Golems were imbued with the will of their creator?"

Sasha nodded.

Armand turned to Pablo. "And it was the leader of the Supreme Coven that you felt when they were here."

Pablo shuddered lightly. "Yes. And they were searching for Amanda."

"If they were after me, there are probably more

looking for Holly and Nicole," Amanda groaned.

Sasha put an arm around Amanda's shoulders. "We'll look after you, sweetheart. Your father is right, though: We're not safe now; we have to go."

"Where?" Amanda asked, her heart heavy with worry.

There was silence for a long minute. It was finally broken by Kari, who had said nothing since the attack. "I know a place."

Alex and Luna: En route to Seattle

Alex sat beside Luna on the plane to Sacramento. A call from one of her covenates before they left L.A. had redirected them here. The plane was nearly empty, and they were the only ones flying first class. Alex looked . . . nervous. *I would be, too, if I were about to meet a long-lost branch of my family and join them in combat against evil.* He turned and smiled at her.

The rest of his coven had stayed behind in Los Angeles, though with extreme objections. In the end, Alex had not ordered them but persuaded them. They had agreed to stay behind at last, not because what he was doing was dangerous, not because he should meet his family alone, not even because he wished it. They stayed because the show had to go on. They had an understudy who could play the Phantom for a few days, but they did not have enough understudies to allow them all to leave. So, with much sighing and ritual blessings, they let him go, bidding the Goddess speed his way back. The bond between the members of the group had astounded her.

It made her nervous that his coven had been operating for several years beneath the Mother Coven's radar. *How is that possible when we both worship the Goddess?* It was a mystery, and she knew she would get no answers from Alex. There would be time enough for the priestesses to puzzle over this. Now she just had to join Alex with his cousins.

They hadn't even been on the plane yet a half hour and it was already painfully clear that one of the flight attendants found Alex irresistible. He seemed to have an energy that radiated from him, and his face shone with an unnatural light. She was not surprised that young women were drawn to him.

To his credit, he did not encourage the young lady. In fact, he barely seemed to notice her at all, as though she didn't even exist. Luna's eyes narrowed as she watched him.

"Would you like something to drink?" the attendant asked, at last turning her eyes to Luna.

"Ginger ale," she said, and under her breath she added, "forget him, child."

The woman blinked and stared at her for a moment blankly before regaining her perky no-one-on-this-flight-has-annoyed-me-yet smile.

The flight seemed interminable, but at last the plane landed. They made their way to baggage claim. Luna pulled out her cell phone and called a member of the Mother Coven who had stayed behind in Seattle when the rest had withdrawn to Santa Cruz. The other woman answered on the first ring. She spoke only three words: *moving, cabin,* and *Winters*.

Luna pressed "end" on her phone and hung up without even saying a word. After retrieving Alex's luggage, they walked outside and hailed a taxi.

"Where to?" the driver asked, looking them over.

"Winters."

"What country you from?" the driver asked, speaking around the gum in his mouth.

"Canada," she said briefly.

"Ah, Canada. Pretty country. You here on vacation or what?"

With a flick of her wrist, Luna dispelled the driver's interest in them and sat back to enjoy the ride. Given the luck of the Cathers Coven, she would need her energies when they met up.

Artemis

Tri-Coven: Winters, California

Richard had won the argument: Of all those present, he had been selected to enter the Dreamtime and go after Jer Deveraux. He had argued that he was in excellent physical condition, and thus more able to withstand the rigors of the place. Armand had wanted to go, but Richard had vetoed that: If those Golems showed up, he wanted him protecting his little girl.

Now, in the cabin Kari had shown them—it belonged to her family—Richard could feel his pulse accelerating, as though he were preparing for battle. *Which I might well be,* he thought. He wished they had been able to get something from Holly about the Dreamtime, but she had only babbled about fire. That and, of course, demons. He grimaced. Barbara had not been much more help. All she had really been able to tell him was that she had been trapped in some sort of cave. Or so she thought.

He stood and accepted the markings as the shaman placed them on his body. He had been warned that, in the Dreamtime, his mind was his most powerful weapon. That worked. He had no magic abilities whatsoever, but he could certainly imagine carnage. Quite a lot of it.

He had mixed feelings about going in to find Jer, but then everyone around him seemed to also have mixed feelings about it. All except for Sasha and Barbara, that is. Barbara had insisted they could not leave him there. She herself had spent more than a year there before Jer and Holly had rescued her. She couldn't stand the thought of someone else being trapped and suffering the hell she had.

In his gut, he had to agree with her. He had been a Ranger, after all. *Rangers never leave anyone behind. We can't afford to have the bodies identified.*

He took a deep breath and lay down in the circle. He exhaled slowly, allowing his mind to become acutely focused while at the same time emptying it of all exterior distractions.

He closed his eyes and opened them in another place. The earth beneath his feet was scorched. A hot wind whipped past him, causing his hackles to rise. Evil was afoot; it permeated the air like moisture until he was afraid it was coating his skin in its dank decay.

He shook his head to remove the fanciful thoughts buzzing there. He had a job to do. He turned slowly in a circle, taking in his environment. He smiled. Not too far away was a huge mountain of rock. That had to be where Barbara had been trapped and therefore was the last place that he knew Jer had been.

He walked toward it slowly, senses alert. In his mind he cast barriers about himself, impenetrable walls. And beyond those he placed alarms that would warn him of the approach of any creature. A year in the jungle had taught him how to put up barriers in his mind, to be master of his thoughts when he chose. He had never dreamed that he would have to go back to that.

He knew Marie-Claire had hated that control. She often complained when he first returned from the war that he wouldn't "let her in." God knew he had tried. She had grown tired of waiting. He had often wondered of late if she would have been pleased to know that his barriers had crumbled around him once she had died, leaving his mind exposed to all.

Those thoughts had no part of him now, though. He had picked up the pieces of his life, and it was time to embrace his instinct for survival.

He reached the mountain quickly. Even the stone had been burned by whatever fire had swept through. Slowly, deliberately, he began to walk clockwise around the mountain, looking for an opening, a fissure, anything.

He had been walking for several minutes before he saw it. It was an outcrop of rock that was shaped like a human hand. Scalp tingling, he stepped in for a better look.

It didn't just look like a hand, it *was* a hand. It was

as though it were pressing out against the rock, trapped inside and seeking to break through. He lifted his fingers to touch the hand and closed his eyes. He reached with his mind, past the layer of stone and inside.

He felt pain, rage, and . . . surprise. He smiled knowing that he had found Jer. He pushed his thoughts from his head, down his arm to his fingers, through the rock and into Jer's hand, up his arm and to his mind. He connected, he felt it.

Are you all right?

The answer came, faint but clear. *Not hurt, but going a little nuts.*

Good, I'm here to help.

Who are you?

Amanda and Nicole's father.

The sense of surprise became almost overwhelming, and he couldn't help but chuckle. *Never count the old man out.*

I won't make that mistake again, Jer answered.

So, what happened here?

Didn't Holly tell you?

She didn't make much sense.

There was silence for a moment, and he could tell Jer was wondering what to make of that. He didn't ask, though.

Well, the rock turned into two snakes who were battling

each other. One of them swallowed me, and then they froze back into stone.

Richard stepped back for a moment and took another look at the stone. It looked like any mountain. He was looking with his eyes, though. He closed his eyes and saw the image again in his mind. Slowly he began to make out two different forms, serpents, biting each other. Jer was trapped in one of them, only a few feet down from its mouth.

He stepped back to touch Jer's hand and felt the other's panic at having been left suddenly alone again.

It is all right. I will not leave you, he reassured him.

The Fire . . .

It is not burning here now. I'm going to disconnect for a moment, but I am not going anywhere.

Jer didn't respond, but Richard could feel his reluctant acceptance. He pulled his hand back again and studied the mountain.

He could see the serpents now with his eyes. He studied them, the position of Jer in the throat of the one. He focused his gaze on the rock around Jer's hand. He imagined the snake's skin stretching, growing thinner, and at last rupturing, spilling forth its prize.

The rock groaned in anguish, and then with a sharp scream began to part around Jer's hand. Slowly, as though it were being born, the hand pushed its way through a tear in the rock. It was horribly scarred, barely human. The tear widened and was followed by the rest of the arm. Then a second hand appeared, and then the arm.

At last the head burst through, and Jer let out a strangled gasp. He looked hideous, but Richard had prepared himself for that. The kid had been burned by the Black Fire, and Sasha had told Richard that it was only because of incredibly strong magic that he was still alive. After gulping in several breaths of air, he yelped, "Help!"

"Help me help you," Richard said calmly. "Imagine the rock parting, imagine the neck of the serpent rupturing and freeing you."

Jer closed his eyes, and Richard could *feel* him helping. He could feel the stone parting faster. In moments, Jer was spilling onto the ground, retching.

Richard gave him a moment to collect himself before moving forward to help him stand. The young man stood slowly, on shaking legs.

"How long have I been trapped in there?"

"Just a few days," Richard assured him.

"It felt like an eternity."

"I'm sure it did. Can you move? We should get out of here," Richard said. As though on cue, one of his trip alarms went off. Something was coming.

Part Two
Fire

☾

Some in fire go to their death
Some by water are bereft
Air may bring death, not birth
But they all return to Earth

So of these three I choose the fire
To dance aflame in death's desire
And as the flesh melts from my bone
You will hear me blissfully moan

FIVE

MAGOG

☾

Witches now are on the run
Beaten by the great god, the sun
They scream and die from the fright
Fading now into the night

Cahors dancing shall return
As we make the Deveraux burn
Someone new within our sight
Hails the watchfires of the night

Tri-Coven: Winters

I hate waiting, Amanda thought as she sat, keeping watch over her father's still form. *That's all I seem to do is wait.*

"Then maybe it's time to stop," said a male voice she didn't recognize. She jumped as the High Priestess of the Mother Coven appeared on the inside of the door accompanied by a gorgeous guy.

"We have to get better wards," Tommy muttered.

Amanda rose hastily to her feet. "High Priestess, blessed be."

"Blessed be," the older woman said solemnly.

Everyone else chorused in.

"Amanda, may I introduce Alex Carruthers, your cousin."

Amanda blinked twice. "My what?"

"Your cousin."

"I never knew you had so many relatives," Tommy quipped. "Cousins have just been popping out everywhere."

Amanda just stood staring. *Another cousin? Did my mother know about him?*

Alex stepped forward, hand extended. Amanda shook herself and stepped forward to clasp his hand. The contact sent electricity through her arm, and her palm burned. It felt like the first time she and Holly had clasped hands, when they had propelled each other across the room.

She broke the contact, stepping back. "Well, Alex, welcome to our little corner of the world. These are the other members of my coven: Tommy, Kari, Philippe, Pablo, Sasha, Armand. Barbara, and my father, over there," she said, waving toward his prone body, "are not covenates, but they do fight with us."

"I thought there would be more of you," Alex commented.

"There were," Philippe spoke up. "However, several were recently killed, and a couple of others are missing."

"My condolences," Alex said, dropping his eyes briefly in a show of respect.

"They are welcome, as are you," Amanda said. "Please, take a seat. We are waiting for my father; he is in the Australian Dreamtime trying to rescue another of our number."

He nodded as he sat in a chair across from the cabin's stone fireplace. "My two other cousins—Holly and Nicole?"

"Both missing," Tommy said.

"Ah, it looks like I have a lot of catching up to do."

"First, we want to know about you," Armand spoke.

Amanda was startled. Armand, the member of the Spanish Coven who had studied to be a priest, rarely spoke up and almost never questioned anyone. It was a good warning for them all.

"Yes," she said, raising her defenses back up. "Tell us all about you."

He smiled in a way that sent shivers down her spine. *He can read my mind. His comment when he appeared wasn't just a fluke!*

"I'm an actor by trade, a witch by practice and belief. I serve the Goddess."

"And you just happen to show up right when we could use another person?" Armand questioned.

Alex raised his hands defensively. "Until a few hours ago I had never even heard of you guys. Then Luna sought me out and told me I had cousins and that they needed my help."

"It's true," Luna said. "I asked the Goddess to show me the lost Cahors witch; I was hoping to find Holly. Instead, she showed me Alex. His branch split off from yours at the beginning of the twentieth century. His family, like yours, forgot their ancestry. Like you, Amanda, and your sister and cousin, he discovered his magical abilities on his own."

"I've been in a coven since I was quite young," he confessed. "I'm the head of my coven now."

"Well, you don't need to do a spell to find Holly anymore," Kari said, her voice trembling.

"You found her?" Luna asked.

"More like she found us," Philippe said ruefully. "She came after us."

"She attacked you?"

Pablo cleared his throat. "I have something to tell you. All of you. I have been communing with . . . the forces that tell me what goes on in the ethers and vapors."

"Holly is in thrall to Michael Deveraux."

A stunned silence fell over the company. The High Priestess visibly paled. The other woman shifted her weight uncomfortably before she finally asked, "You know this for sure?"

Philippe glanced at Pablo and then nodded.

He had already told Philippe. But Philippe doesn't trust Alex, else he would have told her before what Pablo felt. Amanda quickly banished the thoughts from her mind. If Philippe didn't want to share some information, then the last thing she needed was to start thinking about it and have Alex read her mind.

Suddenly Pablo lurched to his feet, wild-eyed. "She's here."

Kari scrambled to her feet. "How did she find us? I never even told Jer about this cabin!"

Ignoring her, Amanda turned to Alex. "Welcome to hell. I hope you're ready."

"What can she do?"

No sooner were the words out of his mouth than a skeletal warrior on a ghost-horse crashed through the wall. The beast's shoulder hit Luna, sending the High Priestess spinning into Amanda and they both fell in a heap.

From the floor, Amanda could stare out of the hole in the wall. She saw Holly, surrounded by a ghost army of dozens, her arms lifted in the air and her hair swirling around her head.

Then the ghost soldiers were charging, heading straight for them. Then a voice cried out, deep as thunder, and the walls of the house shook. She looked up and saw Alex standing with his arms open wide.

"Ego diastellomai anemos o apekteina eneka!" he cried.

"What?" she asked. Her words were snatched from her lips by a wind that seemed to spring from nowhere.

"It's Greek," Armand shouted. "He's commanding the wind to fight on our behalf."

Amanda watched in awe as warriors flew apart, tiny tornadoes exploding upon them. At last only Holly was left. She opened her mouth as though she were shouting something, but a blast of wind picked her up and hurled her through the air.

She lay still, unmoving, for a long minute, and Amanda's heart caught in her throat. *Is she—?*

Slowly, Holly stood up. She stared for a moment, and Amanda realized she was making eye contact with Alex. Suddenly Holly turned and melted into the shadows.

The winds died instantly, and Alex seemed to slump a little. Amanda shakily rose to her feet and brushed herself off. "Is everyone okay?"

"Fine," Philippe answered. He turned to stare at Alex. "How did you do that?"

Alex shrugged. "Air—it's one of the basic elements. Everyone in my coven gravitates toward one more than the others. I've always been good with wind."

"And apparently Holly is not. I think we've found a weakness," Luna noted as she, too, stood up. "We can't stay here, though. We need to move someplace safer, where she can't find us."

"We can't go until my father comes out of the Dreamtime," Amanda protested, panic rising in her.

"You say he went in to rescue someone, a witch?" Alex asked.

Amanda hesitated. "Actually, he's more of a warlock . . . it's . . . complicated."

Alex raised an eyebrow. "It must be. I could go in and try to get them out."

"We've already sent too many people there," Philippe protested.

"Ah, but did any of them have experience with astral traveling?" Alex asked with a smile.

Amanda shook her head ruefully. "No. None of us has experience with that."

Alex's smile broadened. "Well, then, it's a good thing I'm here, because it just so happens that I do. It's one of the attributes of those who claim air as their element."

"Of course it is," Tommy muttered under his breath for Amanda's ears alone. She had to agree with him. It was awfully convenient. Still, anything was worth a try if it could bring her father back.

"All right, you're hired," she said, forcing a smile that she knew didn't reach her eyes.

Richard and Jer: The Dreamtime

The fire was burning all around, rushing toward them faster than Richard could push it back. The wicked black flames writhed like something alive, and he could feel their heat upon his cheek. He pushed and the flames pushed back, inching closer until his skin began to blister. Beside him, Jer was chanting, but the roar of the fire was drowning out the words.

A man approached them, his body seeming to cut a path through the flames. Within a moment he was in front of them. "Uncle Richard?"

Richard hesitated only a moment before nodding. There was something familiar about the young man, though he didn't think he'd ever seen him before.

The stranger lifted his arms and shouted in a strange tongue. Suddenly wind was everywhere, so strong that Richard and Jer began to stagger. The stranger, though, seemed to remain unaffected. Then, as though the flames were from a thousand birthday candles, the fire was snuffed out.

The silence was almost deafening, and into it the stranger spoke: "I am your nephew."

Heaven help us all, he thought as he stood blinking in disbelief.

"I am Alex. Let's go. Your daughter is waiting for us."

Then, within a minute, Richard was opening his eyes and staring up into his daughter's face. "Baby," he gasped.

"Daddy," his Amanda cried as she threw her arms around him.

"Jer?" he said.

A voice croaked from beside him, "I'm here."

"And—your cousin?"

"Well, thank you, Uncle." The young man came into his range of vision, a pleased smile plastered on his face.

Richard slowly sat up, all the images of the Dreamtime flooding him at once. "No one's possessed, right?" he asked.

"Doesn't look like it," Amanda assured him.

"Good." He turned to look at Jer. Someone must have tossed him a towel, because he had it wrapped around his head and face.

"Anything happen while I was away?"

"Holly attacked us again."

"Holly . . . attacked you?" Jer asked, sounding dazed.

Amanda knelt down and placed a hand on Jer's shoulder. "When she came back from the Dreamtime, she wasn't alone. Demons or something are possessing her."

"No!" Jer gasped.

"There is more that you should know," Philippe said, also placing a hand on his shoulder. "She is in thrall . . . to your father."

The cry of anguish that came from Jer was like no sound Richard had ever heard from a human being. Out of respect, he ducked his eyes, the only gesture of privacy he could offer him.

When Jer finally spoke, though, Richard heard the steel in his voice. "I will find her and free her, if I have to kill my father and myself to do it."

Let us all pray it doesn't come to that.

San Francisco: April 17, 1906 8:00 P.M.

Veronica Cathers waited in the hotel room at the Valencia for Marc Deveraux. She could feel him coming; it was a fever in her blood. It was a trap, it had to be, but still, she waited. She had not seen Marc in the six months since they had battled in the basement of the Coronado Hotel in Los Angeles.

Veronica had been visiting her sister, Ginny, in Los Angeles and had been staying at the hotel. Marc Deveraux had been another guest at the hotel, and it had not taken them long to find each other. She shuddered at the memory.

The hotel had burned down completely, she had heard, though she had never returned to see the wreckage. She had fled into the night to return home in time to bury her husband, who had died that same day.

Veronica, her son, Joshua, and her friend Amy were in San Francisco now. Amy had insisted Veronica needed a holiday, a chance to get away from all the pain present in her little house in Seattle, which was haunted by the memories of her dead spouse. *Some holiday it's turning out to be!*

Marc Deveraux had called for this meeting, claiming a kind of truce so they could talk—about what, he did not say, but she could guess. His telegram had arrived this morning and had rocked her to her very foundation. *How did he find me?* She nervously smoothed down the skirt of her pale pink dress. The lace covering the upper part of her chest and throat scratched painfully. The thin, clinging sleeves restricted her movement, and she cursed her choice of garment.

Anxiety filling her, she lifted her hand to stroke the

locket she wore around her neck. Inside the small piece of jewelry she kept a lock of Joshua's hair. He would be one in another month. He was with Amy now, and the other woman knew not to wait up for her. She had promised Joshua that she would see him in the morning. She only hoped it was a promise she could keep.

There was a knock on the door. She crossed and opened it quickly, before she could lose her nerve.

He strode into the room, and she closed the door. When he turned and faced her, her heart flew into her throat, choking the words of a protection spell that she had been about to utter. He stared at her with his coal-black eyes burning into her. He looked like a panther, muscles coiled and ready to spring upon its helpless prey.

And inside her head she could hear Isabeau whispering, *Jean.*

She couldn't look away from his eyes; they pinned her to the spot and probed her soul. The air between them became charged with electricity until she could feel the skin on her hands and cheeks tingling. *Does he feel it too?*

Then he pounced. She threw up her hands to ward him off, but it was too late. They were crushed against his body as he wrapped his arms around her and kissed her. "*Moi,* Isabeau, how I hate you," he breathed in between kisses.

As she looked at him it was no longer Marc's face she saw, but another's, wilder and fiercer. *Jean!*

From her mouth poured words strange to her. Still, she tried to keep herself; she struggled not to let Isabeau consume her completely even as Jean seemed to be consuming Marc.

He swooped her up in his arms and carried her to the bed, whispering words that were both fierce and tender. He laid her down and sat beside her. He picked up her hand and began to kiss her fingers, then froze at the sight of her wedding ring.

It was Marc who looked at her and asked, "You are someone's wife?"

Veronica shook her head. "I am someone's widow."

Then he was crushing his lips to hers. She heard the ripping of fabric as he tore her dress away from her body. She, in turn, tore at his clothes. At last he lay down on top of her, their flesh touching.

"*Mon* Jean," Isabeau murmured.

But it was Veronica who took Marc into herself.

When their passion was spent, they lay in each other's arms. Veronica had never felt so alive and so complete.

"You are my only love," he whispered.

"Isabeau is Jean's only love. You and I are just the pawns in their game."

"No," he denied it. "I love you and hate you as Jean did Isabeau, but it is not his emotion alone that I feel, it is mine as well. In Los Angeles, I wanted you then. I have spent every night since thinking of you, searching for you."

She stroked his hair, damp from perspiration. "I feel the same for you," she confessed. "I have tried to stop, but I cannot. I do not know much about my family. All I know has come from Isabeau. She spoke to me first on the night that we met."

"As Jean did for me."

"I know that our families have battled."

"And still do," he affirmed.

"I don't believe it has to continue," she breathed.

"Nor I. I pledge to you, Veronica Cathers, that my feud with you and yours ends here. I will do everything in my power to turn the Deveraux from their vengeance."

"And I will work for peace between our two families for the rest of my life."

They kissed, biting each other's lips until their blood mingled together and sealed the bargain.

"For the rest of my life," she repeated.

"For the rest of my life," he answered, whispering.

And as they began to make love again, neither had any idea how short those lives would be.

The earth groaned in anguish as though in the pangs of labor. And as a tremor passed through it, it did give birth to pain, anguish, and loss.

The earthquake struck without warning, jarring Veronica from sleep. Her limbs were tangled with Marc's and he, too, sat upright. Before she could shout a spell, there was the sound of screams and explosions. A mighty groaning ripped through the room, and then the floor collapsed.

Fire had raged through the city following the earthquake. Thousands were dead or dying, and the city was under martial law. It was a high price to pay, but well worth it.

Duc Laurent and Gregory Deveraux stood, looking at the ruins of the Valencia Hotel. All four floors had collapsed into the basement. Gregory stood, not offering even a tear for his brother. The ghostly Duc smiled. "There were no survivors?"

"None," Gregory intoned.

"Excellent. You have done well."

Los Angeles: April 18, 1906, 11:50 A.M.

Ginny Cathers stood with thousands of others, reading the huge bulletin boards that proclaimed the latest news from San Francisco. *God protect her,* she thought. She'd had a telegram from Veronica the day before, telling her that she was going to be in San Francisco and was thinking of coming to Los Angeles for a few days when her business in the city was done.

Names of the dead and missing were posted every few minutes. As more buildings collapsed from aftershocks or the fires raging through the city, their names were listed on the board. *So much death, so many lost,* Ginny thought. Her mind turned toward her husband and infant son safe at home several miles away from where she stood. *God protect them.*

This is useless. I don't even know which hotel she was staying at, she thought. Suddenly the earth shifted beneath her feet. Screams rippled throughout the crowd as the earthquake hit. It was small, not large enough to cause any damage, but those who were waiting for word of the final death toll in San Francisco did not know that.

The crowd turned, running away, *as though they could actually escape, somehow.* Ginny was caught up in the tide of stampeding people. She ran because she could do no differently. A screaming man careened wildly through the crowd, and bounced off Ginny. He kept running, but Ginny stumbled. Someone else slammed into her from behind and she fell, landing hard on her wrist. She tried to push herself up, but someone stepped on her back, shoving her down into the dirt. Suddenly the mob was running over her. She tried to scream, but her cries were lost in the crowd.

Someone kicked her as they rushed by, and she felt her ribs cracking. Pain knifed through her lungs, and she began to cough. Someone else stepped on her back, and another on her good arm.

She tried to get up, but it was no use—bones cracked, and muscle gave out as they trampled her. *I'm going to die,* she realized in horror. She lifted her eyes, blood dripping into them from a wound in her head. Before her, she saw a woman in white standing serene in the throng. People seemed to pass by her, and Ginny blinked fiercely as she saw a couple pass *through* her.

"*Ma petite,* I shall watch over your child," the woman said.

I believe you, Ginny thought, with her dying breath.

SIX

FREYA

☾

Playing now our deadly game
The evil that you know by name
Decisions at last must be made
Betrayal is our stock-in-trade

Goddess hear us in the night
Help us now to choose the right
Give Cahors strength to persevere
And banish now our every fear

Avalon: Nicole

Nicole sobbed as pain ripped through her. She was chained to a dungeon wall, not far from the spot where James had once attempted to place her in thrall.

James was attempting now to break the thrall between Nicole and Philippe, her beloved. The two men could not have been any different. James was evil and had married Nicole against her will and kidnapped her twice now. Philippe was good and kind and had entered with respect and reverence in thrall with her in a ceremony that was a marked difference to the dark wedding James had orchestrated. *Rescue me, Philippe,* she begged mentally, wishing he could hear her.

Thoughts of him calmed her, steadying her nerves and helping her fight the pain. Still, she could feel parts of her mind slipping away. She let part of it go, the part that was horrified at what James was doing to her. The rest of it she tried to keep intact, knowing she would need it when her moment came. *Came. Came, game, same. Same game different name,* she thought to herself.

In front of her, James was cursing. Eli was there, too, standing back in the shadows and watching the proceedings.

Eli was staring at her through narrowed eyes, and she could all but see the wheels in his head turning. *Turning, burning, churning,* she thought, trying to distract herself from the pain.

James cut a thin line across her abdomen. She could feel the blood spilling out and running down into her jeans and underwear. *Yearning, spurning, learning.*

James next cut a line in her forehead; blood rolled down her face and she tasted it on her lips. *Earning, concerning, kerning . . . is* kerning *even a word?*

"Witch!" James shrieked, and cut a circle around her heart. *Witch, hitch, ditch.*

"I cut him from your mind, heart, and your organs," James crowed.

Pitch, rich.

"I shall cut him from your loins as well."

Her eyes narrowed, and she focused her sight on the knife he held in his hand.

Bitch.

She kicked, and the knife went flying in a wide arc, landing at Eli's feet. She stepped away from the wall. *"Libero!"* she said in a singsong voice, and the chains fell from her wrists.

Eli stared at the knife where it lay at his feet. He bent and picked it up, brushing his thumb slowly along the blade. It was stained with blood, Nicole's blood. Before Nicole had belonged to Philippe or James, she had belonged to him. *She was my girlfriend and she adored me.* He stared at James as he grappled with Nicole. *He took her because I was intimidated by him. He had no claim to her but he took her, anyway. He is arrogant, proud, and he doesn't care whom he crushes, just like my father. Just like me.*

Nicole fought back tooth and nail, like a wildcat, and he couldn't help but feel a stirring of pride. *I remember when she couldn't have hoped to defend herself with magic or with fists. She has learned so much the last two years . . .*

. . . and I wasn't the one to teach her.

I should have been. Back when she was starting to dabble in magic. I should have shown her. Maybe then she would be in thrall to me *. . . maybe she would be* my *wife. . . .*

He shook his head fiercely. *I don't want her.* It was a lie, though, and he knew it. He had never really stopped wanting her.

Maybe I should help her, he thought, as James threw Nicole into a wall. He took a step forward before he could stop himself. *Fool, she's probably put a spell on you.*

He forced himself to breathe deeply as he crossed his arms over his chest. *She means nothing to me,* he told himself as James knocked her unconscious.

Nicole's body slid down the wall to the ground. He stared at her crumpled, battered form. James stood panting, blood streaming down his face from scratches around his eyes.

"Hellcat," James spat. "She's useless now. We'll sacrifice her tonight, a gift to the Horned God."

Eli blinked, not entirely sure what he thought of that.

Supreme Coven: London

Every corner of the Supreme Coven shook as a roar of rage ripped through it. Every creature residing within, from the most powerful demon to the tiniest mouse, trembled with fear. Sir William's wrath had no bounds.

The skull throne cracked from top to bottom, shards of bone flying through the air and impaling the warlock who trembled before it. He died as his organs ruptured. His companion fell to her knees before Sir William, her head bowed. "My lord, I am, as always, yours to command."

Sir William stared at the young woman. She was one of the female members of the Supreme Coven. Outnumbered by their male brothers, they often worked harder to gain power and recognition. This young warlock had proven herself time and again in his service.

"Rise, my child," he commanded her.

Eve rose to her feet but kept her head down. He probed her mind. A myriad of emotions washed over him. Women, be they witch, warlock, or mere mortal, all had a complicated emotional makeup. He slowly peeled back the layers of anger, lust, sorrow, and joy. At last he reached her core, and she shuddered slightly. He pulled back out of her mind, satisfied. The one emotion he had been looking for was absent. She was not afraid of him or of what he had done to her companion.

He smiled slowly, a wicked grin that he knew made him look even more the fiend. Then he rose to his feet and made his proclamation, projecting his voice throughout every room and cavern.

"Michael Deveraux has broken faith with the Supreme Coven. From this moment forth he is to be hunted by all. Whoever brings me his head will receive my favor and riches beyond his—or her—wildest dreams."

Eve met his eyes and nodded.

He lifted his hand to her slowly, as in benediction. "Happy hunting, my dear."

She turned and vanished from sight.

Sir William sat back down on the throne. Michael Deveraux was persona non grata now. Every warlock in the Supreme Coven would be seeking him.

"Michael Deveraux has betrayed us," a voice hissed from the shadows.

Sir William sighed. "Yes, no surprise there. We should have destroyed House Deveraux years ago."

"But they alone know the secret of the Black Fire."

"We've been holding out for it too long already," Sir William growled.

"So surely a little more time cannot hurt."

"Unless he brings me Holly Cathers's head, I will have Michael Deveraux's."

As the voice from the shadows began cackling, Sir William stood. "Guard!"

A warlock swiftly entered the room, eyes probing the darkness. The laughter continued and it visibly unnerved the man. Sir William allowed himself to smile at the other's fear. "Bring James to me. I shall brook no delays."

The man nodded and disappeared.

"James, your son," the shadow whispered.

Sir William nodded. "We will soon find where his loyalties truly lie."

Nicole: Avalon

Nicole woke with a gasp. The last thing she remembered was fighting James. She had been about to try to crack his skull open when he had hit her. She tried to sit up but found that she was tied to her bed. A feeling of dread rose in her. *What has James done?* She managed to turn her head slightly to look at the chains anchoring her left wrist. *Or what is he about to do?*

She shivered as she gave the chains a tug. The clanking metal grated upon her ears, and she winced. She raised her head and noticed that her legs were similarly manacled. *Great.* She exhaled slowly. *Goddess, come to me, be with me.*

She closed her eyes and tried to center herself, to focus her energy. She concentrated on making a small ball of heat in the center of her being. Her mind cleared, and she focused. *First the chains around my right wrist.* The metal around the lock groaned and creaked as she willed the pins to start moving. *Eli once taught me to pick a lock the old-fashioned way. I wish instead he had taught me to do it the magical way.* The process was agonizingly slow, but one by one the pins moved into place until only the last remained. She pushed, pouring more energy into the stubborn metal until the entire band about her wrist grew hot and started burning her.

Ignore the pain, she coached herself as she kept working at the lock. She wrinkled up her nose as she began to smell her flesh burning. *Ignore the smell.* Then suddenly the pin moved, clicking into place, and the metal cuff sprang open. Gasping, she shook her hand and it fell off.

She stared at the burn marks around her wrist. The skin was beginning to blister. *Not good.* She closed her eyes and prayed. *Goddess, take this wounded arm and repair all its harm, heal the flesh and numb the pain, renew that which now is lame.*

She watched in awe as the blisters dissipated. The pain subsided as well. After a minute there was only a slight red ring around her wrist. *Scar?* she wondered. She couldn't help but think suddenly of Jer and the scarring that the Fire had done to him.

It's a miracle he lives, she thought. *I wonder what dark force kept him alive and healed him enough to function as a human being?* She shuddered. *Whatever it is, I hope I never have to meet it.*

Then, out of the darkness, a voice whispered, "Too late."

Mother Coven: Santa Cruz

Anne-Louise Montrachet was uneasy in her skin. Something is coming. *I can feel it in the earth, in the water, but, most especially, in the air.*

Thanks be to the Goddess, and the healers of her coven, she was well again. The pain of healing had nearly killed her, but now she could move with little effort and only slight pain. She stretched out her legs as she walked the wooded paths and breathed in the rich air.

This was her first time at the Mother Coven retreat in the hills of Santa Cruz, California, though she had heard many things about it. For five years now the coven had owned the property and used it. Behind her, Whisper, a gray cat that had mysteriously appeared and adopted her, scampered after a lizard in the undergrowth.

Santa Cruz was a strange place, with a natural, mystical energy unlike any she had ever felt. Strange happenings were also being attributed to the area. There was the famous "Mystery Spot," where gravity seemed to work in reverse. It was but one of several spots like it on Earth, but it had seemed to draw the most attention. Alfred Hitchcock was inspired by a flock of birds that seemingly went mad and flew into houses, killing themselves, and attacking the people caught outside. The incident that became the basis for *The Birds* was just one of the strange things that had happened in the area.

More than any of these stories, though, Anne-Louise had always been fascinated and disturbed by the stories of the Satanic rituals performed in the very hills she was walking. Every year, ignorant, bored, rebellious college students from UC Santa Cruz and elsewhere gathered to perform bizarre rituals and sacrifice untold numbers of animals. She glanced protectively at Whisper.

The cat paused to look at her, half a lizard in her mouth, and cocked her head questioningly to the side. In almost every instance the children involved in such events knew nothing of magic—white, black, or gray. The "rituals" were just an outlet for their own twisted, sadistic natures. A very few of them, though, were worshipers of the Horned God who used the rest as cover for their activities. Since the Mother Coven had taken property in these hills, they had worked to eradicate such horrors. *True witches don't kill cats,* Anne-Louise told herself. *All the more reason to fear Holly.*

The younger witch had scared her from the first. She had too much power, especially for one so young in years and young in the Craft. *They all do.* Anne-Louise herself had had to work and study for years to accomplish even some of the most minor magics, except for wards. Wards were her specialty—her "gift," as the High Priestess called it. Every witch had a special gift, the thing at which she excelled. What made Holly dangerous was the fact that she excelled at everything and had never had to learn discipline to do so.

The trees moaned as the wind picked up, and Anne-Louise glanced around self-consciously. *Yes, something is coming,* she thought. *And when it gets here, we're all going to be in a lot of trouble.*

Nicole: Avalon

Nicole trembled. "Who's there?" she called.

A low, mocking laugh was all the answer she received.

She saw something move out of the corner of her eye, a whisper of something not quite there. She twisted her head, and it was gone. "Goddess?" she whispered, praying that it was but knowing that it wasn't.

"No."

She twisted her head back to where the sound came from, but there was nothing. "The Horned God?" she asked, swallowing around the lump in her throat.

Another laugh. "No."

"Then, who, what are you?" she demanded, pulse thundering in her ears.

"Something . . . else."

"What?" she gasped.

"Something you can't understand," it roared, and then suddenly it was on top of her, pressing against her, moving through her.

"And now—I'm not alone."

As it merged with her mind, she felt evil, ancient and mysterious. She felt rage, lust, and deceit. And there was something else . . .

. . . there were two.

Kari: California

Kari sped down Interstate 5, leaving the town of Winters behind as fast as she could. "Come on, come on," she shouted, punching her horn to punctuate it. She swerved around the car in front of her and hit the accelerator as she looked at the clock on the dashboard.

Any minute now they would know she was missing,

that she wasn't coming back. She had to get as far away as she could before they sicced the bloodhound Pablo on her—or, worse, the mysterious new cousin, Alex.

They had all been hiding in her family cabin near the town of Winters, which was situated next to the university town of Davis. While everyone got used to Alex and began magical and physical preparations for the evening, she had volunteered to go get food. Somehow, miraculously, they had let her go alone.

She had bypassed the general store, speeding toward the freeway as fast as she could. *I can't handle this anymore. I'm sick of waiting around to be killed like the others. And Alex . . . Alex terrifies me.*

She didn't know why, but there was something about him that made her uneasy. She pushed her foot down harder on the gas pedal. She had to get clear, she had to think. Despair filled her, though, with a sinking feeling that even if she escaped the coven, she wouldn't be safe. Into the blackness of her thoughts, a single small light appeared.

What if I can get the two sides to stop fighting? What if I can get them to call a truce? There must be a way we can all live together in peace.

She narrowed her eyes. Jer had once said his father had a place in the desert, sort of a spiritual retreat. It was in New Mexico. *If they won't listen, he might.*

Nicole: Avalon

Nicole woke up and began to vomit. She tried to curl on her side, but the chains still binding her ankles and right wrist wouldn't let her move too far.

From behind her, a familiar, hated voice commented, "You look like hell."

James! She turned her head slowly and stared at him. "What is on this island?"

"What?" he said, sounding puzzled.

"You heard me," she spat. "What is on this island? There is something here."

He hesitated for a moment, and in that moment he almost seemed human to her, frail and filled with uncertainty. "Once, when I was young, I thought—"

"Thought what?" she pressed.

"Nothing," he snapped, his veneer sliding back into place.

"Tell me!"

He shrugged, an evil grin spreading across his face. "I guess you'll just have to ask the ghosts, once I turn you into one." He threw a dress down on the bed beside her. "Be dressed in that when I return in five minutes."

"Or what?"

"Or, I'll dress you," he said, bending down to give her the full effect of his leer.

Sickened, she turned her face away. She heard him move to the door and open it. Then, with a great clanking, her chains fell from her wrist and ankles. She heard the door shut behind him as she sat up.

He intends to sacrifice me, she thought as she stared at the dress. *Well, he's going to find out I'm not that easy to kill.*

Astarte leaped up into her lap with a soft *mew,* and Nicole stroked her soft fur for a moment before moving her aside so she could begin dressing. Astarte had the most uncanny ability to make herself scarce when James was around.

"That's because I have not chosen him," the cat opened its mouth, and a strong yet feminine voice spoke.

"Goddess," Nicole gasped.

"Yes, child, I have been watching you, guiding you. Your time is not yet over. It has only just begun."

"Those things that attacked me?"

"The betrayer and his apprentice."

"What did they want from me?" she asked while pulling her shirt off over her head.

"What they always want—to corrupt, to pervert."

"Why me?" she asked, as she stepped into the dress.

"Because you are the future."

Nicole zipped up the dress and was about to ask what that meant when there was a sound at the door.

The cat disappeared, and Nicole turned to face James as he entered.

He looked her up and down appreciatively. "You'll make a lovely sacrifice for the Horned God tonight." He sidled close and grasped her upper arm. He pulled her close, so that they were inches from each other. "Too bad we both know you're not a virgin."

She smirked. "Yeah, remind me to thank Eli for that."

"Slut!" he hissed as he raised his other hand to slap her. She just looked up at him, a smile twisting her lips. She had gotten to him. *That's it, James. I win.*

He knew it too. She could see it in his eyes. With a snarl, he turned and started dragging her toward the door. Instead of fighting him, she shook her arm free—*How did I do that?*— and walked beside him.

When they reached the dungeon he locked her in a cell. "I'll be back for you in a little while."

"Do you really think this cage can hold me, James, if I will it not to?" she asked mockingly. The tides had turned and, somehow, despite the fact that she was the prisoner, she had all the power.

James nearly killed the messenger. "What do you mean, my father wants to see me right away?

The man kneeling at his feet didn't lift his eyes.

"Your presence is wanted at once, no delays."

James felt his blood boiling with frustration. The sacrifice of his bride would have to wait. He was still playing his father's game, pretending to be the dutiful son, and he wasn't ready yet to end the charade.

As James got in the boat to cross the waters back to England, he didn't notice another boat that was docking a hundred yards away. The thick fog obscured its occupants from sight. The island had been heavily warded for centuries, even more so since Nicole's escape. As soon as she'd left they had installed barriers that made it impossible to open a portal on the island.

That was why the four huge, lumbering beasts were crawling out of the boat they'd had to steal to attain the island. Because they landed at the same time that James's boat was leaving, no sensor alarms went off. They were lucky, but then the Golems knew nothing of luck. All they knew was the task that they were assigned, and they had been trying for a couple of days to find and kill Nicole Anderson.

SEVEN

MORDON

☾

We waver now in our quest
Green Man tell us what is best
Shall we kill or shall we bleed
And where shall we plant our seed

Betrayal now all around
Weeping is the only sound
We shall die with Wind Moon rise
Victims of warlock lies

Kari: New Mexico

As Kari swerved around the orange barrels rerouting her path across the freeway lanes, the torrential rain pummeled the top of the car like fists in metal gauntlets. She wasn't sure why the barrels were there, but they made her progress even harder . . . and it was difficult enough already.

Her windshield wipers could do nothing against the onslaught; water rushed down the glass with the speed and power of a waterfall. Fanning across the highway, the rising waters sent her hydroplaning, and she cried out and grabbed the steering wheel hard.

Kari was struggling across high desert country. Her neck and upper back were knotted with fear; when she had awakened in her motel room, she had listened intently to the news reports about tonight's flash floods. But something told her to drive, anyway, and to keep driving, and she didn't know if the demanding voice inside her head was that of friend or foe. Now that she had bolted, it could be one of the coven members trying to catch up with her; or one of those hideous Golems . . . or Holly herself.

Her stomach clenched. She was scared to death of what Holly had become. What would Jer think of his precious "soul mate" now that she had practically no soul at all? She, Kari, could almost forgive him for dumping her in favor of Holly. Hell, she was the strongest witch alive, and he was a warlock. But she was also the one who'd left him to die in the Black Fire in the gymnasium. His terrible scars were evidence of her "love" for him.

Maybe Kari wasn't as exciting as Holly, but she sure as hell was more loyal. She'd stayed in the coven even though it had meant risking her life, and had offered her apartment as the place to hold Circle until things got too dicey. She hadn't signed up for any of that, but she'd stayed on board when the others needed her. All she had wanted to do was go to grad school, be Jeraud Deveraux's lover, and learn a few bits and pieces of his magical tradition.

How was I to know his family was into Black Magic?

It was as if she were being punished for having ambition. Wanting to learn about things that would stretch her limits; needing to explore beyond the mundane world. . . .

You knew, she told herself harshly. *You knew about his family. Somewhere deep down, you accepted how bad they were.*

No . . .

And you always felt guilty about your relationship with him. He's so much younger than you. You were using him, because it was always a bargain between you and him—pleasure for magic.

Hey, not a bad trade for either of us, and he was old enough to know what he was doing . . .

. . . and then you fell in love with him, for real.

Tears welled.

Now Holly's gone completely dark. If I don't stop her and Michael Deveraux, they'll kill us all.

The car suddenly hydroplaned; she felt the water lift the wheels from the road and rush it forward. It teetered and threatened to carom in a circle, and she cried out, swerving, riding the current until, miraculously, the wheels found the road again.

She had ignored dozens of warnings on TV. A number of people died in New Mexico's flash floods every year, many of them while driving. It appeared that everyone else had stayed home; she could see no other lights in the darkness, though for a time, strange, fiery plumes had bellowed from the tops of concrete towers way off in the distance, as if from some kind of refinery.

There they are again, she thought, squinting through the windshield. Then she gasped.

They weren't like the plumes she'd seen before. These three towered much higher in the sky, and they glowed with the radiant blue of magical energy.

As she watched, they flickered, vanished, and reappeared again, more brightly this time.

They're closer, she realized.

They went out again, reappeared again.

And closer.

She stopped the car.

The three plumes rushed into being about ten feet away from her car, illuminating the black highway, casting the interior of the vehicle in blue light.

"Oh, God," she whispered. Her breath caught in her throat.

Then the flames extinguished. Before she had time to react, fire banks erupted on either side of the car, at ground level, their blue fire geysering past her line of sight and piercing the rain-soaked heavens.

Kari screamed aloud, inadvertently jerking the steering wheel to the left and pushing her foot down on the gas. She kept screaming as she headed straight for the wall of blue flame, pulling her hands off the wheel and raising them above her face. She shut her eyes tightly, screaming for all she was worth.

Then the car began to hydroplane again; or at least that was the sensation she felt. She dropped her hands back onto the wheel and opened her eyes.

Although still pelted by the rain, her Honda was now entirely surrounded by the blue glow. As the individual flames whipped and undulated, she had a clear view of blackness outside her window; she craned her neck and looked down.

Tinted a dull yellow, a thin stretch of highway was visible, and beyond it, the twinkling lights of a town.

Oh, my God, I'm flying, she thought, throwing herself away from the window. She whimpered and stared out the front window, then the other side. Without realizing what she was doing, she raised her feet off the floor.

Huddling behind the wheel, she murmured a

protection spell. The car dipped, and she shrieked. Then it righted itself and kept going.

As the flames separated, she saw again the pinpoint lights of the town through the driver's side window. The car was gliding away from them, and toward the vast expanses of the uninhabited desert.

What if it drops me? What if I land in the desert and the car gets swept down an arroyo, and I drown?

"Goddess, help me," she murmured, clenching her hands as one did in Christian prayer. She felt no reply, no comfort. She never had. She wasn't certain there was a Goddess. She didn't know who made the Coven's spells work. Or who answered the summons of the Deveraux. She had begun her exploration of magic as a folklorist, and she was aware that, despite popular assumption, the religious varieties of Wicca, paganism, shamanism, and other magic-using traditions employed slightly different interpretations of their supreme deities. One witch's Goddess was not necessarily the same as another's.

On impulse she reached forward and turned on the radio. The noise of the heavy rains had made it nearly impossible to listen to the faint signals she had managed to pick up.

There was nothing, not even static.

She pushed the horn. It, too, was dead.

"Help!" she shouted. "I'm sorry!"

And she *was* sorry. She felt a flood of guilt and remorse, although for what, precisely, she wasn't certain. But she knew deep in her soul that leaving the coven and trying to find Michael Deveraux had been wrong, no matter what her reasoning had been.

No matter what lies I told myself. And now I'm going to pay. Now he's found me and he's going to kill me, because that's what he is, an evil killer, and . . . and . . . what the hell was I thinking?

Batted by the rain, the car glided along. Kari began to cry—huge, heavy sobs that forced her stomach to contract. Bile rushed up into the back of her throat, making it burn; when she tried to swallow it down, she found she couldn't. She sat with her teeth clenched, crying harder and harder, until she was wailing like a crazy person.

Next she heard herself reciting the Lord's Prayer by rote, without a thought as to the words and what they meant. It was simply a reflex from childhood, and although once she realized what she was doing she listened carefully to the words, she found no comfort.

All the gods and Goddesses have left me, she thought bitterly. *These are demons I have to face alone.*

Literally.

She had no idea how long she floated along,

buoyed by the magical glow, but she gradually grew exhausted from all the crying, and her head began to bob forward. Fuzzy images drifted across her closed eyelids—happier times with Jer, holding hands and smiling at each other; getting slick and dizzy in the sweat lodge. Kialish and Eddie were there, and now they were both dead. . . .

Oh, God! I'm so tired of all the dying! I'm so scared!

Then she heard the screech of birds and opened her eyes. She caught her breath and swallowed hard, balling her hands into fists in her lap, then gripping the steering wheel—as if doing so made any sense at all.

Surrounding the car, their bodies sheened with moonlight, dozens of falcons flew on either side of the car. One ticked its head in her direction; its eyes glowed bloodred, and it opened and shut its beak like an automaton. She shrank back, blinking at it. It continued to stare at her, then shut its beak and straightened its head.

Next, she heard a strange sound that she took to be her own heartbeat, a rhythmic *whum-whum, whum-whum.* She listened, pressing her palm against her chest. The two sounds were out of sync. Her heart was beating much faster, and she realized the sound was coming from outside of herself.

She stared at the vast flying field of birds. *It's their*

wings, she realized, terrified. The birds were soaring in unison, each one's wings undulating up and down, up and down, in the rain; as she stared, a picture formed in her head of galley slaves chained to tiny benches below the decks of a great barque, raising and lowering massive oars to the steady beat of the oar master.

Whum-whum, whum-whum . . . and then the sound slowed and blurred; she felt her head fall back against the seat. Though her eyes remained open, she no longer saw birds and night sky and the moonlight. Her field of vision shimmered; colors ran like rain on a chalk painting, and then a new place burst into her reality; and a new . . . or very old . . . time.

A very old time.

France, the 13th Century

"Allons-y!" cried the splendid man on horseback. It was the heir of the House of Deveraux, Jean, and this was the Great Hunt that would provision his wedding feast. He was to be married this very night to Isabeau of Cahors, daughter of the Deverauxs' witchly rival in the region.

And then he will think of me no longer, Karienne thought dismally. She rode her horse astride like a man, at a discreet distance. Though most in the Hunt retinue knew her to be his mistress, they also knew that she was being cast aside. He must save his manly virtues for the marriage bed, and get a child on Isabeau as soon as possible. It was the unspoken bargain between the families.

As always, Jean was astonishingly handsome. His ermine-tipped cloak fanned over his saddle and the cropped tail of his warhorse. The rider raised his left gauntlet into the air, and the magnificent falcon, Fantasme, which had been perched there, hurled himself into the golden sky and flew toward the dense thicket just ahead.

A cheer rose from the hunters, mixing with the steady rhythm of the drummers who walked ahead. *Whum-whum-whum,* their measures bold and merciless. *Catch and kill, catch and kill . . .* For the moment, they sought birds, and hares, and bucks.

But soon they would begin to flush out the serfs who would be sacrificed to the Horned God this very night.

Whum . . . whum . . .

Karienne lifted her chin and sternly denied tears from welling in her eyes.

I have pride. I am still beautiful.

But had I the chance, I would kill that bitch of the Cahors, and magick him into taking me to wife . . .

Had I the chance . . .

Had I the chance . . .

Whum-whum . . . whum . . .

With a sharp gasp, Kari opened her eyes and raised her head off the back of the seat.

Whoa, was that a dream? It was so real. Did I actually go back in time? Was I . . . was some part of me actually Jean's mistress? Because, in a very weird way, that would make sense given what's been going on with all of us these days. . . .

She had no time to consider it further. The car tipped downward, floating at an angle toward the ground. The birds' wings continued to flap steadily, and the car was surrounded with the same blue glow as before.

Frightened, she put her foot on the break, then realized how silly that was, and took it back off. She forced her breathing to slow down—she had begun to hyperventilate—and whispered to herself, "Karienne."

With that, the rain stopped abruptly, as if someone had turned off a faucet. One moment the sky was clashing with the storm, the next . . . peace.

The metal of the car *ticked-ticked-ticked* as the engine cooled down. Kari caught her breath again, and slowly exhaled. Her heart was throbbing in her chest; she could hear it roaring in her ears.

The car continued to descend. To her right, a soft yellow light glowed through the darkness, and she made out the low-slung angles of a New Mexican–style adobe building. A path wound its way toward the structure. Otherwise, the landscape was barren.

As she gazed at the building, she saw over its silhouette the gauzy images of trees and lush undergrowth. It was the forest of her dream.

The wings of the birds echoed the drumbeats of the Hunt.

Slowly, one by one, the birds began to fade, and then disappear. The forest vanished as well. Soon, only the car and she remained in the sky, and the dimly lit building below.

It appeared to be the front entrance to a house. The ends of large logs extended from either side of the entrance, and there were three steps leading up to a front door, which appeared to be made of wood.

It's got to be Michael's house, she thought. *He's brought me to him.*

She made no sound, only stared hard at the door, bracing herself for it to open. On impulse she made sure all her car doors were locked—they were—and then she smiled grimly at how ridiculous that was. The futility of it. Whoever was behind that door had made her car *fly,* for heaven's sake.

Her unhappy smile had not yet faded when the lock on her door unclicked by itself.

Then it swung open.

"No way," she murmured. She didn't touch it, didn't move. Her heartbeat grew even more rapid, and she began to breathe so shallowly that she began to get dizzy.

The door remained as it was, insistent that she get out.

Fresh tears welled in her eyes, and her face prickled with fear. A dizzying wave washed over her; she hadn't realized how exhausted she was from fighting the storm, and she had no reserves to deal with her terror.

After a few more seconds, she tried to move, but she remained strapped in place. She still had on her seat belt. It took a supreme act of will to unfasten it, her shaking fingers pressing uselessly until she grimaced and pulled herself together, jabbing it so hard, she broke her nail. The belt slithered back into the retractor like a serpent.

The lights on the porch glowed. A cold wind whipped sand against her thigh, and Kari finally stirred. As if leaping from the car, she swung her left leg out, found her footing on loose gravel, and scooted the rest of the way out of the car.

Unsteadily, she straightened up. Her gaze fixed on the house, she shut her door and made her way around the front of the car, her hand extended as if she were admonishing it not to turn itself on and run her down.

Then the rain started again, drenching her from head to toe. She cried out and shielded her head. In the frigid torrent, she felt her makeup sluice down her face, all in one piece, as if it had been a mask.

Despite the rain, she didn't hurry her pace—she couldn't—but walked unsteadily across the gravel, inching toward the three steps that led to the porch.

She climbed them, remembering that, back in Seattle, there had also been three stairs to the porch of the Deveraux home. *Three* was a magical number, and Michael Deveraux was an architect. If he had built this house, he put those stairs there for a reason.

On the porch, she stepped onto a hemp welcome mat decorated in red and green—the Deveraux Coven colors—featuring a silhouette of a black bird, a falcon, in the center. She was careful not to step on the bird, and then she thought better of it and ground her boot heel hard into its face.

I won't let him intimidate me, she promised herself, then nearly laughed out loud. *Okay, I will let him intimidate me.*

I just won't let him kill me.

She reached forward toward the door. The moonlight cast a glimmer on a door knocker in the center of the carved door, which was a brass rendition of the Green Man, an aspect of the God as a nature deity.

She took a breath, and knocked.

She wasn't surprised when the door swung open.

Summoning every last vestige of her courage, she took a step across the transom. She was standing inside now, in the pitch-black darkness, in a cocoon that muffled the steady patter of the rain on thc gravel.

I'm going to betray them all to their worst enemy: Michael Deveraux. The man who's been trying to destroy all of us.

Yes, and he's going to succeed . . . if I don't find a way to stop him. I didn't want this. I didn't want any of this. From day one, they bullied me and made me go along with them.

Cold and fear penetratcd her bones. She was trembling, and her knees were beginning to give way; her tears of frustration ran down her cheeks, salty and warmer than the icy rain.

Then a soft golden light bobbed in front of her eyes, and she blinked, startled.

Michael Deveraux stood less than a foot away from her. His palm was outstretched, and above it, a ball of fire the size of a golf ball floated, casting shadows from beneath his chin onto his features, giving him an incredibly sinister aspect. He had long black hair, a black beard, and heavy lashes. His eyes were quite deep set, and his brows were angled slightly back from his nose. When he smiled, she shrank back involuntarily.

He reminded her of the Devil.

"Come on in," Michael Deveraux said jauntily, taking a step back to allow her entry. His heel rang on the stone floor. "Kari, isn't it? We've never formally met, even though you've been sleeping with my son for years."

Her lips parted, but she didn't know what to say in response, so she kept silent.

He was dressed all in black—black sweater, black jeans, black boots—and in his other hand he held out a heavy earthen goblet. She didn't remember it being there before. "Hot buttered rum," he said, smiling. "It'll warm you up. Nasty night out." He raised one brow. "Not fit weather for warlock or witch."

She hesitated. "I'm not a witch. I just know a few spells."

His chuckle alarmed her. "Oh, I know what you are, Kari, and what you're not." He gestured at her with the rum. "Come. Drink." When she still hesitated, he added slyly, "It won't kill you." As if to prove his point, he took a sip, sighing contentedly before he lowered it from his mouth.

She said unsteadily, "I-I made a mistake coming here."

"No. You did exactly the right thing. Believe me."

He turned and glanced at her, indicating that she should accompany him. When she stepped toward him, the area around them suddenly lit up and she stumbled, startled. There was track lighting overhead, and on the wall in front of her, a mirror framed in beaten silver. She winced at her own reflection. Her makeup had collected under her eyes. She looked like a zombie.

"No magic," he said airily. "Just motion detectors."

He led her through the hallway, the soles of their shoes noisy on the hard surface. The walls were crowded with images of fantastic, swirling birds of red and green flying through a verdant forest, the designs painted directly on the white plaster walls. Even the low ceiling above her had been painted with heavy foliage and crazed, vicious birds. Their dark beady eyes seemed to follow her as she walked past them.

At the end of the hallway, Michael opened a set of wooden double doors, revealing a shadowed room illuminated by the glow of flame inside the distended belly of a stone statue of the Horned God. The God's goat-face gleamed cruel and lusty, its taloned hands raised and extended slightly forward as if it were about to pounce on the next hapless person who dared to walk into the room. It sat back on haunches that ended in goat hooves. Kari shivered, looking away.

Other statues stood in the flickering darkness, none of them very distinguishable. All she saw was a vast array of fangs, talons, and horns. Everything sharp, everything ready to cut and wound.

The room was as cold as a meat locker. Her soaked clothes wrapped around her like ice packs.

"Warm yourself," he invited, gesturing to the statue.

She wished she could refuse, but there was no other source of warmth. She edged uneasily toward the figure, stretching forth her left hand as she took another sip of the rum. This time it tasted good, its alcoholic heat spreading through her chilled veins.

"Where are they?" he asked without further preamble.

She licked her lips. *What was I thinking?*

"W-who?" she managed to say.

"Kari, dear," he said kindly, "there's no other reason you would come to me than to strike some sort of bargain. From what I know of you, I'm guessing that you want to give me the Coven in exchange for my saving my son."

"You . . . should save him, anyway," she replied. She bit her lip and stared into the fire. "He's your child."

"Did you come here to argue with me?" He

sounded amused. "I don't think I've met anyone as brash as you since my wife left me."

She licked her lips. "You might be able to turn him, make him be . . . like you."

He shook his head. "Years of trying puts the lie to that, Miss Hardwicke. Jer's bound and determined to make my life difficult. Trust me: I'd be much, much better without him."

He came up beside her and watched the fire. She was aware of how closely he stood next to her; she could smell expensive soap and aftershave, and his body heat mingled with her own. She was shocked to realize that she was becoming aroused.

He's making it happen, she told herself. *Because I would never . . . he's so evil.*

So powerful, another voice whispered in her head.

"Talk to me," he invited. "It'll only be difficult at first."

Still, she kept her silence. Her heart was pounding again, and she was beginning to worry about having a heart attack. Or that she would faint and he would . . . would do something that he shouldn't. . . .

I'm getting really excited. She glared at him. "Leave me alone," she blurted.

He burst into laughter. "It's a little late for that." He grinned at her and added, "Kari, you made the right decision." He grabbed her hand and wrapped both his hands around it, blowing gently on her knuckles.

"Just tell me," he urged. "Tell me where they are. I'll save Jer—if he can be saved."

She took a breath. "They're in Winters."

He nodded. "Tell me about this new male witch from the missing Cahors line. Alex Carruthers."

Her eyes widened. She felt the blood draining from her face and she wished she could stop feeling his skin against her own. "You know about him?" She didn't know why she was surprised. She cocked her head and looked at him. "If you know he exists, you should know everything else about him." Her fear emboldened her, and she added, "Don't you have scrying stones? Haven't you been spying on us?"

A careless shrug was the only answer he gave her. He took her goblet from her and raised the rim to her lips. Then he tipped it forward, forcing her to take a sip or let the rum and butter splash down her chin.

She let the alcohol warm her veins and give her a measure of courage. Then she cleared her throat and said, "He's very powerful."

"Really." He sounded intrigued. "He's their cousin, correct?"

She wondered then if he had tricked her, making

her assume he knew more than he did. It was too late to go back and repair the damage, if she had caused any.

"If"? I'm destroying them all.

"He's a distant cousin, at best. I'm not sure exactly how they're related." She moved her shoulders. "It's all so complicated."

He looked unconvinced. "And yet, you're getting a PhD in anthropology. I would think you'd be extremely well-versed on kinship systems."

"I'm getting a doctorate in folklore," she corrected.

"Ah. My mistake." He eased her goblet of rum from her hand and took a hefty swallow. Sighing with contentment, he handed it back to her. "You came here of your own free will," he reminded her.

Did I? she wanted to ask him. Now she wasn't so certain. . . . "His powers are strong," she continued.

"They would have to be, to defeat Holly."

There was a strange clattering on the stone floor, like the nails of a dog, followed by a high-pitched cackle. The cackling echoed around the room as the clattering skittered toward Kari; she whirled around, glancing at the floor, then cried out when something flashed past her and landed on Michael's shoulder.

It was an ugly, troll-like creature, almost reptilian in appearance, with long, pointed ears and sharp features. It was unclothed, and leathery-skinned, and it hissed merrily at Kari, then cocked its head and began to babble at Michael.

"She'ssss trying to break free, free she issss," it announced, jabbing a long finger over its shoulder. "Going crazzzzzy."

"Thank you. It's not a problem," Michael said, patting the thing on its head. "Go find a dead rodent to eat, will you?" He swept the thing off his shoulder. It soared through the air and landed on the floor, then scrabbled away into the darkness.

Kari's knees buckled.

"Oh here, here, how thoughtless of me. You must be exhausted."

Michael snapped his fingers. An overstuffed chair upholstered in brilliant crimson materialized behind Kari, bumping against her calves. She fell backward into it, sinking into the softness, which was also very warm. Her drink sloshed onto her wrist, sending the scent of nutmeg into the air.

She took a drink to steady herself and leaned back. To her amazement she realized she was about to fall asleep. *He must be casting a spell on me. I was a fool to come here. I was so scared. . . .*

"You did the right thing," he assured her. "This is really the only reasonable choice you could make. I'm going to kill the rest of them. And I'm going to begin with Holly." He looked pleased with himself.

"Jer . . . ," she murmured.

"I haven't decided." He leaned over her, smoothing her wet hair away from her forehead. His eyes were compelling; his smile, a terrible thing.

"I have Holly here," he told her. "Did you realize that? And in two nights, I'm going to kill her. On the Wind Moon, and when I do it, I'll absorb her power. No one in the history of Coventry will be stronger than I will become."

He lifted his chin and focused his eyes toward the ceiling. "Your timing couldn't have been more perfect, Kari. For coming to me, I'll spare you. By that, I mean that I won't kill you." After a beat he added, "That's a good thing, honey."

She followed his line of sight, and her blood ran cold.

Painted onto the ceiling was an enormous black falcon, its wings stretching into the dark recesses of the room. In its massive, wicked-looking beak it clutched a human heart, and from that heart, blood dripped onto the breast of the huge creature itself. Its eyes—enormous, even for a creature its size—glared down at her, seeming to follow her.

"Fantasme, the spirit of the Great Falcon." Michael made a motion with his hand. "He lives in the spiritual Greenwood, and there he hunts Pandion."

Kari heard again the thrumming of the drums of the Great Hunt, a counterpoint to the quicktime wing-beats of the birds that had flown beside her car. She was incredibly dizzy; the room was spinning. She held on to the arms of the chair and began to gasp. Her lids fluttered, and she heard herself moan.

The evil bird lifted its head and screeched. The cry was ear-piercing, shaking her brain inside her skull. The heart in its mouth dropped from the painting, erupting into the real world, and tumbled in a slow-motion float toward Kari.

She lurched to her feet, knocking over the chair, then whirled on her heel and raced awkwardly for the doorway. Michael's laughter trailed behind her.

At the doorway, a wraithlike figure stepped from the darkened hall and blocked her escape. Shorter than she, it was wrapped in a glowing blue gauze, which it slowly lifted as its maniacal laughter trilled from beneath the layers, like the echo of the bird.

Seeing who it was, Kari gasped. Her knees buckled, and she fell hard against the stone floor.

"Bonsoir, ma belle," said the figure.

It was Holly, her eyes spinning with madness.

But inside those eyes, cloaked more deeply, were another set of eyes, and they glared at Kari with fury.

Get me out of here! they demanded. *Maintenant!*

"Isabeau," Kari whispered. "Isabeau, are you trying to communicate with me?"

Holly herself made no response. Kari wasn't sure she had even heard her. But the eyes said, *Oui! Get me out! He will destroy us all!*

Behind Kari, Michael Deveraux said, "Put her somewhere safe, Holly. We'll make good use of her later."

Holly's face cracked into a mad, bewitched smile.

The Tri-Coven: Santa Cruz

The others drew around the fire as Alex stood with his hands spread for warmth. The dual scents of smoke and wood reminded Jer of the old sweat lodge on the University of Washington campus—the one he, Kialish, and Eddie had built together. Of the three of them, he was the only survivor.

And God only knows where Kari's gone off to. . . .

"It's nearly Wind Moon," Alex said, looking up at the pearly orb in the sky. He looked across the fire at Jer, who wore his hooded robe low over his face. Now that Holly was gone, he saved his magickal reserve for things other than creating a glamour of his former appearance. Still, it bothered him when the others glimpsed his features, then grimaced and looked away. He knew they didn't even realize they were doing it, and that Amanda, especially, would be mortified to know how much her revulsion wounded him.

But it's not about me now. It's about all of us surviving long enough to defeat my father.

Alex looked at Jer and said, "You know what that means, right, Deveraux?"

Aware that Alex continued to use Jer's hated last name even though he had asked him repeatedly not to, Jer nodded grimly. The Wind Moon would be ascendant when his father struck hardest. When Michael Deveraux tried to bring Hell to Earth.

He stared into the fire as if he could will it skyward. Witches spoke of drawing down the moon; if only they could, so he could set it ablaze and throw it back up into space and watch it burn. Then Wind Moon would never come.

The ensuing silence made the others nervous. Jer could feel the tension in the air. He took a sip of his coffee and found it bitter. But to him, all of life was bitter.

I'm staying alive to bring him down. And then . . .

Amanda frowned and drew closer to Philippe, saying to him, "What? What does Wind Moon mean?"

"I don't know," Philippe replied, shrugging. He gazed first at Alex, and then at Jer.

Jer looked up at him. Amanda flinched, but Philippe did not.

"It's the Horned God's moon. Any witch or warlock who dies during the next full moon becomes the damned servant of the God for all eternity."

"Well put," Alex said. "Accurate."

"Dios mio," Pablo murmured, crossing himself.

"Why didn't you two bring this up before now?" Armand demanded, looking angry. "We have hardly any time to prepare."

"I wasn't sure," Alex said. "I threw the runes."

The others turned to Jer. "Not every Wind Moon is charged with the same energy. But Alex is right about this one: This is a bad moon."

Amanda sighed heavily. "It never ends," she murmured. "It just gets worse and worse."

Pablo said to Jer, "What do we have to do?"

Before Jer had a chance to reply, Alex cut in and said, "We should kill a warlock to get his power, just like Michael Deveraux is planning to do."

He stared straight at Jer . . . who gazed steadily back.

"A witch serves the same purpose," Jer replied.

The two glared at each other.

One of us is going to die on Wind Moon, Jer thought. *And it sure as hell isn't going to be me.*

"That's enough," Richard snapped. "The two of you, back off, now," he said. He stepped between them, giving them both the benefit of his eyes, which were threatening.

Alex dropped his gaze, but Jer could still feel his threat lingering in the air, a promise for him alone. For his part, Jer unclenched his fists and turned his attention to Richard. He owed Holly's uncle his life, and it was a debt he would not soon forget. Alex might have come along and beat down the Black Fire, but Richard had been the one to free Jer from the rock, and Jer secretly believed that they would have escaped without Alex's help. *In fact, the fire didn't even appear again until after he entered the Dreamtime.*

He had no proof, though, and if Alex could help them defeat his father, then he would be grateful for the assistance. *My father . . . I wonder where he is, what he's up to.* Jer clenched his fists again reflexively. *It's like I can feel him, his presence. He's coming for us, and we're not ready. We need some intel, and we're not going to get it sitting around here. I could find him, though, discover what he's up to . . . see if he knows what happened to Holly. . . .*

He waited for the others to sleep. He rose from his bed, slipped on his shoes, and snuck quietly outside. As he passed Pablo, the young man twitched, a frown clouding his features. He held his breath, but the young witch didn't waken.

He eased the door open and made it outside, closing it behind him. He took three steps away and let out the breath he had been holding. Something moved in the corner of his eye and, he jumped, startled.

Richard was standing there, his gaze almost kind. Jer didn't know what to say. He had thought the older man asleep in the cabin with the others.

"I know where you're going and I just wanted to wish you good luck."

"Thank you," Jer said.

Richard clapped his hand on his shoulder. "Be careful. If you find Holly or Kari, get them out if you can."

"I will."

"We won't be here when you get back, I hope you understand. If you need us, though, try to call to Pablo. That boy's got incredible abilities."

Jer nodded. He knew the Mother Coven safe house was somewhere close by, but he didn't know where, and he wouldn't be likely to find it. After a moment, Richard reached out and hugged him. Surprised, Jer hugged him back. Tears stung the back of his eyes. "Take care, son," Richard whispered.

They broke contact, and Richard smiled before stepping back and disappearing into the darkness.

★★★

The day dawned clear and cool. Amanda stood with the two men she cared most about: her father and Tommy.

"It is good that he left," Tommy said. "It was not working with both of them here." He wrinkled his nose. "Testosterone poisoning for both of them."

Her father chuckled as he nodded agreement, but Amanda still felt bereft. It wasn't bad enough that so many had died or been kidnapped; people were now leaving willingly. Strange as it sounded, Jer had been her last solid link to Holly.

"Time to go," Amanda said as she saw Luna walking toward them. Her voice was raw from fighting to hold back tears for so long.

Within minutes they were all piled back into cars, Luna driving the lead car and Richard driving the other. Sooner than she would have thought, they were pulling up to a large house on a hill. Standing outside, her arms crossed and a large gray cat wrapping itself around her ankles, was Anne-Louise Montrachet.

Amanda got out of the car with a feeling of relief upon seeing a familiar face. She walked up to Anne-Louise and, almost without thinking, hugged the other woman. Amanda could sense her surprise as she returned the embrace.

"You are safe here," Anne-Louise whispered.

Amanda began to sob, unable to contain it any longer. "I haven't felt safe in so long."

"I know, I know."

Amanda felt rather than heard someone walk up behind her, and when he placed a hand on her shoulder, she knew it was Tommy. Anne-Louise pulled back, and Amanda turned, collapsing into Tommy's arms.

She heard Anne-Louise address the others in a strong, clear voice, "Welcome, all of you. We offer safe refuge and a place to heal. Blessed be."

"Blessed be," the others chorused.

"Blessed be," Amanda whispered against Tommy's shoulder.

EIGHT

EPONA

☾

Cahors fall into our hands
Victims of Deveraux plans
We do with them what we will
Savor it now as we kill

Goddess deliver us we pray
Help us live beyond this day
Twist our hearts away from pain
Keep us now safe and sane

Eli: Avalon

Despite the fact that he had had an easy time sneaking into the dungeon where Nicole had been imprisoned, Eli wasn't happy.

It's been too easy, he told himself as he snuck along, slipping on the wet stone floor. He had exchanged his usual 'kickers for a pair of soft-soled high-tops, and they were getting soggy. His feet were icy. *It's got to be a trap.*

The back of his cloak—and beneath that, his black leather jacket—were both soaked with foul moisture from the dripping, moldy wall. The castle was said to predate Arthur's Merlin, and the ancient Druid wizard was also said to inhabit it to this day. The mere thought made Eli's chest tighten with fear. If Merlin was helping Sir William, he, Eli, could be a pile of ashes by the time this day was over.

Or a warty old toad, like Laurent . . .

He meant it as a joke, but he shivered nonetheless. He was terrified, and that was not something a Deveraux warlock should ever admit to, not even to himself. Too much had happened to shake his faith in his family's power. It had been said that Deveraux magic was the strongest there was, at least on the side of the shadows, and that the Moores had usurped Eli's family's rightful place as the head of the Supreme Coven. After all, no other House could conjure the prize of the Black Fire . . . and many had tried.

This dungeon is nothing to me. It's for sure no threat to somebody as powerful as me.

But now, slinking along in the dark, smelling the stench of death and filth, hearing distant shrieks of agony as torturers practiced their art on various enemies of Sir William, Eli wished himself away. He wouldn't do that; even if the new wards on the island would have allowed it, he couldn't go through with that impulse—wouldn't transport himself—but the temptation to do so rose inside him like a hunger.

Nicole doesn't even like me anymore. Why should I bother saving her?

Because she's valuable, he told himself, frowning at his own wimpiness. *She's a Cahors descendant, and she and her sister and Holly make an unbeatable triumvirate. And besides, James took her from me.*

No man, warlock, or mere ungifted human takes what's mine.

With a seething grimace of jealousy, he continued on, mincing his way down the narrow tunnel that his finder's spell had led him to. Using his left hand to shield the light from potential onlookers, he examined the iridescent green glow in the center of his palm. The glow, in the tiny image of a Deveraux falcon, had "flown" slightly forward toward his middle finger, which indicated he should continue moving directly forward. There was always the chance that someone had managed to tamper with it, and was using it to misdirect him. He could unknowingly be walking straight into a trap.

But his magical compass appeared to be clean, and the tiny falcon was an image only a Deveraux could conjure.

There were other Deveraux alive in the world.

Jer's stuck in the Dreamtime, he thought, *and he's probably dead by now. I don't think Dad would go through all this to work some scheme he hasn't shared.*

But it's been too easy, he told himself again.

He tugged at his cloak of invisibility, slung over the black leather jacket. He had placed dozens of wards and amulets all over his body, but he had expected at least a few obstacles—a threshold guardian or two, perhaps an invisible demon force that detected the presence of an intruder. But thus far, sneaking around the cliffs above the shoreline, then snaking his way through a field of heather to the cavelike entrance of the dungeon, had proven to be uneventful. Even boring.

Then a silhouette rose against the dark wall—blackness on black—and Eli knew he had relaxed his guard too soon.

The shape was that of a round, bulbous creature with an ax slung over its shoulder. Its head was disproportionately large, giving it an almost apelike appearance.

It was a Golem, a creature fashioned of mud, whose mind was not its own. It would obey the commands of its creator; it could not be reasoned with or turned from its path. And they were very difficult to kill. Not impossible, but if Eli could accomplish it, he would have to make a lot of noise.

Eli turned his head, expecting to see the Golem standing on the other side of the tunnel. But nothing was there. Alarm prickled up his spine, bone-cold fingers skittering up the center of his back. Golems were very solid creatures. They could not cast apparition silhouettes, like ghosts or wraiths.

Damn it. Where the hell is it?

He closed his fist over his scrying stone to hide the glow and melted into the shadows himself. Narrowing his eyes, he tried to breathe as quietly as he could while he studied the shape. What he was seeing made no sense, unless some form of magic he was unfamiliar with was being employed.

Then, as he stared, the silhouette disappeared.

He blinked. Then he understood: The shadow had not been projected across the tunnel; rather, he had seen through the wall. One of his wards must have empowered that ability.

The Golem shambled along on the other side.

It's been sent after Nicole.

Then all I have to do to find her, is follow it.

He murmured spells, trying to remember which amulets he had put where—he'd been in a hurry—and finally clasped his hand around the sun disc that hung from a leather band around his neck. Its warmth told him he had picked the correct token. He murmured a spell of seeing, and sure enough, the wall thinned again. Again, he saw the Golem, lurching implacably along, a stone-mud monster as relentless as the Terminator.

He trailed slightly behind it on his side of the wall. The thing stumbled, stopped, and then began to recede from Eli's line of sight.

It's turning to the right, he realized.

He hesitated for a moment, then waved his hands and whispered words that melted the wall. He hoped that, with its back turned, the Golem would be heedless; but there was always the possibility that other beings in the same tunnel—if there were any— would notice what Eli was doing.

Soon, a hole big enough to crawl through materialized at waist height; Eli bent down and climbed through, his fist still tight around the scrying stone. He had not forgotten that his purpose was rescuing Nicole, and he knew that he might have to wait for the proper moment to battle the Golem. Where there was one Golem there could easily be another. And another.

As soon as he got through the hole, he trailed the massive stone construct. He was still on alert for guards, and still baffled that none advanced on him.

Then all hell broke loose, and he realized he'd been right: It was a trap.

As the Golem whirled around and began swinging

its ax at him, what had looked to be crumbling pieces of the stone had now detached from the walls and flung themselves at him. They were misshapen creatures made up of gelatinous bodies and long, taloned arms. They slashed at him as they catapulted themselves toward him.

Skilled warlock that he was, he immediately protected himself with a spherical barrier, aiming fireballs at the projectiles and deflecting the swinging ax of the Golem. He was aware of a blur of larger shapes racing around the sphere; and when he had a moment to look at them, he almost lost his rhythm: Three more Golems had joined the first. One had an ax, one a mace, and one a net of chain mail, such as Roman gladiators had once used. All of them were battering at the sphere; and he realized his only chance to survive would be to keep the sphere intact. That was made more difficult by the fireballs he was lobbing at the enemy.

More of the wall-creatures pushed off from the walls and slammed against the sphere, flattening and collapsing into heaps of gelatinous goo as they slid down the sides of the sphere to the floor. There were perhaps a dozen of them now. The four Golems continued to hack and batter the sphere, and its integrity began to give way. It wobbled and began to crack.

Then the Golem with the mace raised the weapon high over its head. The spiked ball of metal crashed down with a bone-jarring impact, and the force of the blow sheered off the topmost section of the sphere. Eli was now trapped inside like an animal in a burrow.

An animal . . . he thought, as he dropped to his knees. *An animal.*

Keeping his calm, he closed his eyes and focused his magical strength, seeing each feather clearly, each shining talon, the beady eyes and greedy beak:

Fantasme, he called. *I summon you across the faceless void. . . .*

Now the Golem with the broadsword arced his blade into the side of the sphere. Cracks like lightning flashes jagged all over the surface, obscuring Eli's vision.

Fantasme . . .

Three of the strange gelatinous creatures scrabbled to the top of the sphere, rose on their haunches, and dive-bombed inside. One of them landed on Eli's head and immediately began digging into his scalp with his long, sharp fingers. Eli roared with pain and grabbed the creature with both his hands; its body squirted between his fingers, and he flung it away from himself, disgusted.

The second one took up where the first one had left off, and Eli smashed that one too. The third had landed inside the sphere at his feet and was trying to crawl up his pant leg; with a grunt, he pushed it off with the sole of his high-top and stomped on it.

Two of the Golems rammed the sphere with their shoulders, trying to roll it onto its side. Eli was tossed to his knees; he spread his arms to prevent himself from slipping forward along the curved surface like a hamster in a wheel.

Fantasme! he commanded.

"There he is!" someone shouted in English, and Eli was aware that human troops had just entered the tunnel.

As if they need reinforcements, he thought. He took the opportunity of the rolling sphere's condition to lob fireballs out of what had once been the top, and now was an open side. He caught the first two human soldiers, who were wearing what looked to be black leather jackets and trousers. The men burst into flame and fell shrieking to the ground.

Damn you, Fantasme, come!

None of the men bothered to help the two who were burning to death. One was blocked by the Golems; it was almost humorous to watch him struggle to bully them out of his way. They paid him absolutely no mind, only kept on taking chunks out of the sphere.

And that is not funny.

The Golem with the mace reached inside, grabbing Eli around the neck. It began to squeeze. The rough dirt of the creature's flesh sanded Eli's neck. Eli grabbed his hands around the thing's thick wrists and fought for air. In another moment or two, the Golem would crush his windpipe . . . and he would be dead.

Bird, he thought, his brain a roar of words he could no longer bring to mind. *My servant . . .*

An explosion rocked the tunnel. The Golem with its hands around Eli's neck was thrown backward. Eli was yanked out of the sphere and onto its chest. The impact loosened its grip, and Eli savagely lobbed a fireball directly into its face.

It made no noise, simply went limp, letting go of its weapon. Eli was surprised—he'd had no idea fire could harm Golems; the fireball had been a reflexive attempt to protect himself—and then he saw a small piece of paper curling into ash inside the Golem's mouth. Of course. As creations of ancient Jewish magic, one activated a Golem by writing a magic spell on a piece of paper and placing it inside its mouth. His fireball had destroyed the spell.

Seizing the moment to gather his wits, he caused a great wall of flame to ignite, sealing off the majority of the guards and the monsters as they raced into the tunnel. Left with a small band to fight, he poured on the aggression and started taking them out one by one by one, as fast as he could.

There was another explosion. Eli mentally took note of it but otherwise spared no attention. The battle at hand took all his focus . . . but he knew that if he lived through it, he would have to deal with whatever was coming next.

There was a third explosion, and the ceiling of the tunnel began to shake apart into huge chunks of stone, crashing down on the gelatinous creatures and the Golem with the broadsword, which had just been about to lunge forward toward Eli. Eli immediately shielded himself with a spell, yet the barrage was so incredible that he rolled into a ball and covered his head with his hands. Then, realizing how vulnerable to attack he was allowing himself to be, he rolled onto his side and staggered to his feet as the floor beneath him cracked apart. One huge jagged mass of it collided with another, forcing both pieces upward like a mountain.

His wall of flame held; yet, incredibly, something so massive rose up behind it that Eli saw its silhouette through the rippling tongues of flame. Then it strode through the fiery curtain, sending the third Golem flying with a punch of its gigantic fist.

It was a hideous creature, leathery and black, approximately ten feet high. As it shambled toward Eli, it had to duck to avoid hitting the top of the tunnel. Its face was an elongated rectangle ending in a strange triangular configuration of flesh and feathers. Its eyes were huge, and there were no irises, only pupils at least half a foot across. Instead of arms, large, fleshy appendages were covered with quills. Its feet were clawed, resembling those of a hawk.

The thing opened its mouth and made a high-pitched, eerie wail. With a start, Eli realized who and what it was: It was the spirit of the falcon, Fantasme, materialized in some bizarre manifestation he had never seen before. "You heard me," he blurted.

The bird-creature reached forward with its arm-parts, scooped up Eli against its chest, and whirled around, lunging forward and opening an enormous mouth at the end of its snout. Its jaws cracked open and expanded; another set of jaws extended forward and ripped open the throat of a gelatinous creature that was sailing through the air in an attempt to land on its back.

Bits of goo flew everywhere. Then Fantasme turned back around and began to lope through the tunnel.

The two remaining Golems took off after it. Craning his neck to see, Eli watched them draw near, then recede as Fantasme picked up speed. The tunnel was filling with smoke and a horrible burnt odor. The acrid, oily smoke poured into Eli's throat before he had a chance to protect himself. He began to cough, his eyes watered. Fantasme gazed down at him and squawked in its incomprehensible speech. Then it jerked toward him and, before Eli could respond, it had engulfed his head inside its beak. It inhaled, exhaled; Eli understood. Fantasme was giving him fresher air to breathe.

The act probably saved Eli's life, and he kept his head inside Fantasme's beak as the bird-creature raced faster, and faster still, hunched protectively around Eli like a quarterback around a football.

He didn't know how long Fantasme ran—it seemed like hours—but the hot, moist breath of the bird grew stale and smoky, as it undoubtedly drew in the poisonous air around itself, filtering as best it could before offering it to Eli. Weakening and feeling ill, he could feel his grip around Fantasme loosening, but the creature held him tightly, and Eli felt a rush of gratitude as they loped along. Throughout the centuries, Fantasme had been a good and faithful servant of his family, in whatever incarnation the bird presented itself.

Of course, that faithfulness had been dearly purchased . . . with the blood of many, many virgins. . . .

But now, he was growing fainter. The air was too polluted; he was suffocating inside Fantasme's mouth. His fingers went limp, and his arm dangled at his side, jangling like a spring as the bird carried him through the dungeon of the castle on Avalon.

I'm not going to die, he thought angrily. *I'm a Deveraux. We don't do that.*

Then everything faded, and his soul screamed in terror, for fear that the Horned God would devour it, and gray and spiritless oblivion would be its final reward.

When he woke up, Nicole was bent over him with her mouth over his. He smelled a delicious fragrance of cloves and roses and inhaled greedily. Witch breath. Magic breath. She was apparently unaware that he had regained consciousness, and he made his lungs rise with the air that she was breathing into his mouth. She was giving him mouth-to-mouth, and he loved it.

She was so intent on what she was doing that when he gently touched his tongue to hers, she continued to work on him.

Then her dark, deep-set eyes gazed directly into his own, and she broke contact.

With a grunt, she sat up and narrowed her eyes, on guard. He made a show of coughing and rolling onto his side, spasming and clenching and unclenching his fists.

She pounded on his back. He grinned to himself and made himself cough a few more times.

"Eli, wake up. Get me the hell out of here," she demanded harshly. "The water's rising."

The water?

Dropping his act, he sat up, realizing that it wasn't so much of an act after all—he was incredibly weak, and the cave—*the cave?*—was spinning around him like a crazed merry-go-round.

"That thing broke me out and brought us both to this cave," she said, pointing to a place behind. He turned. Sure enough, Fantasme loomed protectively over him, its beady eyes reflecting back nothing but the darkness. There was a source of light somewhere in the cave, and Eli glanced around in search of it. A small globe bobbled beside Nicole.

She must have created it, he thought, and reminded himself sternly that she was a Cahors witch and, as such, still his enemy. The old days of high school and her having the hots for him belonged to two inhabitants of a past, foreign country.

"If this is a plan to deliver me to your father or James, I'll kill you," she said. As if to prove that she had the moxie to do it, she pulled a dagger on him and held it to his throat.

Fantasme lunged toward her, but Eli held up a restraining hand and said, "Back."

He recognized the dagger from rituals he had performed with James. It was one of his athames. Wicked-sharp, it had sliced through the breast of a goat with one easy stroke—but he doubted Nicole knew that.

"I'm not here to give you to James or my father," he said. "I'm here to rescue you. Period."

"Why?" she demanded.

He thought about telling her that he loved her, but she would never believe that. Or that he wanted her, which she would probably find offensive. So he told her the truth. "You're powerful, and you're valuable. I need some bargaining chips. You're good in my back pocket." He chuckled at his nonsensical but vaguely sexual turn of phrase.

"Don't you touch me," she said savagely, showing her teeth like a feral cat. That turned him on. "Don't you so much as get near me."

"No worries." He held up his hands. "Down, Sheba." Then he smiled and said, "But if I need mouth-to-mouth again, I'll be sure to let you know."

"I saved your life," she hissed. "But not out of any

compassion for you, Eli. I need you to get me out of here. But if you try anything, I'll kill you."

Fantasme took another step forward. Again, Eli motioned to it to stay put.

"Fair enough, babe," he tossed off. "Same here. Let's agree to a truce until we're out of this mess."

"And then . . . ?"

"Then we'll see where we're at. As we used to say back when we were kids."

She scowled at him. "I never talked like that. Neither did you. Your father did, maybe. He was always trying so hard to be 'cool.'" She tossed her hair, and it was hard for him not to grab her and kiss her. He loved sassy, bitchy chicks.

"My dad is cool," he retorted.

"You know what, Eli? I really don't care," she said.

She was dressed in a shapeless rustling gown of satin and black lace, which was quite fetching on her. It was richly embroidered with Cahors silver at the low-cut bodice and long sleeves, which half-covered the backs of her hands. Though she had been a prisoner slated for death, she was also the bride of a Moore—until such time as she was the dead bride of a Moore. Her dark, curly hair had grown since they'd been together, and it was twisted at the sides and hung long down her back. She was incredibly beautiful.

For a moment he imagined what it must have been like for her, with James. James had shared some of the brutal details with him, and Eli had been angry, jealous that another man touched her. Until now, though, he had never stopped to think what it must have been like for her. He shook his head.

Fantasme made a strange scrying noise, and for a moment Eli had the ridiculous, giddy thought that they were in a *Scooby-Doo* episode and Fantasme was the guy in the suit. Then he sobered as icy, brackish water sloshed over his already-sodden track shoes. "All right, so where are we? I'll skip the Kansas cliché."

"We're at sea level," Nicole informed him. "It brought us to a cave. The water's been coming in steadily. I think the tide is rising."

"Are we still being hunted?" he asked her.

She snorted. "Of course. There are a couple of these icky guys made out of mud—"

"Golems," he informed her.

"Whatever. And demons and goo monsters. All kinds of things. Your birdman outran them and then I put a glamour on this cave so they couldn't see the entrance. But I don't know how good of a spell it was, and I don't know when they'll break down my wards and stuff. I used your cloak of invisibility," she added. "It's a good one." That sounded like a difficult admission for her to make, so he didn't reply.

"So. Did you have a plan?" she demanded.

"Of course," he shot back. "It was based entirely on stealth," he added, so she wouldn't press him for details he did not have. "James knows this entire island. He spent most of his childhood here. He'll figure out where we are." He frowned. "If he hasn't already."

Nicole cast an anxious glance over her shoulder. All he saw was rock, but he guessed that that was where his cloak was shielding the entrance. For all either of them knew, an army of Supreme Coven minions, human or otherwise, was massed on the other side, waiting for them to come out.

He could have taken the knife from her then, but he liked her cute little show of power, so he gave up the chance. Maybe she sensed his thoughts, because she whipped her head back at him and pressed a little harder on the knife. He doubted that she realized that it turned him on even more.

It was too much for Fantasme. The creature arced back an . . . appendage . . . and whacked the knife out of Nicole's grasp. She screamed in agony and crumpled onto the cave floor. "My wrist!" she managed, her voice a raspy shriek.

Eli smoothly picked up the athame and slipped it

inside his black leather jacket. Then he roughly covered her mouth to muffle her screams. That made her scream harder, so he murmured a spell of silence, which rendered her mute.

And for old times' sake, he took away the pain and told her wrist to start healing itself.

Jer: Gorman, California

Jer had stopped to gas up the car on the top of the Grapevine before starting the descent into the L.A. basin. From there he would head east toward New Mexico. The night was dark, clouds covering the face of the moon as he glanced anxiously skyward. *Wind Moon is coming,* he thought with a shudder. *There's a good chance none of us are going to survive it.*

"Not if I can help it," he vowed out loud, startling a woman pumping gas into a red minivan five feet away. He narrowed his eyes; there was something about the woman that didn't seem . . . right.

Her short hair was plastered to her head, and there was something distinctly European about her features. He stared at her hand as it replaced the gas nozzle. She was gripping it tight, the muscles in her forearm knotting. Impressive muscles they were, too. He narrowed his eyes and tried to make out more details in the fluorescent light.

There was scarring on her arm, a long, straight line consistent with self-mutilation. It was on the top of her arm, so it couldn't have been a suicide attempt. No, it looked familiar, like something one would inflict doing a ritual—

She lunged at him, throwing him to the ground and landing on top of him. His head hit the concrete with a dull thud, and a roaring sound filled his ears. His vision blurred, but he felt a sudden stabbing pain in the area of his throat.

"Tell me where your father is," the woman hissed.

His vision snapped back into focus as he realized she was pressing a knife to his throat.

"I'm not entirely sure," he answered honestly. There was no need to lie to a woman who could and would kill him for doing so.

He could tell by the way she pursed her lips that she knew he was telling the truth.

"Don't tell me, he jilted you and you're looking for revenge?" he joked, not knowing what else to do. She had him, and could slit his throat before he could do a thing, magical or otherwise, to try to escape.

She laughed soullessly. "Nothing so exciting. But I am going to kill him."

Jer swallowed hard, trying to ignore the feeling of

the blade cutting his skin. "You'll have to stand in line, then."

"Why should I believe you? Why should I believe you are going to kill your own father?"

"You know who I am and who my father is and yet you have to ask?"

She nodded, seemingly satisfied, and stood up in one fluid motion. She extended her hand, and he took it. As he scrambled back to his feet, he put a few feet between them with a sense of relief.

"Sir William has ordered your father executed. You, however, he said nothing about."

"I never thought being ignored could have such advantages," he quipped lamely as he touched his hand gingerly to his neck. Spots of blood came back on his fingertips, and he cursed under his breath.

"Trust me, he's not ignoring you, he never ignores anyone, which is why he's still alive."

"Sounds like you speak from personal experience."

She glanced up at him with a shake of her head. "I've seen what he can do. I'm not anxious to have him do it to me."

Jer smiled at the double entendre. It was a grim testament to the world that the woman had chosen to live in, the side she had aligned herself with.

"Leave the car. You're riding with me," the woman ordered.

He looked at her warily. "So, I'm your prisoner?"

"Think of yourself more as an accomplice. As I see it, we're both pursuing the same goal."

"If you don't mind, I'll just meet you there," he said, backing toward his car and preparing to erect a barrier between them.

"I wouldn't do that if I were you," she warned as he touched the handle on the car.

"And why is that?"

She smiled, a little wicked smile that felt like daggers of ice being showered at him. "Because while you were inside buying soda, I rigged your car to explode."

He froze, his hand still on the handle. With his mind he began to probe the car, looking for something, anything. It was his eyes that saw it, though. There, lying on the passenger side seat, was a tiny black box with wires running out of it. *It could be a fake,* he thought.

"Are you willing to risk it?" she asked. "Not only your life, and my life, but also the life of the poor slob behind the counter, and theirs," she said with a nod. He turned to watch as a family poured out of a station wagon that had just parked at a nearby pump. They were all wearing matching Mickey Mouse shirts, and it was clear from their exhausted yet happy faces where they had just come from.

A bead of sweat trickled down the middle of his back as he instinctually turned his face away so that the children wouldn't see his scars. *Strange,* he thought, as he stared again at the woman. *I didn't care at all what she thought of them, even before she attacked me.*

"If I go with you, you'll defuse the car so that no one will be injured after we leave?"

She hesitated for a moment before nodding.

"All right," he agreed.

"Take your hand off the handle, gently," she instructed.

He did as he was told and then stepped back away from the car.

"Good boy," she crooned. "Now, get in the van."

He gave her a wide berth as he did so. As soon as he closed the door, she headed for his car. The mirrors in the van were angled to let him see what she was doing, and before she could adjust them she had appeared at the van's driver-side door. She opened it and hopped in.

"Finished?" he asked, surprised.

"Sure," she answered as she started the engine and put the van into gear. As they merged back onto Interstate 5, she added, "There was no bomb."

He put his head back against the headrest and sighed. She was clearly not to be trusted. "So, do you have a name or shall I just call you Deceiver?"

"How about Temptress instead?" she asked in a coy voice. "My name is Eve."

It was going to be a long trip.

June Cathers: Santa Paula, California, March 12, 1928 11:57 P.M.

Four-year-old June Cathers lay awake, too excited to sleep. In the morning it would be her birthday and she would be five. In the bed next to June, her twin brothers, Timmy and Tommy, were sound asleep. She held her breath so she could listen to them breathing for a moment. They were younger than she was, and when they had been born her daddy had told her that she had to look out for them.

She let out her breath with a *whoosh*. There was going to be a party tomorrow, with cake. Her grandmother was going to be there, and both her grandfathers. She only had the one grandmother. Her daddy's mommy had died when he was younger than June. It always made her sad for her daddy when she thought about it.

She rolled onto her side, squeezing her eyes tightly shut as she did so. She had forgotten to shut the closet door when she went to bed; she had been too excited, thinking about her birthday. The closet frightened her; there were things that moved in at night. Once, she had opened her eyes and seen shadows in her closet, shadows that stared at her.

She had screamed and screamed, and when her mommy came she had told her she was just imagining things. She hadn't been, though, she knew it. There were monsters in the world. She saw them sometimes and she knew they wanted to hurt her and her brothers.

The grandfather clock began to chime midnight. She jumped and then forced herself to breathe deeply, calming herself down. She slowly began to drift off to sleep. From somewhere far off she heard something . . . a deep, low sound. She pulled the blankets over her head, but the sound grew louder, increasing to a dull roar. She clamped her hands over her ears, but it just got louder. At last it was deafening, and she sat up. She turned and looked at the closet just as a wall of water came rushing out of it.

She screamed just as the water washed over her. Suddenly, a light appeared, shining brighter than anything she had ever seen. A woman stood in it, with long, flowing hair. She picked June up and held her close. The water passed around them, but did not touch them. June coughed out the water she had already swallowed as she clung to the dark-haired lady. "What's happening?" June wailed.

"The St. Francis Dam broke," the lady answered, holding her closer.

The house collapsed around them, and they remained untouched. The water washed away the debris, and they stayed where they were. At last the deluge passed, and the shining lady set her down on her feet. The mud sucked at her legs, and her nightdress was wet and dirty.

"Be safe, *ma petite* June of the Cahors," the lady said, and then she disappeared.

June Cathers looked around at the destruction of her home and her town. Her family, her parents, and her little brothers were gone, they were dead. She was five years old, and it was her birthday.

NINE

BAST

☾

Something now in the wind
Reveals to us all our sin
We meet this darkness with more hate
This alone a Deveraux's fate

Cahors watch and Cahors pray
Wish away the light of day
For in the night alone we sing
Dancing in a silver ring

Tri-Coven: Santa Cruz

"Goddess, how I miss Nicole," Philippe prayed, as he lay in his narrow bed. "Let me find her well and safe."

He rolled onto his side, preparing for another sleepless night. He couldn't rest since Nicole had been taken—*again by James and Eli!*

He found Pablo staring at him. "What is it, *hijo*?"

"We will find her," Pablo whispered.

"Thanks, Pablo," Philippe answered. "I only pray that it is sooner rather than later."

Pablo nodded at that. The other surviving member of their coven, Armand, snored quietly from his cot. Philippe raised a head to look at him.

Leadership is a difficult burden. I do not know how José Luís bore it so long, he thought.

"He was able to bear it so long because you were there to encourage him," Pablo answered, reading his thoughts.

Philippe reached out and touched Pablo's shoulder briefly. *Thank you,* he thought.

"You're welcome," Pablo answered.

"Any luck in finding any of the others?"

"Sí," Pablo admitted. "Holly is with Michael Deveraux."

"Where?"

"A place called New Mexico."

"And Kari and Jer?"

"Kari is there, too, and Jer is traveling there to kill his father."

"Goddess grant him success," Philippe half-said, half-prayed. "And Nicole?" he asked after a moment, afraid to hear the answer.

Pablo shook his head, clearly frustrated. "Nothing, still."

"Is it possible they took her back to Avalon?"

"I do not know, but I would guess there or London."

"Thank you for trying."

"I will not give up hope, as you must not."

Philippe sighed. There were days that was easier said than done. With thoughts of his missing covenates allayed for the moment, his mind turned to the other concern that had been weighing on him. "Have you sensed anything from Alex?"

"No, he is very closed. It is hard to feel anything from him—and he is always watching, like he knows I am watching him."

"That makes me nervous," Philippe confessed.

"The High Priestess, too," Pablo told him.

Interesting. Maybe she and I should talk, he thought.

"That would be good," Pablo said. "I have worked on it so that he will not be able to read us three," he said. "I will work on the others, as well."

"Thank you, again."

After lying awake for another hour trying to meditate, Philippe drifted off into a fitful sleep. He was awakened in what seemed like minutes but was really hours, by Pablo's excited exclamation.

"I found her!"

Philippe sat up, instantly alert. "Where is she?" he demanded, knowing exactly who Pablo was talking about.

"She is on the island of Avalon. She contacted me briefly. She was trying to reach you, but couldn't quite," Pablo said, suddenly sounding embarrassed.

"It is all right, Pablo," Philippe said gently. The younger man was clearly embarrassed at having intercepted a signal meant for him from his beloved.

"She said that she is fine and that Eli is helping her escape."

Philippe sighed deeply. "Goddess be praised that she is safe. I do not like that Eli is with her, but if he is to become a friend to us, I will welcome him gladly."

"Shall I wake the others?"

Philippe glanced at the clock on the nightstand. "They should be up in another hour. Let them sleep. We will all need what sleep we can get. You should try to rest more too."

Pablo nodded and lay back down slowly. He closed his eyes, and after a moment his breathing began to even out. Philippe sat for a moment until he was sure Pablo was asleep, and then he rose and went downstairs. He found Sasha making breakfast.

"Pablo has found Nicole," he offered by way of greeting. "She is alive and safe on Avalon. Eli is helping her to escape."

A look of relief passed across her face, and she lit up like the sun. A cloud soon obscured the radiance, though, as she asked, "And what of Jer?"

Philippe nodded. "He is on his way to confront his father."

She sagged against the counter, a stricken look crossing her face. "I knew in my heart that that was where he was going," she admitted.

"It doesn't make it any less hard to hear it," he said sympathetically.

"True," she said, forcing a smile. She visibly shook herself. "It is good to hear that Eli is helping Nicole. I wonder what has brought my son to that?"

Philippe shrugged. "Maybe he has realized that he has been serving the master when he should have looked to the mistress."

Sasha smiled. "More likely it has something to do with Nicole."

"Yes, she can be quite persuasive when she wants to be. If he ever did love her, I am sure she can turn him to her will," Philippe said, hating to admit even to himself that the words stung.

The others began to straggle in slowly until everyone was present. They all looked tired, but everyone took renewed courage from the news about Nicole. Her sister, Amanda, was especially relieved.

Last to arrive was Alex, and he, in contrast, looked fresh and rested. Philippe envied him that. Members of the Mother Coven, some of them having already been up for hours, seemed to be avoiding the kitchen. Even Luna was absent, and she had spent much time with them in the last couple of days.

Philippe looked around at the few of them who were left. Sasha and Richard stood together. They were the parents whose children played some of the key roles in the battle that was being fought. He knew that they had taken great solace in each other's presence of late. Barbara Davis-Chin sat at a table, sipping tea and staring around at the others. He knew Armand and Pablo were standing slightly behind him and had been engaged in earnest conversation in Spanish about everything Pablo had told him in the middle of the night. In a corner, also having their own private conversation, were Tommy and Amanda. He had his arm around her, and Philippe didn't need Pablo's psychic abilities to see that Amanda was both excited and upset with the news about her sister. Alex Carruthers made ten in the group.

At last everyone had heard the news about all their missing comrades. Alex cleared his throat, and they all turned their attention to him.

"I have spoken with Luna, and she has graciously offered us the use of the Mother Coven's private jet and whatever they can spare in the way of equipment and people.

"We need to rescue Nicole, and we need to take the fight to the enemy. The leader of this coven is gone, and we have to face the fact that she might not ever return. If she does, we shall welcome her back with open arms. Until that day, though, this coven needs a leader. I am the leader of my coven back home, and I propose to lead this coven into battle. To that end I pledge to you my life, my allegiance, my skill, and my knowledge."

There were murmurs, but no one said anything. Of all those present, Philippe was the only one who had led a coven. He had never liked leading—he was always more comfortable as the lieutenant—still, it was his place to speak for the other two coven leaders who were not present.

Can we trust him? he asked Pablo silently.

I do not know, but I do know that we need him, could really use his help, the boy answered in his mind.

Which he's not likely to give us if we oppose him in this?

I cannot tell.

Philippe nodded slowly. *I guess we will have to take a chance. If he can help us rescue Nicole, we must.* Out loud, he said, "I would consent to your taking leadership temporarily while our other two coven leaders are absent."

"Is it agreed, then?" Alex asked.

"It is agreed," Amanda answered, her bright eyes on Philippe.

"Good. We should do the proper rituals and then we all need to rest up. Tomorrow we fly to England. Half of us will go to Avalon to rescue Nicole, and the other half will attack the Supreme Coven."

As the others gasped, Philippe thought, *By the Goddess, what did you just do?*

That night, Philippe could again not find rest. He relived the events of the day, from the decision he had made in the kitchen, to the ceremony installing Alex as leader of the coven. All of them were to have spent the rest of the day resting and meditating, but Philippe had not been able to do either.

Alex had retired before the rest. The others were just too worn out and too shell-shocked to rest. He glanced at Pablo. The boy was dreaming, and for a while Philippe watched him. Joy and pain passed in rapid succession across his youthful face, and Philippe wondered what his dreams were and if they were true visions of the future or fanciful flights of the mind.

He flipped back onto his back and stared up at the ceiling. He had never felt as out of sorts as he had since Nicole had been taken. *She is a part of me as I am a part of her. It is as though a chunk of my soul has been taken as well,* he thought. *I don't think I'll ever know rest again unless she is at my side.*

From Nicole, his mind drifted to her newly discovered cousin. *I wonder what she would say about everything that has happened?* He smiled. The what-would-Nicole-say game was quickly becoming one of his favorite distractions.

He heard gentle snoring from Armand, and more snores from the room beyond. *Alex, are you asleep? If so what are you dreaming? If not, what are you doing?*

June Cathers: Santa Paula, California, March 12, 1928 11:57 P.M.

Four-year-old June Cathers lay awake, too excited to sleep. In the morning it would be her birthday and she would be five. In the bed next to June, her twin brothers, Timmy and Tommy, were sound asleep. She rolled onto her side, squeezing her eyes tightly shut as she did so. Her closet door was open, and it was bothering her.

It was growling and rumbling, louder and louder. She was trying not to listen to it, but it was getting so loud, she wondered why the others didn't wake up.

She turned and screamed.

A wall of water rushed out of it: A river was gushing right out of her closet!

Then suddenly, it stopped, frozen as though in

midair. A light appeared, shining brighter than anything she had ever seen. A woman with beautiful, long flowing hair stood inside the light. She picked June up and held her close.

Then a man appeared, also shining with a brilliant light. His hair was light-colored, and he was beautiful.

He picked up Timmy and Tommy, one in each arm, and all of them huddled close together. Then the water began moving again, flowing around them. But the shining people held June and her brothers in their arms, standing easily in the water.

"What's happening?" June wailed.

"The St. Francis Dam broke," the man told her. "There is a curse on your family, that they will die by water. But we have saved you. You are our future."

"Are you an angel?" she asked, touching his face in awe.

"No," he said, with a faint smile. "My name is Alex, and I'm not an angel. I am someone, though, who owes his very life to you."

He leaned over and kissed her. "Happy Birthday, June."

Then he and the lady disappeared.

And June woke up to a lovely day . . . and she was five years old.

Bast

Mother Coven: Santa Cruz

Anne-Louise sat up in bed with a gasp. "Something is wrong," she whispered out loud.

Whisper stared at her, her head cocked to the side and her yellow eyes boring through her.

"Something is different—changed, somehow," Anne-Louise said, looking at the cat and praying for answers.

The cat spoke. "The time line has shifted around you."

"What has caused such a thing?" Anne-Louise asked, horrified.

"Someone has changed the past. Look to House Cahors for answers."

A chill shot up her spine. It was serious business to change the past. In the Mother Coven, it was an act that demanded the death of the one who had performed the powerful magic to accomplish it.

She argued, "But if the time line has shifted, how come I'm aware of it?"

The cat blinked at her. "Because I have allowed you to remain an observer of both."

Anne-Louise felt her mouth go completely dry. "What has changed?"

"Much."

Eli and Nicole: Avalon

Within minutes, Nicole's wrist was healed. Eli had taken the time to think about how they were going to get off the island. So far he had come up with nothing, but he wasn't willing to admit that. He looked at her. *She is so beautiful, and she glows so bright.* He swallowed hard. He had to know. The question had tormented him, and now it had to be asked. "Is—is the baby mine?"

Nicole flushed scarlet as she placed a hand over her extended abdomen. "I don't know," she whispered.

"When are you due?"

"The night of the Wind Moon."

"That's just a few days from now!" he exclaimed, beginning to panic slightly.

She gave him the sweetest smile he had ever seen, and he began to calm. *It could be my child,* he thought, a sense of wonder filling him. Almost before he could stop himself, he started to stretch out his hand. He stopped, though, and stared her in the eyes.

She nodded ever so slightly and took his hand, pressing it to her belly. He could feel movement within, life stirring in her, and something more: a slight tingle of electricity.

"The baby has power," he breathed.

"Yes, he does."

"You know it's a boy?"

She nodded. "I can feel it."

"And he might be mine."

"He might be."

He began to shake uncontrollably. Nicole wrapped her arms around him and held him close as he began to cry.

Nicole felt like crying herself. She was moved by the softening in Eli. *He's been changing, right before my eyes,* she thought. *I used to think I could tame him, maybe I was right.*

What she had told him was true: Eli could be the father; she really didn't know who was. She hoped it was Philippe, though they hadn't been together very long. *The funny thing is, I don't remember much about being pregnant. I know it's a boy and when it's due, but other than that, there's not much there.* She shuddered. *What if it's James's child?* She suddenly felt sick to the bottom of her soul. The truth was, there was magic of some kind being done. Nine months ago she hadn't been with anyone in order to become pregnant. She and Eli had broken up before that. She and Philippe had been together only a short while, and James had—done what he had done to her—relatively recently as well.

Another thought whispered through her mind:

What about the thing in my room? Could it have done this to me? She began to cry as well, her tears mingling with Eli's. The truth was that neither of them was likely to make it out of this alive. She had loved him once, and if it brought him comfort to think he was the father—and she really didn't know if he was or not, then it could not hurt to let him think he was.

Jer and Eve: New Mexico

They had stopped across the border at an all-night truck stop for food. Jer's attempts to get more information out of Eve had been met with resistance. They had eaten in silence, and Jer didn't even remember what he had ordered. All he knew was that the food was tasteless and that he didn't care. There was too much to worry about to care.

He waited in the van while Eve used the rest room. He could sense his father's presence, feel his stench even from here. *He's like a plague. His evil spreads, infecting those near him, even the land around him and the sky above. He has to be stopped while there's still some light in the world, some good that is as yet untouched by his hand.*

He turned to look at Eve as she climbed into the minivan. She had changed into black jeans, a black turtleneck, and a black leather vest. The vest looked thick, more like something he would have expected to see used as a bulletproof vest by a police officer rather than used as a wardrobe accessory for the occult-minded. She also wore black leather boots that came up to her knees.

"I feel underdressed," he commented dryly.

"Isn't that like a man," she tossed back at him. "Forever wearing the wrong thing."

He was about to make a snappy retort when something crashed into the windshield, or rather, crashed *through* the windshield. It was an imp and it chortled wildly before stabbing at Jer's eyes with its wicked nails. With a shout, he twisted his head to the side just in time. Eve backhanded the creature, sending it flying back through the windshield.

She started the engine and threw the car into reverse in a single motion. She hit a car parked in a stall behind her and threw the car into drive. Anguished tires screamed as she peeled out.

"I guess they'll be taking away my international driver's license," she noted grimly.

Jer braced himself as she made a hard turn to exit the parking lot. He flew forward, though, when she came to a screeching halt. There, lined up in front of the car, was a row of demons standing shoulder-to-shoulder. They ranged in type and size.

Eve gunned the engine as Jer stared at the demons.

One extended a casual arm, waving them forward. *Red Rover, Red Rover, send Jer on over,* he thought. *If we break the line, we live, if not, we get to join the dead.*

Eve pulled her foot off the brake, and the minivan leaped forward. He wanted to close his eyes, to look away, but something wouldn't let him. Together, he and Eve shouted as the minivan hit the line of demons. Body parts went flying everywhere. A hand came soaring through the broken windshield and landed in Jer's lap. With a scream of revulsion, he picked up the twitching appendage and threw it in the backseat. Meanwhile, demons had leaped onto the van, clinging by hands and feet and tentacles.

One put his fist through the passenger-side window, and a shower of glass flew into Jer's face. He instinctively squeezed his eyes shut. The shards of glass almost felt like rain pelting his skin until the pain began to register.

The demon suddenly demanded his full attention by wrapping his hand around Jer's throat. He desperately grabbed the creature's head with both of his hands and started banging it against the frame of the door. The creature tightened his grip, and as Jer's lungs became oxygen-starved, his actions became more frantic. At last he headbutted the creature. Pain exploded along his temples, but the demon's grip loosened for a moment.

Jer grabbed the creature's fingers and tore them from his throat. It was momentarily off balance, and he took advantage of that to push it backward. It fell to the ground, and the minivan bounced as a rear tire drove over it. An unearthly scream ripped through the night air, and Jer clamped his hands over his ears, gritting his teeth in pain.

It passed in a second, and the van swerved wildly to the right. He turned his attention to Eve. She was fighting a small, scaly red demon for control of the steering wheel. Another demon was hanging half inside the door, clawing at her head.

Jer lobbed a fireball at it that whipped right past Eve's head. It exploded in the demon's face, toppling it backward with a cry. Jer could smell the stench of burning hair and realized that he must have clipped Eve.

"Depart!" he roared at the little red demon, too agitated to think of the Latin word for it.

The creature turned and cackled toothlessly at him, bouncing up and down on the dashboard. It ceased laughing, though, when Eve hit the brakes and it went sailing through the air to land on the ground several feet in front of them. She floored the van, and it ran over the demon with a sickening crunch. Bits of yellow blood and goo sprayed in through the open windows, covering them both.

Eve got on the freeway doing ninety and didn't slow down for half an hour. Jer charmed their passage so that the three police cars they passed didn't see them. They were only an unexplained blip on the radar. At last she pulled off the road at a small town and parked in front of a motel. "Someone knows you're in town," she remarked.

"It would seem so," was all he could say, trying not to vomit as he tasted the demon blood on his lips.

Kari and Michael: New Mexico

The imp jumped up and down in front of Michael, in a state of great agitation. "We tried to kill him, but he had someone with him, a girl," the thing hissed.

It was so upset, Kari could barely understand what it was saying.

"Die, die, he wouldn't die, and neither would she. Warlock she is, powerful one."

"He has a warlock with him?" Michael mused. "That can't be a good thing. Let me guess, that weakling Sir William has finally decided it's bad PR to keep me around?"

"She is strong, stronger than he."

"That wouldn't take much, would it?" he asked with a dismissive wave of his hand.

Kari stood up slowly, her knees shaking. She didn't

remember much about the last twenty-four hours. Everything was hazy. It still felt that way, but she needed to know who they were talking about. "Who?" she asked, her throat dry and her voice barely a whisper.

Michael and the imp ignored her. Instead, the creature just continued to jump up and down, blathering on and on about something. Michael was stroking his chin and looking thoughtful.

"Who?" she asked, her voice cracking but sounding slightly stronger.

They continued to ignore her, and for one wild moment she thought she might be a ghost. *Michael Deveraux has killed me, and now I'm trapped here, seeing but unseen, hearing but unheard.* She picked up a lamp and hurled it to the ground. It crashed and broke.

Michael turned and stared at her. "What's with your coven and breaking lamps?" he asked in an almost amiable tone. "That's all Holly wanted to do at first too."

"Who?" she shouted.

He lifted an eyebrow. "The woman, I don't know—though there are very few female warlocks in the Supreme Coven, so it shouldn't be too hard to figure that out."

"The man, who is the man?" she asked, speaking slowly and enunciating each word.

He smiled bemusedly. "Oh, it's just Jeraud."

"Jer?" she asked, afraid she hadn't heard him right.

He nodded.

"He's alive?"

"Apparently so. He seems to have made it back from the Dreamtime, and now he's on the way here."

She grabbed a chair and sat down before she could faint. *He's alive!* Her heart lifted for one glorious moment before crashing back down again. "You're trying to kill Jer," she accused.

"Why so surprised?" he asked with an evil smirk.

"He's your *son*!"

"And I've tolerated his antics long enough. Every parent hopes that their children will grow up to make them proud, to do better than they did, to be a glorious branch on the family tree."

"But?"

"Well, as any good gardener knows, every tree needs pruning from time to time. Jer, unfortunately, is just an unproductive limb that I'm going to trim."

"But you promised."

"No, my dear," he said, moving closer to her. "If you think back, you'll remember that I never did promise you anything. That's one thing my son and I share in common," he ended with a sneer.

"He's coming here?" she asked, her head still fuzzy.

"Yes."

She lifted her chin high. "Then he's coming to rescue me. You'll be sorry."

Michael laughed, an honest, surprised-sounding laugh. He knelt down next to her so that his face was on a level with hers, and stared deeply into her eyes. "My dear, are you so deluded as to think that he's coming here to rescue you?" He clucked his tongue. "Let's be real, pet. He's on his way to rescue Holly."

His words cut her to the quick. He stood slowly as he drove the final nails into the coffin that contained all her dreams. "Not you. It was never you." He turned and walked away, his imp trotting beside him.

Kari sat on the chair, overwhelmed with grief. *Jer is alive and he is coming here to die.*

Let him die, another voice inside her head whispered. *Look what he's done to you.*

He hasn't done it. It's Holly, it's all her fault. Jer would still love me but for her.

Holly should die in his place. After all, you would die for him. If she loves him, she'll sacrifice herself. Or, you could kill her and then Jer wouldn't have to risk himself, and you could have him back.

You deserve more.

With that, she crumbled and began to sob. "No, I

don't!" she cried aloud. "I don't, I don't deserve anything. I've betrayed them all."

Mother Coven: Santa Cruz

Anne-Louise had spent hours on the Internet doing genealogy research. Every time she had thought she was about to break through, though, she had come upon another dead end. Sometimes you just had to do things the old-fashioned way.

She locked her room and set wards up at the door and window. She burned some incense and lay down on her bed. She had taken a herbal mixture, potent, the equivalent of what a shaman would take when preparing to embark on a vision-quest.

That was what Anne-Louise was on. She had a special quest in mind, though, and she would need the Goddess's help. Whisper jumped up and lay beside her, purring.

Anne-Louise breathed deeply and closed her eyes. *Show me all of the Cahors family.*

Part Three
Water

☾

I drown in thee which gave me birth
From within my mother's girth
The tides alone we all must bear
Witness of the Goddess fair

Within the tides, within their flow
We learn to breathe and then to slow
To savor that which we now claim
For tomorrow is never the same

TEN

RHIANNON

☾

Round and round the sun wheel goes
As we vanquish anew all our foes
We revel and dance while they mourn
Cursing the day that they were born

In visions now we seek the truth
Secrets that were lost in youth
For there is evil we cannot hide
Lurking now deep inside

Holly: New Mexico

In a small corner of her mind she sat upon a little stool and watched all the commotion. *There are demons big and small and creatures I don't know at all. They're making such a mess, jumping all around and breaking things, so many things. If I sit very still, though, they won't notice me. They won't look. They won't see. But I've been sitting so very still for so very long, and it is hard to sit up so straight.*

She wiggled a toe, just a toe, and the pinkie one at

that. *This little piggy cries wee*—and a big, hairy demon with bloody stumps for hands slapped her with one of his bloody stumps. And there was blood on her dress. *Is it my blood or his?* It didn't matter, nothing did, except for sitting very, very quiet and not moving, not even a toe.

And now the dark-haired man was moving outside of her mind. He was there, in another room and he was talking. She really should pay attention; he liked that. When she paid attention she could hear him and for a moment no one else, not even the beautiful woman demon with the long hair who brushed it a thousand times every day but had the face of a snake when she was angry.

What is he saying? She grew even more still, listened even harder, stopped her heart so that it wouldn't roar and drown out the sound of his voice. Pesky demons kept restarting the heart, though. *How am I supposed to hear if they keep doing that?*

" . . . Jer . . . kill . . . London . . . good Holly."

Does Holly get a biscuit? He wants something, now. I'm supposed to do something. Maybe talk. I'll try.

She opened her mouth, and they all turned to look at her. An old imp with wrinkled gray skin who smelled like formaldehyde limped over to her. He held out a bullhorn for her to shout into. She leaned, spoke. "Kill." She could hear herself, it echoed around in her head.

And the dark-haired man smiled.

I got the right answer. A plus, gold star.

Then the imp took away the bullhorn, and they all went back to talking among themselves. *And I'll sit really quietly and they won't know I'm here.*

Michael straightened. He wasn't entirely sure that Holly had understood what he had asked of her. She had at least repeated "kill," so that was a good sign.

He had spent the past hour in contact with his demonic spies and using his scrying stones. Sir William had indeed ordered him killed, and New Mexico was soon going to become a lot hotter than it already was.

He had thought briefly of appearing before the Supreme Coven with Holly's head on a silver tray, but had quickly rejected the idea. It may or may not have served to appease the leader of the Supreme Coven, but appeasement was no longer Michael's goal.

It's time the Deveraux took back what is rightfully ours, he thought. He had learned that Eli was on the island of Avalon, trying to rescue Nicole Anderson. *He always did have a soft spot for that witch.* It was something Michael could use to his advantage.

He went about packing his bags. Jer and his warlock friend would arrive in the morning, but he would be long gone. Instead, they would find Holly. If his luck held, the three of them would kill one another. If it didn't, well, at least one of them would die, and that was good news for him.

If Holly was the one left standing, Sir William's Golems would make short work of her. When he had realized that the Golems had been sent to find and kill her, he had worked to cover her psychic signature. Like bloodhounds, Golems could be thrown off the scent if you knew how.

It had not been easy, though. Her aura was normally so powerful that it would have been impossible to conceal her had it not been for the possession. Yes, Holly definitely wasn't herself.

What to do with the Judas, Kari, was another question. Normally his first instinct would have been to kill her, but he had a feeling she had not outlived her usefulness. He made a decision quickly: She would be coming along.

Finished, he shut off the light in his bedroom with a twinge of sadness. It was a shame, really. It was a beautiful place. He was also more than a little sorry that he'd miss the fireworks. He had pressing business, though, overseas, and now was the time to go.

He found Kari huddled in a chair in the living room. For a moment he thought the girl had gone catatonic. He waved his hand in front of her face and snapped his fingers, but she didn't flinch. He picked up a suitcase and dropped it with a thud and she turned her eyes. *Good.*

She looked at him. "I killed all of them."

"Yes, sweetie, I'm afraid you did. We have to go now, so be a good girl and help me out."

She stood listlessly. *Ah, the quandary of those who like to think themselves moral! How it hurts them when they discover the truth about themselves.*

"Where are we going?"

"To the airport."

As he closed the door he called out, "Holly, remember what we talked about."

Like a wraith, she appeared from one of the shadows. "Kill," she whispered.

He smiled. He was going to miss her on some level. It was too bad he had never truly gotten to enjoy the fruits of their bond. "Good-bye, Holly."

"Good-bye."

And after the dark-haired man shut the door, she added, "Michael." And then she was alone again in the darkness.

Jer and Eve: New Mexico

"So, what is the game plan?" Jer asked as he finished washing up.

"You know your father best, you tell me," she answered.

"Yeah, I know him." He winced as he touched the scars on his face. "He has a witch in thrall, a special witch. I don't want her hurt," he said, quickly changing the subject.

"Holly Cathers," Eve said. "She's more than 'special,' I would say."

"Yeah well, I want her alive," he said.

Eve smirked. "There's a reward on her head, too."

"If you want my help, you'll leave her alone," he warned.

"I don't need your help. I could just as easily kill you."

"That isn't true or you would have done so at the gas station."

He could see the wheels in her head turning as she looked at him. At last she nodded. "Help me get your father, I'll leave you your precious witch."

"Agreed."

"Good. Now, do you have a plan?"

Three hours later all their plans were worthless. As they pulled up to the cabin Jer could tell that his father was gone. Still, they got out and circled around the building. Everything was dark, silent.

"I don't feel anyone," Eve said.

He was about to agree with her, when a fireball clipped his shoulder. With a shout, he dropped to the ground as a hailstorm of them passed through the air where they had been standing. He rolled onto the shoulder that had been hit, extinguishing the fire.

Eve had jumped behind the minivan and erected a barrier. Jer rose to his feet and, ducking, ran to get behind it.

"Who is it?" Eve shouted.

"I don't know," Jer admitted. The fireballs had come from inside the cabin, through an open window next to the door. They suddenly ceased. A minute later the door creaked open, and a slight figure stepped outside into the light.

"Holly!" he shouted.

Holly cocked her head to the side as though she was listening to him.

"Holly, it's me, Jer!" he called.

"What's wrong with her?" Eve hissed.

"She's in thrall to my father . . . and possessed," Jer admitted.

"You couldn't have mentioned this earlier?"

Someone was shouting at her, calling her name. Who was it? She strained to see, but the others were in the way, their big heads blocking her view. *I want to see the picture too,* she thought. *If only I were a little taller, I could see around them.* She wanted to try to sit up just a little higher, but then they would notice and they would yell at her, and hurt her.

The voice was shouting again. ". . . Jer."

Jer, Jer, where do I know that name? It seemed familiar. Why couldn't the devils sit lower, so she could see? *Maybe if I could pull myself up just a little taller, an inch or so, they wouldn't notice, would they?*

But they would, she knew it. They noticed everything, and they had told her not to move. They had said if she moved, they would hurt her and the Golems would come, whoever they were. The Golems were beasties who would kill her.

The voice kept talking to her, and it was familiar. *I should know it. Who's there?*

They said to hold still because of the beasties. Beasties without, beasties within.

"Holly!" the voice shouted.

And she stood up off her little stool and yelled, "What?"

Holly shouted something back, and almost instantly Golems appeared from thin air. Jer shouted a warning, but she didn't move until the first one grabbed her. Jer ran out from behind the shield, with Eve on his heels.

"How do we stop them?" she shouted.

"Either destroy the paper in their mouths or rub out the first letter on their foreheads!"

"Which is easier?"

"Your guess is as good as mine," Jer answered as he tried to grab the nearest Golem's head. The thing brushed him off as though he were no more than a fly. He landed in the dirt and tried kicking at the creature, but to no avail.

He turned just in time to see Eve jump on the back of one and reach around and rub out the first *e* on the thing's forehead. It fell headlong to the ground, and she leaped off at the last moment.

Meanwhile, fireballs had begun to fly off Holly's fingertips, and Jer found himself suddenly busy dodging those. One struck the Golem next to him full in the face and it, too, fell, the paper in its mouth turning instantly to ash.

That left two, and looking at them, Jer wasn't sure they would be so easy to kill. The one had Holly by the throat. Her eyes were bugging out of her head, and the fireballs were still shooting off uncontrollably from her fingertips. Suddenly her face changed, took on a demonic appearance. *"Gande ipse rodal!"* she roared, in a language he had never heard. He watched in amazement as an invisible hand slowly rubbed out the *e* on the creature's forehead. The Golem and Holly tumbled together to the ground, both still.

"Holly!" he cried, rushing forward. He knelt beside her and felt for a pulse. There was none. He laid his hands on her chest and willed electricity to flow from them into her. Her body convulsed as the charge hit. He checked for a pulse and could feel one, though it was faint. He turned just in time to see Eve rip the paper from the final Golem's mouth. It picked her up and began to crush her, but she tore the paper in half and he dropped her before falling.

She stood panting and tore the paper into a dozen tiny pieces, which she then tossed to the wind. She put her hands on her hips.

"So, what's with her?"

"Unconscious."

"Sounds like a good thing."

"It probably is," he said grimly.

She walked over and crouched down to look at Holly. She didn't look impressed. "So, she's what everyone's making a fuss about?"

Jer nodded.

"I don't see it," she said, and stood back up.

"Well, I'm wasting my time here. I've got to find

your father. Got any idea where he's headed?"

Jer looked down at Holly. His father had left her to kill him and be killed herself. Wherever he was going, he must have considered her a liability. Given all of her power, that was hard to believe. *Where would he be going that he wouldn't have to worry about watching her?* he thought.

It came to him in a rush. He was right, he knew it, he could feel it. "He's headed to London."

Tri-Coven: San Francisco International Airport

Amanda sat next to Tommy on the Mother Coven's jet, holding his hand and wishing she were somewhere else. It was relatively crowded: Sasha, Alex, Amanda, Armand, Pablo, Philippe, Barbara, Tommy, and Richard were aboard. Any minute they would be taxiing for takeoff and it was back to Europe for the lot of them. The copilot, a woman and a witch, came back to address them.

"We've received a message from the tower. It seems someone in Albuquerque is requesting that we land there and pick up three more passengers. The message was sent by someone named Jer."

Amanda's mind raced. *Three passengers! Jer must have found Holly and Kari!* Before she could say anything, Alex spoke: "We don't have time to take a detour."

There was a sudden chilled silence in the air as the new leader of the coven found himself the focus of all eyes. Tommy was the one to speak. "As I see it, if he has Holly with him, we can't afford not to stop. She's our greatest asset and, in the hands of the enemy, our greatest liability. We need her and we can't afford to not know where she is."

Alex narrowed his eyes, and Amanda knew he was judging how best to respond to this challenge to his authority. He smiled after only a moment, and the tension passed. "Well-spoken, Tommy. To Albuquerque it is."

The copilot nodded and returned to the cockpit. Several more minutes passed, and then the plane maneuvered itself into position. As soon as the wheels left the ground, Amanda breathed a sigh of relief. *What can Michael Deveraux do to us in the air?*

"Quite a lot, probably, if all I've heard is true," Alex said.

Amanda stiffened. She had let her guard down for a moment, and he had gotten in. She didn't mind Pablo reading her thoughts, but Alex was different. Maybe it was because he was older, or the leader of the coven or a relative. *Maybe it's because I don't entirely trust him*. Whatever it was, she needed to watch herself more closely.

Still, she wasn't going to allow him, or his allusions to Michael's power, to ruin her flight. She sank down in the seat, put her head on Tommy's shoulder, and promptly fell asleep.

She woke when the wheels touched down in Albuquerque. A hard knot settled in her stomach. *What if Jer didn't send the message?* she thought, sudden fear gnawing at her. *Well, we'll know soon enough.*

"Soon enough" took twenty minutes. At last the hatch opened, and she heard a collective intake of breath from the group. When she saw Jer, she sagged in relief. In his arms he was carrying a woman. Her face was turned inward into his shoulder, but she recognized her, anyway: Holly!

Philippe rose quickly and helped Jer settle Holly into a seat. She was unconscious, but Amanda could see the steady rise and fall of her chest. A new feeling suddenly washed over her, a chill dancing up her spine. She turned, expecting to see Kari walking onto the plane. Instead, it was a stranger, a woman with short hair, clad all in black, and there was something about—

"Warlock!" Pablo hissed, lunging toward her.

Jer threw up an arm and caught him. "Pablo, no! She's a friend."

"I wouldn't go that far," the woman said sarcastically.

"Explain yourself, Deveraux," Alex commanded.

Jer glanced over. "Who put him in charge?"

"Don't ask," Tommy muttered.

"Eve's tracking my father, to kill him. She and I had a common purpose. She helped me save Holly. In exchange, we're giving her a lift to London."

Amanda stared thunderstruck. At last she found her voice. "Is it such a good idea to let a member of the Supreme Coven know where we're going?"

"Technically, Jeraud's a member of the Supreme Coven," Eve pointed out.

"Not anymore. I have my own coven," he snapped.

"And where would it be?" Alex asked. His voice was light, mocking.

Amanda watched the muscles in Jer's jaw begin to jump. When he spoke, his voice was a dangerous hiss. "Someday, I will kill you."

"Not if I kill you first."

Amanda's father stepped in between them. "Down, gentlemen, let's not do this." Power and authority surrounded him, encompassing him. "I promise you that if one of you starts this, *I* will finish it."

Silence descended, neither man wanting to be the first to back down. *This is ridiculous,* Amanda thought. Into the silence, she asked, "What happened to Holly?"

* * *

Jer turned to her, the fight leaving his body. "We were fighting Golems. One of them was choking her. Something took her over, and she killed the Golem and was knocked unconscious."

"Witches and warlocks, please take your seats and prepare for takeoff," the pilot announced over the loudspeaker.

Amanda wasn't sure if she was going to laugh or cry.

Holly was asleep on her little stool in the corner of her mind. Everyone was asleep. It was peaceful, for a moment, but soon all would wake and everything would be chaos again. Chaos and fear. She didn't remember much anymore, much other than fear. Fear. How well she knew it, how she had tasted it time and again, lived with it, eaten it, slept it, dreamed it. Just like that night so long ago, in her own room in her own home. . . .

The Cathers Family: San Francisco, 2001

Holly sat, munching popcorn and watching television with her parents. It was Tuesday night, and Tuesday night was movie night. It had been tradition for as long as she could remember. Even the trip to the video store was tradition, complete with the perennially chick flick—shoot 'em up controversy.

Now, as they were watching *The Sixth Sense,* she was starting to think she should have given in to her dad's pleas for a John Wayne movie instead. When the little boy told Bruce Willis that he could see dead people, she thought she was going to cry.

"At least it's not as violent as I thought it was going to be," her mother commented.

"This is worse than violence. This is just messing with your head," her dad protested.

Holly tended to agree with her father. *I can't imagine anything more frightening than seeing a ghost.*

When the movie was over, she ran down the hallway to the bathroom, throwing on light switches along the way. She shivered as she stared in the mirror. *I can't believe I let it get to me like that,* she thought.

She thought she saw a shadow move behind her, and she jumped. She brushed her teeth and got ready for bed while avoiding looking into the mirror again.

After she had laid out her clothes for the next day, she felt a lot calmer. When her mom came by to say good night, she was in bed and her eyelids were drooping.

"I love you, honey."

"I love you, too, Mom."

"You okay?"

Holly smiled. "Yeah, are you?"

"Of course," her mom said, laughing lightly.

Holly's smile widened. It was her mom's nervous laugh. The movie had gotten to her, too. "Sleep tight, Mom, don't let the bedbugs bite."

"You either," her mom said, shaking her head and laughing.

My parents are great. I can't imagine having grown up with different ones, she thought as she slid into sleep.

"Wake up, Holly," a female voice cajoled.

Holly squirmed and flipped onto her back. She could tell through her closed eyelids that the room was light. "Don't want to," she said sleepily.

"Wake up," the voice grew more insistent.

"No."

"You must wake up, Holly."

"Mom, let me sleep."

"I am not your mother," the voice snapped.

Holly's eyes flew open, and she sat bolt upright.

It was still nighttime. The light in the room was coming from a woman. She stood in the center of Holly's room, in an old-fashioned dress. Her dark hair hung in waves down her back. Her eyes burned like coals, and she was glowing.

"I'm dreaming," Holly said out loud. "This is just a dream."

"It's no dream," the woman assured her. "I am

Isabeau. I am your ancestress, and it is time for you to discover who you are."

"I know who I am. I'm Holly Cathers."

"No, you are Holly Cahors of the House Cahors, and you are a witch."

Holly began to shake uncontrollably. "I must be dreaming."

"And I tell you that you are not."

"Are you dead?"

"Yes."

She thought she would faint. The room began to swim before her eyes. "This isn't real, this isn't happening."

"It is real," the woman said, drifting closer. She sat down on the edge of the bed next to Holly. "You are of my House, my blood. You are a witch and you need to discover what that means now rather than later. The Deveraux are your enemy, you must remember this. They will kill everyone you love if you let them."

She reached her hand toward Holly, and Holly tried to scramble out of her reach. Her body seemed frozen, though, and she wanted to scream as dead, cold fingers touched her cheek. "*Ma petite,* so much to learn and so little time. I will help you."

Isabeau pressed her hand to Holly's forehead. "I will be with you, sharing my strength, my power with you. Now," her voice deepened into a commanding tone, "light the candle on the dresser with your mind."

Holly felt compelled to obey, as though she had no will of her own. She turned and stared at the candle in question and suddenly, with a whoosh, it was on fire.

Holly began to scream. Within moments she heard footsteps pounding down the hall, and her parents burst into the room. Her mother screamed, and Isabeau turned to look at Holly's parents. For a moment they all stayed, frozen as though in a tableau, and then Isabeau was gone and the only light in the room was from the candle.

"Holly! What happened?" her mother cried as she rushed forward. Holly threw herself into her mother's arms, and they both collapsed onto the bed, crying.

"Mom," she gasped between sobs, "I'm a witch and I see dead people!"

"It was the movie, that's all, it gave you nightmares, it was nothing," her mom said, her hysterical tone belying her words.

"But, Mom, you saw her, she was here."

Her mom was silent, and Holly pulled away to look at her. There was fear in her eyes. "What am I going to do, Mommy?"

Just then her father stepped in close. He placed his hand on her forehead, much as the woman had done.

When he spoke, his voice was deep, deeper than she had ever heard it. “Sleep and forget.”

She slipped into blessed oblivion.

When she woke in the morning, Holly had the nagging feeling that something was wrong. She had slept well, but she was tired, and something just felt off.

Downstairs in the kitchen she found her parents at the breakfast table. Both were silent when she walked in, and both looked as though they had been crying.

“What’s wrong?” Holly asked, feeling herself begin to panic.

“Nothing, honey,” her father said with a forced smile that made it nowhere near his eyes. “How’d you sleep?”

“Like a log.”

“No nightmares?” her mom asked.

Holly turned, puzzled and worried. “I don’t think so, why?”

“Nothing. I just thought I heard you tossing a lot last night.”

“No, no nightmares, no dreams. I just slept really solid. Are you two okay?”

“Fine,” her father said quickly, too quickly. “We’re fine, honey. We just didn’t sleep well.”

“I told you not to let the bedbugs bite,” she tried to tease her mother.

The joke fell flat, but her mom gave her a sickly smile. Not sure what was going on but convinced they weren't going to talk about it, Holly ate quickly.

Finished, she headed for the stairs to get her back-pack. She was halfway up the stairs when she heard her mother say, "She doesn't remember anything about last night, what she saw, what she did."

"I told you she wouldn't," her father said.

She froze, listening. *What happened last night?* she wondered, her pulse beginning to race. They had stopped talking, though, and she slowly finished climbing the stairs. In her room she picked her watch up off her dresser.

She turned to go but froze in midmotion. On her dresser was a candle made in the shape of a horse that her best friend, Tina, had given her for her birthday. It was beautiful, and Holly had never used it, happy to have it more as a figurine.

The top of the horse's head had melted, the wax dripping down and covering its eyes. *Someone burned the candle,* she thought, stunned, *and the horse is blind—just like me.*

Tri-Coven: Over the Atlantic

On her stool in the corner, Holly dreamed, and she remembered. Isabeau had come to her long before, and her father had hidden it from her. Her mother had been frightened, so had he. That was why they had fought. That was what had happened.

Still sitting perfectly upright on her stool, Holly slowly opened one eye and looked around. The demons were all sleeping, crashed out on the floor, lying in heaps, some atop one another. Past them, now that they were lying down, she could see more, she could see outside, and she saw Amanda.

The hairs along the back of Amanda's neck lifted on end, and she had the sudden and unnerving sensation of being watched. She turned her head sharply and saw Holly, her eyes open, staring at her. "Tommy," she whispered, "look!"

Tommy did, and came to the same conclusion she had: "It's Holly."

Amanda quickly unbuckled her seat belt and moved over in front of Holly. "Holly, it's Amanda. Do you recognize me?"

Holly blinked her eyes once, strongly and clearly.

In a moment, Pablo was beside Amanda. "I can feel her," he said.

"Holly, can you help us get rid of the demons?" Amanda asked.

Holly just stared straight ahead, and Amanda wasn't sure she had understood her.

"She can't," Pablo said. "She's afraid."

"Holly, honey, don't be afraid. We're going to help you, we're going to get them out of there. Do you understand?"

She blinked. Then, slowly, her eyelids closed.

"No, Holly, come back, come back to us," Amanda begged.

Pablo laid a hand on her arm. "She's retreated. I can't feel her anymore."

"But at least we know that she's in there," Tommy said.

"We need to find a way to bring her back," Jer said.

"We tried exorcism. It didn't work," Sasha told him. "That's how Tante Cecile was killed."

"I believe I can do it," Armand said.

Amanda turned to him. "Armand, I'm not sure we can risk losing another person."

Philippe interjected. "Let him help. Armand studied to be a priest before he began to explore the ways of the Goddess. He knows things and has seen things that none of us have. I believe he can do it."

"I say we take the risk," Jer chimed in.

Amanda turned on him. "You weren't there last

time. You don't know what it's like. We have to find a way to help her, but I'm not sure an exorcism is it!"

"Amanda, if he's willing to try, I say we let him."

She looked from face to face. They all looked so earnest, so hopeful. At last she turned to Alex. He hadn't said a word. "What do you think?"

He raised an eyebrow. "If multiple demons are in there, they might not all be from the same faith paradigm. Someone who has experience with multiple religions might succeed where others have failed. I say you let the priest try."

It made sense. She wasn't sure if that's because it was what she wanted to hear or because it really did. She looked at Holly. *We need her back. We're returning to the mouth of hell, and we need her with us.* She turned to Armand. "What will you need?"

ELEVEN

MARY

☾

Time now to make our move
Deveraux have much to prove
We show them now all our power
We rule them all in this hour

God and Goddess hear our cry
We lift our hands unto the sky
We cast out those who cause us fear
Enemies both far and near

Tri-Coven: London

Amanda's nerves were frayed. Getting from the airport to the safe house had been harrowing. They were treading on Supreme Coven ground. Moreover, at least one member, the woman Eve, knew that they were here. *What's to keep her from alerting the others to our presence? I know Jer trusts her, but that doesn't mean I do.*

As soon as they had landed Eve had taken off,

thanking them flippantly for the ride. She was hunting Michael Deveraux, and in that, and only in that, they were on the same side.

She looked around the house where they were now. It was located just outside of London and was quite large. Armand had roamed through it like a lion, until he had found the room where he wanted to perform the exorcism. Everyone had spent the last hour stripping the room bare so there would be nothing Holly or her demons could use as weapons.

The witch who owned the house had left before they'd arrived, but had left them with all the supplies they could use and carte blanche to use the property as they needed to. *I don't blame her for taking off. I would, too, if I could.*

Her father had left half an hour before, to get . . . something . . . he hadn't said what. He had had a hard look in his eye when he'd left, though, and it had made her nervous.

Tommy came up beside her and kissed her cheek. She smiled and turned into his arms. It felt so good to have him hold her. She just wanted to be held, forever.

"I love you."

"I love you too," she whispered.

"We'd better see if Armand needs anything else."

She looked up at him. He looked like a man.

Where was the boy she had once known? How had he managed to change before her eyes without her noticing? He smiled, and she saw the boy again, but it was only part of him now. There was something good and strong about him. He was more than she had ever known, more than she had ever dreamed. He was everything she needed and wanted. *I will do anything to keep hold of him.*

Arm in arm, they walked into the room. It was empty. Even the paintings were gone. It was more than just furniture and paintings, though. Pablo and Sasha had worked hard and scrubbed the room clean of any psychic imprints as well. She had never felt a place so hollow. It chilled her. *Is this what death is like? No, it can't be. I refuse to believe that it's emptiness.*

They all stood together in the room, gathered around, staring quietly at Holly. She was slumped in the middle of the floor. She hadn't come to again on the flight, or in the car ride here. Amanda had begun to fear she wouldn't wake up again.

"When you leave, close the door and stand ready with the swords we prepared. If anything comes through that door, kill it," Armand instructed.

Pablo spoke. "The demons are beginning to stir."

"Everyone leave," Armand said quietly.

"I want to stay," Amanda protested.

"No, you must go, quickly."

"Come on, Amanda, it will be okay," Tommy said, half-dragging her from the room.

Armand turned back to Holly and breathed in deeply. In a strange way, he had been preparing his whole life for this. His grandfather had been a priest and an exorcist. Armand himself had studied to be a priest. Then, on the eve of taking his vows, he had turned aside to study the ways of the Goddess. Still, in his heart, he had never betrayed his first God. Instead, he worshiped them both, and he had found others who did the same.

Holly's eyes snapped open, though it wasn't Holly who stared at him from their depths. Gazing at Holly as she sat shivering, madness flickering in her eyes as untold demons battled one another within her, Armand thanked both deities for all the years of training. It was all that was going to save him and her.

He lit the purple candles and began.

The words flowed off his tongue, though it had been years since he had studied their meaning and memorized them. *"Exorcizo te, omnis spiritus immunde, in nomine Dei."* He made the sign of the cross over her. *"Patris omnipotentis, et in noimine Jesu."* Another cross. *"Christi Filii ejus, Domini et Judicis nostri, et in virtute Spiritus."* He inscribed a third cross in the air over her.

"I exorcise thee, every unclean spirit, in the name of God the Father Almighty, and in the name of Jesus Christ, His Son, our Lord and Judge, and in the power of the Holy Spirit."

"Filthy creature, you are of witchblood and have no right to invoke that name," a demon hissed, speaking through Holly and twisting her face into a hideous reflection of its own features.

"God loves all His children, and He aids those who have faith in Him and call upon His name."

"He won't listen to you," another spirit taunted. "He will not share you with the Goddess."

"I don't believe that's true," Armand forced himself to answer calmly. "But even if it is, he is also a merciful God, and I am sure He will forgive me. Depart from her, all you demons within, in the name of the Goddess who rules her heart, you have no place within her."

"She likes us," a third demon spoke in a high, shrill voice. "She wants us to stay."

"*I command you to leave. Sancti, ut descedas ab hoc plasmate Dei,* Holly Cathers, *per eumdem Christum Dominum nostrum, qui venturus est judicare vivos et mortuos, et saeculum per ignem." Depart from this creature of God named Holly Cathers through the same Christ our Lord, who shall come to judge the living and the dead, and the world by fire.*

Holly began to thrash back and forth as the demons

fought her, one another, Armand, and the Deities he invoked. There was a sudden scream, and one flew out her mouth, a tiny, red-spotted thing with a tale like a dragon and wings like a sparrow.

Armand drew his sword from his belt. He sliced through the creature's body. "I send you back to the hell from which you came."

The creature exploded in a small, sulfurous cloud of red dust. It sprinkled to the ground.

Only one. This is going to take a long time.

He picked up a large wooden bowl filled with frankincense, crushed garlic, peppermint, cloves, and sage. He touched the flame of the purple candle to the mix and then set it on fire. He blew on it gently until the flame went out, but the mixture continued to smolder. The scent filled the air, and the demons inside Holly began to squeal.

Armand walked to Holly. He spit carefully into his hands and then touched her right ear then the left. *"Ephpheta, quod est, Adaperire." Be opened.* Next he touched her right nostril, then the left. *"In odorem suavitatis. Tu autem effugare, diabole; appropinquabit enim judicium Dei." For a savor of sweetness: And to you, O devil, begone! For the judgment of God is at hand.*

"Holly," he commanded her. "Holly, listen to me. Help me cast out these demons."

There was a flicker in her eyes, a moment of what he could only call understanding, before the demons pushed her back down with a roar.

"You cannot have her, priest. We shall not leave this body. We are grown . . . comfortable . . . here," one of the voices hissed.

"How many are you?" Armand demanded.

"Hundreds."

"Then hundreds of you shall die."

Holly sat on her little stool and watched in surprise as a little red demon left. It went, crying the entire way. She almost felt sorry for it, but she remembered it had spit on her earlier, so she didn't feel so sorry anymore. Rather, she was glad it was gone. There was one less voice ringing in her ears, one less body blocking her view.

Then she heard a man, commanding her, pleading with her to help him get rid of the demons. The demons were busy, looking out, talking to the man. They weren't looking at Holly. She moved her little toe, and this time no one noticed, no one cared.

She sat very still again. In a moment, she would try moving her entire foot.

Armand took the holy water and sprinkled salt in it. Demons were supposed to fear salt water—it was supposed to hurt them. That was what he had learned. That was why, when Jesus had cast demons out of a man and let them enter a herd of pigs and the pigs had stampeded into salt water, the demons had died. At least, that's what was said. He confessed in his heart that he didn't know. *But then again, that's what this is all about: It's all about faith.*

He picked up the bowl of water and crossed over to Holly. He looked down at her. Her hands and legs were bound with rope—something you're never supposed to do to an exorcism recipient, but, then, nothing about this was normal. There was magic binding her as well, courtesy of Alex. It made sense. Holly knew what the rest of them knew, practiced the same magic, knew the same spells. Alex, at least, was a bit different, as were his ways.

He poured the water over her head in the shape of an *X*. He did it three times. Demons screamed, and he could smell sulfur and burning flesh. A dozen demons poured out of her, and he let them go. They were dying—he could tell it by the way they rippled, as though they were fading in and out of being. If they even made it to the door, Philippe would handle them.

He put down the bowl and picked up another filled with herbs. He pressed his thumb into the dried herbs and then anointed Holly with them, touching first her forehead, then her chin, then her right eyelid, then her left.

"Pax tibi." Peace be unto you.

"Blessed be," Holly wanted to say, but she didn't. She was afraid. The stench of death filled her nostrils. More demons had gone, but the ones who remained were growing more agitated, more dangerous. She twitched her left foot. None of them noticed, though. She exhaled slowly, and no one turned to look at her.

She licked her lips; maybe she should try speaking, maybe it would help. Her heart began to pound louder, so very loud and so very fast. She parted her lips, and nobody stopped her. She flicked her tongue across her teeth. The demons were all jumping up and down, shouting and screaming at the man outside.

They hated him, and she could feel their rage; it bubbled around her, making her heart pound faster. It frightened her and exhilarated her at the same time. It had been so long since she had felt something other than fear. *I'm going to do it!*

"Blessed—" a dozen demons jumped on top of her. One clamped a hoary hand over her mouth while the rest began to hit her and spit on her. They whispered vile things in her ears, told her that she was nothing, no one. *They must be right. After all, they would know.*

***

A wizened, dying demon slid underneath the door, and Philippe stabbed it, sending it into oblivion. "Something he's doing is working," he noted. "That demon was all but dead already."

Amanda paced in front of the door, playing with her sword as though it were a baton. He felt sorry for her as he watched her. *She has lost much, and stands to lose so much more.*

"Have I mentioned how much I hate waiting?" she asked.

"You have mentioned that," Alex commented. "We need to start gearing up. As soon as Armand is done, we need to move out. Half of us will go to Avalon to rescue Nicole. The other half will begin the assault on the Supreme Coven."

"Isn't it dangerous to split up like that?" Tommy asked.

"It's dangerous not to, at this point. We need to move, and do so quickly. We can't brook anymore delays. We must strike before we are expected." Alex glanced at Jer. "For all we know, we're already expected."

Philippe noticed that Jer bristled, but said nothing. He turned his attention back to the door. *Goddess help him,* he prayed for Armand as he kept watch for more demons.

★★★

Armand heard Holly speak, or at least try to. "That's it, Holly, work with me, fight them off, you can do it. You are stronger than they are. Cast them out. You have the power."

"She has no power over me," a voice hissed. A wind suddenly whipped through the room, and Holly seemed to be at the center of it. "Neither do you."

"Who are you? What is your name?" Armand demanded.

"Bunyip."

Bunyip? Where have I heard that? The wind continued, and that seemed familiar. *Bunyip. Whirlwind.*

"You're an evil spirit that lurks in the whirlwind. Stories are told about you amongst the aboriginal people."

"You know of me, good. Then you know to be afraid."

Armand gestured to indicate the wind. "So far, I am not impressed. So, unless you have plans to turn Holly into a bird, I think you should leave." He stood, awaiting the creature's response and racking his brain as to how to expel it.

In aboriginal legend, the rainbow serpent shaped the land and created all the spirits. It's a start, at any rate.

"I command that you part, Bunyip, in the name of

the spirit that breathed life into the people of your land. In the name of the rainbow serpent, I bid you depart!"

There was a howling as the wind picked up in the room. Armand saw the demon flow out of Holly's mouth in a rush. Then the whirlwind began. Round and round, the wind swirled, harder and faster. It tore at Armand's clothes and stung his eyes.

He opened his mouth to shout out an incantation, but the wind ripped the words from his lips and they were lost even to his own ears. *Goddess help me,* he thought as the wind continued to pick up speed, twisting in upon itself, *else it will rip both Holly and me apart.*

In the corner of the room, a tornado began to form. Fear raced through Armand as he realized the creature could destroy them all.

The door suddenly opened, and Alex stood in it, his arms lifted. He was screaming something, but Armand could not tell what it was. The wind died instantly, leaving an eerie stillness in its wake. The door slammed back closed, and Armand was once more alone with Holly and all her demons.

I'll have to thank Alex later, he thought, turning back to the job at hand.

There was only chaos in her mind. At least the wind was gone, but it had left a lot of bodies strewn around, demons dazed, demons unconscious. None of them were looking at her. She took a deep breath and stood up.

Nothing happened. No one noticed her. There was a brown, scaly demon lying on the ground next to her stool. He was small, only about half her size, and very scrawny. His mouth was open, and he was drooling thick yellow liquid all over the floor of her mind. *Gross.* She nudged him with her toe, but he didn't move. *He's not so big. I could take him,* she thought, glancing around furtively at the others.

She made small movements with her left hand, inscribing a pentagram in the air over the creature. "Goddess, cast this creature out, it does not belong here about," she whispered.

The demon's eyes flew open, and it made a gasping noise before it went flying out, out through her mouth. The rest who were awake turned to her. *Uh-oh.*

Armand stared in surprise as a tiny brown demon flew out of Holly. He grasped his sword and sliced it in half. Brown goo dripped off the edges of the sword and tumbled to the floor before slowly dissolving in midair.

"Good, Holly, keep it up."

***

Holly, however, wasn't listening. She was back on her stool cringing as they all stood around screaming and striking her with fists and biting her with teeth. She was crying and bleeding, and there was no one there to help.

Armand stared hopefully at Holly, but there was no sign that she understood, and no more demons forthcoming. Holly suddenly started babbling; it sounded like Aramaic. Armand lifted his hands and placed them in the air over Holly's head. *"Allaahumma jannibnash-shaytaana wa jannibish-shaytaana maa razaqta-naa." O Allah, keep Satan away from us and keep Satan away from what You have bestowed upon us.*

A dozen demons came screaming out of her, and Armand whirled this way and that, skewering one, dismembering another. The last one he had to chase around the room for a minute. He stood panting after he had slain it, trying to regain his breath.

"Help me!" he heard Holly gasp behind him.

He jerked around and saw her sitting, staring wide-eyed at him. "Help me!" she cried again.

He rushed back to her. Just as he reached her side, her eyes rolled back in her head and her body started convulsing. She fell backward, and Armand caught her and held her. "Fight them, Holly, fight them," he urged her. "You can do it, I believe in you. Come back to us. Cast them out. Goddess, I beseech you, remove the unclean things from Holly, restore her mind and soul. Let all the creatures who lurk within be banished and shine your light upon her."

More demons went flying, and Armand let them go, praying the others would catch them.

"I command thee, unclean spirits, begone from this girl. You have no business here, and I command you, in the name of Jesus Christ, whose blood was spilled on the Cross, to leave now!"

Anguished screams ripped through the air as more demons poured out. He could feel a couple of them clawing at him, trying to latch on to him, but he brushed them away with hand and mind.

"In the name of the Lady and the Lord, depart from here every evil thing. I claim Holly as a holy vessel for the Goddess. Consecrate her and make her clean."

From his pocket he drew a white linen cloth and placed it on her head. *"Accipe vestem candidam, quam perferas immaculatam." Receive this white garment, which mayest thou bear without stain.*

There was something like an explosion. There was a blinding burst of light and the rush of air and *things* passing by him. Holly's eyes flew open, and she looked up at him.

***

Holly was standing in the center of her mind. *Where are they all going?* she wondered in awe as demons flew past her. One reached out and grabbed at her, its claws raking down the length of her arm. She shook it loose, and it, too, went flying.

At last she was alone and everything was silent. Quietly, cautiously, she tiptoed forward until she pressed her face to her eyes and she could see out. She took a deep breath, and air rushed into her lungs. She looked up, and there was Armand.

He was holding a white candle. The flame flickered bright and clear. He handed her the candle, and after a moment she was able to lift her hand and take it from him.

"Accipe lampadem ardentem. Amen. Blessed be."

"Blessed be," she whispered. *I'm back.*

She began to cry.

Armand held her as she sobbed, thanking the Goddess and Christ that he had been able to bring her back. After a few minutes there was a tenuous knock on the door. "Come in," he called hoarsely.

The door opened slowly, and he glanced up. Philippe walked forward slowly and knelt down beside them. "How is she?" he asked.

"Philippe," she whispered.

He smiled and touched her cheek. "It is good to see you again."

"The demons?" Armand asked.

"We killed them all," Philippe answered.

Relief flooded Armand, and he felt himself sag slightly. His body began to shake as the exhaustion overwhelmed him.

"Holly?" Amanda called from the door, her voice filled with uncertainty.

"Amanda," Holly choked out.

Then the two cousins were embracing, Holly still lying half in Armand's arms.

A sound from the doorway caused Armand to turn and look. Alex stood there, an inscrutable look on his face. "She's back?"

Armand nodded.

"All right," Alex said in a loud voice. "Everyone get ready to move."

Richard: North of London

Richard was driving on M-11 North. He was about a half hour outside London. He slowed slightly, eyes searching. Finally he saw a tree-lined country lane, nothing imposing. He turned down it. He drove for a while until at last the lane dead-ended at an abandoned

World War II U.S. Army airfield. He parked and got out, cautiously.

Every sense was hyperalert as he looked around slowly. He walked quietly, barely touching ground as he glided forward toward the buildings. He made his way inside and quickly found what had once been the officers' bar. The room looked as though it had been untouched since 1945. Dust lay thick along the tables. Broken glass lay everywhere, and several windows were missing.

Cobwebs hung from the ceiling, and a mouse scuttled across the top of the bar as he passed by. He headed for the back of the room, where there was a door. It would have been easy to overlook, tucked back in the shadows, but he moved to it with surety. As his hand touched the knob, he knew he was in the right place. The doorknob was free of dust.

He opened the door and started down a long flight of stairs. He walked carefully, waiting to be challenged. He reached the bottom and came face-to-face with the guards he had been expecting.

Wordlessly, he reached into his pocket and pulled out his identification. The guards took it and examined it. After a minute they nodded him over to a machine on the wall. He placed his eyes against it and held them open as his retinas were scanned.

Almost immediately the guards opened another door, and one escorted him through the halls of the underground structure, a training ground for a British commando unit and the SAS. Within moments he was seated in a British army colonel's office.

The other man leaned forward across his desk, peering at him intently. "Richard Anderson?"

Richard nodded.

"Your reputation precedes you, sir."

"I was just a guy trying to serve his country."

The colonel raised his eyebrows but didn't respond to that. Instead, he asked, "What can I help you with?"

Richard took a piece of paper out of his pocket and passed it across the desk to the colonel. "I need a few things."

The colonel read the list twice before nodding. "I think we can take care of this." He pushed a buzzer on his desk, and a soldier came in. The colonel handed him the list. "Please assemble these items for the gentleman."

The two rose to their feet and shook hands. "Would you mind if I ask exactly what you need them for?"

Richard shook his head. "It's better you don't know. Besides, I don't think you'd believe me if I told you."

"Fair enough," the other grunted. "Good luck to you."

"Thank you, Colonel."

Ten minutes later, Richard was back in the car and on his way to the safe house.

Tri-Coven: London

Amanda hugged Tommy and prayed she would never have to let go. She didn't like the idea he would be heading to Avalon while she would be staying in London with the group that was going to launch the attack on the Supreme Coven.

She needed to stay with Holly to help keep an eye on her, to help keep her grounded, especially since she had only just met Alex. If Tommy stayed with her, though, that would leave her father, Sasha, and Philippe to sneak onto Avalon alone. They really needed another person. Philippe had to go, since Amanda could not. Because he and Nicole were in thrall to each other, he would be the one most likely to be able to find her.

Still, the tears coursed down her cheeks at the thought of being apart from Tommy. *It isn't fair!* she thought. She'd had all the time in the world to get to know him as a friend, but they were just now truly discovering each other in the love that they shared. *In fif-*

teen minutes we'll have to part, though, and what if something happens to one of us?

"I have an idea," he said, his voice husky.

"Yeah?"

"Why don't we do a spell to, you know, keep us together."

"Throughout eternity?" she breathed. "So that if we die, we'll be together?"

"You're such a dork," he said affectionately. "To keep us safe, and together, no matter what."

"Yes, we can do that. We must hurry, though."

Amanda quickly drew a rough circle on the ground while Tommy found and lit some incense. In a minute they were in the circle together, their knees touching.

She grasped his hands in hers, and for a moment all the world seemed to slow and then stop. She breathed in and he inhaled at the same time. She could feel her heartbeat slowing to match his, could feel the pulse in his fingertips mingling with her own.

An athame lay between them beside a single white candle. She let go of Tommy's hands and picked up the athame. Tommy lit the candle. "Future and past, we remain together until the last," he intoned.

She sliced her palm with the athame, wincing at the pain. She then sliced Tommy's. They clasped their bleeding hands together over the candle. Blood dripped down into the flame, causing it to hiss.

"As pure as the flame, my love for you," Amanda whispered.

"I am yours in this life and the next," Tommy replied.

Next Amanda pulled a hair from her head, and Tommy pulled one from his. Together they dropped the hairs onto the flame.

"Goddess, keep us in safety in this life. And grant we live together in the next," Amanda implored.

"Eternity," they whispered together. They leaned forward and kissed over the candle. As their lips touched, Amanda felt a great surge of power ripple through her and then leave.

When she pulled back, Tommy was staring at her wide-eyed. "Did you feel that?"

She nodded. "I don't know what it was."

"Well, let's hope it was good luck, 'cuz we're going to need some about now," Tommy said, looking over Amanda's shoulder.

"It's time," Alex said from behind her, making her jump.

TWELVE

BRIGITTE

☾

Death and destruction we always bring
Evil is what makes our blood sing
Deveraux will finally rise to power
See us in our most wicked hour

The Goddess has made us whole again
Made us stronger women and men
The circle has come full round at last
Cahors make up now for the past

Richard, Sasha, Tommy, and Philippe: Avalon

"Would someone mind telling me again—why are we in a boat?" Tommy asked.

Philippe had to admit it was a reasonable question. Given that the loved ones of Cahors witches died by drowning, what they were doing would qualify them for the Darwin Awards.

"Because this is the only way we may reach Avalon," Sasha said, answering seriously.

"Thanks to our last rescue, they've obviously warded the island against teleportation."

"So, what, the Mother Coven didn't have helicopters?"

Philippe shook his head, images of Tommy hanging from one of the struts filling his mind. "What, and miss out on all this bonding time?"

Tommy made a sour face, and Philippe's heart went out to him. *He is worried about Amanda, and I understand that. Half of me is lost until Nicole is found.* He grimly turned back to the job at hand.

A dozen times they wanted to turn the boat, but didn't. Twice, the boat tried to turn itself, but they straightened its course back out. All the magic had been put in place years ago to keep the island from being accidentally discovered.

The magics used to hide the island weren't the only strange thing he had noticed. He kept catching himself glancing backward, trying to see something in the water behind them. Always, though, nothing was there. Still, he couldn't help but feel as though they were somehow being followed. He closed his eyes and tried to reach out with his mind, to touch something, but he only touched air and sea. Frustrated, he gave up. *It's just in my imagination.*

They didn't see the shore until they were nearly on

it. Her breath catching in her throat, Sasha whispered a spell that Philippe hoped would allow them to land safely and without detection.

The boat ran ashore. After a few seconds and nothing had happened, they all breathed a collective sigh of relief. Philippe hopped out, and together he and Tommy tied the boat up so it wouldn't slip off the rocky shore back into the water.

"Can you feel her?" Sasha asked as she joined them.

Philippe shook his head in frustration. He glanced over at Nicole's father. Richard stood a few feet apart from them, tension evident in every line of his body.

A sniper rifle was slung across his back, and he was carrying ammunition on his person—and a few other things he hadn't bothered to identify to the group.

We really are at war, Philippe thought.

They were standing on a rocky shore. A faint path led upward, wrapping around the base of a mountain. Sasha set out upon it, and the rest of them fell in behind her. Philippe strained his senses. *Nicole is somewhere on this island, and I should be able to feel her.*

They wound their way up and around the mountain, tripping on loose stones that seemed to suddenly twist beneath their feet. "This whole place is cursed," Tommy muttered, and Philippe had to agree.

At last they stopped for a rest on a small plateau.

The trail blanched here, part of it continuing upward and part of it beginning to head back down. A large rock stood on otherwise level ground, and all but Richard sank to a seat on it. The wind whipped past them, taking Philippe's breath away.

He touched Sasha's arm, and she turned to him. "How do you know where we're going?" he asked.

"I've spent much time on this island," she admitted.

"A prisoner?" he asked.

She smiled faintly. "Yes, and no."

"I don't understand."

"I used to come here at night, when I was sleeping. I would astral-travel—my body lay in my room in Paris, and my spirit roamed here."

"What were you doing?"

She shook her head. "I never really knew. It wasn't an active choice on my part. At first I thought there was something here I could use to help my sons, but all I ever found here was evil. When they brought Jer here, I was overwhelmed with sorrow and joy. I tried to speak with him, to comfort him, but I don't think he ever heard me.

"Holly heard me, though. She came one night to see Jer."

"You were the one who showed her where the island was," Philippe said.

She nodded. "I thought then that maybe that was why I had roamed the island every night for so long. If it freed my son, it was worth it."

Her eyes took on a faraway look. "There's something here, something I can't explain. . . ."

As she drifted off, Philippe felt a cold chill sweep through his body. She was right: There was something here. It felt ancient, evil. It tainted everything. Sitting beside Sasha, he could barely even sense her; the evil was acting as some kind of filter, muting the feel of her presence. He closed his eyes, trying to ignore the evil, trying to push past it, to reach beyond it . . . and then, he felt—Nicole!" he exclaimed, leaping to his feet.

"She's not far away," he said excitedly.

"Which path?" Richard asked, his voice strained.

"Down," Philippe said. He could feel it in his soul.

Eli was angry with himself. *The witch is playing me, she has to be*. Still, part of him didn't care, and that's what got to him. Fantasme sat huddled in a corner looking miserable and angry at the same time. *He's probably as confused as I am by the fact that I'm sitting next to a Cahors witch and I'm not trying to kill her.*

"Fantasme, find us a way out of here," he ordered.

The hideous, birdlike creature screeched once and then disappeared.

"Alone at last," he joked.

"Uh, not exactly," Nicole answered, staring toward the back of the cave.

"What do you—"

And then he saw the three Golems lumbering out of the darkness.

Philippe, Sasha, Richard, and Tommy: Avalon

They had been on the island for almost two hours. They had worked their way down the path and were now standing on the crown of a hill facing east.

"Where is she?" Sasha said in a voice that was barely above a whisper.

"She is here. I can feel her presence, and she is very frightened," said Philippe. He had been able to keep her presence with them since he had first felt her on the plateau. The hard part was, they had probably been only within a few hundred feet of her then, but the winding of the trail had taken them on a circuitous route.

At that instant there was a loud rumbling down the hill by the shore. A large dust cloud was rolling along the sand, and when it cleared, Eli and Nicole were lying in the water and three very large creatures were emerging from the ground.

"Golems!" yelled Philippe. With that, Tommy was

off running, stumbling, and rolling down the hill toward Nicole. He was still over a hundred yards away when one of the Golems reached Nicole. Nicole tried to kick it but to no effect. It reached down and picked her up by the front of her dress like a rag doll. A second Golem was reaching for Nicole's legs as if to tear her apart.

"Do something, hurry!" Sasha yelled in a near panic.

At that moment the hairs on the back of Philippe's head lifted, and four more Golems raced past him, heading directly for Tommy. Philippe shouted, panic flooding him.

Richard, who had been slightly higher up the hill than the others and was looking the other way, whirled around. In a movement so sudden and yet incredibly smooth, he had unslung the sniper rifle, raised it, and fired twice. There was almost no sound, just a soft *phfft, phfft,* and two Golems dropped to the ground, the first *e* on each of their foreheads neatly replaced by perfectly round little holes. Philippe was stunned by the look of controlled rage on Richard's face. Before he and Sasha could even react, Richard was racing past them and was about fifty feet behind Tommy.

Tommy reached Nicole just as the two Golems were beginning to pull her in opposite directions. He jumped on the back of the one closest to him, bringing his right arm up and around the Golem's forehead. The Golem tried to shake Tommy off, but that only served to wipe away the *e*. Three down. As Tommy was riding the back of the Golem to the ground, three more shots rang out and the Golems who had just reached Tommy fell. Philippe felt his jaw grow slack.

The last remaining Golem had Nicole by the head. *He's going to kill her.*

Another *phfft* sound, and the final beast dropped to the ground still clutching Nicole. Richard had fired again while at a dead run.

As though in slow motion, Philippe watched as Eli rolled up to a sitting position and raised his hands into the air. He could see his lips moving but could not hear what spell Eli was chanting. Richard reached behind his head and unsheathed a long, wicked knife that had been resting between his shoulder blades. It went sailing end over end before driving itself into the ground between Eli's legs. Even from that distance, Philippe could see the warlock turn ash white.

"You just sit still," Richard boomed. "Breathe wrong and I kill you."

As Philippe scrambled down the hill, his heart was pounding. Eli was sitting absolutely still, not even blinking.

Tommy rolled off his dead Golem, turned, and

shouted at Richard, "You could have hit her."

"No, there was six inches above her head," Richard said as tears of joy rolled down his face. He was cradling his daughter in his arms, and she was clutching him and sobbing.

As Philippe ran up, Richard extended an arm to him and he joined them in the circle. He reached out and touched Nicole's arm, and an electric shock went through him.

He gasped and looked down at her distended abdomen. *She's pregnant!* His head reeled with the possibilities. He reached down with a shaking hand and touched her stomach. *What magic is this?* Then, with a sudden, devastating certainty, he knew—*it's not mine!*

"Where, where did those other Golems come from?" Tommy panted.

"I think they were following us," Philippe said.

Sasha stood, taking in the whole scene. Dead Golems lay everywhere. She reached down and touched one lightly, shuddering at the contact. "These last went after you, not Nicole," she noted to Tommy. "I think they're the same ones that were trying to find Amanda."

"But that makes no sense. Amanda's not here," Tommy protested.

"It makes perfect sense," Philippe answered quietly. "We've blocked Amanda's essence from them, so they turned to the only person who carries a piece of her inside himself."

"Yes, you and Amanda are in thrall, a part of each belongs to the other. When we left the group, the Golems must have been able to sense Amanda in you and came after you."

Tommy shuddered. "Do you think there are any more?"

Sasha shook her head. "Jer said four came after Holly. We know these four"—she gestured—"were after Amanda. We may be able to assume they are searching in groups of four. If that's the case, though, only three were attacking Nicole."

"One of them was dead already," Eli said quietly. "I killed it back in the castle."

Sasha turned to stare at him. "Thank you for getting her out."

"Don't thank me," he snarled. "I didn't do it for you, or for her. Trust me, I'll kill all of you the first chance I get."

"I say we don't give him that chance," Tommy muttered.

Sasha could tell that Philippe agreed wholeheartedly but compassion for her kept him from voicing his feelings.

She looked down at Eli. There was hate raging in his eyes. He stood slowly, head half-turned toward Richard, who kept his eyes riveted on him. "The Horned God will destroy you, all of you," he hissed.

"Eli! I did not raise you to be a servant of evil."

"No, that's right. You didn't. You didn't raise me at all," he snapped. "No, you bailed out and left that to Dad. Now you want to come back into my life and judge *me*? How dare you! Instead, you are the one who needs to be judged. You are the one who abandoned your children and never once looked back! And now, what, you get to act all surprised and hurt that we take after Dad. Gee, big surprise, he was the one who was there. He gave me my first lessons in magic, he taught me how to drive a car, he told me how to treat women. You left me with him knowing what he is and you're surprised at how I turned out?" He was screaming at the last, his face crimson, and spittle flying from his mouth.

He raised his hands as though he was going to attack her. From the corner of her eye she saw Richard draw another knife, and then suddenly a shiny black demon knocked Eli off his feet.

The thing resembled a giant cockroach, complete with exoskeleton. It scrabbled on six legs and twisted around, its fangs headed for Eli's neck. He punched the thing in the head, though, and it whimpered and skittered away while he leaped to his feet.

"Say good-bye," a voice hissed from somewhere behind her. Sasha twisted around to see a nymph aiming a crossbow at Eli.

"No!" she shouted, lunging at Eli and trying to knock him out of the way.

She hit Eli, and both of them began to fall. She felt the arrow as it pierced her back, burrowing through her body and toward her heart. Then, there was a great *whoosh* and a blinding light.

They hit the ground, which was made of stone and covered with straw.

"Welcome," a silky female voice purred.

Sasha looked up, amazed that she could still do so, and began to laugh hysterically.

"Who is she?" Eli asked, his voice dripping with fear.

A stately woman in black and silver robes, crowned with black veils and a diadem of silver, stood over him. Her mouth twisted. "I am Isabeau of the House Cahors, and you are most welcome."

"Where did they go?" Nicole shouted.

A moment before, Eli and Sasha had been falling.

They had hit the ground and vanished. Their disappearance had been accompanied by a sound like a sonic boom.

The demon who had shot Sasha staggered backward, a dagger in its chest. It collapsed to the ground, wheezing and gurgling. Tommy had grabbed the cockroach creature and twisted its head off.

Tommy stood slowly, looking sick. Purple blood covered the lower half of his face.

"I'm not sure, but I think it might have something to do with a spell Amanda and I cast."

"Explain," Philippe demanded.

"We did a spell so we would stay alive and together. When we were done, there was a surge of power. Just now, I felt it again, just before they disappeared."

Nicole felt a wave of nausea rush over her. "Maybe Pablo can figure out where they went," she gasped when it had passed. "Where is everyone, anyway?"

She saw Philippe and Tommy exchange a quick glance. *They're wondering how much to tell me,* she realized.

"Let's just say they're on the Continent," her father said cautiously.

She glanced up at him, seeing him with new eyes. "You never wanted to fight again, to use your training again, did you? You never wanted us to know who or what you are, and Mom never wanted to know either."

The look on his face was validation, and she could feel all the pain that he had kept to himself for so long. "Mom recoiled from your scars and never let you talk, so your soul could heal. So you just turned into a simple, quiet, fade-into-the-background kind of person. Well, it's out now, Dad. You are—"

"Ssh, honey. It's okay," he said, interrupting her. "All that matters is that you're safe." His face was full of tenderness, but slowly his look changed to one of grim resolve. "Now, let's go find your sister."

With her father on one side and Philippe on the other, Nicole rose shakily to her feet. "My men," she joked weakly, and they both laughed, humoring her.

She could feel the baby move inside of her and she winced. *What I wouldn't give for a nap.* She glanced around quickly, wondering if Fantasme had come back, but the hulking creature was nowhere to be seen. *Go, find your master and Sasha,* she bid him silently, knowing he would never listen to her.

France, 13th Century

"We're dead," Sasha said as she rolled over onto her back and stared up at Isabeau.

"No, Madame, you are not," the Cahors witch assured her, and though she was speaking in medieval French, Sasha understood every word she said.

"If we're not dead, then where are we?" Eli asked, looking around suspiciously. "How do we know if—"

"You are in my home, my time." The beautiful princess inclined her head. "Inside the castle of my husband, Jean de Deveraux, and his father, Duc Laurent."

Sasha sat up slowly, confused and unsteady. She saw the gray stone walls, adorned with battleaxes, picks, and maces. A long wooden table was covered with the remains of a recent feast, and rushes were strewn on the floor.

"We're in France, six hundred years ago?" Sasha asked her. "How did this happen?"

A cloud passed over Isabeau's face as she regarded her surprise visitor. "A portal was opened between our two times. It was an accident. I stepped through and pulled you from your time."

"Why?"

"To save your life," Isabeau answered.

Sasha slowly stood to her feet. She wanted desperately to reach out and touch the other woman, to assure herself that she was flesh and blood. *Is it she, or her spirit? Does the woman still live, or has the Massacre already occurred?*

Isabeau reached out her hand and touched Sasha's. Her skin was soft and warm. "I am flesh," she said simply. "I was told to look for you."

And then in her mind, Sasha heard her speak. *He is Deveraux.*

He is my son, she replied.

"You worship the Goddess," Isabeau asked her out loud.

"I do, yes."

Then you understand my pain.

"Your husband. Jean."

My love.

Sasha felt a sudden rush of giddiness. *I can stop it,* she thought. *I can keep it all from happening.*

"You can stop nothing," Isabeau told her, her voice filled with sadness. "Nor can I. All we can do is watch and pray."

"What are you two talking about?" Eli asked, standing.

"Her future," Sasha whispered.

Isabeau smiled, and it broke Sasha's heart. *She knows! On some level, she knows all that is to come.*

"A choice has been placed before you both. You may remain here, to live out your days, or you can return to your own place and time."

She nodded to Sasha. "If you should choose to return, you will die from your wound."

The arrow! So, I was not far wrong in thinking I was dead already.

"Indeed," Isabeau said to her. "But how many days you will live, I cannot say. Wild days and nights will unfold soon. Of your own fate, I have no knowledge. Of my own . . ." She turned her face away and sighed. "I have it in me to stop it from happening."

Sasha's lips parted in surprise. "Would I be able to do anything to help you? Could we manage it together?"

Isabeau stared at her. "I have no idea," she answered frankly.

"Perhaps the Goddess sent me here," Sasha told her. "So many die, do they not, once our families clash in the flames? If you and I could change the future, would the Supreme Coven still rise? Will the Mother Coven become so weak, if you and I together worked magic now, in your time?"

"I . . . I don't know," Isabeau murmured.

"What of your mother?" Sasha asked, her blood warming. "Would she join us?"

Isabeau smiled bitterly. "For her, the fate of all in this castle is sealed. They shall all die."

"I shall stay," Sasha replied. "Even if we fail to change what is to come, I'm a survivor. Better to live, no matter what century. And no matter if for a few days or a hundred. And whether we can stop the Massacre or not."

Eli stood, emotions that she couldn't read colliding inside him. She could see the struggle, but there was nothing she could do to help him. Death could conceivably await him no matter which he chose. He could die in the Castle Massacre along with dozens of Deveraux, or he could die in his time by the hand of the Supreme Coven, or his own father's.

She could see his fear, his confusion, and for the first time since she had left, she felt close to him. *He's just a child, still searching for his way in the dark,* she thought.

He turned to her, his eyes full of questions she could not answer, and her heart began to break. She reached out and touched his cheek, and for a moment he let her before he jerked away.

Our whole lives have been leading to this, she realized.

He took a step back and turned to Isabeau. "I choose to return."

The young woman inclined her head.

He lifted a hand. "Can you return me to London instead of Avalon?"

Isabeau nodded. "The portal was initially formed in London by two who wanted to shield themselves and their love for eternity. I can return you there."

"Good."

"What do you intend to do?" Sasha asked.

He looked her in the eyes. "I don't know yet."

She grasped his hand and swallowed around a sudden lump in his throat. She hadn't been a part of his life for years, but there had always been the possibility that that could change. Now, that would be lost to them both. "I will try to come to you," she whispered.

He nodded that he understood, but he didn't say anything. He let go of her hand, Isabeau made a motion in the air, and with a rush of wind, he was gone.

Michael Deveraux: London

It was nearly time. In a few hours it would be Wind Moon and blood would be shed. Michael Deveraux smiled. In a few hours House Deveraux would take its rightful place as head of the Supreme Coven. His ceremonial robes flowed about him as he walked toward the altar. He had prepared several sacrifices to appease the Horned God, that he might look with favor upon Michael.

Duc Laurent was there, smiling wickedly and dressed from head to toe in black leather. "Tonight, the Black Fire will consume our enemies, and will visit destruction upon all who stand in our way."

Considering that the Black Fire had, at least, indirectly, been the death of the Duc, Michael admired his fearlessness. "You're sure my son will be there?"

Laurent nodded. "He and what's left of the Cahors Coven are planning to attack the Supreme Coven tonight."

Michael shook his head at the audacity, and at the foolishness of it. "What can they hope to achieve by such an assault? They are weak, divided, and Holly is still possessed." *At least, last my imp saw her, she was.*

Laurent laughed. "Who cares—so long as they are there, we can use them."

Jer is the key, Michael thought with bitter amusement. *That was why we were able to conjure the Black Fire in the high school gym. Eli and I were chanting, but his presence was key. The son who disobeys me and tries to break with our magic will lead to the destruction of all. How poetic. I guess he can't help it. Deveraux are just born bad.*

"What do you think, pet?" Michael called out.

Kari walked in from the other room, listless and dazed. "That's nice," she said, though she clearly had no idea what was nice.

"How long do you plan on keeping her like this?" Laurent asked, pursing his lips.

"Oh, a little while longer, at least."

"You should kill her now, before the battle. The mesmerism takes some concentration, concentration you could easily lose during the fight."

Michael shrugged his shoulders and sneered. "Look at her. Do you really think she's a threat? Besides, I'm saving her for the after-Massacre celebration."

Tri-Coven: London

Jer was nervous. The coven wasn't prepared to take on both the Supreme Coven and his father, yet in a few scant hours they were going to war with them both. He touched his face, feeling the scars that lingered there. The last battle his father had been involved with hadn't ended well.

Now I'm hideous, disfigured, a monster outside to match the monster within. He searched his heart and still found himself lacking. He knew not which deity he owed his allegiance to, and he was filled with rage and bitterness.

What would I have been like had I grown up in a different family, one who worshiped the Goddess? Would I be more like Alex? Can he really be as good and pure as he seems, or is it all a masquerade?

He wasn't going to find the answers to his questions, at least not in time to help with the battle to come.

"Jer?"

He looked up. It was Holly. She seemed different to him—older, quieter. *I would be, too, if I'd gone through what she has.*

She came and sat beside him, the springs of the bed creaking ever so slightly. In the darkness she couldn't see his scars, and he was grateful for that. She touched his hand, and he flinched.

"Jer, I want to be close to you. Don't shut me out."

"You deserve someone who is whole," he whispered.

"There's nothing wrong with you," she answered, her voice cracking slightly.

"We both know that's not true, Holly."

She laced her fingers through his, and he thrilled at her touch. "I need you."

"You need someone who can take care of you, someone you don't have to hide in the dark with."

"Your face is not our problem," she answered, her voice gaining strength. "Your fear is. I've seen horrors I can't even express. You think a few scars bother me, especially when they're yours?"

"You don't know what you want," he said bitterly. "You and I, if we begin something, it's going to be forever. 'Till death us do part,' even if we're the cause of that death. You're not ready for that. You're a child."

"I'm not a child," she said, her voice rising. "I'm a woman, but you've been too wrapped up in your own self-pity to notice."

He turned toward her. He could see her eyes gleaming in the dark, large and round like a cat's. He ached for her. He wanted to take her in his arms and never let go. He had dreamed of it for so long. . . .

She lifted her hand to touch his cheek, and he jerked back.

"Don't pull away from me. I'm not afraid of you, of us."

"I am," he whispered.

"Don't be."

And then her lips were on his, hungry, demanding, and he could not deny her. He kissed her with all the passion that was in his heart, his soul. He felt her hands plucking at his shirt, unbuttoning it, and then her warm hands moved against his chest.

With a groan, he closed his eyes. *It would be so easy to make love to her, we have both wanted it for so very long.*

Yes, oui, *take her,* he heard Jean whisper in his mind. *She is ours, and we will have her.*

"Mon amour," whispered Holly—or was it Isabeau?

"You are the fire that burns me," he answered, his lips against hers.

"And you, me."

Holly stared into Jer's eyes and could see the passion within. His face swam in her sight as Isabeau began to take her over, even as Jean was claiming Jer. She felt everything that Isabeau had felt as she had lain in the marriage bed with Jean: the passion of a lover, the duty of a bride, the fear of a virgin. Holly knew all these because the same emotions coursed through her, the same feelings held sway in her heart and mind.

Our lord, our husband, we must be with him, Isabeau demanded, her words ringing clear in Holly's mind.

"I love you, Jer," Holly whispered, gazing at him through lowered lids.

He paused for a moment, staring into her eyes, and all the world around them seemed to stand still. "I love you, Holly," he answered in a voice so savage, it made her quake.

His hands were on her shoulders; she could feel the weight of them, and their heat burned through her shirt. He slowly slid his hands downward to the front of her shirt. Her back arched uncontrollably, pushing her harder against his hands. She could hear his breathing heavier now, and his breath warmed her neck.

"My husband, *mon homme, mon amour,*" she whispered.

With a groan, he tore her shirt open and pulled it off her. She gasped as he trailed kisses down her neck and to the tops of her breasts. A fire kindled in her belly, and all she wanted was to be his. Bodies moving, flesh entwining, as it has been it always shall and must be. He circled his arms around her and crushed her to him.

And then he pushed her away again with hands that shook. "No," he said, voice hoarse.

She felt as though ice water had been poured into her veins. She tried to lift her hands to touch his face, but he grabbed them and held them still.

"This is Jean and Isabeau, not us, Holly."

"It *is* us," she breathed. "It always has been. They can only play upon the emotions we already feel. We belong together."

"I can't pull you into my world of darkness. You deserve to live your life in the light."

"I want to live my life with you."

"No, we have to stop, even if that means I have to be strong for both of us. We need to stop before there's no turning back."

She stood abruptly, pain rolling off her. "You say that you are being strong, but you are weak. A strong man embraces his emotions, he doesn't run away from them."

Jer sat helplessly watching as she clutched up her shirt and threw it back on, awkwardly holding together the ripped edges in front. His heart ached for her. He could feel her pain and humiliation as though they were his own.

She started to leave, and he wanted to call her back but knew that he couldn't. At the door she stopped and turned back toward him. Her voice was quivering as she told him, "Jeraud Deveraux, you are nothing but a coward."

And as she left, he knew that she was right.

THIRTEEN

DIANA

☾

And now at last our journey's done
We give praise to almighty Sun
We kill and maim and claim our right
To triumph using power and might

Bleeding we lay in the dust
Goddess protect us, you must
With our last breath we pray to thee
If you wish us dead, so mote it be

Tri-Coven: London

Wind Moon. It had come at last. Holly didn't know whether to feel fear or relief. One way or the other, it would be over tonight. Everything would be done. She looked down at her hands, clasped tight in her lap. It still seemed so strange to see them, to know that she could control them. She breathed in deeply, centering herself. One thing she had learned from the possession, and that was the value of patience, *and how to be still.*

She was still now, waiting and listening for the voice of the Goddess. Isabeau sat beside her, impatient but quiet. At last, Holly turned to her. "If he doesn't want me, then there's nothing I can do."

"But he does want you, you can feel it, you know it as well as I."

"Maybe I do," Holly answered. "But he is going to have to come to me."

Isabeau made a hissing sound but said nothing.

Holly sat for a few more minutes, gathering strength, focusing her thoughts and calming her heart. At last she rose to her feet. She was wearing a black turtleneck and loose-fitting black trousers. She had removed all her jewelry and braided her hair back, entwining it with silver and black thread.

All the others were similarly dressed. She took her place in the circle they had formed in the living room of the safe house. She looked at their faces and was stirred by sorrow. *Not everyone is going to survive tonight. Maybe none of us will.*

Armand met her eyes and nodded encouragingly. He had been very kind to her the last couple of days. He alone of the group truly understood what she had gone through.

Nicole smiled bravely, but Holly's eyes were fixed on her cousin's belly. *She shouldn't be fighting.* The cat

Astarte sat on her lap. The cat had found Nicole before she and the rescue party had left the island. The cat gazed at Holly as though she knew exactly what was happening and the nature of that which they were about to undertake. Philippe sat next to Nicole, one hand protectively on her stomach and the other stroking the cat. *He'll die before he lets anything happen to Nicole.*

Amanda and Tommy huddled together, arms entwined and legs touching. *The magic they did opened the portal that Sasha disappeared through. Their magic alone, though, couldn't have done it. They must have combined it with someone else's inadvertently. It wasn't mine, so that could only leave . . .*

Alex. He sat there staring levelly at her. *We know so little about him, but he's a Cahors, and he's helped us so much already. The extent of his abilities is unknown to us, though, perhaps also unknown even to him.*

Next to Alex sat Jer. She could feel the hostility flowing through them both. *Something has passed between them that the others haven't told me about. Goddess, let them put it aside for the battle.*

Pablo stared at her, clearly reading every thought she was having. Since she had come back she had noticed that he had given up every pretense of not reading people. *We may need your insights yet,* she told him. He nodded.

Barbara sat looking nervously at the rest. *Of us all, she doesn't belong here, and I don't know what help she can be. It's likely we sacrificed so much to rescue her, and she will be killed tonight, anyway. The others have worked hard with her, repairing her mind, teaching her some protection skills. Goddess, let it be enough.*

That left Richard. He sat, dressed all in black, but with black markings on his face. They made him look like some sort of devil. He had cut his hair to within a half inch of his head as well, military style. Of all of them, he had surprised her the most. Everyone had written him off so long ago, and that had been a mistake. His particular skills were going to prove especially useful now. Her uncle had spent the last forty-eight hours discussing the layout and security of the Supreme Coven with Jer.

The two had formed a plan that was brilliant and daring and, Goddess willing, that just might work. Richard sat quietly, and it was clear that he, too, was preparing himself mentally. Around him lay a small arsenal. She hadn't asked where he had gotten the weapons; she didn't want to know.

Just as Jer and Richard had worked on a plan of attack, Alex, Tommy, and Philippe had worked on enhancing the weapons magickally. *That should surprise Sir William,* she thought. *I wonder if anyone has thought before to combine technology and magic in the way that we have?*

Her army waited. It was a good army, one that had stayed loyal despite all the hell she had put it through. Many had been lost, but those who remained were undaunted by that. They were ready to fight, and to die, for what they knew was right.

"Tell me again about the weapons," Holly said quietly.

Philippe let go of Nicole and Astarte and picked up a bullet. "These are depleted uranium bullets. As I understand it, they are incredibly deadly on their own. One bullet can rip through a tank, turn into shrapnel, and shred anything inside so that it is unrecognizable."

"That's correct," Richard said.

"What we've done is, tried to put a charm on each bullet so that it can also punch its way through a magic ward. Most wards are designed to block much larger things—a creature, a melee weapon, or other magic. We figured that something this small, if enhanced slightly, might be able to make it through the barrier."

"Excellent," Holly said, impressed.

Philippe put down the bullet and picked up something that vaguely resembled a grenade. "This is a concussion grenade. Instead of spraying shrapnel, it compresses sound waves and air."

"It's like when you have the bass on the TV set

really high and you can feel it more than hear it."

"Like when the sound vibrates your breastbone?" Holly asked.

Philippe nodded. "These should cause a ripple effect that can theoretically tear through wards as well."

Philippe put down the grenade and held up a knife and a baton like police used. "We only have a couple of these. Barbara's going to show us all some of the most effective places to strike to cause damage or death."

Barbara? Holly's eyebrows shot up as she turned to look at the woman.

Barbara stood up, her hands shaking slightly. "Well, who better than a doctor to teach all of you how to hit someone to cause the most damage? Tommy, will you help me out?"

Tommy rose with alacrity, and the two positioned themselves in the center of the circle. "First off, some basic physiology," Barbara said, her voice growing stronger. "As I understand it, most of the warlocks you'll be fighting are men, so we'll focus on gender-neutral techniques, and then some that will work specifically on men.

"If you hit your opponent hard on the nose, it will cause him to lose his vision for a couple of seconds. If you hit his nose really hard, it can drive blood and bits of bone into his eyes, further impairing his vision. If you can hit the nose at the bottom with the palm of your hand and push upward hard enough, the breaking bones will drive up into his brain and kill him."

Barbara slowly and gently mimicked the motion she was describing. Tommy looked distinctly uncomfortable. Holly glanced over at Amanda. Her cousin looked green, and for a moment Holly thought she was going to throw up.

Apparently ignoring the reactions around her, Barbara continued. "If you take your hand like so," she said, demonstrating, "and drive it upward just under the breastbone, you will crush his heart. Avoid actually punching your fingers into the chest cavity, because you could get your hand caught in there."

Amanda got up and fled from the room, her hand pressed over her mouth. In a moment the sound of retching could be heard coming from the bathroom. Even Holly was beginning to feel queasy, and the sound didn't help.

"Kick your opponent in the side of the knee to fell him instantly," Barbara continued.

"Now for some gender-specific points. Men have Adam's apples. Strike the Adam's apple, and he won't be able to breathe for about thirty seconds. Strike it harder and you can dislodge or crush it, causing him to choke to death. Notice even the slightest pressure there is uncomfortable," Barbara commented as she gently touched Tommy's Adam's apple with one finger and he instantly backed up.

"Now, men and women stand differently. Women stand straighter, whereas men hunch their shoulders forward slightly. This makes a man's collarbone more vulnerable. If you can strike it, you can break it, and it is one of the most excruciatingly painful bones to break. That is because of its proximity to the head and neck. The nerve centers in the collarbone link up with the head as well as the chest, so the pain will pretty much incapacitate most people."

Holly felt herself start to sweat slightly and she squirmed as she imagined the pain.

"Now, this is especially important," Barbara said, pausing to look at them all. "You all know that you can kick a man in the groin to cause him extreme pain. It's more effective, though, if you actually grab the testicles and crush them."

An anguished shout rose from every man in the room, and Tommy leaped back, shouting, "Stay away from me!"

Amanda, who had just made her way back into the room, went running again.

Barbara sat down, her lecture done. It took a minute

for everyone to calm down, and Holly noted that when they did, every man was sitting with his legs crossed.

"There is one other thing," Philippe said, still visibly shaken. He picked up a pair of ice picks. "Richard wants each of us to carry a pair of these with us. He's going to show us what to do with them later."

Pablo's face suddenly went deathly white, and he, too, went running from the room, his hands clamped over his ears.

"Okay," Holly said. "And now for the plan."

Headquarters of the Supreme Coven

The plan was simple, and it involved marching into the Supreme Coven's headquarters. Of course it helped that Michael wasn't going alone. He was being smuggled in by James Moore. Between the two of them, they knew where all the trip alarms and wards were. With Duc Laurent and Kari in tow, they made their way into the heart of the underground kingdom as the last ray of the setting sun touched the earth above them. *Sunset for Moore, how poetic.*

The alarm wasn't raised until they were nearly to the throne room. Guards caught sight of Michael and shouted, there was the sound of footsteps as warlocks came running, and Michael smiled, knowing many of them were loyal to him.

Then, from the darkness behind him, he heard a female voice purr, "Hello, Michael, I've been waiting for you."

He threw himself to the side just as a lightning bolt ripped through the air where he had been standing. He glanced up to see a young female warlock standing, smiling wickedly.

Eve.

Tri-Coven: London

Jer hated Alex. There was something about him that drove him crazy. *Maybe it's the fact that he threatened to kill me on Wind Moon,* he thought dryly. *Maybe it's because he's everything I'm not. He's what I could have been had my father served the Goddess and not the Horned God. Whatever it is, I'm not going to let him out of my sight. Of course, that's going to be difficult since I'm point and he's bringing up the rear.*

Next to him, Richard lifted his hand in the air and Jer stopped, bringing his mind back to bear on the task at hand. They had already passed through the outer defenses that the Supreme Coven had placed on the streets of London surrounding the entrances to the Coven. They were thin wards that acted more like "magic detectors" than actual barriers. Richard had been able to pass through easily, having no witchblood in his veins. Jer had passed through easily, though not without notice. He was a warlock, though, so no alarms were raised.

Through the fog, two men converged on them, warlocks both. They were sentries, guarding the entrance to the underground headquarters. Jer didn't recognize them—a good thing, else they might have raised an alarm upon seeing him.

"Hail the Green Man, guardian of the day," Jer murmured as they stopped before them.

"You have entered ground consecrated to the Horned God. Woe be to any who trespass here."

"I come as a fellow servant."

Satisfied, the two men turned, indicating that Jer and Richard should follow. Jer pulled his two ice picks from his belt and waited for Richard to nod. When the other man did, they both moved in tandem. Jer jabbed one ice pick into each ear of the man in front of him. The warlock died without a sound, without even a breath being expelled from his body. Holding on to the ice picks, Jer lowered him slowly to the ground so there was not even the thud of his falling to alert anyone. Beside him, Richard did the same. Then they stepped over the bodies and moved forward.

Jer was shaking from head to toe. It was the first human he had killed, and he felt like he was going to be sick. He glanced over at Richard and saw the steely look in his eyes. *It's not his first, and if this night goes as planned, it won't be his last,* Jer realized.

He shuddered. Adrenaline was rushing through his body so that all his senses felt alert, heightened. *He would have killed me if I'd let him,* he told himself, thinking of the fallen guard.

They entered a dead-end alley. At the back was a door, set low into a brick wall and blending so well with it that it would go unnoticed by most. The glamours on it were strong.

Jer nodded to indicate that this was the entrance. He took one of the concussion grenades from a pouch on his belt. He pulled the pin and sent it sailing through the air. It exploded against one of the wards with a low boom. Windows rattled in the buildings around them, and Jer could feel it in his bones. *Hope that did the trick,* he thought.

Moments later, the rest of the Coven raced up to him. When no portals opened spilling forth demons, Jer realized that it must have worked.

"All right, everyone inside quickly before they realize what's happened," Jer instructed, opening the door.

They all spilled inside. Holly touched his hand as she passed. Once they were all in, he stepped in and closed the door behind him.

"'Into darkness deep as hell,'" Alex muttered.

"What?" Jer whispered.

"It's a *Phantom of the Opera* reference," Holly explained quietly.

She and Alex exchanged a glance that made Jer instantly uncomfortable.

"Quit the chitchat," Nicole hissed.

Jer moved back forward to re-establish himself at the front, leading the way through the twisting corridors. They hadn't gone more than a hundred feet when all hell broke loose.

Suddenly there were warlocks everywhere, bursting from side passages and hidden doors. It seemed as though they were coming out of the walls. And, then, bewilderingly, they rushed past the group and kept going.

Jer blinked. *What is this, the Twilight Zone?* And then he heard it, a deep keening sound—it was supposed to indicate a breach of the premises. *If we're not it, though, what is going on?*

Another warlock came thundering down a side passage.

"What's going on?" Jer shouted.

"Michael Deveraux," the man panted. He turned to glance at Jer and then stopped dead. "Hey, you're—"

Before he could finish his sentence, he died in his

tracks, a knife buried in his chest. Philippe strode forward and yanked the weapon back out, wiping the blood on his clothes.

"All right then, let's go," Jer said.

"Can you tell where they're headed?" Holly asked.

"Looks like the throne room," he said grimly. "Makes sense. The Deveraux have been wanting to take that throne back from the Moores for generations."

Eli Deveraux stood next to James Moore as they both surveyed the carnage. *I had no idea my father had recruited so many of the Supreme Coven,* Eli thought.

He ducked as a stray fireball exploded in the air above his head. He straightened slowly and turned to look at James. "You know they don't care about us," he said.

James turned to eye him coldly. "What?"

"Your father and mine—they don't care about us. Neither of them has ever been able to see beyond himself. We'll always be pawns in their games."

A warlock raced by, engulfed in flames, and Eli watched him for a moment before turning back toward James.

"He threatened to kill me," James said so quietly, Eli had to strain to hear him. "He told me it was time to choose sides and that if I sided with your father, he would flay me alive. For starters."

"I think the only reason I'm still alive is my father's been too lazy to kill me."

James snorted. "They think we'll be content to live our lives in their shadows, never wanting more than what they give us."

"I'm tired, tired of watching my back. We need to stop fighting each other and start fighting those who oppose us."

James nodded. "We should do something about it."

"Agreed," Eli said. "And, James, just one more thing."

"What?" thc other grunted.

"When this is done, I want you to divorce Nicole."

A lightning bolt shot into the wall between them. When the smoke cleared, James turned full toward him. "Divorce her? I planned on killing her. Why?"

"Because I want to marry her," Eli said, hardly believing the words that were coming out of his mouth. "I think the kid could be mine."

"It could as easily be mine," James said, a subtle threat in his voice.

"I'm willing to take that chance," Eli told him, looking him square in the eye.

A week before—hell, an hour before—they would

have tried to kill each other. Now, though, James nodded slowly. He extended his hand. "Agreed. Now, let's go kick some ass."

Holly couldn't help but gasp as she stood surveying the scene. Everywhere she looked, warlocks were engaged in combat. *They're so busy fighting one another, they don't even notice us,* she marveled.

The same could not be said of the other denizens of the dark. The demons she had been expecting at every turn suddenly exploded upon them, as though they had all been waiting to attack at once.

"Heads up!" Holly yelled, hurling fireballs off her fingertips. Several demons dropped to the ground. One, though, continued to stride forward, laughing. It looked human but for its twisted face and the fact that the fireballs splatted against him with no effect.

Before Holly could react, Amanda exploded into action. She rushed forward, shouting and twirling a baton. For one moment she looked like a crazed member of a marching band. The illusion faded, though, when Amanda smashed the end of the baton into the creature's nose.

With a roar of pain, the thing fell to its knees, clawing at its face. Amanda pulled back and then drove the end of the baton upward into the nose again. The creature fell backward, dead.

"Works," Amanda said shortly. Another demon rushed them, roaring. Amanda twisted around and drove her fist up into the creature's abdomen. It, too, fell with a thud. Amanda turned and gave Holly a brief nod.

Holly said the first thing that came to mind: "You go, girl."

Then there was no more time to stand and wonder how her cousin had soaked up so much information while in the bathroom puking her guts out. It was Holly's turn to put down some demons.

She spun in a circle, fireballs rolling like waves from her fingers. A high-pitched scream caused her to twist and throw her hands up. *Too late!* A shiny black demon breathing smoke was upon her. Then suddenly it exploded before her.

As bits of demon fluttered to the ground, Holly stared through the smoke to see Eve. The warlock gave her a brief salute before limping on toward the fray. Holly stared after her. She had seen only a glimpse of Eve, once, but Amanda had told her enough about the warlock that there was no mistaking her.

Something hit Holly hard, and she tumbled to the

ground. She lay still for a moment, the wind knocked out of her. She glanced up expecting to see a demon and instead came face-to-face with a grinning warlock. He slammed her head into the floor, and her vision dimmed for a moment.

Jer knocked the warlock off of her with a sideways blow. Amanda stepped up from behind and hurled a fireball directly into the man's face. He fell to the ground, writhing in agony for a moment before dying.

Suddenly a wave seemed to ripple through the air, and Amanda gasped aloud. *Wind Moon, anyone who kills a witch or warlock on this night gains their power,* Holly thought.

Then Amanda and Jer were off again, whirling dervishes dealing out death at every turn. Holly lay still a moment, trying to regain her breath as she assessed the battlefield. Everyone seemed to be holding their own. She struggled to a sitting position.

"Holly!" Barbara Davis-Chin shouted. "Are you okay?"

Holly turned to look at her just in time to see a demon walk up behind Barbara and cut her in half.

"No!" Holly screamed. Shock ripped through her. All the effort to save Barbara had been in vain.

A hand grabbed the back of her collar and hauled her to her feet. She swung around, a fireball in hand.

"Keep moving!" Richard shouted at her, his face inches from hers.

She nodded through the haze of pain. Richard clapped her on the shoulder and then he was off.

Holly turned in time to see a wave of warlocks descending upon them. Suddenly they were all flung backward as though by a gale. Out of the corner of her eye she saw Alex, his hands raised in the air. The warlocks hit the far wall and were pulverized against it, bits of blood and bone flying everywhere. A ripple shimmered back across the room and slammed into Alex. The powers of the dead warlock were bestowed upon him in that moment.

Shaking her head in amazement, Holly turned to punch a horned demon that had its hand around Pablo's throat. She waded into the creature, and it dropped Pablo. She poured all her rage into every blow and kept pounding until the creature slumped to the ground. She didn't know if it was dead or only unconscious, so she took a step back and fried it with a fireball for good measure.

There were more demons to fight, and Holly loosed her rage on them. From time to time the others entered her line of sight, and so she knew they were still alive.

She downed one and turned just in time to see

Tommy ripping the head off another. She heard the sound of the rifle as Richard shot monster after monster. They exploded in a fabulously grotesque manner, showering each of them with gore. She noted that in every case Richard fired at creatures only when they were in front of walls, careful not to send bullets toward any demon standing in front of a member of the Coven.

She stood panting, looking around at the bodies of the dead demons. She glanced at the others, and they all shook their heads, not knowing if that was all.

Jer motioned them to follow, and in moments they were in another room. In the middle of it she saw Michael Deveraux.

"Jer!" someone screamed.

Then she saw Kari, running toward them. Michael Deveraux must have heard her as well, for he looked up and threw Holly a mocking salute. To his son, he called, "Welcome, Jer, the devil take you."

He threw a metal sphere toward Jer. Holly screamed a counter-spell but was unable to deflect it. Kari twisted, saw it coming, and dove in front of it. It hit her full in the chest, exploding as it struck her, and she fell backward against Jer.

Jer grabbed Kari as she fell against him, falling to his knees and lowering her to the ground. Her head lay on his leg, and she stared up at him, eyes wide. Around them the battle began anew, Holly's coven against his father's followers, but he didn't care. All he cared about was the shadow that was passing across Kari's eyes.

Kari lay in his arms, her blood covering his hands and face. "Jer," she gasped, looking up at him.

His father had tried to kill him, and Kari had sacrificed herself to save him.

"Ssh, it's all right now. Everything is going to be okay," he lied, looking down at what was left of her chest.

"No, it's not," she gasped. "I'm so sorry. I was wrong, and afraid. I thought you were dead. All I ever wanted was to love you, be with you."

"And you can, Kari, I swear. You'll be okay," he told her in a shaking voice. He tried to take her pain, tried to pass healing warmth through his hands, but he couldn't. Deveraux hands could only give death.

She whispered to him, *"Je suis la belle Karienne. Mon coeur, il s'apelle Karienne. Ah, Jean . . . mon Jean . . . "*

"Oui, ma belle," he found himself answering in French, finding love deep inside himself for her. *"Vives-toi, petite."*

The light began to fade from her eyes, and he felt himself begin to die. He had been so cruel to her, had treated her so badly. He had loved her once, or, at least, he thought he had. She had been shallow and vain, but no more so than he was. And when it had counted, she'd been there. *She'd always been there, even when I had refused to see,* he realized. He felt as though he couldn't breathe, as though his heart were being squeezed in his chest. "Live," he begged her, knowing that she could not.

"Kill me, Jer," she whispered. "Don't let your father get my magic."

"I can't," he sobbed.

"Yes, please, for me," she whispered.

His tears fell on her cheeks.

She reached up and touched his scarred face. Her fingers were cold. "You are beautiful," she said. "Like Jean."

He turned and kissed her hand. Then he pulled his dagger from his belt and cut her throat.

The ghost of a smile touched her lips. Then her hand fell, her eyes rolled back, and she was gone. And nothing he could do would bring her back. He felt the power passing from her into him, strengthening him and bringing him some bleak comfort. *A part of her will always be with me.*

Karienne.

★★★

Eli saw Jer and Holly enter the throne room, but they were the least of his worries. Eli maneuvered close to his father, who had nearly reached the throne of skulls. Only four guards stood between Michael and the leader of the Supreme Coven. Eli hazarded a glance toward Sir William and saw James at his side. With a wave of his left hand, Michael Deveraux sent three guards flying and, with his right, hurled a fireball into the chest of the fourth.

And then Eli was standing beside his father in front of the throne. Sir William had changed to his demonic appearance, his visage a terrible thing to behold.

"Deveraux," he bellowed. "You will pay for this."

"I think not," Michael said with an arrogant laugh.

Eli pulled his athame from his belt. "Actually, Father, you will."

Michael turned to look at him, surprise on his face. At that moment, Eli plunged the athame up under Michael's breastbone and into his heart. From the corner of his eye he saw James do the same to Sir William.

Michael tumbled to the ground, a look of astonishment on his face. Blood began to spill from his lips. They moved as though he was trying to speak.

Eli knelt beside him. "Why so surprised, Dad? You were the one who taught me to kill. You also taught me one other thing: 'Do unto others before they do unto you.'" He bent and kissed his father's brow before twisting the dagger and pulling it out.

In a moment, the light faded from Michael Deveraux's eyes and he was gone. A wave of power washed over Eli. It had belonged to his father, and now it belonged to him—not as his heir, but as his killer.

Eli stood shakily as a roaring sound began to fill the room. He looked up and saw James kneeling over the body of Sir William. The corpse shook and convulsed; Sir William's eyes bulging and then popping from their sockets. His chest expanded, contracted, then blasted outward. His skin slithered and steamed; and then, a hideous-looking demon clawed its way out of Sir William's chest, howling. Its form was black and leathery, and as it got free, its many-jointed, skeletal limbs began to unfold like collapsed metal rods. With a series of cracks and scraping noises, it unfolded itself until its furled, lizardlike head brushed the ceiling of the great chamber.

Its eyes were snakelike, yellowing and glowing, with a pinprick of darkness in the center. Its tongue was black and forked, and it flicked it once, twice, at James, who repelled the attack with fireballs, one of which lodged itself just beneath one of the monster's eyes, where it continued to burn, apparently unnoticed by the creature.

It roared, and then it flung back its head. Sir William's human laughter cannonaded out of it, making the walls shake. Then it hopped forward on massive, taloned feet, raced across the room in three steps, and disappeared into the far wall.

The skull throne cracked from top to bottom with the sounds of thousands of dying animals pouring from it and everyone stopped to stare.

Eli fingered his athame for a moment before hurling it at James. At the same moment, James threw his weapon. Eli fell, the dagger lodged in his shoulder. He turned his head slowly and saw James lying on the ground as well, his body draped over that of his father's ruined corpse.

Eli turned away. *Bastard*. Then, slowly, everything went dark.

Pandemonium broke out. Warlocks raced toward the fallen bodies of their leaders as Holly stood, mouth agape. She turned and glanced at Nicole. The other girl was white as a ghost, and her hand was pressed to her stomach. Then she began to totter, and Holly watched in horror as her cousin's knees buckled and she began to fall as though in slow motion.

Philippe threw himself forward, hitting the

ground beneath Nicole and reaching up to wrap his arms around her, cushioning her fall with his body. "She's going into labor," he shouted.

Holly turned and stared toward the remnants of the skull throne. Those they had come to fight were dead, the Supreme Coven was in a shambles. *Time to go, to get out while we can,* she thought, *before they turn their attention to us.*

Too late, she realized almost instantly as several nearby warlocks launched a sudden volley of fireballs their way. She lifted her hands to spin a barrier, but before she could, a rushing wind filled the room, extinguishing the fireballs.

"Everyone out!" Alex boomed in a voice that rolled and echoed like thunder. He stood, the center of the windstorm, his eyes flashing like lightning.

Holly didn't have to hear the scream that issued from Nicole to agree that it was a good idea. Philippe and Armand picked up Nicole and, carrying her, set out at a run led by Richard.

Pablo, Tommy, and Amanda followed close on their heels. Jer stood, stock-still, a look of shock on his face as he stared toward the throne. Holly touched his shoulder. *What must he be feeling about his father's death? Joy, sorrow, both? Only he knows,* she thought. "Let's go," she urged.

He let her lead him out of the room and into the passage. She could hear Alex as he brought up the rear behind them.

Getting out would prove harder than getting in, she soon realized. Demons crawled out of the walls. A strange sucking sound exploded around her, though, and the demons suddenly were trapped, pinned to the walls as though by some invisible force. She could feel a slight movement of air.

Wind, she realized, *Alex is keeping them at bay, somehow.*

As they raced through the seemingly endless tunnels, her thoughts flew ahead to where Nicole was. She could feel her pain; it rippled in waves off her, and her screams bounced off walls and ceiling and floors. *Nicole is strong, but none of us knows what to expect.*

Then, suddenly, they were at the exit and they all burst up onto the street outside and into the fresh air. Alex slammed the door behind him, muttering a spell to bar the way.

Holly stood, gasping in the clean, crisp air and listening to the labored breathing of the others. The stench of death and decay still hung about her clothes and being, and she worried that all the showers in the world would not change that.

A cloud moved in the sky, and directly above them

the full moon burst into sight, shining down upon them. *Wind Moon and most of us are still here, praise the Goddess.*

Back in the safe house, Holly felt as if an age had passed since they had left. Nicole lay in a bedroom upstairs, in the final stages of labor. Armand was tending her and had chased all the rest but Richard out with a worried look on her face.

I can't believe that it is over, Holly thought. *Michael Deveraux is finally dead. I am free of him—we all are. It is done. I feel strangely robbed that he did not die by my hand, but relieved as well.*

"It is not over," Alex announced, standing and facing the group. "Michael Deveraux and the Supreme Coven were just the barest tip of the iceberg. There are thousands of covens, on this world and others, and not all of them worship as we do. For every Michael Deveraux who falls, there are a dozen who stand ready to take his place."

And Sir William escaped, Holly thought.

"Indeed he did," Alex said, gazing at her. Then he said to the others, "I belong to the Temple of the Air. My coven and I have spent years fighting those who use the dark magic."

"You mean, tonight, this was not new to you?" Amanda asked.

"Hardly," he said, his face inscrutable. "I and others of the House of Cahors have fought many battles in the name of good and light."

"Other Cahors?" Holly asked, astonished. "But we—"

He nodded. "We four here are not the only descendants of House Cahors. There are many, many more, and we are all fighting to bring the covens together, to lead Coventry into a new era of peace."

"You didn't tell Luna any of this," Amanda accused him. "You let her think you were ignorant of your heritage."

"Yes, I did," he said. "The Mother Coven is weak. I have no use for them."

"I have a lot of experience with people who want 'to lead Coventry,' none of it good," Jer flung at him.

"Your experience all comes from the dark side of magic," Alex retorted, and it was clear that no love had been gained between the two of them. "Join us and help bring light. You can atone for your family's evil."

"I don't think so," Jer said. "Not that way."

"The Supreme Coven and the Mother Coven are both just two covens in a much larger world. The time for age-old battles is past. Covens need not fight each other. Houses need not fight each other," Alex said pointedly. "Not even yours and mine," he added, looking straight at Jer.

"I'm tired of fighting," Holly said quietly. "But I can't allow others like Michael Deveraux to roam free, killing all those in their path."

"You would be welcome in our coven, Holly," Alex said, pinning her with his gaze. "You have lost so much in this battle, and you have become so hard. You don't need to stay that way, though. We can help you. We can restore your faith."

Suddenly there were tears streaming down Holly's face. She *was* hard inside; her heart was a piece of flint. And yet . . . tears. They were magical, a miracle. "Is such a thing even possible?" she found herself asking.

Alex came and sat beside her. He picked up her hand and stared into her eyes, and she felt his heat, and his strength. His power.

"It *is* possible, Holly. We can help you, and you in turn can help us. You could be my High Priestess, and I will be your Long Arm of the Law. Together, we could lead with strength and mercy. Imagine what we could accomplish *together.*"

And as he said that, she knew what he meant by the last word. *Together.* She broke his gaze and turned to Jer.

He locked gazes with her and for a moment, one

single instant, she saw . . . something. And then it was gone—extinguished or hidden, she couldn't say which.

Jer shook his head bitterly.

And Holly's heart hardened again.

Alex was still holding her hand. Warmth suffused her skin, and where the heat traveled, feeling returned to her. Alex was offering her something that Jer couldn't—or, more accurately, wouldn't.

Alex released his hand and stood. Holly could feel the weight of Amanda's stare on her, but she wasn't quite yet ready to meet her cousin's eyes.

When Amanda spoke, though, it was directed at the group at large. "We've done our bit for Coventry; we've fought our battle. Tommy and I need time to rest, to just be together. And I'll be honest, I don't know if we'll ever be ready to go back to fighting again."

Holly risked a glance at her. Amanda sat, arm entwined with Tommy, who was nodding agreement. *They are so close, so in love. What would it be like to have the kind of bond that they do?* She glanced again at Jer. *If I wait for him, I may never know.*

"I understand," Alex said. "Nicole should also stay behind. She has a baby to raise—a very special baby, unless I miss my guess."

Holly cocked her head to the side, wondering what

he meant by that. He didn't elaborate, and she knew that now was not the time to press him.

Philippe cleared his throat. "The survivors of the Spanish Coven wish to join yours."

"But your heart is torn," Alex answered.

Philippe nodded. "I wish to fight with you as well, but I must be with Nicole."

"Then you have a choice to make, for you cannot do both," Alex said.

"I'm going out," Jer announced abruptly, grabbing a coat and heading for the door.

Holly watched him go with an aching in her heart.

Everyone was silent for a moment. Holly heard her heart beating; it was a sound so foreign that she wondered if it had actually stopped for a while . . . ever since she had sacrificed Nicole's first familiar, Bast . . .

"So, Holly of the Cahors, what will you do?" Alex asked her.

She looked at him and felt a blush mounting her cheeks. She loved Jer, but he was damaged. He had worshiped the darkness for so long that his soul was more deeply scarred than his body.

Then again, so is mine.

She looked at Alex. His straightforwardness was refreshing, and he was offering her a chance for healing, a relationship with one who worshiped as she did and a place in the battle against evil.

His face shone with an unnatural beauty, and she knew that it would be easy to say "yes" and go with him. She was tired of fighting losing battles, and it felt good to know she could be on the winning side. She glanced at Pablo and Armand. She trusted them both, and they were going with Alex. *I won't have to be alone.* She looked in Alex's eyes and realized she would never be alone again.

He extended his hand to her.

EPILOGUE

☾

Anne-Louise Montrachet had been gone a long time, her body still, but her spirit seeking the answers to so many questions. Whisper, the cat, walked slowly around her, careful not to tread a paw on her. The woman should be coming back soon, with answers to old questions and more new questions than she would be able to count.

At last Whisper walked gingerly up onto Anne-Louise's chest. Slowly, the cat sat down, an Egyptian Goddess waiting for her tribute.

Then, with a gasp, Anne-Louise awoke, eyes flying open, body twitching. Blood began to appear oozing from wounds that seemed to spring up in the witch's flesh as if by magic.

Anne-Louise looked wildly around for a moment before bringing her eyes to bear on Whisper. "You?" she asked.

The cat dipped its head in acknowledgment.

"We must get to the others, warn them," Anne-Louise gasped. "We need to tell them *that's not Alex Carruthers.*"

USA Today bestselling author Nancy Holder has received four Bram Stoker awards for her supernatural fiction. She has served on the board of trustees for the Horror Writers Association. Her work has been translated into more than two dozen languages, and she has more than seventy-eight books and two hundred short stories to her credit. Her books for Simon Pulse include the Wicked series and the novel *Spirited*. Nancy also recently published the novel *Pretty Little Devils*. She lives in San Diego with her daughter, Belle, and far too many animals.

Debbie Viguié is the author of several books including *Midnight Pearls* and *Scarlet Moon*. Debbie has been writing for most of her life and holds a degree in creative writing from UC Davis. When Debbie is not busy writing, she enjoys traveling with her husband, Scott. They live in the San Francisco Bay Area. Visit Debbie online at www.debbieviguie.com.